A Deity Rose: Nature's Wrath

KIM MCCORMICK

Acknowledgements

Book Cover - Etheric Design

Contents

For the incredible people who saw potential in me and my story, even when I struggled to do so. Your support and belief in me has made this dream a long awaited reality. Thank you from my whole heart.

To Brad, I never stopped hearing you shout my name from Heaven. *Beastman Strong* forever.

To Aurora and Saxon, never stop chasing your dreams.

One

There was something about the aged cottage in front of Calla Moro. A wave of unease rippled through her stomach. Her senses fueled the reasons for her distress, from the birds singing to the warm afternoon glow scattered through the trees. Everything gave her a churning mess of mixed emotions and memories that she would rather not think about. It only made her miss her mom that much more. Her vivid blue eyes told her that the cottage didn't need much work, at least on the outside, and she was grateful for that.

Her mom had such an immense love for gardening that despite her old age, she spent most of her day tending her plants. The lawn was bright and green. Calla's mom, Nancy, had prided herself in that. Nancy had hired someone for leaf and snow removal, but Calla was hoping the house would be out of her hands before the leaves fell. An assortment of fall flowers lined the front, back, and walkway of the house, adding to the fairy tale aesthetic. Their family home could have been straight from a world far away, it was that picturesque.

Nancy and Calla had loved to sit on the back porch at sundown to watch the woodland animal's frolic. Nancy would tell young Calla to listen for the creatures of the forest chattering back and forth. Calla smiled at the memory. No matter how hard she listened, the conversation was just out of her ear's reach. But Calla knew Nancy caught their words. Coming back all these years later, after so much had changed, Calla couldn't have asked for a better place to grow up.

Calla started to head inside, then paused at the ancient oak and its tire swing that had seen better days. A faint smell of rubber brought memories of her younger self spending hours on that thing floating through her mind as a gentle breeze tossed the golden waves of her hair. She pushed such thoughts from her mind. She was here for a greater purpose. She pulled out her key and advanced upon the house with trash bags and plastic bins in tow. There was a moment of hesitance before she crossed the threshold into her childhood home.

She was still in awe that Nancy had lived to be ninety and had still been sharp as a tack. Tears welled in her eyes as the stark realization that her mom was gone was even more prevalent inside. Pictures of the two of them surrounded Calla, hung on the walls, sitting on tabletops, even printed on a blanket. She grabbed her favorite picture off an end table. She was eight, and it was the day that Nancy had adopted her. Both had smiles across their faces and tears running down their cheeks. That was eighteen years ago, years Calla was grateful for. Nancy had treated Calla as her own daughter. When Calla was younger, Nancy would tell her stories of when she was a nurse on the Navy ships during the Korean War. She had a gift of telling stories filled with brave men and women, nail-biting battles, and everything in-between. On those nights when Nancy's war stories replaced Calla's bedtime fairy tales, she had always been too excited to sleep. They would read a few chapters of a book together until she had fallen asleep to the printed words.

With a soft sigh, still holding back tears, Calla placed the photo down. She was here to clean out the house and sell it. As much as she wanted to keep the charming home, she lived with her best friend, Felicia, in the city. She hoped another mother-daughter team would move in, which would warm her heart. Calla planned on spending the week to sort through everything. She worked as a freelance writer for various companies. Felicia didn't have a typical nine-to-five job either. She was a model with dreams of walking in one of the world's most coveted fashion weeks. Now Calla was on her own for two months as Felicia was gone while she visited her parents in Indonesia.

A peppy tune broke Calla from her morose thoughts. She reached into the back pocket of her jeans for her phone. "Hey, Felicia! I thought you boarded your flight." Calla dropped the bins and trash bags by the door. She thought of locking it but waved a hand at it instead. This was a safe neighborhood. She would be in and out anyways to take the trash bags to the bin at the end of the driveway.

"I did, but a storm came in. So, I'm sitting on the plane, waiting for them to cancel the flight."

A smile spread across Calla's lips as she picked up a picture of Felicia and herself at their prom, their forgotten dates behind them. Felicia's face has always been small, with a tiny, flat nose. Her smooth, tawny beige skin glowed in sharp contrast with the mischievousness of her dark umber eyes. Even as a teenager, she hadn't been afraid to stand out as she wore a tight-fitting red dress beneath sleek black hair that fell straight past her shoulders. Calla had taken a softer approach with a deep sapphire ball gown that complimented her sandy complexion and a half-up, half-down hairdo. The picture reminded her of simpler times.

Calla winced, "Ouch. I'm sorry. Well on the upside, this is your last flight." She decided to bring this photo home. Felicia would get a kick out of it.

"Calla, this whole trip has been a nightmare, let me tell you," Felicia started. "I'm starting to ask myself if this was a good idea."

"You know it is. Your parents have always wanted to see their ancestral village. It means a lot that you're going with them."

Felicia scoffed on the other end. "But we have to hike through the middle of the jungle, up mountains, and through who knows what. All to reach this tiny little village that my great-great-great-grandparents came from or something like that." Calla was about to speak, but Felicia cut her off, "Since when have you ever seen me hike? And my mom confirmed there is no electricity there. I don't know how I'll survive. Oh, and the bugs... What if one bites me and I'm allergic? My face will swell, and my modeling career would be over like that!" Felicia's finger snap mirrored her angst.

"Oh, stop being so dramatic. I'm certain that there are no mutant bugs in Indonesia. As far as electricity goes, isn't that the idea to unplug and reconnect with your roots?" Calla felt the eye roll from Felicia through the phone. Their relationship reminded Calla of oil and water, but somehow, they were the best of friends. Ever since fourth grade, they'd been thick as thieves, and no one could break them apart.

"Yeah, that's great and all, but like... what if I don't care about my roots? You know? Like, is where I came from more important than who I am now?"

The fact that Calla was more alone in this world now than ever since her mom's death stopped the words in transit from her brain to her mouth.

"Hey... I didn't mean it like that. You know I speak without thinking like I don't have a filter on myself. I should get one. It's about time I did."

Calla smiled with a small chuckle, "It's okay, Felicia. You know I've come to terms with it." On the inside, Calla laughed at what she said. She had not come to terms with it, but it sure was easier to tell everyone that she had. A tiny part of her always wanted to know who she had once belonged to and why they hadn't wanted her. It was a constant struggle. She was afraid to find out the truth.

"I'm over talking about this trip. I sense a stress pimple coming. How was your date last night?"

Calla suppressed a groan while gathering all the pictures she wanted to keep in a plastic bin. She didn't have the heart to throw any away, even the ones she wasn't in.

Calla pressed her lips together, unsure of what to tell her. "Well, it... um." She sighed knowing she had to tell the truth. "Felicia, it was a complete disaster. He isn't my type. I know you were so excited about him, but I don't think it's going to work out."

"What? Get out! Zach was perfect for you," Felicia complained. She was hellbent on finding Calla a handsome model to date. Each one was either as arrogant as the days are long or stale with zero personality. Last night was a disaster. Zach had gotten bored with her and was checking out other women at the restaurant. "He was tall, strong, funny, and sexy! Oh, and he had blonde hair and blue eyes, just like you. I was so excited for your little bright-eyed Viking babies running around."

Calla laughed, "I don't think I'm having babies, let alone little Viking babies, any time soon."

"Way to crush my dreams. I want to be Auntie Felicia! I'd spoil them so badly!"

"Oh, I know, but I don't want to be mommy Calla yet." Calla paused for a moment, "I think you have your hopes set too high for me."

"Of course, I do! You're my best friend!"

"What if I'm meant to be single for the rest of my life and not have little Viking children?"

"Oh, hush. I just haven't found you the right guy yet. I know I will. I think I'm getting close to your perfect match," she squealed at the end.

Calla fought back a sigh, Felicia was more stubborn than Calla was, and Calla was stubborn. "Shouldn't you worry about your own love life first?"

Felicia scoffed, "Me? Please! I don't need a man impeding my career."

"And you think I want one?"

"Well, duh!"

"You're something else. You know that, right?"

"Yeah, but you still love me," she sang out in a mocking tone.

"And you love me too, with or without a man."

Felicia paused, "Hey, my mom is calling, she sent like a million texts about the flight. Whoops! I'll text you. Kay?"

"Sounds good. Tell her I said hi."

"I will!"

Calla ended the call by tossing her phone onto her favorite armchair. She pressed her hands into her waist with a soft sigh. Nancy kept a clean home, but there was a lot of stuff. Feeling bummed out by Felicia's call, Calla wandered to Nancy's bedroom. As she entered the room, she closed her eyes and memory after memory came flooding back. Calla almost saw her younger self sitting on her mother's bed in tears. She'd been bullied at school quite often as she was an easy target, what with being adopted and having an older single parent. And, she had a faint tattoo of a strange flower on the back of her right hand. Nancy had always told her it made her special, but when she sat on Nancy's bed in tears, she never felt special. Everything made her feel different, like a freak.

As time went on, the words hurt her less. She learned to stand tall, proud of her tattoo. Letting go of the image of her younger self, Calla noticed a dark wooden box on the bedside table. There was an envelope leaning against it. She went through her memories of that day trying to remember if it had been there when she had taken her mom to hospice. She had been so concerned about Nancy, there could have been an elephant in the kitchen and Calla wouldn't have noticed. With a curious intent she lifted the box from behind the envelope to get a better look at it. Her eyes grew wide and her mouth parted a little in shock. The polished walnut box had gems of all shapes, sizes, and colors encrusted all over it. What made Calla's heart drop was the design on top. It was the same odd flower as her tattoo. She brought her hand next to the box, and her stomach dropped as well. Calla put the box down where she found it and with shaking hands, opened the envelope. It was a letter from Nancy, she recognized her perfect penmanship anywhere. She held the folded piece of paper in her hands for a minute, trying to anticipate what could have been inside it. She wondered if this held one of the answers she'd been seeking her entire life. Taking a deep breath, she opened the envelope and began to read.

Calla,

I suppose that I am gone by the time you're reading this letter.

Calla struggled to read through the fresh tears.

I didn't want to leave you, but the Lord says when it's our time, and mine has come and gone. I know you're confused about the box on the bed and why I kept it from you. I hope the truth doesn't tarnish how you think of me. From the moment I found you, my every action was to protect you. I kept back the truth in how I found you, but I suppose it's time to tell you the whole story.

You remember Nina Barclay, right? The one with the black curly hair who would pick you up from school sometimes. She had lost her mother that morning and needed time off. I was at the hospital that night covering for her. Being sixty-four at the time, I didn't have many extra shifts in me, but I always helped where I could. I was at the reception desk waiting to talk to the secretary who was on the phone, Jenna Folton. She was a good friend at the time. The doors to the ambulance bay opened with no one around them, and cold air rushed in. I went to close the doors manually, but I heard something. A cry from a baby. It was you. I rushed outside to find a basket bundled up in wool with a hand-woven blanket tied tight. I peered in the basket to see you, crying up a storm. I picked up the basket to bring you inside right away, but that box that you're curious about fell from the basket. I was in awe of how beautiful the box was, it had to be the most expensive thing I'd held in my life. Besides you, of course. We called the police to file a report of infant abandonment, but a deep part of me knew this box belonged out of their hands. I shoved it in further into the bush and out of the light hoping no one would find it for the rest of my shift. You know this next part... You were found to be in perfect health, a true miracle from God. There were no signs of hypothermia. It was as if you weren't outside at all. That minute I spent outside made my nose red and bones cold.

The next day I came to check in on you after the police filed their report and the social worker came. That tattoo on your hand perplexed them to no end. They came up with theories from motorcycle gangs to cults, but they never found an answer. The social worker wanted to place you in a foster home, and before I could stop myself, I had told her I would foster you. I knew in my heart and soul that I was to be your mother. While I waited for you to come home to me, I tried everything in my power to open that box, but nothing worked. I couldn't bring myself to destroy it either, so I hid it away, postponing this talk.

I do not know what lays inside, and I was nervous that it would take you away from me. My gut feeling says that your life won't be the same once you know the contents, but that seems like the simple answer. You know that nothing is ever that simple or easy.

It was selfish that I didn't want you to know about it until after I was gone from this Earth. I'm so sorry Calla, and I hope you can forgive me. I wanted you to have a normal life not affected by whatever is inside that box. But please know that I love you, and I thought I was doing the right thing. You're my only child, and I would do anything for you. I will always love you, regardless of what's in that box.

All my love,

Mom

Calla let the letter slip from her fingers as her eyes fell to the box. She fought back tears as she picked it up again, letting her fingertips graze over the gems studded into the wood. In a sudden need for answers, Calla tried to pry the top off the beautiful yet mysterious box. She sucked in a short breath and pulled with all her might all while feeling betrayed by Nancy. She hid the box from her all this time. Hiding beneath the wood, the contents of the box held the answers Calla always yearned for. The top didn't budge, not a fraction of an inch, just as Nancy documented.

Calla let out a cry of frustration as she spiked the box onto the bed, no longer caring for how delicate it was. Calla left the room in a flurry and got a hammer from the hall closet. She was going to find out about her past, no matter what. Calla set the box on the worn beige carpet. The top of the box gleamed back at her. It mocked her, like it had a secret that she had longed for her entire life. Calla raised the hammer high with a white-knuckle grip. Her resolve faded fast as a sob escaped her lips, and the hammer fell next to the box. "Damn it!" Angered, Calla slammed her palm on top of the box, her tattoo matching up with the identical symbol on the box.

Her tattoo started to tingle. Calla swallowed hard, pressing her palm further down with caution. The tingling became stronger, and the box began to shake. Calla looked around and realized the whole house was shaking. She could hear precious memories fall from shelves and shatter on the wood floors. Calla ripped her hand off the box, but nothing stopped the shaking. She looked between her tattoo and the box, what was this thing on her hand? And what had she done? The wood of the box splintered and Calla dove for the other side of the bed. She covered her head with her arms, not knowing what was going to happen. A burst of golden light slammed Calla into the wall. The lights in the house blew out with quick pops and fading sparks. She rolled away from the wall and onto her back. Her entire body felt so weak. Her muscles screamed in agony with every inch she moved. Sunlight drifted in through the open window and splashed over her face. Closing her eyes to shield them from the light, she surrendered to her body's distress.

Two

By the time Calla became conscious it was dark outside, and she couldn't see anything. For a moment she forgot what nighttime was like out of the city. No lights to wash out the stars, no people, no noise to drown out the concert the crickets played for her in the background. She sat up. Everything hurt. She rubbed her face, trying to rationalize what had happened. Struggling to remain calm, she crawled to the box. The wood had splintered from the implosion but was still somewhat intact. She slid her hand inside to feel around the box, but it was empty. Calla turned the box over and shook it. Still nothing. "No," she cried to herself. "You were supposed to have all the answers!" Calla tossed the box at the wall, hard enough for it to scrape a chunk out of the plaster. "Stupid box."

Calla sat in the darkness for a few minutes. She didn't want to think about the wall she now had to fix. It took time for her to gather strength to arise and continue on with her life with no answers about who she was. She went to turn on the hall light and found that the power was out. Calla sighed, trying to not let her headache run rampant. She remembered where the flashlight was, under the kitchen sink. With a nervous swallow, she hoped the batteries still worked.

Calla weaved through the house, with the floor plan engraved in her memory. Broken ceramic and glass littering the floor rekindled the fear she felt when the house was shaking. She hoped nothing precious was lost. Her body ached less with every move she made, but the soreness still stuck around. After she found the flashlight and turned it on. The light flickered a few times then went dark. She hit the flashlight on her palm, but it remained dead. "Of course," Calla muttered to herself as she let the flashlight roll from her hand onto the counter.

"Are you sure it's this house?"

Calla froze at the unknown voice. The voice was deep and on the other side of the front door, the same door that she'd left unlocked.

"The portal opened near this house, Hector. The Hybrid must be here." The second voice sounded female, with a raspy tone to it.

Calla's eyes glanced down at her hand. Was this her doing? She reached along the familiar counter. Her hand wrapped around the largest hilt in the knife block and slowly removed it, afraid to make even the slightest noise. She crouched under the small kitchen table with the knife at the ready. Her heart pounded. Each thump of her heart crept up her chest and throat. Everything seemed wrong, so very wrong.

"Let's move in before we miss the Hybrid. We must not fail our Queen. She's been waiting a long time. If we fail…"

"We stay in the human realm or don't come back at all," the female finished.

"The human realm…" Calla mouthed as her eyebrows scrunched together in confusion. What sort of new drugs were these people on? Halloween was in a few days, but it seemed like the crazies started early this year. Her eyes caught the small light from her phone blinking on the chair. An idea popped into her mind, if she moved fast enough, she could grab it and sneak out the back, then call for help. As Calla moved out from under the table, she heard the knob to the front door jiggle. She squeezed back under the table and reaffirmed her grip on the knife. She had never hurt anyone, but she's never been in a life-or-death situation before. Calla watched two figures enter her childhood home.

"Where do you think the Hybrid is?" the male asked in a hushed voice as she could hear glass crunching underneath his boots.

"Close by, I'd bet, it's only been a few hours since the realm shook." They split up.

Calla watched from the dark shadows as the taller figure came towards her side of the house. She gripped the knife even more tightly as she thought about the most lethal place to stab someone. She saw feet at the threshold of the kitchen. Her heart galloped at a speed that lodged in her throat. Her eyes were drawn to the dark shape of a sword sheathed on the figure's side. She held her breath, afraid to breathe.

"Hector! I found a box. It must be the signal. It's open and has the Hybrid's sigil marked on the inside!" Hector turned away and went into Nancy's room.

Calla let out a quiet but ragged breath and made a silent dash for the opened front door, grabbing her phone on the way out. She hoped the intruders stayed in her mom's room for as long as possible.

Calla pressed herself against the tree that held her beloved tire swing. The dark of the night had abandoned her, as the low moon was bright, and the stars sparkled as diamonds in black sky. She looked behind her, no one was there. She couldn't hear them talk, nor could she see their shadows in the house.

Crouching, she dashed to the tree line and into the forest. A strange light deep within in the woods caught her attention. Calla checked the house one more time, and seeing no movement, she cautiously crept into the woods to investigate. When she got close, she ducked behind a tree. She saw the light was a shimmering wall of lavender mist off in the distance. "What the hell is going on," Calla whispered to herself.

A strong hand clamped on her arm. Calla gasped and whipped around. "You're coming with us, Hybrid," Hector said.

"Let me go!" Calla tried to pull the man's hand off her arm, but he whipped her around and locked her arms behind her.

"You made it easy for us, coming to the portal," Hector laughed into the back of her head.

Calla squirmed to get away. "Please let me go, I have no idea who you're looking for."

Hector finished tying her hands behind her back.

Tears fell down Calla's face, and her heart pounded.

"You see..." the woman had come out from the trees and stopped just short of a moonlit spot near Calla. "Our Queen has been awaiting your return. When you opened that box you sent a signal to all of Midelle..."

"What are you talking about? You're crazy," Calla shrieked as she vainly struggled against the man. He only gripped her arms tighter.

"You, the Hybrid, sent the signal. We came to retrieve you. Simple."

These people were unhinged, and she had to change her approach. Thinking on her feet, Calla stopped fighting Hector. "Then let me go, and I will go with you on my own accord." Calla kept trying to look at the woman's face, but it was hard to see. She was waiting for her to step into the light of the moon that broke through the trees. "In fact, I'd like to meet your Queen."

"Hector, untie her. Seems the Hybrid has changed her tune, and we were instructed that no harm would befall her."

Within seconds, Calla's arms broke free from the loose rope. She rubbed her wrists and rotated her shoulders.

"Let me see your sigil, the mark of the Hybrid," the woman demanded.

Calla covered her hand, "It's just a tattoo?"

Calla jumped when Hector grabbed her shoulder. "Show Anita your sigil."

"Okay, okay..." Calla put her hand out and tilted her mark towards Anita. A rough hand to Calla's back pushed her forward, and she caught herself right before the light. Anita stepped forward into the moon's glow.

When Calla's eyes landed on her face, her heart dropped into her stomach. The tips of fangs rested on her lips, and her eyes were a dark crimson. A piercing scream left Calla's throat before she could stop herself, and she ran as fast as her legs could take her. The two were immediately on her tail, but Calla knew these woods. She hoped they didn't.

Calla ran towards the hazy wall of lavender mist, knowing she couldn't run back to her house. If she kept running in that direction, she'd reach a neighbor's backyard.

"Capture her at all costs," Anita screamed from further back.

Calla could hear Hector's feet swiftly crunch against fallen leaves and twigs. He was gaining on her, but the wall was getting closer. If it was a portal, she hoped that she was light enough on her feet to trick the red-eyed monster into it. She kept running, her lungs burned as a cramp stabbed her side. She prayed that she wouldn't fall. The wall was now in reach, and she saw hazy figures on the other side. At the last second, Calla veered away from the shimmering wall, hoping to shake off Hector. To no avail, he grabbed her ankle. The two of them tumbled and wrestled onto the ground.

Hector pinned Calla to the ground with ease. His eyes were burning red as well, and he had patches of dry skin on his face and arms. The closer his face came to hers, the more hideous he looked.

Rope thumped on the ground right before Anita pounced onto Calla and shoved a cloth into her mouth.

Calla thrashed against Hector's strength.

"Where's the rope," he asked, pressing his hips down to pin her as he blindly reached for the rope.

Seizing the opportunity, Calla grabbed the woman by her arms and used every bit of panic-infused strength to toss her to the side.

Anita's body rolled through the hazy veil, causing the wall to break up. "No! That was our way back," Anita said as her head popped up from a pile of leaves.

Hector turned his attention back to Calla. "I have a spare portal, but we need to tie her up first. Hybrid, you are coming back to Midelle with us."

"I'm not a Hybrid!" Calla's plea got lost in the fibers of the cloth gag.

Hector grabbed the front of her t-shirt and pulled her up to him. His knuckles pressed into her sternum. "You will be one of us," he roared in front of her face.

Calla closed her eyes tight, but all she could see was the dark red of his eyes.

Minutes later, Calla sat propped against a tree. Her hands and feet were tied, and her mouth was still gagged. Calla so wanted to run, but she couldn't wiggle free of her bindings. The cloth muffled her sobs and erratic breaths, but nothing was stopping the heavy stream of tears from running down her face.

The two of them had their backs to her, talking in hushed voices. Calla heard them talk about opening another portal. She had never believed that things like this existed. Her brain was running a million miles per hour, and she couldn't wrap her head around any of it.

"Hector!" A voice boomed through the trees.

Calla jolted from the confident tone of the voice. Goosebumps crawled over her skin. Her eyes were wide and alert, but it was still pitch-black in the forest.

Hector slowly spun around the area. A deep growl escaped his throat, and his hand wrapped around the hilt of his sword. "Come out, vampire. Come to steal what's mine again?"

Vampire? Calla's heart couldn't beat any faster. Anita joined his vigil, brandishing two short blades of her own.

With a snap of a twig, a figure burst from the trees brandishing a sword. Calla couldn't get a good look at him as he was in the moonlight for only a flash. She heard flesh give way to the power of his blade. Anita's head bounced off the ground and landed a foot in front of her. Calla shrieked through the gag and kicked the head away. She fell forward on her face to scramble away from Hector.

He growled with pure anger when the mysterious figure was once again cloaked by the trees. "Come out and fight, coward," he yelled, swinging his sword in the air, his red eyes blazed with anger.

Laughter echoed from the trees, but Calla couldn't pinpoint where in the woods it came from. A tense moment of silence hung in the air before the figure charged Hector. Their swords met with a ferocious clangor and a shower of sparks. "This is where you disappeared to, I see," the figure taunted as he raised his sword backward.

Hector swung with wild intent while grunting, but the man blocked with ease. "I will end you!" Hector swung again.

The figure dodged every thrust and slash with ease.

Calla rolled to witness the fight.

"I thought Jedrek taught you better than this," he laughed as he slashed Hector's arm. Hector howled but persisted with a quick jab to his antagonist's stomach.

The figure side-stepped the jab and brought his sword down, the blade leaving a deep gash in Hector's thigh. Hector swung again and managed to slide the blade of his sword on his opponent's arm.

The figure ignored his wound and with a swift move sliced Hector's stomach.

Calla gasped into her gag and closed her eyes as the contents of Hector's abdomen spilled out onto the forest floor. She couldn't take it anymore. She heard what had to be Hector's body hitting the ground, followed by one more sickening slice. She did everything she could to keep the bile down.

"Hybrid? Are you okay?" the figure's voice called.

Calla kept her eyes shut, positive that this had to be a nightmare. There was a gentle touch to her shoulder. Calla turned her head and finally got a good look at the figure. He looked like no monster she had ever dreamt about. His skin was smooth but pale, with green sea-glass eyes and short cut hair that mimicked copper.

"Here, let me help you." His voice was cold. He flicked his sword in one movement and freed her hands and feet, then helped her up.

She reached out to a nearby tree to steady herself as the man untied her gag.

He fell on one knee before her and rested the tip of his bloody sword on the ground. With a bowed head he began, "Hybrid, allow me to introduce myself. I am Finnegan Quinn, Captain of the Royal Guard, but many call me Finn. I will take you to safety." He raised his head as if awaiting his next command.

Calla held up a hand to him. She felt bile boil up her throat and land at the base of the tree.

"I don't want to rush you, but there will surely be more Corrupted coming. We must make haste."

Calla wiped her mouth. Her throat burned and she needed water. There were too many questions running through her brain but all she could ask was, "What's happening?" Calla kept her eyes on Finn knowing there were two corpses on the ground oozing blood into the dirt. She took a second to glance at his arm. His sleeve was ripped and darkness seeped around the gash.

The tall man watched her every move. He glanced at his arm too. "He barely got me. It looks worse than it is." Finn brought his attention back to her. "Hybrid, we must move. Time is of the essence, more of The Corrupted are going to come."

"More?" Calla shouted, "Who were they? What the hell is the Hybrid? And move where? I'm not moving anywhere unless it's back to my car and straight to the police."

Finn took a step back from her, "Not here, Hybrid." She watched him go to Hector and dig around in his pocket. "Shit." He pulled out a cracked vial, drained of the liquid inside. "If only life was that easy." He turned his attention back to Calla. "We must move, Hybrid."

Calla snapped, "Let's get one thing straight here, my name is Calla Moro, and I'm not any kind of Hybrid. You've got me confused with someone else. And whatever shit you're in with these red-eyed freaks, keep me out of it. Unless I get answers right now, I'm going to the police."

Finn held up his hands and gave Calla a cautious look, "You can have all the answers you want, but not here."

"Yes here!" An owl flew from the trees, it was too late for this. "Who was that?" She asked, pointing to the beheaded man. "And that!" She added, gesturing to Anita's body. "And what are you? They called you a vampire!"

Finn sighed. "They are The Corrupted." He ran his hands through his hair and stopped talking.

Calla crossed her arms and raised an eyebrow. "Would you care to elaborate?"

Finn took a moment. The sounds of the forest filled the silence. The wind ruffled the tops of the trees, rubbing leaves against each other. Calla glanced upwards for a moment, but her eyes fell back down to Finn. He was digging in his pocket. "They are The Corrupted..."

Calla sighed, "Yeah that's great, but what does that mean?"

"Let me finish!" Finn said, losing his temper. Calla clamped her jaw shut and after a few seconds, Finn started talking again.

"The Corrupted have had something terrible happen to them..." He paused, and Calla listened, making sure she clung onto every word. "Something the heart can't overcome and slowly they become twisted, dark..." Finn stopped again, running his hand through his hair. It molded back to how it was. "There is no curing it. It used to be rare to see one, but now? It seems they are converging to fight. Like someone is leading them."

Calla opened her mouth to speak, but Finn held up a finger. "They have a Queen," she continued with her thought. "The woman said something about not failing their Queen."

Finn nodded his head, digesting her words. "Interesting. Good job, Hybrid."

Calla ground her teeth at hearing that name again.

"The Corrupted need a powerful weapon to take control of the realm, and you're that weapon."

"Me?" Calla scoffed with a cheeky grin. Her mother used to tell her fairy tales as a child, but this took the cake and then some. "That's impossible!" She held up her hands and took a step back. Her eyes drifted over to her right hand. Time seemed to stop at that moment as Calla swallowed hard. Her tattoo. Calla brought her eyes up, and Finn nodded his head as if reading her thoughts.

"That is the Hybrid's sigil," Finn stated while wrapping her cold hands in his.

Calla furrowed her eyebrows at the odd gesture.

"The Oracle says the Hybrid is the one who can either save or destroy our realm. We thought it was all a lie, but the signal you sent was..."

"I never sent a signal," Calla said immediately after she ripped her hands back from Finn. She stood there in disbelief that any of this was happening. Her head was spinning again, not that it had ever stopped.

"I hate to break it to you, but you did."

"When?" Calla took one deep breath after another, trying to keep herself from passing out.

"A few hours ago."

"I did not send," Calla started, then gasped as she covered her mouth.

"What?" Finn asked, taking a step towards her but then stepped back, locking his hands behind his back.

Calla's icy eyes grew wide. "It all makes sense," she mumbled, looking around like the trees had answers. She paced a few times, away from Hector and Anita's bodies. Finn watched on confused. "The box."

"The box?" Finn repeated, unsure what that meant.

"This!" Calla held up her hand to him, "I opened a box with my tattoo. A bright light exploded from it, and I woke up hours later feeling like I got hit by a truck." When she said the words out loud, she thought they sounded ridiculous. These things don't happen.

"That sounds like it was the signal." His hand dug around in his pocket and pulled out a small vial. It looked like Hector's vial before it broke, and it held a purple substance too. He held it open in his hand and gave Calla a look.

"What's that?" She asked, trying to keep her cool.

Finn encased it in his palm and crushed it. His face winced for a moment. The thick purple liquid and his blood danced together in the air and started to pool on the ground.

Calla looked at Finn and back at the ground, "Are you crazy?"

"It's too dangerous to stay here. We're going, now."

"To where?" Calla asked, watching Finn. Her mind raced as adrenaline pumped through her veins. Despite that, a fascination still gripped her.

"Midelle."

"Where's that?" She crossed her arms. Her annoyance faded when the pool stretched out on the ground and lifted into a hazy lavender veil. Calla watched in awe.

"On the other side is Midelle."

She was oblivious to Finn's words as the portal grew taller and wider. Through the haze, Calla saw the middle get darker with outlines of different shapes appearing. Incoherent whispers started coming from within the portal. "Do you hear them?"

Finn gave her a strange look, "Hear who?"

Calla forced herself to walk around the portal. Everything in her wanted to reach out to see if there was another side. The whispers were still faint, but they called to her. Her heart drummed in her chest. The more Calla investigated the portal, the stronger the voices became. She took a tentative step closer, her breathing shallow.

"Lady Calla?" Finn asked as she took another step closer.

The voices were calling to her... no, they were begging to her. "The whispers..." She mumbled, reaching out into the portal. Her fingertips touched the veil, appearing on the other side.

Finn watched her, not saying a word.

The whispers drew her in like a siren's song and she was lost at sea. Every cell in her body was screaming to move into the lavender haze. Calla took a step into the portal, hesitating with her next step. She felt a force pulling at her from the other side. Her breathing stalled as her back foot joined the front one. Before she could stop herself, she was through to Midelle.

<h1 style="text-align:center">Three</h1>

The voices stopped the instant Calla passed through the portal. The only light was from the moon's glow sneaking through the low clouds. A sudden wind tossed her hair. She wrapped her hands around her bare arms to fend off the chill and realized she was standing on a stone balcony. She took several cautious but quick steps to the edge of the balcony, encased by a railing made from columns of ornately carved stone.

Her stomach twisted once she realized how high she was. Down below, a plateau gently sloped into a brief patch of forest before leading straight into a grand city. Calla was surprised by just how far away the city below was. A pit hardened in her stomach. She never had a problem with heights until this moment.

Finn came through the portal, waving his hand through, to break it up in the same manner to when Anita fell through the first one. Hazy lavender droplets floated away with the wind. Calla whipped around in a fury, marched up to him, jabbed her finger in front of Finn's face and shouted, "Where are we?"

Finn's calmness surprised her as he moved her hand away from his face. "You already know, Midelle."

Calla shook her head in anger. "No. It doesn't exist! You're lying!"

"Lady Calla, it does, and you're here," Finn said.

"Take me home!" The moon peeked past the clouds at her demand. The wind carried shouting from the city below to her ears. She paused for a moment at the sounds, then quietly proclaimed, "I don't want to be here!"

"I can't do that," Finn replied. "Let's get you inside. You're not dressed for our fall weather. You look cold."

"No!" Frustration swirled in her head. "I'm not the Hybrid or whatever you're looking for, and you will take me home. Right now!"

"Lady Calla," Finn started slowly, "I can understand this is difficult for you, but..."

"Take me home," she punctuated each word. Her fists clenched at her sides and her nails bit into her palms.

"Lady Calla," Finn said again before he opened a grand set of doors.

"No!" She took a step back from the doors. "Get away from me!"

Finn shook his head and stepped inside. "Fine. Stay out here and freeze to death if that's what you want." He slammed the doors.

Calla's bottom lip shivered as a sharp wind ripped through her thin t-shirt and jeans. She crossed her arms again while looking around the balcony. Besides a bench, unlit torches on the wall, and pots of blooming flowers everywhere, that was it. No way out, and no way down without killing herself. Angry in this defeat, Calla opened one of the doors. Finn deliberately lit a bedside lantern, then turned to face her. It was the only source of light aside from the sparse moonlight slipping past the doors. Finn stood tall with his hands behind his back. The flickering lamp light illuminated one side of his face. "So, you've changed your mind. Good."

Calla closed the door, thankful to not be in the cold anymore. "Just because I came inside, does not mean I am going to stay here." She waved her hand in the air, "Get another one of those purple portal things and take me home."

"Hybrid..."

"Calla!" She stomped her foot, "My name is Calla Moro, and..."

"Lady Calla, it's not that simple," Finn gave her a beseeching look and clasped his hands behind his back.

"Oh, but it is. Didn't your mother ever teach you to put things back where you found them?"

Finn's face hardened. His eyes narrowed in on her, and Calla returned the look. He didn't move an inch and neither did she.

A knock on the door turned both of their heads to the sound. Finn stalked across the room at a quick pace while Calla had her hand on the door to the balcony, ready to hide. She only had a sliver of trust in Finn, but he had saved her life after all. Watching the door with pointed interest, she saw it open a crack and heard someone whispering to Finn.

He whispered something back, then shut the door. "I must leave you now."

Calla's eyes grew wide. She darted across the room to Finn, grabbing onto his arm as if he was keeping her from falling from a cliff. His muscles tightened under her desperate grip. Her eyes dipped down to the dark stain on the sleeve of his other arm. "Don't leave me alone here." Her voice was frantic, "You said I was in danger! Aren't more of those corrupters coming?" Calla couldn't define how she felt, but she knew she didn't want to be alone, even if it meant Finn staying with her.

Finn coldly shook off her hands. "You're safe here, in the castle," he said, stepping away from Calla. "Get some rest."

"How do you expect me to sleep after what happened?"

"Lay on the bed and close your eyes."

"That is not what I meant," Calla shrieked in vain.

Finn cracked open the door, then slipped through and shut it behind him before she had finished the sentence.

"Open this door right now!" She banged her fists on the door. Calla tried to open it, but the heavy door wouldn't budge. "Captain Finnegan Quinn!" She pounded on the door. "Let me out!"

After a few minutes, it was clear that the door was locked. If someone was there, they weren't going to answer her or open the door. The moon and the lantern provided a little light as she huddled in the corner by the door to the balcony. From that perspective, she could make out a large bed a few feet away from her with the bedside table next to it. A long and thin table sat along the wall to her right. On the wall opposite of her the dark square of a fireplace stood out against the light-colored walls. Two arm-chairs sat facing the fireplace and what looked to be a bookshelf nearby. She wanted to start a fire so she could see better, but her body stayed put by the balcony door.

Looking away from the room, a sudden wave of fear and anx-iety crashed into her. "This can't be happening," she whispered to herself. "This is a dream. Close your eyes, and when you open them, you'll be at home and in bed." She closed her eyes and repeated those words again and again. Her eyes cracked open, and her lips quivered as she realized that she wasn't dreaming. "No, no no..." Her fingers twirled strands of her hair in angst. Calla's stomach turned at the prospect of never seeing Felicia again. Her best friend was all she had left in the world. Would Felicia even care that she went missing? She had to, but how would she ever find out that Calla was missing? She was off the radar for two months gallivanting in the jungle. Calla chided herself for being so stupid. She should have bolted from Finn the second he untied her. The gravity of her situation had tears pouring down her face and light sobs filling the room.

A gentle knock rapped on the door. Calla looked up in fear. The tears left her eyes puffy and face wet. Adrenaline surged through her as another set of knocks, somewhat louder, sound-ed on the door. She grabbed a heavy golden candelabra off the thin table next to her then placed her hand on the balcony door. She didn't know if she had it in her to hit anyone, but her life could depend on it. She needed to escape this room and find a way to get home.

"May I come in, Lady Calla? I am Violet Gund, your hand-maid." The voice was kind.

Calla didn't answer, her grip only tightened on the candelabra.

"I'm going to come in."

Calla heard the lock unlatch, and she swallowed hard. The door opened, and Calla caught a glimpse of a female guard outside peering in along with light from the hallway. A woman came in, taller than Calla by at least a few inches. Violet looked older than Calla, with a wide-set frame. She wore a stiff cotton dress and apron. She carried a tray with a teapot and two cups on it. Calla noticed her gentle smile, and kind brown eyes first.

Violet stopped near the two plush chairs, placed the tray on the table between them and knelt beside the fireplace. Calla watched her, not saying a word. Every so often, she glanced back towards Calla, who hadn't moved. After a long and silent minute Violet had a small fire started. As the fire strengthened, she placed more logs on top to bolster the flame. Even with the new source of light, the room still flickered with darkness. Calla saw the four-poster bed with more clarity. She had a hard time looking away because it looked more expensive than anything she had ever slept in.

"That's much better, isn't it?" Violet smiled, sat down in a chair, and poured tea for herself. She looked at Calla, who was ready to bolt out to the balcony. The woman had a square-shaped face and a strong chin to match her sturdy shoulders. Her graying hair eluded at a jet-black past with the locks tucked into a low bun at the nape of her neck. "I'm sure you have a lot of questions."

Calla kept a tight grip on the candelabra as she nodded her head. "Where am I?" She fought back a wince at how aggressive it sounded.

Violet sipped her tea first before answering, "You know where you are, Midelle."

"No," she sighed, "Where is Midelle?"

Violet thought for a moment, taking another sip of tea. "I will cut right to the chase. You are not in the human realm anymore."

Calla's heart sank, in utter disbelief.

"Think of Midelle as another world, connected by magic."

Calla shook her head. "This is crazy. I must be dreaming."

"I am afraid you're not." Violet patted the other chair. "Why don't you come sit by the fire and drink some tea. It will calm you. You can also put down the candelabra, I'm not going to hurt you. I may look a little scary, but I could never harm a fly."

Calla's grip on the heavy golden candelabra loosened somewhat, but her feet stayed still. "I'm fine right here," she lowered the candelabra a little. "There's been some mistake, I'm not this... Hybrid everyone keeps calling me."

"I can only understand how confused you are," Violet sympathized. "The realm has been waiting a long time for your return."

"Return?" A spike of anxiety pierced her gut. "You don't understand, I've never been here before."

Violet's low chuckled was punctuated by a pop from the fire. The rogue sparks fizzled on the stone hearth. "What other questions do you have?"

Calla licked her lips, noting Violet hadn't answered her question. "What's going to happen to me?

"Well," Violet began, but she stopped and then started again, "Captain Quinn didn't tell you?"

Calla's jaw tightened. "He wasn't exactly forthcoming with helpful information"

"Oh well, he fulfilled his most important duty by bringing you here."

A sudden rage flamed up inside Calla, who exactly did Finn think he was? She slammed the candelabra on the table in anger.

Violet jumped, "Oh my word. Captain Quinn will be back in the morning if you need to speak with him. For now, why don't you come and sit." Violet patted the chair next to her.

The fire inside Calla was spent as fast as it had ignited. Her anger was with Finn, not Violet. She was at least being helpful. "Okay." She took a step and stopped, wanting to bring the candelabra.

"You don't need the candelabra," Violet stated as if she could read Calla's mind.

She placed her makeshift weapon down and walked away from the table with an awkwardness that embarrassed her. "I wasn't... I... um," Calla stuttered, "I wanted..."

"It's all right, you're scared."

Calla took a seat and watched Violet pour tea for her.

Violet's skin was a warm, moderate tan with what looked like hard and cracked patches in certain places. It resembled the way Hector's skin looked. The patches didn't look painful, but like a natural part of her. Violet held the teacup out for Calla.

Calla dropped her eyes to the teacup when she realized Violet caught her staring at her skin. The apples of her cheeks grew hot from embarrassment.

"It's okay to look, but not to stare. You'll find thousands like me out there."

Calla took a small sip of the tea, welcoming the warmth in her sore throat. "What are you?"

Violet smiled and crossed her thick fingers in her lap. "I am a troll."

"A what?" Calla gasped while holding back a laugh. This had to all be a crazy and elaborate dream.

"A troll. There are no ordinary humans in Midelle, Lady Calla. The realm used to be void of people. Only animals, until the deities came..."

"I'm sorry," Calla cut in, "You've lost me. Vampires don't exist. Trolls don't exist. And I know for a fact that deities don't exist."

Violet drummed her fingers on the teacup in thought. "I want to tell you a story."

Calla sucked in a breath to say something but drank her tea instead. She paused with the teacup on her lips for a moment thinking it was a mistake to drink the liquid. She internally laughed at herself to shake the notion away.

"A long time ago, the heavens above blessed these lands with four deities with unique powers. Vitala could harness the power of life and nature. Auan was in tune with the tides. Tera could control the heartiness of the land. The last deity," Violet sighed and glanced at Calla, she was watching with curiosity in her eyes.

"Morta found that she connected with the shadows of death and darkness.

"Each of the deities made a home of their own within Midelle but longed for companionship. They decided to work together to fill the realm with wondrous citizens who would love their creators. By combining their magic, they turned to the human realm. There they took hundreds in secret. They experimented to find they could infuse a touch of their magic into these people. Excluding Morta, the deities created beautiful creatures... druids, mermaids, and dragons." Calla's eyes grew wide. "Vitala and Tera noticed Morta could not create creatures on her own. They assisted her with their gifts of magic and thus created vampires and trolls.

"As time passed, Morta grew envious as her creations were never as beautiful as the others. Her envy grew into a hatred that grew day after day until one day, Morta created a creature of pure hatred. The hate from this creature's heart spread like a plague among those not strong enough to fight it. The citizens of Midelle feared this disease that they called The Corruption. The three deities sought to destroy The Corruption, and that was the First War of Midelle. The citizens of Midelle won in a glorious battle, and the deities confronted Morta. They brought her back to the heavens to pay for her grievous crimes. The citizens learned to live in peace without their beloved deities. Since then, there were rare sightings of The Corrupted, but now..."

Completely enthralled by Violet's story, Calla found she had finished her tea. She poured herself another cup. "So, there are no humans in Midelle?"

Violet readjusted herself in the chair. "No. Every human to step into Midelle was transformed hundreds of years ago."

"I'm human," she stated with a tone of nervousness in her voice.

Violet didn't say anything, she avoided Calla's eyes and stared into the fire.

"...Right?"

"There's a little more to the story which will answer your question."

Calla's breath stalled in dread of the answer.

"Thirty years ago, patterns reemerged in the realm that were very reminiscent of before the First War. People disappeared only to come back Corrupted or not at all. The disappearances spread fear across the realm. The citizens hoped Vitala, Auan, and Tera would descend from the heavens to lead them in a war against The Corrupted. Instead, the three deities created a weapon. This weapon will end The Corruption once and for all."

"What kind of weapon?" Her heart was racing. Despite drinking the tea, her mouth went dry.

Violet smiled and grabbed Calla's free hand, "You." She turned Calla's hand to show her tattoo. "The three deities created you, the Hybrid, to end The Corrupted. This sigil proves it. It is the mark of the deities."

Tears threatened to spill, but Calla didn't know if she had any left. All her life she thought she was normal, but her birthright, if she could even call it that, was to stop an evil she never knew existed, and her sigil proved it. The thought was dizzying.

"Created?" Her voice was meek. "How?" A tiny spark of interest lit in her heart, the answer she sought could be here, in this crazy fantasy land.

"By the deities' hands, Lady Calla. I remember that night when I learned about the Hybrid, from the Oracle. I was twenty-five or so years younger and the Queen's handmaid," She reminisced. "It was a cold winter's night, and the snow wouldn't stop. The air was thick with something that I could feel in my bones. I was up late that night. The Oracle came to the gates, demanding to see the King. The guards brought her in as it was dreadful outside, but to our amazement, she was blind. Her eyes were cloudy and white. Somehow the Oracle looked straight into my eyes and demanded to see the King once again. I never ran so fast in my life. I awakened the King and Queen and explained the situation as best I could. We hurried to the Oracle, who told us that the deities had created a Hybrid of life, land, and water. The Hybrid was born to save the realm, but she cautioned that the Hybrid must not fall into corrupted hands. If that were to happen, the end of all life would surely follow. The Oracle also said a great tremor would shake the realm as a signal when they Hybrid was ready to return." She paused for a few seconds. "The signal was you telling us that you were ready to return to end The Corruption once and for all. It also awakened your powers."

Calla furrowed her eyebrows and removed her hand from Violet's grasp. "So, I don't have parents? I was created...?"

"It would seem so."

Calla's shoulders slumped forward in disappointment. Her broken heart continued to break into smaller pieces.

"I'm sorry if that's not what you wanted to hear."

Calla pushed past the disappointment and tears. "I need to get back to the... human realm."

"You can't leave. They know exactly who you are, from your sigil. It makes you different from everyone else."

Calla looked at her hand. The intricate lines and curves intersected to create a mystery flower. Her mark looked different in a way, but it was the same one she grew to accept.

Calla looked up at Violet. "They? As in," her voice broke recalling their wicked red eyes, "The Corrupters?"

"Corrupted. But yes, since you sent the signal, they will stop at nothing to find you." The fire sparked again, and a log tumbled down in the pile to the back of the fireplace.

"I thought I was safe here?"

"You are, but it won't take long for The Corrupted to figure out that we have you. And where else is better to protect you than the capital city of Midelle, Japhia."

Calla rubbed her sigil with her other fingers. She couldn't fathom that trapped within the lines was a power that could change the fate of a world. "What about my powers? I haven't exactly tried to use them, but I don't feel any different."

Violet pursed her lips, frowned, and wrung her hands together. "The night I learned of the Hybrid, the Oracle had more to say. She mentioned that even though when the signal shakes the realm, you'll only have half of your powers. The Oracle safeguards the other half, hidden away in the depths of the Library of Midelle. To have the best outcome when you fight The Corrupted, you will need your complete powers."

"Where's the Library of Midelle?"

"The Library is on the far coast of Midelle at the Cape Toria. Even on horseback, it would take two months to cross. I am told that Captain Quinn has a few ideas about how best to escort you across the realm."

Calla rolled her eyes in disbelief. "Can't the Oracle come here? She's done it before, right? There has to be another way."

"The Oracle is too frail to travel. Even if we send to retrieve her, she will not come. All those years ago, the Oracle was adamant that the Hybrid must go to her." Violet drank the rest of her tea.

Calla fought the urge to roll her eyes.

"During your crossing, Captain Quinn will keep you safe. It's his duty, and he will die for you to fulfill this duty. Since you have the power to save or destroy this realm, you can't be allowed to fall into the hands of The Corrupted."

"If," Calla frowned, "I am this Hybrid then how can I be The Corrupted's weapon too? You said the Deities created me to stop the evil." Calla got up and paced the room at a slow pace with her brain working overtime.

"You can become Corrupted too."

Calla gasped. Violet's words slapped her hard. Picturing herself with red eyes made her want to vomit.

"You're not immune, no one is."

Calla sat on the edge of the bed, her mind running away with what if's.

"Dark times have fallen upon our realm. The Corrupted are becoming stronger, smarter, and more dangerous by the day. They used to lose themselves to The Corruption and become mindless, but we're seeing less of that. It's treacherous out there, and the citizens of Midelle are becoming more and more frightened. The number of disappearances is increasing at an alarming rate. I know you didn't ask for this, but you are the Hybrid."

Calla shook her head and a lone tear tumbled down her face. A vice wrapped around her chest and her breaths fell in shallow puffs.

Violet only watched with soft eyes.

"I can't do this," Calla pushed out.

Violet cleaned up the teacups, grabbed the tray, and stopped right before the door. "I'll let you be. You are safe here in the castle. There will always be a guard posted outside your door. The door will remain locked for an extra layer of protection. If you are to need anything, knock and request for me. I will come."

Calla looked up, her lip quivered, but she forced a small smile. "Thank you."

Violet nodded her head and left Calla alone once again.

Calla heard the door lock, a noise that made her stomach drop in sickening loneliness. She was stuck in this realm. There had to be a way to get home. She knew she had to get one of those purple vials that made a portal. Both The Corrupted man, and Finn had one, but that was a task for the morning.

Feeling defeated and exhausted, she slipped off her sneakers and fell into bed. The mattress hugged every part of her in a welcoming comfort. It made her think of her bed at home. Home, Calla sobbed into the sheets. All she could think about was home and how to get there. After a while of thinking, her eyelids grew heavy, and she slipped into a restless sleep.

Four

Calla stood in a large field of endless waving grass. Her simple white cotton dress fluttered in a wind that didn't exist. "Hello?" Her voice echoed on and on. There was no sky, no stars, no sun or moon. Only the overgrown grass in a black abyss. She stepped forward, not sure if this was the right way... if there even was a right way. She stopped to admire a large patch of flowers. It was the only thing she saw besides grass. The flowers radiated a familiarity that she couldn't place. On each flower the shimmering white petals overlapped, each layer alternating the peaks and crests of the petals. The layering created a beautiful, cupped shape. Calla lay down next to the patch and touched one with a gentle downturn of a finger. Calla drew back her finger, but the petal she touched reached back out to caress her skin. She gasped but smiled. "Why hello there, little one." Calla kept stroking the petals of the flower. She felt at peace, it was her and the flowers.

Her brow furrowed when thorns slithered from the ground and choked the flowers. "Stop," Calla screamed, it echoed. She started pulling at the thorns, their sharpness cutting her hands. She could feel the flowers dying all around her. Calla felt pricks on her toes. She ripped her feet from the weak grasp of the sharp vines. The thorns grew more aggressive and wound up her legs to her knees. Blood trickled down her legs as she pulled at the thorns, and panic grew within her. Dead vines of thorns snapped from the ground and tied down her wrists. She bled from a thousand cuts as her body was bound by the vines. Calla's eyes grew wide as she watched her blood swirled and moved her skin to take the sigil's form.

"Hybrid..." A cold voice called through the dark sky. "Come to me."

Calla screamed, fighting the thorns even harder.

"It's only a matter of time."

Calla awoke drenched in sweat which glistened from the sun's rays that reached into the room. She thought for a moment that she was back home, but no, she was exactly where she feared she was. Midelle. A pit opened in her stomach as she realized it wasn't a dream. This was real.

The fire had reduced to embers while she slept. Through her bleary eyes, Calla noticed how beautiful the room was now that the early morning sun chased the night away. A golden chandelier dripping with clear crystals hung from the high ceiling in the middle of the room. She was mesmerized by the way the sun's early rays danced off the crystals, spreading soft rainbows throughout the room. The bed had thick ivory curtains tied back at the posts and soft cream duvet and sheets. There was the shelf that she'd seen near the fireplace last night was filled to the brim with books of all sizes. Both of those things near the fireplace and sitting area where her and Violet talked last night. Heavy double doors to her room were on her left and the doors to the balcony on her right. The presence of the tall windows that surrounded the balcony doors allowed Calla to catch the fading purple-pink wisps of dawn. Straight across from her was a smaller wooden door, then a larger one. Delicate ivory covered the walls decorated with golden accents, drowning her in splendor. Calla felt like this would be well-suited to a five-star resort, but she didn't feel like a five-star VIP.

She felt like a prisoner.

Still shaken from her nightmare, Calla pulled her knees up to her chest and rested her chin on them. How was she going to get through this? She knew they weren't going to let her leave. Not until she did what they wanted, but she couldn't fight anyone or anything. Especially those monsters with red eyes. She had to leave today, and that was that.

Calla got up, slipped her sneakers back on, and stood before the gilded door to the outside of her room. "Is anyone out there?" Calla heard rustling; someone was outside.

"At your service, Hybrid," a woman said through the door. "Do you need Violet?"

"It's Calla, actually. No, thank you. You need to let me out," Calla replied with unease. It couldn't be that easy, could it?

The woman sighed. "I'm under strict orders from Captain Quinn not to let you out and to guard you with my life."

Captain Finnegan Quinn. That name only lit her with anger and... something else. She decided it was fear.

"I don't belong here, I'm not the Hybrid," Calla replied while fighting back tears. "Please..."

There was another voice outside the door, a lot peppier and energetic. "Good morning First Commander Varden. Hybrid?" The voice sounded younger.

"Calla," she corrected, annoyed.

"May I come in?"

"Sure," Calla said, then muttered, "What choice do I have?" She had a quick thought to grab the candelabra, but Violet said she was safe in the Castle. Violet seemed trustworthy, but so did Finn.

The door unlocked, and a carefree girl stepped into the room rolling in a small cart. She couldn't have been more than ten. The young girl smiled, but Calla couldn't stop staring at her eyes. They were big, bright, and her irises a starchy white. Her hair fell to her waist in long, soft waves of lavender. A raspberry dress embroidered in white hung from her youthful body. To accommodate her tiny frame, she had rolled the sleeves up, but the hem still pooled on the ground some.

"Who are you?" Calla made herself look anywhere else but her eyes.

The girl laughed, it was light and boisterous. "Forgive me for barging in. I'm Philomena Castob, the Resident Witch of the castle! And you're the Hybrid," she said the last part with awe. The witch stopped the cart by the chairs. The top had a tray with a plate covered by a cloche, a pitcher of bright yellow liquid, and a teapot with a teacup. The bottom half of the old wooden cart had bowls of herbs and different looking liquids and a neatly folded blue fabric that she could make out as a dress. "I offered to bring you breakfast since I was on my way up here anyway." Her smile was infectious, if it weren't for the situation, Calla would have smiled back.

"My name is Calla," she corrected, not wanting to hear the h-word. She did have a name. "Did you say you were a... witch?"

"Yes! The youngest to ever serve the realm at eleven. I took over for Rose two years ago." Philomena clapped her hands together, "I'm still kinda new at this."

"Who's Rose?" Her stomach growled loud enough that Philomena had to have heard it. She covered her stomach and looked away in embarrassment.

Philomena smacked her lips together. She had an ivory hue to her skin, a little button nose, and plump cheekbones.

Calla thought this girl was adorable and so energetic.

"She was the previous witch to serve the realm. She took ill because she's old, like Violet, and left once she felt I was ready. It's a tradition that the outgoing witch continues to train their replacement until they die. Violet says I'm doing good so far." Philomena put the tray on the table in the middle of the chairs, being careful not to spill. "Here, you should eat." She smiled.

Calla nodded her head and stubbed her foot as she walked to the table. She winced in pain as she mumbled words not meant for an eleven year old's ears under her breath.

"It's so dark in here!" Philomena raised her hands towards the fire. A small ember of fire glowed in the palm of her hand. The fire came alive with a small whoosh after she tossed the ember into the fireplace. "That's much better, isn't it?" Philomena moved to put more wood in the fireplace.

"Yes. Thank you," Calla said with a small smile while looking at the fire in amazement. She lifted the cloche and her mouth watered looking at all the delicious items. Sausages, fruit, eggs on toast, and some sort of porridge made her debate on what to eat first. She was never a breakfast person, but she felt like she hadn't eaten in days.

Philomena went back to the cart, pulled out and unfolded the blue fabric so Calla could see it. "This is one of the Queen's dresses. You should change. Violet is working on getting you more clothes after you meet with the King and Queen. Only the best for the Hybrid."

Calla paused with the cup filled with a sweet citrus liquid to her lips, "King and Queen?" She recalled Violet mentioning a King and Queen last night, but they felt like mythical creatures in a fairytale then. Everyone did, even herself.

"Yes, as soon as you eat and change, you will meet with them. They are quite eager to meet the Hybrid."

Annoyance dug under her skin as she reminded Philomena, "Calla."

"Oh right, my sincerest apologies, Lady Calla." Philomena did a curtsey that only made Calla feel like a jerk. Philomena rocked on her heels, biting her lip. "So... what's it like?"

Calla looked up from the food, her stomach was all but begging for her to eat. "What is what like?"

Philomena looked at Calla with her eyes wide and a large open grin, "To be the Hybrid!"

"Oh." Calla didn't want to break her spirit, nor lie to the little creature. "It's different."

"I can't wait for you to defeat The Corrupted," Her words made Calla fill with guilt. Philomena believed that she could save the realm. "You couldn't have come at a better time."

"Philomena..." Calla began, but she stopped as the witch held up a finger.

Philomena grabbed a wrapped package from the cart. "Here. It's Captain Quinn's request." Philomena held out the package, and Calla took it with a tiny scowl on her face. His name made her stomach churn.

Calla pulled the simple string which unwrapped the simple cloth. A pair of gloves fell into her lap. They were a soft taupe leather and finger-less. "Gloves?"

"To hide your sigil, you'll be wearing them a lot. Captain Quinn wants you to get used to wearing them. I don't think it's much of a request from how he shoved them into my hands on my way up here this morning."

Calla tossed the gloves onto her tray, not caring about what Finn wanted her to wear. "Right." Calla started eating, her stomach wouldn't allow her to wait any longer. She wasn't going to let Finn spoil her appetite. She had no idea when she'd get the chance to eat again. Calla pushed aside a pang of guilt from giving Philomena the cold shoulder and spooned into the porridge. If her stomach growled one more time, it would eat itself for breakfast.

Philomena laid the dress on the open armchair then placed the discarded gloves on top. "I guess I'll take my leave now. Captain Quinn will be up after the morning bells." Her eyes were cast down.

"Philomena?" Calla asked through a mouth full of creamy porridge.

The witch turned around with hope in her eyes.

Calla swallowed. "Thank you. I guess I'll see you around... the castle?"

The witch smiled, nodded and left with a tiny hop in her step. Calla resumed shoveling food in her mouth as quickly as she could. She was so eager to speak with the King and Queen. They would understand that this is all a mistake and let her return home in one of those portal walls.

With a full belly, Calla ventured to the unexplored room to find a bathroom. It was a shame she wasn't staying because the golden claw-footed bathtub was calling her name. She was able to pump water into a marbled basin to wash her face and arms. Her hair was still a wild golden mess, but she braided it as best as she could to fall over her shoulder, tying it with a short ribbon. She let her fingers trace the soft cobalt blue dress. Calla had difficulty slipping on the dress because it fit so snugly onto her body. Not that she was fat, but the Queen must be a stick. She could see herself in the reflection from the windows and did a soft spin. A part of her always dreamed of wearing dresses like this, living in a castle, and saving the world. Never did she imagine that things like that happened. Her fingers traced over her sigil. It felt foreign to think of it that way, but it never felt right calling it a tattoo either. A chill ran down her spine and over her skin as she thought about if Finn, Violet and Philomena were all right.

A distant but loud song of crisp bells tolled through the air. Calla counted nine tolls. A sharp knock snapped her from her thoughts. "Who's there?" She pulled on the gloves, feeling the soft lining caress her skin. Her fingers moved as she tested the gloves.

She heard what sounded like a person on the other side of the door clearing their throat.

"Captain Quinn."

Agitation rose underneath her skin as she muttered for him to come in. The lock lifted, and he slipped in standing tall. He wore a leather tunic with a crest of a dagger stabbed into the ground sewn onto it and a long sleeved linen undershirt. The thick leather belt wrapped around his hips carried the sword he had employed to save her life. "Good morning, Lady Calla. I hope you slept well." His voice was calm and curt. That got under Calla's skin even more.

"I did after Violet answered all my questions," Calla replied with the same curtness as Finn.

"Are you ready to meet King Nakosi and Queen Shea?"

"Yes, I have a lot to discuss with them." She opened her mouth again, but then closed it.

Finn gave her a look, but Calla didn't know him well enough to decipher it. "Is there something on your mind?"

"Now that you mention it, I believe you owe me an apology for abandoning me last night. I asked you to stay and you left anyway. I would think that with how important everyone makes me out to be, you'd want to ensure my safety."

Finn squared his shoulders back, rejecting her idea. "I am here to protect you, not hold your hand. Do I make myself clear? The King and Queen are waiting in the throne room."

Calla bit back the want to roll her eyes. She thought it was a reasonable request, but if this was what Finn wanted, then so be it. "Right. Let's go." When the door opened, Calla felt free, but she knew she was far from it. The hallway was lit with torches, adding to the natural light coming through a mix of clear and stained glass windows. Her room was at the end of a long hallway, with other hallways branching off left and right at the other end. Tapestries, statues, and exotic flowers lined the corridor. She'd never seen anything so grand.

They were steps ahead as Finn ran into someone. "Oh," a voice squeaked. "Forgive me, Captain Quinn." It was Philomena. A quick look of fright flashed on her face.

"Move, witch," Finn ordered. Philomena scrambled past Finn to stand behind Calla.

"Captain Quinn," Calla scolded, she had no idea what she was doing, but a grown man had no reason to terrify a young girl like that. She brought a cold gaze up to meet his narrowed jaded eyes. "Not very Captain-like of you to speak to the Resident Witch like that." Finn took a step toward Philomena, and Calla's arm shot out to protect her. "Aren't we headed somewhere?"

Finn growled, "I'd watch your tone if I were you."

Calla knitted her eyebrows together. Finn was putting on a good show before, but now his true colors were showing.

"You watch your tone, I am the Hybrid after all," Calla hissed, not believing she called herself that name.

Philomena cleared her throat, "I wanted to come by to see how breakfast was."

Calla bent down to face the girl, "It hit the spot. Thank you. Why don't you come by later tonight?" She glanced up at Finn in time to see him huff. "We'll talk more then. Okay?" Not like she'd be here, but she wanted to calm the witch's nerves.

Philomena beamed. "Okay! I'll see you after supper." She kept walking to speak to the guard standing watch at her door.

Calla wanted to introduce herself to the female guard with soft wheat-colored hair. She thought it wouldn't be a bad idea to befriend her.

"Let's go," Finn ordered, cutting her thoughts off. He turned on his heel and continued down the corridor.

The halls were laden with torches, paintings, and tapestries, much like the corridor outside her room. All the art depicted places or perhaps stories, but all were a mystery to her. Calla wanted to take in the artwork, but all she got was fleeting glances as she made fast strides to keep up with Finn. Never did she stop rehearsing her case in her head, how this was all one big misunderstanding, and they should allow her to go home.

They came to a doorway that led to a tall and wide spiral staircase. When they started their descent, she saw more floors above hers. Calla's stomach erupted with nerves when they reached the main floor. If she hadn't been so nervous, she would have been in awe by the opulence of the castle. Floors of marble parquet led the way to a balcony above the main foyer. On each side of the foyer, a staircase against the wall connected the two floors. Her head was dizzy with the number of expensive metals and gems that were everywhere. No matter where she looked, there was an element of elegant splendor to it.

"This way," Finn severed Calla's thoughts. They went under the overlook, through literal golden doors and into a massive room. On the far side from the door was a low platform where two people sat on glimmering thrones. Calla gulped, but her mouth was dry. On each side of the doors a staircase that led to a balcony that, supported by thick marble pillars, encased the circumference of the room stopping short of the thrones. Calla froze, only steps beyond the stairs, as the King and Queen focused on her.

"What are you waiting for," Finn hissed under his breath.

"I...uh..."

"It would be best if I were to escort her the rest of the way, Captain Quinn." Violet appeared next to Calla, making her jump. Her nerves were getting the best of her. Finn stepped aside and locked his hands behind him. His face was void of any emotion, but his eyes never left Calla. She could feel his gaze on her back as Violet pulled her arm with a gentle touch to get her to walk. "No need to be afraid, my dear. King Nakosi and Queen Shea are bursting at the seams to meet you. They would have come last night, but I told them you needed some rest and time to digest all this. Remember to breathe."

Calla took deep, timed breaths to slow her anxious heart down. After a few steps she didn't feel about to collapse anymore. "Thanks."

Calla, Violet, and Finn approached the royal pair. Violet dropped into a curtsey and Finn bowed. Calla copied the female troll, but her courtesy was less than graceful. The King was a tall man, with rich brown yet wrinkled skin, bald head, and eyes that reminded her of cola. A thick, golden crown studded with gems sat upon his head, and he wore a regal outfit of navy blue and white.

The woman next to him, the Queen, had a tight face and was pale as could be with early signs of aging woven into her skin. The tight curls of her ginger hair were woven into a braided crown about her head, topped by a delicate tiara of silver. The large emerald in the center of the crown stood out against her coppery hair. She too had eyes that reminded Calla of cola. Her hands laid clasped in her lap, and she wore a dark gray dress with a thick black fur cape. Calla felt the eyes of the king and Queen upon her. Hell, she knew everyone's eyes were on her.

"Hybrid," the King began, his voice calm, "I am King Nakosi Adel of Midelle, welcome. I wanted to give you some time to adjust. I hope you've enjoyed a proper welcome so far."

Calla let go of Violet's arm to smooth her dress, "My name is Calla Moro, King Nakosi." Everyone remained silent, waiting for her to speak again. Calla glanced at Finn. "Everyone has been very kind, thank you for the hospitality." Her voice shook more than she thought it would. She tried to remember the speech she had planned. She should have written it down.

"I am Queen Shea Adel of Midelle," the woman said with a curt tone, not moving one inch.

Calla smiled and averted her hard gaze. The thick red hair matched Finn's. Calla's eyes darted between them; she knew they shared blood. Shea could pass for Finn's sister, perhaps even his mother.

"I can understand this must all be," Nakosi paused for a moment, "hard for you." Calla nodded her head, afraid to speak. "Captain Quinn and Violet informed us of your skepticism about the situation."

"Um, yes." Calla felt like a sheep in a lion's den. "I can't be your Hybrid. I am Calla Moro, nothing more, and I'd like to go home to the human realm. Right now." She felt every eye upon her, and she did what she could to keep herself together.

Nakosi rubbed his chin, his dark eyes watched her with intense interest. "I do believe there's been a misunderstanding."

"Yes," Calla agreed with eagerness. "A huge mistake. I'm so glad you see…"

"No, did you not grow up with the knowledge that you were the Hybrid?" Nakosi interjected.

Calla's stomach dropped into her feet. "No… I had no idea, Your Majesty. I'm not what you think I am."

Shea tilted her head. The emerald caught the light beaming through a window from the balcony. "You bear the sigil of the Hybrid, do you not?"

Calla pulled off her glove and tilted the back of her hand towards the King and Queen. "This? I was born with it. It's nothing more than a mere tattoo."

"Come now, Hybrid," Nakosi laughed. "That is no tattoo. It is the sigil of the deities, a deity rose."

"No..." Calla couldn't remember her planned reply to correct him. Her strategy was spiraling out of control.

"You are the Hybrid," Shea added with the corners of her lips upturned in the most subtle of smirks. "The proof is woven on your skin by the deities themselves."

Calla so wanted to smack that look off her pale face.

"Now about your powers. All those years ago, the Oracle mentioned baseline powers. Let's see them," Nakosi ordered. He leaned forward on his throne with an intense interest.

Calla's face twisted in confusion, "I don't have any powers."

"Nonsense," Shea laughed, "You are the..."

"I'm not the Hybrid!"

"Absurd," Nakosi cut in. "My love spoke the truth, look at your hand, the sigil is there. Clear as day."

"No. I am not your Hybrid. I am not the savior of your realm. My name is Calla, and I demand that you take me back to where I came from!" Her chest rose and fell dramatically.

Everyone was silent until Nakosi was the one to finally break it. "You are the Hybrid, Lady Calla."

Calla at least felt somewhat rewarded for Nakosi calling her by her name.

"I can't let you go, not until you defeat The Corrupted. Their army is rising again and with a smart and dangerous leader. The deities created you to kill off The Corrupted once and for all."

Calla felt her lip quiver, but she refused to cry.

"Captain Quinn?" Nakosi looked past Calla.

Finn straightened up his already ramrod straight back. "Yes, My King?"

"I agree with your course of action that we discussed last night. Around the clock protection and a sparring session with a member of the Royal Guard once per day. As soon as her powers come to light, you will leave for the Library of Midelle. I want daily reports on her status. That is all, you may leave... Perhaps straight to the sparring yard."

Calla felt her heart drop to her toes. Powers come to light? She didn't have any powers! Her frustration mounted higher with each passing second. She got no say with anything that was happening to her and everything she said was politely acknowledged, but ultimately ignored.

"Yes, My King," Finn said, bowing his head. "Lady Calla, follow me." Finn gave her an expectant look, but her feet stuck to the ground in defiance.

"I'm not going anywhere except home." Her voice was as firm as she could make it.

Finn stepped forward, grabbed her arm to yank her after him. Calla caught herself with a quick step. She heard Violet gasp but remained still, clearly outranked. Finn's eyes narrowed in on Calla. "I wasn't asking."

Fear overtook her body as she followed him. This was turning into a nightmare, one that she hoped she would soon wake up from.

Five

Sitting by the fire, Calla watched the flames dance in the night's silence. She was at a loss for words as she kept replaying the last twenty-four hours over and over in her head. It always started with her at her mom's house going through her belongings and then a wave of grief hit her, and she thought about the strange box. That beautiful box that shook her childhood home and called those red-eyed monsters to her like a strange beacon. Then Finn came to her rescue and brought her here. Now she's been labeled as this Hybrid and tomorrow her and Finn start sparring with training swords, all because of some supposed powers everyone thought she had. Calla broke her stare off with the fire to glance at her sigil, not tattoo. It felt different to think of it that way, but it felt like there was at least a little truth in all this madness.

When Violet had brought her dinner earlier, she wasn't hungry. Now her stomach growled at the cackling fire, and Calla debated going to bed to ward off the hunger. She knew she needed to sleep, but it eluded her as the minutes ticked by. She didn't want to wake up to who knows what the next day.

"Lady Calla?" She picked her head up to a familiar voice. "It's Philomena. I know it's late…"

"Come in." She could use a distraction. Calla heard the lock lift, and the young witch came in. "Hey."

"Good evening, Hybrid." She winced when she realized what she said, "Lady Calla. Sorry."

Calla got up from the floor, wiped her nightgown off and gave Philomena a sympathetic smile. "It's okay. Don't worry about it." Bells started to toll in a melodic song, signaling sundown. She glanced behind her to confirm with the darkening sky with her own eyes. "Shouldn't you be in bed? It's late."

Philomena shrugged. "I fell asleep while waiting for a batch of portal potion to mature, and I ruined it from bubbling too long. It had our only sample of a way to get to Cape Toria in it," her head cast down, but Calla's perked up. "So, I'm not tired now."

"Portal potion? Like the purple liquid in the vials? Do you make those? One can get me to Cape Toria?"

"Yes, Rose made sure I had mastered the task before she left. If only I hadn't fallen asleep. She would have smacked the back of my head, then said, 'witches must be attentive and watch their potions for the precise moment of perfection.'"

Calla calculated the words in her head, making sure she picked the right ones. This could be her chance to escape and go home. "How exactly does it work?"

"Um, well. It's kinda complicated."

Calla fought the urge to sigh and roll her eyes. Of course, it was.

"So," Philomena paused to rethink her words, "you don't know anything about Midelle, right?"

"Right."

"I'll start with the witches then. Since the deities created the realm, traces of their magic still grace the land. Every fifty years, a new witch is born from those traces of magic."

"How did your parents know that you're a witch?" Calla's stomach growled. She wished that she hadn't refused dinner.

"I don't have parents, just like you. We were both born from the deities, but I don't have nearly the power you do."

Calla sat up straight, "I had a mother back home. She recently passed, but..."

"You were born in Midelle. The Oracle said so."

"But someone gave birth to you," Calla retorted in disbelief.

"Not me. A man outside the Falls of Goldtown found me when I was a baby. He brought me to the Emissary of Goldtown, and she brought me here!"

"Wait." Calla rubbed her temple, trying to keep up. "Where is Goldtown?"

"West of here, but besides being born there, I've never left Japhia. Especially now because of The Corrupted. King Nakosi says a corrupted witch is almost as bad as a corrupted Hybrid." Calla tried to keep her face neutral, but Philomena noticed. "Sorry."

"Okay, um." Her head pounded, but she wasn't sure if it was from the tsunami of information or the lack of food. "What's an Emissary?"

"Each city has one. It doesn't matter how many people live there. The town, village or whatever, chooses an Emissary to hear their needs. Then they bring it to King Nakosi's attention at the capitol. Every summer there's an Emissary's Ball where they all come, and most of the city comes too. It's a lot of fun, even if I'm too young for the good stuff. Too bad you missed this year's ball by a couple of weeks." She frowned, "Sorry. I got off topic again."

Calla's headache relaxed into a gentle pounding after a few calming breaths. "So, the portal? How does it work? You said you had one to Cape Toria? That's where I need to go."

The young girl's shoulders slumped forward. "Rose had the foresight to save hair from the Oracle when she came all those years ago. When the portal potions reach maturity, they turn purple and last for a few months. The length of the maturity period depends on the quality of the potion. Once they turn gray they're no good. When you came to Midelle, I started working on that one to get you to Cape Toria, and I ruined it!"

"I don't understand. Hair from the Oracle?"

"Oh yeah! Sorry. Um. I make the potion, and it's useless." Calla's confusion showed on her face. "There are two parts to the potion. Oh. I should have started with that." She licked her lips. "The potion needs a place to open up to, so anything from the location where you want to go. Plants are a hit or miss because the magic can channel to any location where that plant grows. Clothes are bad. Food is bad..." Calla thought about her words while she was off on another tangent. Her face deflated when she realized that she had nothing to bring her back home.

"What's wrong? Are you gonna cry?"

Calla shook her head. She believed all her tears had been spent during her sword-wielding lessons with Finn. "I'm curious how I would get back home. I don't have anything."

"Captain Quinn was thinking of that while he came to rescue you. He put some dirt where he found you in a vial for safekeeping. I have it down in my workroom. It could have been something better, but combined with your hair, it will still get you close to home."

"Well, at least he was thinking of me returning. I'm grateful for that." Calla kept her thoughts of Finn short. He only made her angry, and... wanting to throw a rock at his smug face. Calla touched Philomena's shoulder to comfort her. "It's okay. I'm sure Captain Quinn has other ways to get there. Is there anything else you can use for the location that would work?"

"I wish I had more of the Oracle's hair. It's unique to the person and easy to get. Which reminds me. Can I have some of yours?" Her eyes became wide, and a smile spread on her face. "I have quite a collection of hair. You never know when you'll need the King's, the Queen's, the Captains, First Commander Varden's, Violet's, the cook's, the guard's, groundskeeper's..."

"Sure, it can't hurt. Right?" Calla smiled, cutting off the unending list.

Philomena clapped. "Right! Oh, thank you, Lady Calla!" She rushed Calla's side, but she held up a finger to stave off the anxious witch. She ran her fingers through her hair, pulling out strands that had given up. "Is this enough?" Calla asked. She held out her closed fingers to Philomena.

"Yes!" Philomena pulled each strand from Calla's fingers to drop them in her free cupped hand. "I should practice! I got it right with you the first time. Rose said hair is difficult during the second brewing period. She wasn't lying. I need to work on staying awake. The portal to Cape Toria would have been fine if I hadn't fallen asleep."

Calla played with a crimped wave from letting her braid down, "Practice away. I have hair to spare." She smiled.

"You should come with me to see my workroom," Philomena gasped with excitement. "I can show you all the potions I have brewing and the book that holds all the instructions! Rose told me it's dated back to the first witch of Midelle hundreds of years ago."

"Philomena." Calla rolled her lips together, conjuring up courage. She placed a hand on top of hers. "Can you brew the dirt from my home, the human realm, with the base potion to take me back?"

Philomena's face grew conflicted. "But you're supposed to help us kill all The Corrupted. You can't leave yet."

"I can't do this. This is all one gigantic misunderstanding. I'm not the Hybrid as everyone keeps calling me. This," she paused to show her tattoo, sigil, or whatever it was to the young girl, "it's a tattoo."

"But it has to be you! The hair I had led to you. That's how Captain Quinn found you!"

A light bulb illuminated in Calla's mind. "How did you have my hair before I got here?"

Philomena gave Calla a quizzical look. "The Oracle brought some to find you once you sent the signal. That was after she hid you away in the human realm years ago."

Calla looked at Philomena in disbelief. "The Oracle had my hair as an infant?" Could the Oracle be her birth mother?

A curt throat clearing made Calla and Philomena turn in unison to the door. The young witch curtseyed immediately but Calla froze under the hard eyes of Shea. She hadn't noticed her entering. "Philomena, your studies require your attention. After the disaster today you should be studying to improve your skills."

"Yes, My Queen." She glanced at Calla, a sad look in her eyes. "Goodnight, Lady Calla."

Calla gave her an encouraging smile. "Goodnight, Philomena." She felt her chances of getting home leave with Philomena. "Queen Shea, to what do I owe the pleasure?"

Queen Shea had a wooden box in her hands, and Calla's eyes were captured by its ornate carving. The door closed, and the thud jarred Calla's attention away from the box.

"Today did not go as any of us had planned."

Calla swallowed her retort and nervously stood in silence before the Queen. She had no idea what to expect from a visit by the Queen. Calla watched her cross the room and stop by the fire.

"Come, sit," Queen Shea sat in one chair and patted the seat of the other.

Calla joined Shea by the fire. "What can I do for you, Queen Shea?" She inquired again, struggling to appear outwardly calm.

"I thought that you could use a friend to talk to." The hard edge of Shea's voice clashed with the kind sentiment of her words.

"I don't need friends." Calla's response was quick. "I need to go home. I don't belong here."

"According to you." Shea drummed her fingernails on the wood. "Everything in the realm has been waiting for twenty-five years for the Hybrid to come and save us all. Imagine our disappointment when you send the signal, Captain Quinn saves you and brings you to Midelle, and you refuse to help us." Shea's face mirrored the disgust in her voice.

"Because I'm not the Hybrid." Calla rolled her hands into fists. She didn't know if she had the guts to attack Shea. Besides being nasty, she hadn't done anything wrong. Philomena's words popped in her head, "How can you even be sure the Oracle had the right hair?"

"The Oracle is never wrong," Shea said. "That's why she's the Oracle. Oh, I remember the day I learned of the Hybrid. I was certain the realm would quake any second. Once the realm trembled, King Nakosi and I came home immediately from our diplomatic trip to Ashburn. Philomena had finished brewing the portal by the time we had arrived. Nakosi and I worried that Philomena was going to fail, but she succeeded. At once, Captain Quinn created the portal and brought you here. It was quite troubling when he mentioned that The Corrupted were also there, but I digress. I know you doubt it, but you are the Hybrid. If you weren't, why would the hair lead us to you? As I said, the Oracle is never wrong."

"It must have been a mistake. Maybe hair doesn't work as great as you think it does."

"What are you so afraid of?" Shea raised an eyebrow.

"Let's start with dying. I could die! I'm not ready to die, nor do I want to. I don't want to fight. I won't fight."

Queen Shea tutted, "Isn't life all about doing things you don't want to do?" This only fed Calla's agitation. Shea raised her eyebrows and her dark eyes seemed consumed by the glow of the fire. "I was born into the dirt," she scoffed, "lower than dirt." She took a calculated breath. "I won't bore you with my memoir, but I've been afraid of death. I've lived much of my life doing things that..." She shook her head. "The point is, you're here to complete a task, and you will do it. Captain Quinn will fight alongside you on the battlefield. But first..."

"My powers need to come to light," Calla finished, knowing what she was going to say. She thought all day about what the hell Nakosi had meant by that. Powers? She didn't have any and sparring with swords wasn't going to create any. "I don't doubt your past, but I don't have powers. You're better off fighting The Corrupted without me."

"I brought this for you," Shea said, holding the box out. Calla took the box and set it on her lap. "Consider it a gesture of good faith from King Nakosi and myself. Once you defeat The Corrupted, you'll need to feel like the hero you are. I've had a dream since the realm trembled. A dream filled with a grand festival here in Japhia. One where all citizens come to celebrate a Corruption-free Midelle. I haven't come up with a name yet, but there will be food, amusement, games, retellings of the heroic battle. All the makings of a true celebration. With you being at the center of it. Can you imagine it?"

"I guess so." Calla wanted to say so much more, but she knew it would fall on deaf ears. No one here would listen to her. Until the Corruption was gone for good, she was stuck here. Calla opened the box, and a soft gasp left her lips. A beautiful crown of dark silver sat on a small pillow of red satin. The crown came to a simple point in the middle, studded with pearls and diamonds set into delicate curves. Her fingers ran over the edge of the crown. It was cool to the touch. Calla closed the box quickly. Despite its beauty, the crown served as a harsh reminder that these people were depending on her. "I can't accept this." A gesture of good faith, her ass. Shea was beguiling her.

"Please keep it. It was the previous Queen's and," Shea wrinkled her nose, "it's not my style."

Calla let her hands fall on top of the box, not wanting to look at it. "So, you want to get rid of it? Then it's not out of good faith that you present this to me."

Shea shrugged. "I couldn't think of a better owner for it than you. Violet led me to believe it was Queen Alina's favorite crown."

Calla felt like she was drowning in her thoughts with the crown pulling her down faster and faster. "Thank you for this. I believe it's time I got some rest." She faked a yawn but thought it to be very convincing. "I have quite the day tomorrow, right?"

"You do. I will take my leave then." Shea stood up and Calla watched her at the door. "Sleep well, Captain Quinn will need you at your best for sparring tomorrow."

Calla turned away from the Queen with the flames once more accepting her icy stare.

"Goodnight, Hybrid." The door closed a bit harder than she expected.

Calla opened the box only to close it again. She huffed as she fought the urge to put the crown on. Sure, it was easy to fall into the glitz and glamor of the bribe, but she wasn't like that. She placed the box on the end table beside her. "I need some fresh air," she said to herself as she pushed the hair from her face.

Her feet led her to the balcony, where this all started. She looked out, and there was a vast line of mountains in the far distance. The moon illuminated the forests between the capital and the mountains.

"I can feel your sadness from here and girl let me tell you, it's bumming me out." Calla turned to see an image of her best friend. She was wearing something Calla has seen her in many times, tight jeans and a crop top with her hair piled on top of her head. She missed jeans already.

"Now you're manifesting inside my head?"

"Don't give me that sass," Felicia chided, "You're the one imagining me. Not the other way around."

"I'm so lost, Felicia. What do I do? Am I dreaming?"

"No, you're not dreaming, and you know it. Remember growing up, we would dream of worlds far away filled with magic, Kings, Queens, and heroic battles with the hero saving the day?"

Calla smiled at the memories. "Yes, I remember."

"Well then, for starters," she snapped her fingers and was in a gorgeous muted red dress. Ivory lace encrusted the bodice and the waistline The sleeves were wide with lace stitched onto the end. "They want to treat you like a Queen, and you won't let them!"

"Yeah, because they expect me to fight some corruption or whatever. They're bribing me."

"So?" Felicia held out her hand and the crown Shea had gifted Calla materialized in it. Her dark hair fell into soft waves. "When life gives you lemons..." She placed the crown on top of her waves. Calla rolled her eyes, for it looked better on an imaginary image of Felicia than it ever would on her.

"You make lemonade?"

"No silly! You wear them like the Queen you are."

"But I'm not a Queen. There's already a Queen. I'm the Hybrid. Whatever that means and that's so not the saying."

"Psh! Queen Shea? You'd make a better Queen, you're far prettier. Fake it till you make it, girl. Nancy didn't raise a coward."

Calla thought about her words for a half second, then ran inside and grabbed the crown from the box. She slipped it on her head and moved before the mirror. Calla smiled as Felicia appeared behind her. "It still looks better on you."

Felicia smiled and shrugged, "What doesn't?"

"I know we're stuck in separate realms, but I don't miss your lack of humility."

Felicia held up her hands, "You imagined me like this. Part of me thinks that you love my lack of humility, which I totally don't see by the way."

A crisp knock on the door made Felicia disappear and Calla gasped at the sudden noise. "Lady Calla? It's me, Bruno. Are you okay? Is someone there with you?" Calla had met Bruno in passing as the female guard and he swapped places for the night.

"I'm fine. Talking to myself actually!" Calla guessed that he thought she was nuts.

"Oh. If you're okay, I suppose."

"I am. Thanks." Calla went back outside, missing her illusion of her best friend.

Felicia popped up, floating around her with her skirt floating back and forth. "A girl could get used to this. You know?"

"Felicia?" she stopped floating around Calla to rest her chin in the palm of her hand. "Do you think I can do what they're asking? To get rid of this Corruption once and for all?"

Felicia smiled, "Yes."

Calla furrowed her eyebrows. "Are you saying that to make me feel better?"

"Well... I am a manifestation of your mind. Part of me wants to say yes, but I'd like to think that if I was here, I'd be your number one fan. Foam finger and all."

Calla leaned forward and set her elbows on the railing. "I wish you were here now."

Felicia entwined her arm in hers then rested her head on Calla's shoulder. "Me too. You can do this. Believe in yourself."

Calla turned towards Felicia and the image was gone. She touched the crown to make sure that wasn't an illusion too. When the metal met her fingertips, she smiled. Maybe Felicia was right, how bad could it be?

Six

"Pick up the sword, Lady Calla," Finn commanded. His dull sparring sword pressed against her neck once again.

Part of Calla wished that the sword was sharp, so this nightmare would be over. For the past week, Finn and Calla had sparred for several hours a day to try and get her powers to come to light. Bruises littered her body along with tiny cuts, and everything was sore. A week ago, her sparring clothes were new and pristine. Now, dirt, sweat, and a little blood stained the fibers. They weren't even sparring anymore, it turned into Finn beating her again and again. At first, Calla fought back, wanting to at least try. Every time they sparred, Finn outmatched, disarmed and, in theory, killed her over and over. So, she had given up, which only added an angry tone to Finn's instructions. He hit harder. He gave her less time to recover and he kept going even as Calla begged him to stop.

"Are we done yet?" Calla couldn't stop the tears from falling. Each night was filled not by meaningful, restive sleep but by relentless, frightful nightmares of The Corrupted and of Finn as well. Her will was fading fast. Calla had shut out Violet and Philomena, refusing to speak to them. They allowed Finn to do this while trying to reason with her that this was her destiny. She felt betrayed by everyone she had met here and couldn't have felt more alone. Her room was a prison and a sanctuary at the same time.

"Pick up your sword," Finn commanded again, slower this time, with more malice in his voice. He flipped his sparring sword in the air with the hilt landing with grace and finesse in his hand. In her head, Calla had hoped that his sword would become sharp by magic and cut his hand off. Wishful thinking. She shook out her arm, knowing that the latest hit to her arm would be a bruise by suppertime.

Calla did as Finn said and lifted her sparring sword from the ground, "Let me go to my room."

Finn ignored her and swung his sword to slice the open air between them. Calla blocked the swing. The reverberations of the dull iron dug deep into her aching muscles.

She brought her head up to look at King Nakosi. He stood on an upper balcony overlooking the yard. Curious onlookers came and went, but Nakosi stayed during the whole session every day. Calla cried and begged to the King for a reprieve. Like everyone else, he ignored her except for calm assertions that this was the only way for her powers to show. Finn went to swing again, but Calla's fingers loosened on her swords' hilt. It thumped into a patch of mud under her feet. "Have mercy..."

Finn paused, his sword hung in the air.

Calla thought that her begging had got to him, but to no avail. Calla felt a quick jab to her thigh, and Finn fell back in his fighting stance. Her legs buckled from exhaustion, and she fell on her knees in a patch of mud. Calla let her head drop in shame. She wanted to hold the sobs in, but they fell from her lips, not caring who was watching. She prayed for someone, anyone to intervene.

"Get up," Finn mused as he circled her.

"I can't." Her fingers curled into fists and mud squished out between her fingers.

Finn knelt next to her, and in an odd gesture, he tilted her head up to look at him. His jade green eyes bore into her blue ones with a confidence that terrified her. "You can. And you will." Calla ripped her chin away from his cold fingers in defiance to his command. He whispered, "Perhaps the deities made a mistake creating *you*."

Calla's head snapped to face Finn. He was a mere hand's breadth from her face. She whispered back, "You're a cruel bastard."

"Captain Quinn," Nakosi called out from the balcony. The sun was warm, and the King had shed his thick fur cape, as he often did outside of a formal audience. If Calla didn't know he was a King, she never would have guessed. He carried himself as a nonchalant guy.

Finn backed away from Calla and bowed his head. "My King?" Calla stood, watching Nakosi. He had a pondering look on his face.

"That is enough for today. Lady Calla, take the day for yourself. We will resume tomorrow." Nakosi nodded his head towards Calla.

"Thank you, King Nakosi," she cried as what remained of her tears fell from her eyes without her noticing. Her aching muscles allowed her only an awkward attempt at a curtsey as Nakosi retired from the edge of the balcony. Right now, Calla couldn't care less that she had to return to this torture tomorrow. They had only sparred for fifteen minutes, at most. Nakosi saved her hours of Finn's beatings. Calla tossed her sword at Finn's feet, "Your parents made a mistake creating you."

Finn only stood there, his eyes narrowed in on her, teeth clenched, and his lips in a tight line.

Calla knew she'd pay for that tomorrow, but right now? She didn't care.

The sparring yard that was next to the quarters of the Royal Guard. Looming behind her was Lucy, a guard who followed her day in and day out whenever she wasn't in her room. It was the only way Nakosi and Finn agreed to let her roam the castle, but Calla never roamed. She only went back and forth from the yard to her room out of a desire to shut herself out from this strange world.

Calla looked out a window as she walked towards her room. Even though she passed through this way many times, she had never looked out of the windows. Calla stopped at the window and looked out over a serene haven. In the middle was a fountain where water babbled from a canted vase into a tranquil pool. Hearty oaks lined the outer rim of intricate brickwork. Sunlight shone through the leaves on bricks and bright green grass. Something moved Calla to make a detour, she turned to her guard who escorted her. "Lucy?" She had attempted to speak with Calla on their first day together, but Calla had only yelled at her to leave her alone. Lucy hasn't said a word since but stayed vigilant and by her side regardless.

"Lady Calla." Lucy bowed to her. Her bright green eyes sparkled with hope. A long braid of her blonde hair fell over her shoulder. "I never got an opportunity to introduce myself properly. I am Lucy Varden, First Commander of the Royal Archers. I've waited my whole life to meet you, Hybrid."

Calla held back a grimace. She glanced at her mud-caked sigil.

"It is an honor to escort you and to one day fight at your side to rid the realm of The Corruption."

Calla rolled her lips together, trying to not hurt Lucy's feelings. It was difficult knowing she was another witness to Finn's cruelty yet didn't intervene either. After a few moments of silence Calla finally could piece a sentence together, "It's my honor. Thank you for protecting me."

Lucy advanced on Calla and grabbed her shoulders. Her arms were strong but were graceful. "Will you save us from the wretched corrupted?" Lucy whispered to her face, their eyes meeting in a moment of seriousness. "I have to ask. Forgive me."

Calla swallowed hard, there was so much hope in her eyes, but Calla could feel the fear creeping up again. "Lucy," she began unsure of what was going to come out of her mouth. Calla watched the gleam in her eyes falter. Even though Calla didn't believe she was the Hybrid, Lucy did. They all did. "I'll do all that I can." Her week in Midelle has taught Calla many things. One of which was that these people truly believed she was the Hybrid, and would save the realm. There was no shaking their faith in this so-called prophecy.

Lucy smiled, dimples dented her cheeks. "As the prophecy foretold."

"As everyone keeps telling me. Would you mind escorting me to the courtyard? I would like to enjoy the weather before the frost comes."

Lucy dropped her arms and nodded her head. "Right this way, Lady Calla." Lucy led the way through the Castle.

Calla noticed the bow and quiver Lucy wore on her back. A grave thought crept into Calla's mind, that Lucy was willing to lay down her life to protect her. Calla wrapped her hand around her sigil, in deep thought, shaking her head and those thoughts from it. She wasn't the Hybrid. Calla knew who she was.

Lucy stopped by a thick wooden door, "This is the side entrance to the courtyard. I will do my best to give you space. Take as long as you need, it's a beautiful day. Think of it as the deities smiling upon you."

Calla gave a few words of thanks and stepped out into the late morning sun. Lucy stayed close but still gave her space. She kept thinking why Nakosi let her go, was he finally seeing that this wasn't working? But when she stopped in the middle of the courtyard, all her thoughts about sparring dissipated.

The courtyard was indeed the little haven it seemed to be from the inside. In the center was the fountain babbling away with its gentle watery tune. Underneath, bricks in varying shades of brown covered the ground and formed a circle outward towards the mighty oaks that grew beyond the immediate courtyard. Benches of wrought iron lined the edge of the brickwork with pots of flowers serving as bright pops of color in shades of yellow, pink and red. The sweet floral scent caressed her nostrils and reminded her of home.

Calla walked up to the fountain and dipped her hands into the clear, cool water. She watched the caked mud float from her hands and dissipate into the water. After she splashed water on her face and dried it with the inside of her shirt, she felt a little better.

A bench on the opposite side of the courtyard seemed like a good place to sit. Next to it was a pot of red flowers. She had the same kind on her balcony. But Calla wanted to blend in. She wanted to disappear for a few hours. She chose the far side of an ancient oak with her back to the castle. The leaves gave a speckled shade from the late fall sun, but the air still clung to some summer warmth.

Calla rested her head against the trunk of a tree and her eyes fluttered closed. She wanted to stay out here forever. This was the first place in Midelle where Calla felt calm and serene. The smell of the tree reminded her of being outside on the tire swing for hours with her mom.

"Care for some company?"

Calla opened her eyes. A man stood before her. It took her eyes a moment to adjust to the sunlight. He was taller than her, with golden beige skin. She thought of emeralds when she saw the color of his hair. It was up in a low ponytail. His strong jaw was clad with dark stubble, and his smile had a slight crook to it, but it was still charming. What entranced Calla the most, was his eyes. They rivaled the most vibrant purple orchids. His muscled arms squeezed through rolled-up sleeves and his shirt did nothing to disguise his powerful chest. A deep breath filled her lungs even though it felt like all the air had vanished.

"Sorry, but no," Calla replied. "I came out here to be alone." Something stirred deep in her stomach. It wasn't fear and it wasn't anger, the only two emotions Calla had been feeling as of late.

The man sat on the ground before her as if he didn't even hear her. Calla noticed a sheen of sweat on his skin and dampened his white linen shirt in places. "Mind if I sit here, on my own then? Not keeping you company? I came out here to be alone too."

Calla rolled her eyes, "I don't care what you do." She crossed her arms, as she finally identified the feeling in her stomach, butterflies. Calla became angry at herself for thinking that romance could fit in anywhere in the mess she was in. She glanced back to Lucy who was near the door leading back into the castle. She was alert, but this man didn't alarm her.

The man stretched his arms out in conjunction with a long-drawn-out sigh, then locked his fingers behind his head. "Beautiful day, isn't it? I love this time of year, even though I'm more of a summer man myself. You can't beat the colors of the flowers, the warm wind and enjoying a good swim on a hot day. Now? Not so much, but when you look out west, the Edulis Mountains are alive with color. The views are-"

"I hope you're talking to yourself because I'm not listening." Calla closed her eyes, raised her chin, and rested her head back on the tree trunk.

"Well, as you stated, you don't care. So yes, I am speaking to myself."

Calla could feel the man smiling at her through her closed lids, but she didn't dare open her eyes.

"As I was saying... to myself... When the leaves change, and you look out west, nothing can compare to the view. It's breathtaking, among other things." He whispered the last part like they were sharing a secret in a crowded room.

Calla opened her eyes. The man's devilish smirk enticed more dancing in her stomach. "I came out here for a moment of solace, and you are ruining it."

"I came out here to see a beautiful..."

"Do not finish that thought because I have zero interest. Go flirt with the trees. You'd have a better chance with them anyway."

The man held his hands up, palms facing Calla, "If you let me finish, I was going to say a beautiful day. I also think the trees would appreciate me. I am a druid, and nature is a part of us."

Calla held out a hand. "A druid?" She remembered Violet listing all the creatures that inhabited Midelle. Calla glanced behind her to catch Lucy staring off into the distance, was Lucy a druid too? She had a hard time identifying who was what creature. Trolls were easy, their skin was a dead giveaway. Most of them were taller and wider than the druids and vampires.

The druid held out his dirt-clad and calloused hand. "That's right. Vihaan Rowan, fourth-generation Groundskeeper for the Castle."

With a sense of hesitance, Calla shook his hand. "I'm Calla Moro," she paused, "no fancy title for me." She went to pull away, but he flipped their hands, so her sigil faced up. Seeing her sigil made her angry all over again. She became hyper-aware of all the bruises on her body. Only the ones on her arms were visible, and part of her was grateful for that.

"I beg to differ," Vihaan glanced down at her identifier briefly, then looked into her eyes, "Hybrid." He smiled as if he were star struck.

Calla's mood turned sour as she ripped her hand away. Her eyes narrowed. "Are you going to beat me senseless too?" Her sudden turn of mood rendered Vihaan speechless. "Excuse me, Mr. Rowan, but I'll be leaving now. Enjoy the beautiful day because you've ruined mine." Calla got up, stalking past Lucy. "I'm going back to my room." Her voice was loud enough that birds took flight from the trees around the courtyard.

"Lady Calla," Vihaan called after her, "Wait!"

Calla spun around, "That's all you people care about! This!" She showed her sigil to him. "Not me. Never once has anyone asked me if I'm okay with any of this. News flash, I'm not!"

Vihaan stood there, stunned. Lucy spread her palms and shrugged her shoulders. "Lady Calla, I will escort you back to your room. If the heat has gotten to your head, resting would help."

Calla felt like screaming at the top of her lungs because no one was listening. She grabbed at the roots of her hair wanting to pull out every strand. In defeat, her hands fell to her sides as her anger subsided. "Escort me back to my prison cell." Her shoulders dropped, and she began the trudge back to her room, not once looking back to Lucy or Vihaan.

Later that evening, Calla finished brushing the tangles from her wet hair and set the brush down. Dark blonde ends curled against her bare shoulders as she stared into the mirrored surface. She did a quick once over of her body, "Back in the human realm they would call this abuse." Bruises in different shapes, sizes, and colors riddled her skin. Calla didn't need any more reminders of how miserable she was. She grabbed her dark cotton nightgown and slipped it over her head. She left her top untied, and her cleavage showed. The evening air felt good against her skin.

There was a knock on the door. Calla allowed entry and Violet came in with a tray of food. Calla narrowed her eyes at the troll then turned her back to her.

"Lady Calla, I know you're angry, but this is to help you. Captain Quinn is positive your powers will come to light this way."

Calla crossed her arms, looking into the dark sky. "Let's switch places. I'm sure you'd be singing a different tune soon enough."

"You should come down to dinner. You may enjoy it."

Calla turned to face her would-be ally, "You're out of your ever-loving mind if you think I'm going down there. They would whip me for entertainment at this rate."

"Lady Calla," Violet scolded. Her body went rigid and eyes wide. "That is no way to speak of King Nakosi and Queen Shea. They have been very accommodating…"

"Just leave me alone." Calla turned away from her again, so Violet didn't see the tears that wanted to fall. "Please."

Violet sighed, "Very well. I take a sunrise stroll through the gardens every morning when the skies permit. You should join me. The fresh air might do you well."

Calla didn't move until she heard the door close behind Violet's footsteps. She rubbed the salty tears from her eyes, wishing the tears would run out. The smell of slow-roasted meat hit her nose, and her sadness gave way to hunger in an instant. She hated how fast her moods swapped as of late. Calla always picked at her breakfast and lunch. Knowing what was coming, it was hard to have an appetite. She scarfed down her dinner faster than she thought she could. After she was full, Calla curled in the armchair by the fire. She watched the flames as her brain worked overtime. Midelle was solidifying as a real place in her mind, but she couldn't fathom that it was her who would save everyone. She couldn't even save herself from the scummy men she went on dates with.

A gentle knock sounded on the door, and she broke her stare off with the flames.

"Who is it?"

"Vihaan."

Calla scoffed as she went to the door. She didn't know why he came. She thought of sending him away with a curt word but found herself walking to the door. She convinced herself she was going to open the door because maybe a slap to the face would knock some sense into him. The iron lock lifted, and Calla whipped open the door, ready to show Vihaan a piece of her mind.

He stood there, holding a bouquet such as Calla had never seen before. The flowers were a vibrant yellow with cascading petals and light blue pistils. He looked different from earlier. He had changed his clothes and washed up. He gave Calla that smile that was stuck in her mind since they parted ways. "Lady Calla, I..."

Calla couldn't stop herself as she slammed the door in his face. Her anger kept getting the best of her, and it made her even angrier. She knew that she never had the guts to slap him. Feeling a wave of regret wash over her, Calla opened the door again. Vihaan still stood there, unfazed by her rashness. She grabbed the flowers from him. Their fingers brushed for a fleeting second that lasted forever in her mind. She gave him a cheeky smile, then shut the door again, softer this time. She pressed herself against the door, like that would do something. The corners of her lips turned upwards as she inhaled the sweet scent of the flowers.

"Goodnight, Lady Calla. Sweet dreams. I do hope to see you again soon."

Calla heard his footsteps fade away through the door. She heard Bruno, the night guard, lock the door again. Calla brought the flowers to her face and inhaled. Her eyes searched the room for a vase.

"Sweet dreams, indeed."

Seven

A light mist fell from the overcast sky. It made the entire sparring yard a morass of mud. Calla's hair was a frizzy mess that clung to her face. Something was different about today's sparring session. There was an electricity in the air that she couldn't place. The energy felt different, but that didn't stop Finn from delivering blow after blow to her battered body. She knew her comments from yesterday would ignite his fury today, and Finn didn't disappoint.

Their swords clanged together, but Finn withdrew, then tossed his sword behind him. He grabbed the dull blade of Calla's sword and ripped it from her hands. He resumed his fighting stance as Calla looked at him dumbfounded.

Nakosi stood from his chair in the balcony. "What is the meaning of this, Captain Quinn?"

Finn circled Calla with the sword mere inches from her body, but she remained still. Only her eyes followed him when he passed her. "I was thinking last night, my King." Finn raised an eyebrow to match the slight smirk on his lips. "About why we aren't successful in bringing her powers to light."

"Go on."

Calla's eyes flitted to Nakosi who's saturated brown eyes watched on with a deep curiosity. A distant rumble of thunder rolled as dread settled in her heart.

"You see, if we want her powers to come to light, she has to fear for her life. What we're doing now is not working because she's not scared."

"I most certainly am scared!"

Finn thrust the sword into the mud, where it tilted but remained upright. "Squire," he barked, "my sword." A teen jumped at his Captain's orders, but he took Finn's battle sword from the sheath. The gold inlays that pressed into the iron stood out amongst the dreariness.

"Captain Quinn, I'm not sure I agree with you. She could get hurt," Nakosi interjected. Finn slashed the air with his sword, the very same one he had used to save her life. The squire ran back to the weapons rack to grab leather armor.

Fear numbed Calla's body.

Finn looked up to the King, "For today only, and if it doesn't work, we try a different strategy. I have a few in mind. And you have my word as Captain of the Royal Guard, no harm will come to her."

Nakosi rubbed his chin in thought, Calla could see that he wasn't sleeping very well from down in the yard.

"That's a real sword," Calla cut into the silence of the King's thought. "He could kill me! What the hell is the matter with you people? Beating me to death is not the way! And neither is slicing and dicing me. Don't you see that?" She couldn't keep it in anymore, anger coursed through her veins. This torture ended today.

"That is no way for any citizen of the realm to speak to the King," Queen Shea chimed in, stepping into Calla's view on the balcony. The rainy morning had frizzed her tight bun of thick curls. Her cheeks were pinched rosy, and the dress she wore was the shade of sapphires. Calla wanted to rip the delicate crown from her frizzy curls and chuck it in the mud to show how much she cared about the way she spoke to anyone.

A short laugh escaped Calla's mouth. "And this is any way to treat," she used air quotes to follow her next words, "the Hybrid? If I am so powerful, why don't I use my powers to destroy the castle? Huh? How would you like that? Then you could only blame yourselves for creating a monster!"

"Lady Calla, please calm down," Nakosi said calmly. He turned to his wife to whisper something in her ear. She gave Calla a terse stare, then turned on heel and disappeared. Calla gave Finn a death glare, and he returned it without hesitation. "Captain Quinn, I appreciate your idea, but it isn't worth the possible injury to the Hybrid."

"Calla!" She screamed her correction at him. Her blood boiled, and she wished she was anywhere but in the sparring yard. With every word that went past her lips, she knew she was making the situation worse, but she couldn't stop. The gates holding her anger and frustration for herself burst open, and there was no closing them now.

Finn scoffed to himself as he tossed the sheathed sword back to his squire. He dropped the armor to catch it before it plopped in the mud. The squire picked up Calla's sparring sword caked in mud, tossing it back to land inches from her feet. "You're lucky." Finn picked up the sword that was still upright in the mud behind him. "Shame that your forest boyfriend isn't here to witness this," Finn whispered to her.

Calla's eyebrows knitted together in confusion, but a vivid image of Vihaan struck her mind. A small smile spread on her lips while she wiped the hair from her damp face. "Forest boyfriend? I believe he has a name."

"Fuck his name," Finn said as he kicked Calla's legs out from underneath her. Her back caught all her body weight as it squished into the mud. A sharp blow to her stomach from Finn had her curled up in a little ball. "What about his name now," he whispered with a hint of envy in his voice as another blow struck her thigh.

"Stop it, asshole!"

Another hit to her shoulder. Calla cried out. There was a sharp sting on her back. Something felt off within her. A whack to her legs. Something slowly bubbled to the surface. Finn's blows were relentless. Each hit was harder, and he did it with the flat side of the blade. Calla had come to learn that the flat side hurt more than the dulled edge. Her sigil started to burn like fire was creeping across the delicate lines. Calla tried to wrap herself in a tighter ball, but Finn knew exactly where to hit to land on top of a bruise.

"Ey, Captain Quinn!" The relentless attacks stopped.

Calla popped her head out of her man-made cocoon. Her sigil felt like she had stuck her hand in icy water, and she could breathe again.

Vihaan strode out into the yard, sparring sword thrown back behind his shoulder. His arms tightened with anticipation. "Why don't you fight a more formidable foe?" On any given day, Calla would have taken offense, but right now? Vihaan might as well have been her guardian angel.

Finn backed away from Calla, the mist turned into a steady rain. Lightning lit up the sky. "I'd mind your own business if I were you, druid."

Vihaan turned to Nakosi, "My King, can't you see she's terrified?" Vihaan pointed to Calla and thunder rumbled in the distance. His voice was calm but deep. She managed to stand up with her clothes caked in mud. The rain too slowly washed the mud from her. "Do you think that this is the way to make her powers come to light? She's right! When she does get her powers, she'll remember how you treated her, and hatred will course through her veins. Is that what you want? You might as well tie a ribbon around her and hand her over to The Corrupted now."

Vihaan paused, letting his words sink in. He gave a quick sympathetic gaze to Calla. "Let her powers come from a place of kindness and respect for Midelle. Not hatred. I'm asking you to allow me to show her how beautiful Midelle can be. I'm sure her powers will come to light. The right way."

Tears mixed with the rain on Calla's face. She felt whole again, someone had finally done something. Nakosi was deep in thought, as always. Calla held her breath. Half out of annoyance for Nakosi's indecisiveness, and the other half out of her anxiousness.

"Vihaan, your courage has not gone unnoticed, and I do agree with you. It is time we try a new method, one filled with respect for Lady Calla. I permit you to show her Japhia, with a guard. We will speak tomorrow on any progress. Captain Quinn, stay in the loop with this. I always want your best guard with her when she's not in her room. Excuse me." Nakosi vanished the same way Shea went. By that time, a few onlookers had gone back to their own business and receded from the edge of the balcony, but there was still quite the crowd looking down on the three of them. Perhaps they wanted to get a closer look at their supposed savior, The Hybrid.

Calla turned to her protector. His emerald hair was darker from being wet and he slicked back to show raindrops dripping down his angular jaw. The way the rain plastered his shirt over his muscles made her mouth go dry. She brought her eyes up from his chest to meet his. "Thank you, Vihaan. I'm sorry for how I acted yesterday... I..."

Vihaan placed a hand on her arm, and her breath escaped. She barely noticed his hand was on top of a nasty bruise. "Don't apologize, it is I who should apologize to you. I've watched from day one of this madness, and I should never have let it go as far as it did. If you would like, you can clean up, then we can take a walk around the castle." He waved an arm at the mud, "I'm sure you'd like to do something other than this?"

Calla smiled. That simple expression felt foreign. "I would like that." Calla felt guilty in an instant. She was able to forgive Vihaan this quickly, even as she had rejected Violet and Philomena's apologies. She put that at the top of her list to rectify.

"Not quite yet," Finn cut in. He held two real swords. Calla gulped, no Nakosi here to save her now.

Vihaan threw out an arm in front of Calla. She moved behind him, grateful for his protection. "You heard the King. This is over. Take your rage out on your poor squire." Calla heard the squire on the edge of the sparring yard let out a disgruntled noise.

"Not her. You." Finn handed Vihaan a sword. He took his time taking it from the Captain. Finn's squire ran up with two pieces of hard leather chest armor. "Care to spar a little?"

Vihaan slipped on the armor and he said with a smile, "I can't wait to wound your pride, you arrogant bastard."

"Do you realize who I am?" The two men went to the middle of the square and nodded their heads to each other as a sign of sportsmanship. Calla had a feeling this had nothing to do with sportsmanship.

They got in a fighting stance, "A sad excuse for a Captain?"

Finn's grip tightened on his sword, "You'll regret that, druid."

Calla stepped off to the side next to the squire. He was shorter than her and had dark sand colored hair. She wondered if he was a vampire like Finn. Purple bruises crept up the neckline of his shirt.

They matched the deep blueberry color of her fresh ones. It would seem that she wasn't the only one subject to his wrath.

Calla's face flinched when Finn took a swing at Vihaan. He dodged the blow with a step back and a parry. Their swords danced together in a flurry of thrusts, slashes, and parries as the two moved around the yard. Vihaan was keeping up with Finn, almost besting him at times. Finn jerked his sword to the left and Vihaan raised his to kiss the two blades of steel together. At the last moment, Finn cut his sword to the right and jabbed Vihaan in the armor. Calla gasped, covering her mouth, but Vihaan only faulted for a moment.

Vihaan gave a quick thrust at Finn's side, but his sword slid down in time to block the blade. Lightning flashed as the two slid their swords to the center. They had turned so Vihaan was facing Calla. She could see the intensity in his eyes and the confidence on his face. Thunder cracked, much nearer now. Calla saw Vihaan wink at her. It was quick, but still a wink. Vihaan put his free arm behind his back, and Calla watched as mud-caked roots snaked up from the ground by Finn's feet. Her eyes went wide at the display of druidic magic.

"Interesting..." she whispered.

Their swords clashed again with the harshness of thunder, all friendliness gone. She couldn't watch this anymore, someone was going to get hurt. She stepped forward, and watched Finn fall from the roots tangling his feet. Calla watched as the roots retreated into the ground so quickly she almost thought she'd imagined them.

Vihaan stepped up to Finn and tapped the tip of his sword at Finn's chest. "Regret what? It seems I have bested you."

Finn's chest rose and fell from his exertion, and after a moment his grip on his sword loosened. Lightning illuminated the men's factious expressions. Rain dripped from Vihaan's sword to fall on Finn's chest.

Vihaan stepped back and handed the sword and armor to the squire. He looked to Calla, and those stupid butterflies got loose in her stomach again. The thunder clapped out of nowhere, making Calla jump. She turned a furious shade of red. Vihaan only held out his arm for her, "Shall I escort you back to your room, so you may change?"

Calla snaked her arm to entwine in his, "Yes, good idea. I have mud in places where it shouldn't be."

"We can't have that now, can we?" The two of them walked into the corridor that went back to the main part of the castle. Calla heard Finn rejecting the squire's help. She kept her head forward, for he deserved everything he got. Perhaps it was time he knew what it felt like to lay beaten in the mud.

"I like to think I showed him a thing or two about humility, huh?"

Calla bit back a smile, "Were you behind the roots? This is all new to me."

"I was, but I'd rather spend my time with you than in a pissing match with that bastard." Vihaan flashed her a smile.

"You cheated!"

"For the right reasons! You have to admit, you liked seeing him down and out."

A small laugh left her lips, "It was nice. Is that something all druids do? Play with roots?"

Vihaan unhooked his arm from hers, turned to walk in front of her, "Not at all Lady Calla. Druids are closer to all things nature than any other creature in Midelle. We can stop by my garden house tomorrow. I'll show you what I mean, but controlling roots is only the start."

"Interesting. What about the other creatures? Vampires for instance?"

Vihaan came by her side again and Calla wrapped her arm in his as soon as he offered. "Vampires have fertility challenges. Most give birth to stillborn, but some couples are lucky and can have children."

"How are there still vampires then?"

Vihaan's face became tight. "Druid orphans. Druids are the only ones that can withstand the change. It's a never-ending cycle."

"What else?" She gave his arm a gentle squeeze after sensing his unease.

The tension in his jaw faded. "Vampires need blood to survive. Most get their fill from animals, but if they don't get the blood, they go into a blood rage. They blackout, drinking as much as their body allows until they pass out and come down from the rage." Calla's eyes got wide with fear. " By that point, their rampage for blood has usually killed someone. By law, they are condemned to die. It's sad, but it enforces some form of self-control over them."

"If they weren't in control of themselves, then it's not fair to kill them," Calla countered.

"I don't make the rules." Vihaan came in close to her ear, "The King kind of does that." His breath tickled the skin on her ear. When he straightened, Calla missed him being close. "Everyone thought after Nakosi took the throne, he would abolish the rule that previous King's put into place. He says it adds accountability to vampires."

"Why would he remove the law?" They turned to a new corridor that passed by the kitchens. Delicious smells enveloped them.

Vihaan looked as if she had grown a second head, "The King and Queen are vampires."

Calla's mouth dropped in shock. She never would have guessed that.

"Oh, and the Captain?" Vihaan rolled his eyes, "Queen Shea's brother. Everyone knows how he got to be Captain, and that's why no one respects him. The Captain of the Royal Guard is an honor. Something someone works towards their entire life. It should not be handed out like charity."

Calla rolled her lips inward, processing everything. "Were you vying for that role?"

Vihaan laughed, "No, I had always wanted to be a member of the Royal Guard, but my lineage forbade it. Fourth-generation groundskeeper, remember?"

"I do," She smiled. "Moving on to trolls?"

"Ah yes. You've met one."

"Violet," Calla jumped on the answer. They crossed the main foyer of the castle, she remembered when she first saw it on her way to meet the King and Queen. So much had changed since then and now. She was able to let herself bask in the splendor now that the circumstances were different. "She came right out with it my first night here."

"She is one to be blunt. Now it's my turn to ask something."

Calla thought on his request but then nodded her head. "I suppose that's fair."

"Is it true you came from the human realm?"

"Yes, but that's home to me. It feels so weird saying 'the human realm'."

"Midelle could be your new home," he said, but there was a cocky undertone to his voice.

Home. Everything she missed back home came flooding in. It wasn't much, but what she had she loved. Thinking of Felicia, Calla wished she could have seen her reaction to Midelle. She laughed out of context, "Don't mind me. My best friend would get a kick out of Midelle." She paused, not wanting to cry, "Tell me about trolls. What makes them special?" Going up the main foyer stairs, Calla was starting to recall her way. They pretended not to notice Lucy discreetly following them.

Vihaan opened a door, letting her go first. He went along with the new subject. "All trolls are identifiable by hard patches on their skin. It's random placement, like birthmarks. Some are completely covered. They are usually wider and bigger than most people with broad shoulders and thick limbs. Despite their looks, many trolls have a calm and patient demeanor. Violet is the perfect example."

"You are the expert on all things Midelle, huh," Calla teased at his wealth of knowledge.

"Among other things." He turned to her with a mischievous glint in his eye.

A faint blush fell over Calla's cheeks, "If I remembered right, there are mermaids?"

"Yes, they live only on the Southern coasts and keep to themselves for the most part. I can't say what they're like because I've never met one."

"And you call yourself an expert," Calla chided with a sly playfulness.

"If I recall correctly, you called me an expert." They separated to go single file up the stairs to let a maid carrying sheets pass by. She gave Calla a quick nod of her head. She was unsure what to do in response, so she gave her a thin smile.

"And if I recall, you didn't deny it." Calla glanced at Vihaan behind her knowing this was all playful banter. He still had that look in his eye and a half smile planted on his lips, like he knew a secret. His eyes caught hers, but she knew once she would go forward again that they would drop lower.

"You caught me."

Calla turned forward again. They were almost to her room, but he would be coming back. She scolded herself for craving his company too quickly. In the end, she was going back to the 'human realm', and that was that. There was no time for whatever Vihaan wanted. "And the dragons? What about them?"

"Like mermaids, I've never seen one. If you ask Violet, she'll tell you about how they used to soar the skies with their colorful wings and scales. They disappeared around the time I was born. The bridge leading to the Isle of Dragons crumbled to nothing around that time. No ship going to the Isle ever came back." Vihaan sighed, "I hope one day they will return. I'd love to see a dragon."

The pair exited the stairwell, and Calla resumed holding onto his arm, but not for guidance. She knew exactly where they were. "How sad. I hope they come back. Do you think it was a disease that wiped them all out?"

Vihaan shrugged, "That could be it." Like clockwork, they stopped at Calla's door. Lucy was in sight, but far enough back to not intrude on the conversation.

Calla felt her cheeks redden like she was sixteen again, "Thank you, Vihaan."

Vihaan unlinked their arms but trailed his hand down to grab her hand. "Stop saying thank you. The pleasure is and always will be mine." He brought her hand up to his lips, but he paused right before they contacted her skin. He dropped her hand and Calla went from floating to mortified. Vihaan then picked up her left hand and pressed a swift kiss on the back of it. "Now that hand can feel special too." Calla's cheeks flushed redder than before, and she lost all capacity to speak. "I'll be back in an hour or two? Then we can take a stroll throughout the castle and talk some more."

Calla opened her mouth to speak but could only find it in her to nod, hiding the giant smile that wanted to burst through.

"See you soon, Lady Calla." Vihaan winked and left her at the door, passing by Lucy.

Once he was out of sight, Calla fell against the door and fanned herself.

"Vihaan is quite taken with you," Lucy mused as she walked up to Calla. She stopped at the windows, looking outside to the dreary plateau.

"I don't see it." Calla's blushing cheeks were finally fading.

Lucy glanced over to Calla with an all-knowing smile plastered on her face, "You keep telling yourself that."

Finn slammed the door to his quarters so hard, the wood of the door cracked down the middle. "Damn her!" He shouted as he swiped a glass off his desk. The glass shattered. Coppery blood dripped down the stone wall. Three crisp knocks rapped on the door. He knew who it was from the knocks alone. "What, Shea?" he snapped.

Shea came in, "What is this I'm hearing about you fighting the groundskeeper, of all people?"

"Hello to you too." Finn glanced out the window. It was pouring now, but the lightning and thunder seemed to have subsided.

Shea scoffed. "Finn!" She was tapping her foot. He hated it when she did that. It reminded him of their mother. "This is serious. You're not helping your reputation."

"What can I do for you, sis?" He turned away from the window.

Shea rolled her eyes. "Don't be an ass."

"I seem to be pretty good at it. This is a disaster!"

"Protecting her isn't a popularity contest." Shea tutted, another mannerism of their mother. "You can't lose control like…"

"I know," Finn roared. His older sister always knew how and what buttons to push.

Shea's face was still set hard, and her eyes narrowed in on Finn. "I did you a favor. Don't let your temper run away with this."

"I didn't exactly ask for your help, did I? I was going to live with my actions until the day I died."

"Which would have been a lot sooner if it weren't for me." Shea had a smirk on her face that lit a dangerous fire in Finn.

"Maybe it would be better that way." A table that laid out as a map of Midelle. Different types of figurines were scattered all over it. Finn grabbed a dagger from the table and held the hilt out to Shea. "Would you like to do the honors?

Shea rolled her eyes and laughed. She swatted the dagger away. It landed with a clang in the corner. "What? One lass gives you trouble, and you want to off yourself?"

"That's not it," Finn growled as he gripped the strategy table too hard, his knuckles went white.

"Then do your job. Or my love and I will find someone who can." She turned on her heel, walked out, and slammed the door, which only made the crack bigger.

Finn ran his fingers through his ginger hair and gasped, "Damn her."

Eight

The sky was aglow in shades of brilliant pink and orange the next morning. The air was crisp with fall's grasp extending further and further throughout the land. Calla knew that soon it would be snowing but hoped to be long gone before then. She also knew she had to make amends with Violet. She clasped a fur-lined cloak over her shoulders and came out to the gardens. Lucy had escorted her without complaint despite the early hour but didn't seem as vigilant as usual.

"Violet?" Calla thought she may not be out here at all.

Violet emerged from an archway of shrubbery and orange flowers. She was clad in a simple dark red dress with a cream-colored apron and wool cloak. Her hair was in a braided crown, her usual. A soft smile lit her face, "Good morning, Lady Calla. I had hoped you would join me. You picked a fine morning."

Calla moved to Violet's side. They went in a direction new to Calla, down a cobblestone walkway, deeper into the gardens. Soft yellow flowers that struggled to survive the chill lined the walkway. Her fingers played with the edge of her cloak. They walked long enough for the silence to echo Calla's nervousness.

Violet filled the silence. "I love mornings. The realm is still asleep, and it's so quiet. It's nice to have that serene moment before you are laden with the duties of the day."

"I'm sorry I treated you the way I did. You didn't deserve it." Calla let out a steady breath of air as she felt better with her apology, now if she could only find Philomena. Finding her was harder than finding a needle in a haystack.

Violet laughed a hearty laugh. "I don't blame you. You were ripped from your world to a place unknown, expected to jump into something that you don't understand. I did try to reason with King Nakosi once I learned what Captain Quinn wanted to do. I disagreed from the start, but I was limited in what I could do to try and bridge the gap." Violet looked over to Calla, guilt written all over her face.

"I like the new plan much better," Calla said, trying to keep her smile under wraps.

Vihaan came back yesterday, as he promised. They had strolled throughout the castle for a few hours, lost in each other's words. Vihaan was so interested in her old life and for once, it didn't unearth sad feelings when she spoke of the human realm. They ended up eating dinner in a back corner of the kitchen, away from the song and dance of the formal dinner with the King and Queen. Calla couldn't have dreamed of a better day.

By the time night fell, he had brought her back to her room with a promise to show her the garden house today. Calla fell asleep with ease that night, but her nightmare returned. The one with her blood dripping to form the sigil and the strange flowers dying. The dream taunted her in the recesses of her mind, but Calla didn't know what it meant or who to talk about it with. She'd awoken drenched in sweat to the early part of sunrise, the sky a mix of light purples and blues. It was the perfect opportunity to join Violet on her morning stroll.

A small cheeky smile spread over Violet's mouth. "I heard Vihaan is to show you around, so you can get a better understanding of Midelle?"

The simple sound of his name made her feel empty and full inside, "Yes. That's the plan. He's going to show me the extent of druidic powers today. I'd be lying if I said I wasn't curious."

Calla and Violet reached the end of the long stretch of the cobblestone. New paths branched out to the sides of a flower covered archway straight ahead. The flowers color reminded her of creamsicles. They kept walking straight under the archway. "Vihaan. He's a good one." Calla cocked her head to the side. "I raised him after his father died by The Corrupted King Raoul." The sun's rays had reached over the horizon, bathing everything in its warmth.

"You've done a wonderful job. He's been a perfect gentleman." Violet and Vihaan's situation made Calla think of her mother. Her death still hurt, but the pain had begun to heal into loving memories.

"I'm glad to hear you say that, Lady Calla. I was never a true mother to anyone, but I tried my hardest with him. You two will be good for each other."

Calla stopped walking to place a hand over her heart in a dramatic fashion. "What? I don't think so. He's an acquaintance. I plan on leaving Midelle once I do what I must do. There is no time for..." Calla battled to quiet the thoughts that she'd have to fight evil at some point. One problem at a time.

"Don't lie to me," Violet scolded. "I wasn't born yesterday."

Calla sucked in a breath, "Okay fine. My feelings may go beyond a harmless acquaintance, but that doesn't mean anything."

"Rest assured the feeling is mutual." Violet gave her a coy smile but as Calla glanced away from her, she stopped in her tracks. Before them towered a giant fountain with four figures carved from marble. Each figure had water falling from a different feature with all four facing her. The figures were set atop four fluted marble columns in an angled diamond pattern, the furthest being the highest one. "The fountain of the four deities. I thought you'd like to see it. These are the deities, your creators, Lady Calla."

Calla stepped away from Violet with her heart drumming in her chest. Sure, they were statues, but she felt there was some truth to the depiction. "Who's the one on top?" The deity stood tall and graceful, with outstretched cupped hands from which water flowed into the bowl held by the lowest and closest deity.

"Vitala, the deity of life."

"And the one to the left?" This one had a kind face and was posed almost turning away from the group. Her water feature gently babbled water off to the side from a simple vase.

"Tera, the deity of stone."

Calla's eyes drifted to the deity on the right with a playful smile on his face. He held an elongated pot high above his head to pour a steady stream of water into the air on the other side of him. "This one?"

"Auan, the deity of water."

Calla remembered the story that Violet had told her when she first arrived when her eyes landed on the last deity. She watched the water cascade from Vitala's hands into the bottom one's bowl. Green deposits of scum streaked down her stoic face from her eyes. "This one is Morta, right?"

"Yes. The deity of death."

Staring at Morta, Calla asked, "If she created The Corrupted, why is she up there?"

"The legends tell us she did help create Midelle into what it is. Morta's statue also serves as a reminder that with life comes death, and that life cannot thrive without death." Violet began walking again, but Calla's feet remained in place. She looked at the statue of Morta, seeing much more than a static face carved into stone. Calla saw anger, sadness, and jealousy carved into the rock, but somehow the face remained the same. "Lady Calla?" Violet turned around from the beginning of a new path that was to the left of the fountain.

Calla turned to Violet. When she glanced back at the statue, Calla saw nothing, but a solid chunk of stone chiseled into a face. "Coming."

Calla checked herself one more time, even though she knew nothing changed. Her hair still fell in waves of gold, and her corseted fir colored dress still fit her like a glove. She ran her bare hands over the regal material as much to luxuriate in the feel of the fabric as to smooth it out once again. She had fought hard, and Finn finally allowed her to roam the castle without her gloves. Vihaan said he would come by when the noon bells sang which gave her ample time to obsess over nothing.

The ornate melody drifted through the air from the citadel in Japhia. Calla counted along with the bells until they stopped after twelve. The seconds passed by, and when Calla didn't hear Vihaan knock, she scowled. What was wrong with her? Calla opened the doors to the balcony and took a deep breath of the fresh air. The cool autumn breeze gave her goosebumps, as the rains yesterday had chased away any lingering summer weather. She could see many leaves had turned to their fall hues, but most of the trees were still green. From her vantage point Calla could see everything at the base of the plateau. Japhia was a bustling city filled with all sorts of creatures who all held her as their hero. Her stomach knotted at the thought of protecting these people. She couldn't even protect herself from the one who oversaw protecting her. The train of thought made her head spin.

"Lady Calla?"

Calla jumped out of her skin but realized it was Vihaan poking his head into her room. "Vihaan, hello. Sorry, I was wrapped up in my own thoughts." She came inside to close the doors behind her.

Vihaan came in, looking more dashing than ever. He wore a more formal shirt with a leather vest and clean pants. "I didn't mean to scare you. I knocked and heard nothing. Lucy was about to barge in."

Vihaan offered his arm to her as had become their custom. Calla accepted and tried to not blush. On the way out, she apologized to Lucy for the scare.

"I have to say," Vihaan started, "You look stunning today."

Calla was about to object the compliment, but smiled and replied, "Thank you." She knew she had to douse these flames between them. They seemed to grow bigger every minute they spent together. As much as she cherished every second they spent together, this could only end in heartache when she left Midelle for good. "Vihaan, I want to make something clear."

He raised an eyebrow. "Go on." They passed by the entryway to the gardens. The image of the fountain flashed in her thoughts.

"I, uh," she took a slow breath in, "I want you to know that trying to win my affections is a wasted effort on your part. I'm leaving when I've done what I'm supposed to do. I don't think you want to go to the human realm, and I'm not staying here. Feelings can be spared..." Calla paused when his finger barely graced her lips. Her eyes darted up to meet his.

Vihaan took a step towards her, and her mirrored foot stepped back. Her mouth went dry. His finger dropped to curl under her chin, "If we're making things clear, you need to know that you are not a wasted effort." His other foot stepped forward and her foot stepped back. "You also need to know that this is only the beginning, I won't stop." Their dance ended with Calla's back pressed against the wall. "Because I am a man with conviction, and I know what I want."

"Until the chase is over," Calla whispered breathlessly before she could stop herself. Warmth grew in her cheeks.

Vihaan's face went level with hers. A purple fire burned in his eyes, "Even when the chase is over, there's a very sweet prize at the end. One that I'd never stop wanting." They were locked in a stare-off laced with infatuation and temptation. Calla forced her eyes to stay on his, knowing the consequences if they didn't. Her breathing felt short and shallow, yet their chests rose and fell in perfect synchronization. Out of the corner of her eye she could see one side of his lips curve into a half smile. He broke the moment by tapping her jawline with his thumb like he was savoring what had happened moments ago. He backed off one slow step at a time, and Calla could breathe normally again. She felt her cheeks burn scarlet from the heat that blazed between them.

Calla needed to change the subject to anything but this. There was a part of her that wanted everything that Vihaan offered without even knowing him, but her brain screamed against it. She broke the gaze by focusing on a grand tapestry of Midelle across the corridor. "That map there?"

Vihaan glanced at it, "What about it?"

"Can you show it to me?" Calla's eyes dipped down the corridor, Lucy had ducked around the corner to give them privacy. The tip of her bow jutted out from the other side of the corner.

Vihaan smirked while his gaze smoldered into her own again, but after a few seconds he backed off.

Calla sucked in a long silent breath and let it out slowly as he side-stepped over to the hand-painted, embroidered tapestry. She was thankful he let it go without fighting. Her brain was still trying to process his words and subtle touches.

"Let the expert on all things Midelle show you the way around it. There's a whole realm at your fingertips, Lady Calla. Where to first?"

Calla's eyes roamed over the map, but only one place seemed logical to start. "Japhia."

Vihaan pointed to the castle sitting in the southeast corner of the map. Only grasslands were to the bottom and right of the capitol. Beyond that was a mix of blues signaling the ocean. "As you know, we are here at the capital, Japhia." Above the castle was a depiction of the city. He dragged his finger north and east from the Castle. Painted was a forest but the trees were shades of red and black. "These are the woods of Ashbury. People disappear in these woods. Brave souls live on the outskirts of it in Ashburn. Legend has it that Morta's forgotten soul haunts the woods." Vihaan made a soft howling noise and ran his fingers up her arm.

Calla laughed to swat his hand away in a playful way, but a shiver ran down her spine.

His finger then went northwest. "These mountains are the start of the Edulis Mountains. Down here," his finger dragged down the depicted mountains and stopped at two high peaks, "are the Shimmering Peaks. There are villages on either side to coordinate crossings but passing is long and cold. Even during the summer months, the passage is drifted with snow. Here," He pointed to a new spot that resembled a lake, still close to the mountain range, but veered a touch southwest. "Are the Falls of Goldtown. Also, located near the falls, are the mines, the city, and a vast lake." His finger then ran across the south coast of Midelle. "These are the coastal villages where you can find mermaids, swamps, and beaches." Vihaan then covered a big area north of the coast and west of Goldtown, "These are the Great Plains, where most of the farmlands are. Beyond the Great Plains is Cape Toria which holds..."

Calla gave him an empty look as she tried to come up with an answer. She watched his finger point to the middle of the west coast at a spiraled peninsula

"...the Library of Midelle, which is where the Oracle is." Calla's heart tightened when he mentioned the library. Vihaan brought his hand up to the top of the map where there were mountains covered in sharp tangles. "Last but not least, the Wall of Thorns. This covers the whole top of Midelle. The thorns grow so quickly that no one can cut through or over the mountain. Trapped in the thorns for all eternity, are countless brave people who tried to cross the wall."

Calla shivered again as her nightmare of blood and thorns crossed her thoughts. She couldn't imagine that happening for real.

"And to wrap up our grand tour," his finger traced a road that cut straight through Midelle, "the Long Road that connects Japhia to Cape Toria. You can reach any destination from this road. What the map doesn't show are little villages and towns that have popped up over the years. This map is very old."

Calla ran her eyes over the map again, soaking it all in, but avoiding Cape Toria. "That's a lot to cover."

"It is, but I promised you my garden house, and I vow to never disappoint. Let's go."

"It's a date," rolled off Calla's tongue before she could stop the thought. Vihaan only gave her a smoldering smile as he popped his arm out for her to take.

Vihaan wasn't lying when he said garden house. Calla was in awe as she stepped inside the glass-roofed building filled top to bottom with shrubs, plants, flowers, and saplings. She wanted to melt against the fragrances of the flowers and the rich earth they grew in. It was heavenly with an explosion of colors everywhere. "It's like a dream!" In fact, Calla wished she dreamed about places like this instead of blood and thorns.

"This is my legacy. All my ancestors worked in this garden house. Seems fitting I do the same."

Calla's nose graced a red flower that faded into white at its center, "So what can you do, druid?" She inhaled to smell the sweet fragrance. "Do you talk to plants, or do they talk to you?" A flirty smile crossed her lips before her brain scolded her salacious actions.

Vihaan went over to an old wooden table in the corner and waved Calla over. She took a longer than direct path and let her fingers grace over different plants as she walked. It felt like her own mini paradise. "I don't have conversations with them, but each plant gives energy, and I can feel it." Calla stopped next to him. "These are seeds from the Falls of Goldtown. This stubborn flower only grows in the Falls, and I thought I could cultivate them here." Calla looked down at the table, laden with loose dirt and clay planters filled with vivid green sprouts. The sprouts had a familiarity to them, but Calla couldn't place it. He pulled two stools up to the worktable.

"I am curious though."

Calla raised an eyebrow, "Oh?"

"Would they grow for you, the Hybrid?"

Calla only sighed. She looked at the sprout closest to her. Reaching out and running her fingertip over the juvenile leaf gave Calla a feeling of déjà vu.

"It likes you," Vihaan stated.

Calla took back her hand, "How do you know? Is it giving you a feeling, plant whisperer?"

Vihaan laughed, "I like that, plant whisperer. Who doesn't like you? Try talking to it!" Vihaan smiled while leaning forward.

Calla's smile fell into a frown, "Captain Quinn doesn't like me, I'd go as far as hate."

Vihaan shushed her as soon as she finished. "He doesn't count. Now go on, speak."

Her mother always talked to her plants, but it was never like this. She always said it helped them grow. "Why hello there, little one," Calla said in a sweet voice, glancing at Vihaan. "I'm supposed to be talking to you, but I have no idea what to say. Please grow? I'd love to see you all bloomed and beautiful." The pair watched in anticipation, but nothing happened. "What now?"

Vihaan rested a hand on her shoulder, "Give it time. Gardening is ninety percent patience, ten percent skill."

"What kind of flower is this supposed to be anyway?"

Vihaan dipped his finger in a bowl of water, and she watched as a few drops fell onto the tiniest sprout. "A deity rose."

Calla immediately glanced at her sigil. She always knew the delicate and interwoven lines were a flower. Before Midelle she never knew what kind, despite countless hours of research. "I thought if you were in touch with the deities, that it could bring your powers to light."

Calla nodded, remembering what this all was about. Her powers. Her saving Midelle. Her being the Hybrid. She wanted to be angry at Vihaan, but she couldn't bring herself to be. The more she thought about it, she had no one to be mad at. It was no one's fault that she was the Hybrid. "What does a deity rose look like? I can't say that I've seen one."

Vihaan pointed to a double-sided bookshelf in the middle of the garden house. "If you look in the big leather-bound one, you'll find it. It's quite beautiful. I also want to crack the code of growing these outside the Falls. I was hoping you could be the key."

"Is that all I am to you, a key?" She gave him a coy smile, and he returned it.

"Among other things, yes."

Calla followed his instruction and with care, flipped the aged pages. She saw faded notes in the margins, knowing it came from his ancestors. "C...D..." She muttered, and when she flipped the page, she gasped. Calla dropped the book and covered her mouth.

"Are you okay?" Vihaan rushed to her side. He picked up the book and thumbed through to the deity rose page.

"That rose links to the deities?"

Vihaan furrowed his brows in thought. "All legends and folklore, until you showed up with the sigil on your hand."

Calla's lip quivered as visions of her nightmare came back as haunting as ever, "I've seen this flower before."

"Where? How? They don't grow outside the Falls."

"In my dreams," Calla croaked, her throat had gone dry. "I find a patch of them in an endless field, and then thorns come out and trap me. Blood flows down my skin, and it all converges on my sigil." She shivered. "I've dreamt that several times now. It ends the same with an ominous voice calling out to me." She gripped his arm and her eyes went wide. "Please don't tell anyone. Especially Finn.

"Your secret is safe with me." He placed his hand over hers. "You said you heard a voice?"

Calla nodded her head. "No matter how hard I try to break free from the thorns and shut out the voice... nothing works. It says it's only a matter of time."

Vihaan brought Calla close to his chest. She didn't bother fighting him, she wanted this as much as he did. He smelled like his flowers, sweet and heavenly. "A matter of time before what?"

Calla wanted to say before she became Corrupted, but she knew better. That thought was the only thing that could manifest itself as a dark voice in her brain. Besides Finn, that was the only thing she feared. Becoming corrupted. "I wish I knew."

Nine

Calla's curled fist hovered in front of a wooden door. She withdrew it for the fifth time as her hand fell into the soft folds of her crimson dress. "Do you think she's in there?"

Calla turned her attention away from the door to Lucy. She leaned along the wall a few feet away with her arms crossed and hip cocked off to the side. "You would know if you knocked on the door."

"Right." Calla raised her fist again and rapped her knuckles on the door. Her heart raced and her palms were sweaty. She wasn't nearly this nervous apologizing to Violet. "Philomena?" She knocked again, a little louder this time. "Are you in there? It's me, Calla."

Lucy stepped closer to reach over to Calla and open the door. They peaked in simultaneously, but it was clear that Philomena wasn't in her work room. Lucy sighed as her hands went to her hips. "That girl is always missing when you need her."

Calla stepped inside, feeling odd just hanging around in the corridor. "She's bound to show up, right?"

Lucy followed her in. "I suppose we could wait for her for a bit."

Calla turned away from Lucy as she took in the foreign space. The wall to the left was a bookcase, complete with a horizontal sliding ladder. She bit back a laugh as she imagined Philomena sliding back and forth to keep herself busy. There was a small desk near the bookcase wall with candles burnt down to stumps. Papers and books covered the entire surface. The back wall held a series of tables and shelves holding vials and bunches of herbs. A lone window sat in an opening from the shelves. On the wall to her right there was a glass cabinet full of neatly organized vials. To fill out the middle of the room, a giant cauldron sat in the middle with the remnants of fire underneath. A long table sat next to it.

"It's always quite a sight, isn't it?" Lucy murmured as she took in the room herself. "I don't find myself in here that often, but it always feels different than the rest of the castle."

Calla nodded. There was something different about this room from the rest of the castle. A low energy hummed beneath her feet, but surely it was just the mystique of the room. She peered into the cauldron, empty and clean. She moved to the glass cabinet that had a heavy lock hanging from the latch.

"It's all her finished potions," Lucy commented from the other side of the room. "When Rose was new here, it was unlocked, but there was a guard that turned Corrupted under everyone's eye. He caused so much damage to this room but was eventually captured. King Raoul decreed a lock with only two keys. One for the Resident Witch and…"

"Another for the master set that the Captain of the Royal Guard has."

Lucy and Calla exchanged glances with each other before turning to the source of the standoffish voice.

"Captain," Lucy immediately bowed her head.

Calla pulled her shoulders back and jutted her chin out. She still pictured him down in the mud from their last interaction.

"Varden," Finn nodded his head back to her. "Lady Calla." His jaded eyes narrowed in on the two of them. "What are you two doing here? Asking about keys, no less."

"I was telling her the story of the lock, Captain. She didn't ask."

"We're waiting for Philomena. I need to speak with her." Calla's reply came out tarter than she expected it to.

"I see. Give us a moment." He glanced at Lucy who slipped out of the room faster than Calla expected. Finn looked up to the ceiling then back at Calla. "I need to report to King Nakosi about your progress. Has there been any?"

Calla shook her head, internally praying that there was never any progress to report. "Vihaan had an idea that I'm quite taken with." Calla rolled her lips in when she witnessed a tense wave dominate Finn's features.

"And that is?" His voice became incredibly low and dangerous.

They locked eyes with a narrowed venom for each other. "Vihaan wants me to experience Japhia."

"No."

Calla scoffed and rolled her eyes. "Of course, you would say no! You're not even giving it a chance."

"Because it's dangerous!"

"Because it's dangerous," Calla mocked him in a goofy masculine voice. "That's a copout answer and you know it." She couldn't place it, but the fear she had for him was waning. On repeat, the image of him down and out kept playing in her mind. It made him less scary and more... human?

"It's not. It is dangerous out there. The castle is the only place where I can ensure your safety."

"If you think it's such a bad idea, then bring it up to King Nakosi. Surely he will agree with you since it's so dangerous." Maybe a quick chat with King Nakosi could indeed change his mind. She was The Hybrid after all and could use that to direct him in the right direction. Ever since the decision to end sparring his decisions were in her favor and not Finn's.

"Perhaps I will. I see you going behind my back on this."

Calla crossed her arms over her chest. "I would do no such thing." Her subconscious immediately called her a liar. "There has to be a common ground here."

"Yeah, you not leaving the castle unless it's to leave for Cape Toria. That's the only common ground I can agree upon."

Calla stabbed a finger in his direction. "You are incorrigible and an asshole!"

Finn swatted her hand away even though she wasn't close to touching him. "I am here to protect you and nothing more. I am not your friend, your confidant, or anything of the sort. I have a job to do, and you seem hellbent on making it as difficult as possible for me."

"Poor Captain Quinn," Calla cooed. "Sorry you have such a difficult Hybrid to watch over." She threw a hand over her forehead for added flair. "If only life were easy."

Finn's jaw grew tense, but he didn't make a sound.

She returned to her previous stance, wondering if she crossed a line. His silence was making her nervous.

"Ah, Lady Philomena," Lucy interrupted from the corridor. "Perfect timing. We were waiting for you."

Finn cleared his throat. "Excuse me, Lady Calla. I am late for my meeting with King Nakosi." He turned and left the room without acknowledging Lucy or Philomena. Calla let out a soft sigh as she felt increasingly guilty for being difficult on purpose. But Finn deserved it.

"Lady Calla!" Philomena dashed excitedly into the room with a bright and wide smile. The young witch had on a sage green dress with golden embroidery. The top portion of her hair was tied back with a white silk ribbon that Calla presumed was once a bow but now has fallen apart. Philomena's smile faded. "Are you still mad at me?"

Calla's heart plummeted to the floor. She waved Philomena closer and sat on her knees to face the girl at eye level. "No, I'm not and I never was."

Philomena's smile returned. The innocence of the gesture warmed Calla's heart.

"I came by to apologize to you."

The young witch shrugged. "As long as you're not mad at me anymore. Violet said to give you some space. I'm not sure what she meant by that, but it was really hard not to visit you."

Calla brushed a rogue strand of hair behind her ear, something she remembered her own mom doing for her. "I'm so sorry Philomena. You and Violet didn't deserve my anger. The two of you were the most kind to me after my arrival. I was angry at my situation, and I took it out on you. It wasn't right and you deserve an apology because we're friends."

"Best friends?" Her eyes went wide with hope.

"Best friends," Calla confirmed, not even thinking twice about it. She opened her arms for a hug from the sweet girl. Philomena crashed into Calla's arms, and she held the witch tight. "I'm so sorry, Philomena. I hope you forgive me." A tear sped down Calla's cheek and dripped on top of Philomena's lavender hair. The little witch didn't notice, but it made Calla hold her even tighter. She couldn't explain the tear, but it was from a place of love and friendship. She never had a sibling, but the relationship she had with her felt like what Calla imagined it would be.

"You're squishing me," Philomena muffled against Calla's shoulder.

Calla laughed as she loosened her grip. "Sorry." She fixed Philomena's hair again before fully standing up. "Am I forgiven?"

"Of course! I'm glad you aren't mad at me."

Calla shook her head playfully giving her a small smile. "Never."

"Oh!" Philomena's face lit up. "Mister Vihaan wanted me to give you a message."

Calla pretended to ignore the flutters in her stomach. "He did, did he?"

"Mhm." Philomena tapped her chin in thought. "Umm, he said that..." She blew out a steady stream of air. "Something about counting seconds until the time moves slow and he sees you then it goes fast when together? I can't remember. He said it in a strange way."

Calla smiled, even though the message was garbled. "Thank you for delivering the message. Do you know where I can find him?"

"I saw him on the way back from the kitchens. He was doing something in the courtyard."

"I think I will pay him a visit. Is that okay?"

Philomena nodded her head before going over to the wall of books. "I have to get some stuff started anyways. King Nakosi wants everything ready to go for when your powers come to light."

Calla's smile dropped, but she was thankful Philomena had her eyes attuned to a book. "Bye Philomena."

She looked up only for a few seconds before bidding Calla a farewell.

When Calla met Lucy outside the workroom, Lucy gave her a presumptuous smile. "To the courtyard?"

Calla ignored Lucy's excitement as she said, "Yes. Perhaps we'll catch Vihaan there."

"Aren't you going to go up to him?" Lucy asked after her and Calla stood in the shadows leading into the courtyard.

Calla spent the last few minutes admiring Vihaan from afar. He hadn't noticed them but was hard at work shoveling out the frostbitten flowers that wouldn't survive the winter. His shirt was cast to the side. Sweat gleamed over his tanned skin and damped the hair close to his scalp. She kept bouncing back and forth on if she was being a total creep or not. "Can't a girl enjoy a view?" She let out a dreamy sigh.

Lucy grinned at her. "You're welcome to do as you please, Lady Calla." She let out a sharp whistle then ducked out of view.

Calla let out an inaudible string of curses aimed at Lucy before she stood there dumbfounded and caught like a kitten that got the cream as Vihaan's magnificent gaze landed on her. He smiled and waved to her.

Calla gave a small wave back, feeling the apple of her cheeks grow warm. "Hello Vihaan. I got your message from Philomena."

Vihaan abandoned his project and met her by the entryway into the courtyard. "That was quick."

"I was actually in her workroom. I needed to speak with her, so it all worked out." Calla didn't miss Vihaan's eyebrows furrowing for a second.

"I hope everything is alright."

Calla waved a hand nonchalantly at him. "Oh of course, nothing to worry about there. But what I do want to know is more about this message." Calla couldn't help laughing at Philomena's retelling.

Vihaan nodded his head, anticipating her words. "Let me guess, she got it all wrong?" He said the words in jest, like he knew that was to be the outcome all alone.

"Did you mean to say, 'something about counting seconds until the time moves slow and you see me then it goes fast when we're together.'"

Vihaan let out a laugh and Calla followed. He gestured to a bench next to where he was working. They sat down with their legs touching. "It was supposed to be along the lines of..." he paused as the corner of his lips turned upwards, "I am counting the agonizingly slow seconds until I can see you again, even if just a glance. When we do meet, those seconds burn faster than oil and before I know it, we are apart once again."

He lifted his gaze to meet hers and Calla could feel the heat pool in her belly. "You expected Philomena to remember all that?" Her voice came out as a whisper.

"No, but I thought it would be fun." Vihaan's eyes dipped to her lips for a quick second. Then his purple irises captured her icy stare once again.

Calla internally stood at a fork in the road. Her body was screaming to give in and to finally learn what it felt like to kiss Vihaan, but it wasn't right. She couldn't lead him on. She would eventually leave and there could be possible heartache on both sides. She turned away from him where a pile of dirt sat within reach.

Vihaan placed his hand over hers that she had resting in her lap. "My sincerest apologies if I upset you Lady Calla. It was never my intention to. I intended the opposite actually."

Calla turned back to him. "I suppose I'm still sorting out feelings on my end." That was as honest as she could be without spilling everything to him.

"I understand."

Calla couldn't stand herself as a blanket of awkward silence wrapped around them. She couldn't meet Vihaan's intense gaze. "I spoke to Finn about going into Japhia." She finally looked up.

Vihaan's hand gently squeezed hers. "And?"

Calla's lips turned downward. "He said no immediately."

Vihaan made a noise of disgust. "That arrogant bastard thinks he can just control you from every angle. I'll speak to the King about this. I promised to show you how beautiful Midelle can be, and I won't fail you."

Calla let go of the tension that unknowingly built in her shoulders. "He said he would speak to King Nakosi, but I don't entirely trust him."

"Entirely?" Vihaan gave her a dry look. "I don't trust him at all. I shall speak to the King and press for this before the snow comes." He picked up her hand that he had been cradling this entire time and placed a swift kiss on the back of it. "I promise to you."

His grip loosened on her hand where it started to slip from his but Calla tightened her grip by wrapping her thumb around his fingers. "I can't wait to see Japhia." Calla winked.

Vihaan's smile grew wider as he grabbed her hand once more and placed a longer kiss over her knuckles all while capturing her gaze with his.

"You know," Calla started with a mischievous intent, "for a groundskeeper, you sure are clean." As soon as the words left her mouth, she wondered if this was right... to give into her whim.

Vihaan raised an eyebrow, and a smoldering smirk slowly upturned the end of his lips.

That look alone was worth it.

"Would you prefer I be dirty?"

Calla bit her lips as she toyed with the idea that flashed in her mind. "You'd fit the image of groundskeeper much more." Before she gave him a chance to digest her words she grabbed a handful of the dirt that was piled high next to her and playfully tossed it on him.

Vihaan played along and smeared it over his skin, mixing in with the sweat that once covered him. "Better?"

They both broke out into a fit of laughter, but Calla managed to nod. "Much."

Vihaan held his hands out to her. "Now it's your turn!"

Calla shrieked playfully as she darted up from her seat and to the other side of the fountain. Vihaan grabbed two handfuls of dirt before attempting to approach her with a sinful grin of his own. "Seems that you're too clean to be around the groundskeeper now. Best dirty you up."

"Oh no you don't," Calla laughed.

Vihaan went to chase after her and Calla ran to the opposite side of the fountain. Every time Vihaan moved in one direction, Calla moved in the other, all while shrieking with fits of laughter. Then he moved to one side and Calla was too invested in their game to stop herself as Vihaan changed directions. Calla screamed as she took off to the shaded grove connected to the courtyard.

They darted in and all around the trees with both laughing and sending flirtatious looks to each other. Vihaan finally caught her and wrapped an arm around her waist to pull her flush against him. His arm lifted high then sprinkled dirt over them. Calla covered her face as she broke out in another fit of laughter.

When he was out of dirt, Calla brought her head up and stuck her tongue out at him. "Still clean." She ran the backside of her fingers across her cheek.

Vihaan cupped her cheek and used his dirt clad thumb to create a single streak over her skin. "Not anymore," he whispered as his purple eyes fell to her lips.

Calla's breathing hitched as her hands went to his chest and her head tilted back slightly.

She wondered if his heart was beating as rapidly as hers was.

"Lady Calla!" A panicked voice rang out in the courtyard.

Calla jumped away from Vihaan as the voice served as ice cold water drenching them and ending whatever was going to happen between them.

Vihaan peered through the trees and a groan immediately left his lips. With a flat tone he said, "It's the Captain."

"Lady Calla, where are you?" Finn again, but she could hear Lucy trying to placate Finn's worry.

Calla gave Vihaan a sad look of longing. "Next time," she whispered before clearing her throat and saying louder, "I'm in the grove!"

Finn found her within ten seconds, the tips of his ear were red with rage, and she was positive a vein kept popping out on the side of his throat. "You were screaming."

"Clearly not out of danger," Vihaan muttered.

Finn pointed a finger at Vihaan. "Stay out of this druid."

"He's not the problem here," Calla said while narrowing her stare at Finn.

"I heard screaming and thought you were in danger," Finn snapped back.

Calla gestured to Lucy. "Don't you think she would have done something?"

Finn huffed and thought about his words for a moment. "That's beside the point. You can't run around the castle screaming everywhere. Got it?"

Calla crossed her arms. "Sure thing."

Finn made a crisp turn around before stalking back inside the castle.

"Perhaps next time?" Vihaan offered with a gentle grin.

Calla returned his grin with one of her own. "Perhaps next time. If you'll excuse me, I have dirt all over me."

"Tsk tsk tsk," Vihaan laughed while shaking his head. Strands of emerald hair escaped their containment. With the dirty, sweaty chest and wild hair, he made butterflies run wild in her belly. "Why do you always get so filthy around me?"

Calla shrugged her shoulders playfully. "Fate?"

Vihaan gave her a parting nod. "Remind me to thank fate later."

She took small steps back towards the main courtyard. "Will do."

Their gazes smoldered as distance grew between them, but then Lucy grabbed Calla's elbow and the feeling between them burned out.

"I don't know what happened there. He just showed up suddenly," Lucy confessed.

"Maybe I shouldn't have screamed. Did I sound like I was in trouble?"

"Not at all."

Calla glanced at the castle, but out of the very corner of her eye, she saw a flash of red disappear from an upper window. She shook the image right out of her mind. "I need to rest. I think I'm seeing things."

Ten

Japhia was everything Calla hoped it would be. From the moment she entered the city, her eyes bounced from one thing to another. Delectable smells of savory and sweet swirled all around her, wanting to pull her in their direction. All kinds of vendors lined the streets, selling things she had never seen before in her life. Rows of simple houses lined the cobblestoned alleys that branched off the main streets. She couldn't tell who in the crowds were druids, vampires, or trolls at first glance. Children weaved in and out of the crowds, smiles plastered on their faces. Calla couldn't help but notice the guards posted at all intersections and gates. There was always one tiny thing that reminded her of what she was. Even still, the citizens blended into the wonderful melting pot of the city that was Japhia.

The past week had been simply wonderful. Each day was filled with Vihaan. Time with Violet had weaved its way in, as did time with Philomena. Calla was starting to look on the brighter side of things. But each night, her curiosity ran rampant as she marveled at the sleepless city from her balcony. The air had been crisp, with sparkles of frost sprinkled over everything when she had awakened that morning. They had melted fast under the intense morning sun. Vihaan had gotten her to Japhia before the first snow, a sweet promise fulfilled.

Getting approval to tour the city with Vihaan was like pulling teeth with tweezers. Finn had been adamant that he would escort them instead of Lucy. Both Calla and Vihaan petitioned to Nakosi against this, but to no avail. The risk would be higher being in the city, and Finn asserted it wasn't worth the risk. The King had set three conditions for the visit. As they strolled the streets of Japhia, Finn trailed behind them. That was condition one. He wasn't wearing his Captain's armor or anything that would draw attention, so to a casual observer he was just one in a crowd of many. Calla tried to pretend he wasn't there, but she could feel his gaze vex her back.

The second condition of the outing was that Calla wears gloves to hide her sigil. That was easy. And the third? What Finn says goes. If he decided that they head back to the castle, then they go without complaint. Despite the conditions, she was still in awe of Japhia. She wanted to spend days walking through the shops and enjoying Vihaan's company. Anything to delay her so-called powers coming to light and having to trek to the Library.

A chilly gust of wind blew down the street they walked on. Calla shivered and brought her thick cloak tighter. Fall had final-ly pushed summer out for good. "I've talked your ear off about everything the past week," Calla softened her voice, "Tell me about you."

Calla looked up at Vihaan. He wore his hair tied back above his thick cloak. Calla liked when he wore his hair back, it showed the strong jawline she couldn't get out of her head since their little moment by the tapestry of Midelle. He looked over to her and smiled. "I am but a simple druid."

Calla rolled her eyes, "Come on now, fess up. Violet told me that she raised you, and I'm curious. I grew up without my birth parents too."

"I can always count on Violet," he joked, rubbing the back of his neck. "My mother, Brook, died in childbirth. Violet says I have her eyes. My father, Bastiaan, died while protecting me from The Corrupted King Raoul."

Ah yes, the different King her cohorts have mentioned as if it were a slip of the tongue. "I here his name here and there. Tell me about him." They passed a bakery where the smell of fresh bread wafted around her head. Her mouth watered.

"Before Nakosi took over, King Raoul ruled with fairness and more importantly, in peace with his wife, Queen Alina, and son, Prince Vallen."

Calla immediately thought of the crown still sitting in its box in her room. Shea said it once belonged to Queen Alina.

"My dad grew up with Prince Vallen, working as the groundskeeper. That never stopped them from becoming best friends. When the Prince was in his teen years, disaster struck. Queen Alina became ill and passed away."

Calla shivered at the thought of wearing a dead Queen's crown. The notion that she was probably dead slipped her mind when Shea gave her the crown.

"After that, King Raoul wasn't the same. He kept a close eye on the Prince and almost never let him out of his sight." Vihaan and Calla walked to an open circular area. A grand citadel stood tall in the center with trees surrounding the white-bricked building. She was listening to Vihaan's story, but her eyes still took in the citadel. "Then the Prince vanished. No one could find him and that enraged the King so much that he became Corrupted. He and his royal guards killed hundreds of innocents trying to find information on his son. There was no stopping him. One day when I was a baby, I was in the wrong place at the wrong time, and the King almost killed me in a fit of rage. My dad protected me. The King accused him of hiding information about the prince. After that, no one ever saw him again. I learned this all from Violet." He was looking straight ahead, but his magnificent orchid eyes looked lost.

"I'm so sorry," she whispered. "That's terrible."

Vihaan gave her a gentle nod. His eyes looked a little less lost. "Years later, an army of free people had enough of King Raoul's torturous ways. Roark, his brother Jedrek and his squire Nakosi led this free army. They started north of Cape Toria, in Ebonrun, and gained traction along their journey. By the time they reached the castle, the Captain of the Guard let them in without hesitation to put a stop to King Raoul. In their battle, Roark received a grievous wound. He ended up dying along with King Raoul. In his dying breaths, Roark gave the throne to Nakosi as Jedrek refused it. Jedrek did honor his brother by serving as Nakosi's Captain of the Royal Guard. He recently retired to East Shimmer and that's when," they glanced behind them to see Finn with a hard-set face watching them. Vihaan whispered, "Finn replaced Jedrek."

Calla bit back a smile. They didn't try to hide that they were gossiping about him. "How long has Nakosi been King then?"

"Twenty-five years?" Vihaan shrugged. Calla noticed his thumb rubbing her arm in slow circles through the long sleeves of her dress. She ignored the butterflies running amok in her stomach. " I didn't get to spend much time with my father or have many memories of him, but there are some days where I wonder if he'd be proud of me. I find his notes everywhere in the garden house and after all this time, I still find new ones."

Calla smiled. "I know he would be proud of you, Vihaan. You've been nothing but a gentleman to me and..." She trailed off, with a faint blush falling over her cheeks.

"And what?" A big smile spread on his face. His arm untangled from hers and snaked around her waist underneath the cloak. Her skin tingled under her ivory dress from where his hand touched.

Calla turned her head to meet Vihaan's gaze. Their eyes met in a sweet flurry of ice and orchids. "And thank you for showing me Japhia."

"The pleasure is all mine."

"Vihaan!" A man came running out of a store. Calla stopped. The dangers of this trip outlined by Finn and the sudden clamor from the man brought a wave of fear over her, and she shrunk behind Vihaan. The man had a long red beard with gems braided into it, all which sat below a shaved head. His mustache curled at the ends, and he wore layers of bright colored robes. The building he came out of echoed his flamboyancy. The bricks were a vivid scarlet red and an eclectic yellow sign hung over the door reading, 'Beastly Beauties'. The shop stood out among the monotony of his neighbors.

Vihaan took Calla's arm again and gave her a reassuring smile. She glanced back to Finn, his hand was on the hilt of the sword sheathed beneath his cloak. As the man came closer, she could see a variety of piercings and tattoos that riddled his skin. "Yocsho," Vihaan smiled as the man embraced him. She caught Finn relaxing his hand out of the corner of her eye.

"My friend. It's been almost three weeks. You haven't been to town since the tremble."

Calla's stomach dropped as she watched Finn circle behind the strange man, his eyes narrowed on him.

"Much to do to prepare for the winter," Vihaan stated. "This is Lady Calla, she's visiting from Goldtown." Vihaan dropped his arm and gestured to her. "Lady Calla, this is Yocsho..."

"Proprietor of unique items within the realm, and owner of the most coveted animals throughout the land," he finished, cutting off Vihaan. He grabbed her right hand to kiss it with a melodramatic flare. His thumb ran over the back of her hand before she pulled away. "Come, come! This is your first time in Japhia?"

Calla could only nod as she hid her hands under her cloak.

"You must see my beauties, but do not touch." He twisted the ends of his oiled beard, then wagged a finger. "Never touch."

Vihaan leaned down to Calla's ear, "He's weird about his animals. Don't take offense to it."

Calla smiled as Finn staked his claim by the storefront, "None taken."

The store was alive with animals of all kinds. Reptiles perched in the sunlight, while birds tweeted to each other in song. Strange four-legged creatures that Calla couldn't identify dashed between shelves of unique items. A large striped cat lay on a deep purple pillow suspiciously watched them enter, then yawned and resumed its nap. In the corner, a beautiful, sleek bird with dark sapphire feathers sang. The enchanting song was high-pitched and all in one note. Calla stopped before the bird, and it spread out its tail to show brilliant shades of blue, purple, green and red. The bird chirped and bowed its head.

"He's a blue ember phoenix," Vihaan pointed out.

"He's amazing," Calla whispered. She reached out her hand but a sharp whack from a riding crop made her recall her hand quickly.

"No touching my beautiful Korios," Yocsho warned her by wagging a finger at her. Rings of different metals and gems sparkled along his fingers.

Vihaan stepped forward, "Forgive her, Yocsho. She's enamored by Korios, can you blame her?"

Calla's eyes glanced outside. Finn had watched the encounter with intensity. She's surprised he hadn't barged in.

Yocsho pondered for a second and smiled, "I cannot. It is interesting..." Calla raised an eyebrow at his words. "He doesn't bow to anyone, not even me." Yocsho's eyes became lost in thought, disengaging from the conversation. His eyes snapped back and he raised ring-clad a finger, "No more touching. Understood?"

Calla clasped her hands behind her back, "Understood."

Yocsho barred his stained teeth with a smile. "Vihaan, remember that snapping sprig tree you found for me?

Vihaan passed Calla, his hand gave her arm a playful squeeze. "I do. I paid good money for that."

"And I paid you even more for it," he joked, but his face fell serious. "There's a slight problem with it."

Vihaan crossed his arms, "Is there anything I can help you with?"

"It's aggression..."

"It's supposed to be aggressive," Vihaan interjected, "That's why it's a snapping sprig tree."

Calla listened, intrigued by the conversation. Faint whispers floated around her and caught her attention. She looked around and saw no one nearby. Vihaan and Yocsho kept going about their business. She remembered when the portal to Midelle opened and the whispers called to her then, just as they did now.

"It's not aggressive enough," Yocsho said with a sly smile.

Vihaan's eyes gleamed at the shop owner's words. "Interesting. Lady Calla?" Calla turned her head from the direction of the whispering, afraid they were going to stop again. "I'll be right back, okay? This is too intriguing to pass up."

"No touching my animals," Yocsho and his finger added as he and Vihaan slipped past a velvet curtain.

"I'll just be outside by Finn. It's hot in here," Calla said.

"I'll be only a minute," Vihaan said with a smile that made Calla weak in the knees.

Calla watched as they disappeared behind the curtain to some sort of vast side room. She focused again on the vague whispering. As she moved closer to the backdoor of the shop, the whispers grew louder. Calla glanced at Finn. He was looking in the shop's window, intrigued by some tiny yellow lizards in a cage. She dashed through the back door before he could notice.

Coming outside, a strong wind blew through the back alley, causing chaos around her. Novelties were blown off tables and carts, bottles smashed against the cobblestone and women shrieked as their skirts fluttered up with the sudden wind. Calla walked around the corner and the whispers grew stronger. She pushed through a crowd of trolls gathered at an intersection and followed the whispers around another corner. The whispers dimmed and Calla panicked. She rushed around yet another corner, she came onto a wider street. The whispers returned, and she followed them down the street and to another alleyway.

Heavy clouds darkened the alleyway. Small torches lit her way, and crudely blown glass bottles rolled against the cobblestone from the wind earlier. Calla pulled a lit torch from its holder and followed the whispers.

They got louder and louder, and she followed without hesitation. So many whispers filled her head she couldn't think straight.

Every cell of her body screamed to follow the hushed voices. She turned another corner and the whispers ended. The air became still.

Calla stood before an ancient building housing a boarded-up shop. She walked to the storefront and ran her hands over the boards that nailed the door shut. She raised the torch to read the faded sign that hung crooked from a single chain. "Bellcott's Apothecary," she whispered. Calla went to one of the broken windows and peered in. The place seemed long abandoned. She used the torch to knock out the remaining shards on the windowsill and climbed in.

A layer of thick dust had settled over everything inside the shop. Empty bottles of different shapes and sizes, upright and knocked over, lined the shelves. She ran her fingers over a shelf to leave four streaks in the dust. She grimaced and wiped her hands on the inside of her cloak. Her steps echoed the emptiness as she walked along the rows. The handwritten cards for each bottle had either faded away with time or were missing.

Calla walked into the back section, the floorboards responding with deep creaks to each step. A large dust-covered portrait with a silver frame caught her eyes. She brought the torch closer to get a better look. The image was of three people in what looked like a family portrait pose. There was what looked to be a mother and father with black aprons and a daughter in a muted green dress seated in before them.

Calla wished she could see their faces, but jitters stirred in her stomach when she realized why it was so difficult. It wasn't dust covering their faces, it was ash. Their faces burned by fire. She touched the ashen spot on the mother only to wipe dust onto her fingers. Someone burned this a long time ago.

"Calla?" Vihaan's panicked shouting floated in the apothecary. His voice was faint, but it brought Calla out of the lull she was in. She took one more glance at the portrait, then left the room.

"Calla!" The panic in his voice was rising. His running slowed when he saw Calla waving from inside the apothecary. "What are you doing in there? I thought something happened to you! Finn had no idea where you were either!" He rushed over to the window and grabbed the torch from her to place it in a nearby holder.

"I don't know what came over me. I wasn't going to go far and then I ended up here," Calla explained while Vihaan helped her out of the window. The bottom of her light-colored dress was gray with dust.

"You scared me half to death... I thought..." He stopped talking as he took Calla in his arms. Calla looked at his eyes, they were alive with an energy that she'd never seen before. His eyes dipped down to her lips then back up to her eyes. "I thought..." He whispered with a small sigh as his eyes fell to her lips once again.

Calla was dancing the line in her brain, deciding if she wanted to kiss him. She gripped his arms and let her nails make gentle indents into his hearty skin. "Thought what?" She whispered at the end of her breath.

Vihaan dipped his head down and their lips met for the first time in a sweet kiss. His hands spread out across her back, pulling her in closer. Calla let her fingers relax on his skin as the kiss deepened.

Fireworks flew high in her mind, and her stomach tumbled. Calla never wanted to stop kissing him, she felt safe in his arms, but like all good things… Vihaan broke the kiss, his chest heaving. He placed an adoring kiss on her forehead, "I didn't mean to…"

Calla smiled, holding back a laugh, "Oh yes, you did."

"You caught me." He brought her in close. Calla's ear pressed against his chest, and she could hear his heart thumping just as fast as hers was. "What were you doing in there?"

Calla looked back towards the old building. The truth danced on the tip of her tongue. Were the whispers part of her powers? Even if they weren't she didn't know their intent, not yet at least. Still, if they were related to her powers coming to light, she didn't want anyone to know. "I was walking along, and I got curious. What happened there?"

"That used to be the best apothecary in Midelle, but someone murdered the family who owned it."

"Who murdered them?" Calla thought of the portrait with the burned faces.

Vihaan shook his head with a sad face. "No one knows. They disappeared one day. Concerned citizens organized a search party since King Raoul refused to."

"Because he was Corrupted?"

Vihaan nodded. "King Raoul only wanted to find his son. The search party found the mangled bodies of Mr. and Mrs. Bellcott in the Ashbury Woods."

Calla made a face of disgust. "That's horrible! What about the other one? There was a daughter?"

"No third body was ever found. The two bodies were a shock to Japhia. Despite the horrors they saw from King Raoul's actions, it was another sign that The Corrupted had returned. No one had the heart to take over their store, so it's gone to ruin. Rambunctious kids throw stones at it at night, but they don't dare go inside."

Calla pursed her lips. "Except me."

"You had no idea. What was it like in there?"

"Dusty."

"Some say it's haunted, see any ghosts?"

The color drained in Calla's face as Finn came stalking up to them. His eyes narrowed on her and his face twisted in anger. "What makes you think you can run off like that?

"I didn't run off!"

Finn grabbed her arm, yanking her away from Vihaan.

"Easy now! She made a mistake," Vihaan said, pushing Finn's shoulder. His grip was still tight on Calla. She ground her teeth against the pain of him squeezing over a bruise.

"This little tour is over. Come, Lady Calla."

Calla tried to yank her arm free from Finn, but he only held on tighter. "You're hurting me! Let go!"

Finn pulled her close to him, "You will not disobey me again. Do I make myself clear?"

Calla's blood began to boil. "Let me tell you something, Captain..."

Angered screams pierced the air, followed by mass shrieking. Finn let her go immediately to draw his sword. He looked over at

Vihaan, "Get her back to the castle! I'll meet you there. I need to investigate."

Calla grabbed Vihaan's hand, frightened. "Come on, we'll take the side roads." Vihaan rushed her away from the commotion. She glanced back to see Finn dash out of view into an alleyway.

A woman came running out from the alleyway, her face twisted in fear. "It's The Corrupted! Run!"

Calla's heart stopped beating, but somehow her feet were running, her hand welded to Vihaan's as they sped through the streets. "What's happening?" Calla asked when they paused to check if the coast was clear.

"It sounds like The Corrupted have come to take you. I'm getting you to safety." Vihaan pressed his finger to his lips and Calla nodded, afraid to speak. They crossed the street, then ducked into an alleyway. Near the end of the alley they turned to cross onto an open street, and both of them stopped in their tracks.

Corrupted.

The Corrupted were running through the streets. All-out chaos had broken out in Japhia. Citizens fled in and out, trying to get to safety. Calla knew The Corrupted were only here for one thing, the Hybrid. "There's the Hybrid," one of many shouted.

"Run," Vihaan shouted as he pulled Calla in the direction they had come from. The horde followed frantically. Vihaan stuck his hand out behind him. Tangles of thorns and bushes burst from the stone walkways to fill the way behind them. The Corrupted tore through thorny bushes with their weapons and bodies, ignoring the thorn cuts.

A figure burst through a window in front of them. It was Finn. He rolled to his feet then threw Vihaan an extra sword. "It's a siege! They broke through the north defenses into the city."

Calla retreated behind them, terrified. "What do we do?" Calla screamed as the horde came closer.

Finn handed Calla a dagger, "We have to hold them off until the Guards arrive!"

Calla nodded her head. Finn and Vihaan both steadied their feet and readied their swords.

Calla glanced up as a shadow flew over their heads. The sleeping cat from Yocsho's shop was anything but sleepy now. The striped hunter landed on a Corrupted woman and sank its teeth into her shoulder. She screamed, but the horde only continued without her.

"Fly my beautiful Korios! Protect your Hybrid!" Calla was shocked to see Yocsho on the roof of a building across the street with the blue phoenix perched on his arm. When he outstretched his arm, Korios took flight. He gave a slow nod to Calla, one that said he knew her not so little secret.

Calla gripped the dagger as flashes of The Corrupted in her mother's house played through her mind. She didn't know if she could end a life but looking all around her... everything was at stake. The swords of Finn and Vihaan sliced the onrushing corrupted without hesitation, but Calla remained behind them. Gallant horns sounded from the castle, she hoped that help was coming. A hard body fell on Calla, knocking her to the ground. The dagger flew from her hands. She rolled underneath the person, and dark red eyes stared at her while he tried to yank her up. "Vihaan!"

Vihaan glanced back towards Calla, but another corrupted man advanced on him. They locked swords. Calla extended her arm out, to reach for the dagger. She reached for the dagger, but it was too far. Her frantic fingertips could only spin the dagger. The Corrupted goon pressed a cloth to her mouth and covered her nose. She thrashed with everything in her, but a screech made the goon look up from her. Korios dove down, and powerful talons plunged into the man's shoulders. The magnificent bird lifted him off Calla with another screech. Blood from the dying assailant fell on her as Korios flew away with him.

Calla regained her feet among the chaos. Now everything moved slowly for her. She saw people running with terror-filled faces. Children cowered alone in corners and cubbies. The cat pounced on another victim and sank it's fangs deep into their arm. Endless fighting. Death. Pain.

She felt an overwhelming power ignite through her body, and her sigil started to burn. She went to clutch her hand, but a dull light shone from inside the glove. Calla ripped the glove from her hand to reveal her sigil glowing with pure golden light. She saw her two guardians become overwhelmed, and something turned on inside her.

With a surge of courage, she ran to them and felt a power over-take her. With a guttural shout, Calla slammed her hand into the ground. A tsunami of golden light exploded from where she hit the ground and surged through the air in all directions. The three of them watched as the wave of light swept over The Corrupted, turning them to dust in the middle of their distressed screams.

A deafening silence filled Calla's ears.

"Calla you did it!" She heard Vihaan shout as the threat disappeared into thin air. He held onto her arms, but her vision was hazy. "Calla?" She felt exhausted, and her strength faded as the glow in her sigil diminished. Her legs buckled, but Vihaan caught her. "Calla?" She looked up at Vihaan as the darkness closed in around him. Her body went limp as everything shut off.

Eleven

"**L**ady Calla will awaken. You need to be patient."

Calla's head pounded, her body ached, and it hurt to move. But she was alive. When everything started coming back to her, her heart raced. Japhia, The Corrupted horde, and her protectors. Vihaan and Finn fighting together. They found something to unite over. Her.

"She's awake." A very familiar voice hit her ears.

Calla groaned and rolled over to crack her eyes open. The room was blurry but was coming into focus slowly. The light of the fire flickered on that distinctive ginger hair she'd come to detest. "Finn?"

"You're okay," he said, coming to her bedside in a hurry. "Lucy, let Nakosi know."

Calla heard Lucy mutter a response, then the door opening and closing. "Is everyone okay? What happened? Where are we? How long was I out?" Calla blurted out as she sat up, still dazed. Finn touched a hand to her shoulder and gently pushed her back down. She felt the familiarity of her bed and could answer one of the questions herself.

"Everyone is okay for the most part. No major casualties, aside from The Corrupted. They stormed Japhia, looking for you. It was only a matter of time. We're at the castle. You've been out for two days." He gave her a small smile. She wasn't prepared for how well it fit his face. "You did it, your powers came to light."

Calla looked at her hands, her sigil was back to normal now. The same dark sandy color it's always been like it had never glowed. She did it, somehow, she found it inside herself to awaken her powers. They were all right. She was the Hybrid. "What about Vihaan?"

Finn's smile fell in an instant with his face becoming tight. "He's fine. We've been watching you in shifts. King Nakosi has ordered around the clock protection to be on you. The Corrupted know you're here up in the castle, and we can't take any chances." Calla watched as he opened the curtains to the room. She shielded her eyes as the sun came in.

"Can you take me to see Vihaan?"

Finn turned back to her. "Now that your powers have come to light, we must make haste for the Library of Midelle. Time is of the essence." Finn paused, looking at Calla like he was expecting an outburst. She knew what getting her powers meant, but she only hoped that they would never come. "If we can keep The Corrupted believing that you're still here, it would give us a head start. I've assembled a small convoy of my strongest guards. We leave at dusk tomorrow. So, today you rest," his eyes gave her an analytic once over, "this won't be a scenic trip. We are moving fast with little respite."

Calla crossed her arms and noticed dried blood on her dress. Her stomach churned. "I'm not going anywhere without Vihaan."

"Why?" There was something in his voice. "So, he can warm your sleeping mat at night?" She knew what it was, jealousy.

Calla's mouth fell open, but she squared her shoulders back. "My relationship with Vihaan is none of your business. Beyond your comments, he's a good friend and looks out for me." Calla swung her legs over the bed to stretch.

Finn turned away from her. Distant voices were floating in from the corridor. "Last time I checked, good friends don't kiss for the hell of it."

Calla half gasped and scoffed at Finn's admission that he had seen them. "You're sick! That was an intimate moment between us." She stood, preparing for the onslaught that was about to come through the door.

Finn's mouth opened, his retort poised on the tip of his tongue when the door burst open.

Nakosi was first, Shea trailed behind him, Philomena, Vihaan, and Lucy followed. Before anyone said anything, Vihaan looked at her. Their eyes connected, and his face gave her the reassurance she needed. "Afternoon, Your Majesties." Finn bowed. "I see First Commander Varden has informed you that Lady Calla is awake."

Nakosi took a step forward, "I'd like a moment alone with the... Lady Calla."

Calla's eyes grew wide as Nakosi gestured to the balcony. Calla followed him, feeling like she was sticking her head into the lion's jaws. The doors closed behind them. The warmth of the midday sun was welcome on Calla's skin.

"Your powers have come to light." Nakosi turned outward towards the city. The gems in his crown sparkled in the sunlight.

Calla nodded, unsure of his statement.

"And Captain Quinn informed you of the plan?" He turned his head towards her.

"Yes, but King Nakosi... Please let Vihaan come. He's a true friend to me and..."

Nakosi turned back to her with a stern look. Calla rolled her lips together. "Do you understand the severity of the situation?"

"I think so."

Nakosi gave a pensive sigh. "What do you know about The Corrupted?"

"They have red eyes, and they want to make me one of them. But I don't want to be one of them."

"But do you understand it?"

Calla shook her head.

Nakosi looked over the city below again. "You see, The Corruption comes from a place of hatred within the heart. People like me and you can reflect it because our hearts are virtuous."

"How does a heart become unvirtuous?" Calla wanted to laugh, Finn's heart filled with virtue? His eyes should have turned red eons ago.

"A tragedy to that person. It breaks the virtuous surface around the heart, and The Corruption seeps in. Some succumb to it quickly while others fight it tooth and nail. But The Corruption always wins. I haven't seen a case where it doesn't."

"Can't you cure it?"

"No. There is no cure. The telltale mark is red eyes, but there's something different to them now. They have a leader and a base somewhere. They haven't been this organized except in the accounts of the First War. As the Hybrid, you must kill their leader. A Queen, correct? You heard them speak of a Queen the night you sent the signal?" Calla nodded. "It is what the deities created you for."

Calla clenched her fists. "I don't want to kill a Queen or anyone else. I don't even know how my powers work." She held her hand out and channeled the same feeling as before, the feeling to protect. While her sigil started to glow, she felt dizzy. Her legs buckled, but she held onto the balcony railing to keep herself from falling. Nakosi helped her stand. "What's happening? Do they not work anymore?"

Nakosi rubbed his chin. "It seems that without the other half, your powers render you unconscious. There is a more pressing need to get you to the Library of Midelle, now more than ever. The Oracle's instructions stand true. Remember, The Oracle holds the other half, and you cannot defeat The Corrupted without that." Calla gripped the railing tight. "After all this time, are you still refuting that you are the Hybrid?"

Calla looked to King Nakosi. Ten years of rest would not relieve the stress his face displayed. "I don't want to be the Hybrid. I don't want these powers. I don't want to save the realm!"

Nakosi sighed. "Lady Calla, do you know how I became King?"

Calla sniffed to fight the tears that wanted to fall, "A little, yes."

"Roark led the charge across Midelle, removing Raoul's occupation from villages. I was only a youthful squire at his side. Between him and his brother, Jedrek, the free army grew city by city. When we arrived at Japhia, the citizens threw their doors open for us. They wanted The Corrupted King dead as much as we did."

"And he became corrupted from Queen Alina dying?"

"Violet recounts that it was his son leaving. Disappeared in the night, without a word to where he went. Forever dubbed, the Forgotten Prince Vallen. Raoul's eyes turned shortly after that."

"I don't understand why the citizens let him reign for so long if he became Corrupted."

"Terror. He killed anyone who stood against him. He started with his servants. Vihaan's father included," he tacked on, but Calla remembered. "By the time we got to the castle, Lady Leola, the previous Captain of the Royal Guard, let us in. She said she had a duty to the realm and to be swift with the King's death. Roark and Raoul fought to their deaths. As his dying wish, he wanted either Jedrek or me to take the throne. Jedrek refused. He knew he was more brute than brains. So that left me. I took the crown as a young buck with a lot to learn. Jedrek became my Captain. He retired to follow his love." Nakosi laughed, "I can't blame him. I'd give up the world for my sweet Shea."

Calla wanted to gag hearing Nakosi talk sweet about Shea. There was nothing sweet about her.

"But we both have positions that we don't love," the King continued. "The point of my rambling is that our duty to Midelle comes before everything else, and we have the most important duties of all." Nakosi tapped the railing, thinking about his next words. "Another point to mention is this; "if you do not defeat The Corrupted, they will make you one of them. That means a lifetime spent consumed by anguish, sorrow, and hatred. You can't run away from being the Hybrid. And take some solace in the fact that those who do not want the position they're in, tend to thrive in it, for they cannot be blinded by power. You'll do well to remember that."

Calla nodded, but she felt hopeless. She was stuck being the Hybrid and there was nothing she could do about it.

Nakosi led her back inside. The room was thick with a tension that slapped her in the face. It seemed the room had split in their absence. Violet had come in. Shea and Finn stood on one side near the fireplace, their resemblance more prominent as they stood near each other. Vihaan, Violet, and Philomena stood by Calla's bed. Lucy seemed a neutral player, standing watch by the door.

"Lady Calla, I'm so glad you're safe!" Philomena crossed the room and hugged Calla's waist. "Captain Quinn won't let me come with the convoy."

Calla wrapped her arms around her head, returning the hug as best she could. "Why can't she come?"

Finn defended his choice, "She's a child."

"But I can be useful!"

"Philomena," Nakosi began as he knelt to her level, "You're too valuable to go. I need you here as the only Resident Witch. Make sure they're stocked with quality portals to come back to Japhia, you will have done your part exceptionally well."

Philomena let go of Calla's waist and sighed. She pouted just a bit and twisted her foot on the floor, "Okay My King. I will check on that right now. I will remain diligent as Rose taught me."

Nakosi nodded, "Very well. Now run along."

Philomena did a quick curtsy to the room and left. Calla felt bad, she was only eleven after all. Calla and Vihaan connected gazes again, her heart danced in her chest when she thought of their kiss. "I demand Vihaan come with us." King Nakosi gave Calla a look of little patience. She knew she was pushing it, but she needed someone with her that was on her side.

Vihaan smiled, "If I may, Your Majesties?"

"There's no room for a tag-a-long," Finn growled.

"I beg to differ, Captain. Lady Calla confides in me as a friend. Given her hesitance towards the journey and you, having a friend would make it a little easier." He turned and spoke to the King, "I have also proven myself a worthy protector, and possess valuable knowledge of flora and fauna. At this point, Captain Quinn could be the tag-a-long. Perhaps we leave him here?" There was a tiny smirk on Vihaan's face. Calla did everything in her power to keep a neutral face.

Finn's face became red as his hair, and his fists clenched at his sides. "You are not coming."

"He has a point, Captain Quinn," Nakosi said, picking up Finn's anger, "there must be room for one more."

Finn thought about his next words. Calla could see it in his eyes. "We leave after the evening bells tomorrow. If you aren't by the South Gate by then, we will leave without you." Calla knew he was only talking to Vihaan.

"Understood." Vihaan bowed his head to the King as they began to shuffle out.

Shea looked Calla up and down a few times, a scowl crossed her dark painted lips. "You should clean up. You're filthy." Calla covered a dried blood spot with her hand in a moment of self-consciousness. Shea picked up the front of her skirts to follow behind Finn.

Calla still wanted to slap her. In every scenario that she had played out in her head, it was worth it.

Violet placed a hand on her shoulder, "Let's get you cleaned up."

Calla stewed in the bath as the steam floated high. Violet sat on a chair in the corner with her side to Calla. Finn was dead serious when he meant that she was not to be left alone. Violet minded her own business by humming and sewing away at something long and blue.

Hugging her legs, Calla rested her cheek against her knees. Nakosi's words kept echoing in her head, *'we have the most important duties of all.'*

"I am the Hybrid," Calla whispered against the steam. This was the first time she said it out loud, and it felt strange. She brought up her hand to watch the water trickle down. Her fingers traced the delicate lines of the sigil, a motion her mind remembered well, but this time it was different. Trapped within the depicted petals was a power that could change the fate of everything. "What will happen after the Library?"

Violet kept her eyes down on the needle, "By then you will have your full powers. I would like to think that Captain Quinn will find The Corrupted's hideout and attack."

"How would he find it?"

Violet's face went tight, "I'm not supposed to know about this, but I know everything that goes on around here. He's torturing them in the dungeons. The Corrupted found by guards are brought to the castle. They go straight down to the dungeons to never see the light of day again. If they don't give him enough information, he kills them."

Her fist clenched tight. "He's no better than they are."

"Captain Quinn? He is far better than The Corrupted, don't you say such things. I know you two don't particularly get along, and his methods may be..."

Calla flipped her wet hair to the side to show a mustard-colored bruise on her collarbone, "Cruel?" Violet glanced up to see her example but went back to the methodical sewing.

"He is doing all he knows how to do to save the realm. I wish I could accompany you on the journey, but my old bones can't do such things anymore."

Calla let her anger go in a long sigh. "I wish you were coming too."

Long after her skin had pruned, Calla got out of the tub, dressed in a warm nightgown, and went out to her balcony. She sat outside with her back to the world under a dark and thick blanket. She was content. Lucy was inside, relaxed by the fire. Calla was already sick of someone being with her nonstop. Being outside was her only relief.

"Lady Calla?" Finn called from outside the bedroom door, knocking twice.

Calla nodded her head to Lucy, not bothering to get up. "Lady Calla would like you to come in," Lucy announced.

Finn unlocked the door and came in with a tray. Lucy acknowledged him with a nod of her head before turning back to the fire.

"Good evening, Captain Quinn," Calla addressed him with a proper tone, suddenly wishing she could just go to bed.

"Lady Calla," Finn placed the tray on the table, grabbed both mugs to come outside and sit across from her. The moon rolled out of its cloudy coverage to put a lunar veil over them. He handed her a drink, and a warm cinnamon smell wafted up to her nostrils. "I want to make amends."

"Oh," she let slip from her lips while she took the mug of the warm liquid and inhaled. The scent of the liquid reminded Calla of spiced cider.

He took a calculated, but deep breath. "I'm sorry. My actions have been anything but Captain-like."

Calla stopped drinking the cider and looked up with the mug still on her lips. She raised an eyebrow.

"If I'm to protect you the way I must on this journey, we need to work together. Hating each other and fighting is how we both die when shit gets thick."

Calla set the mug down next to her and folded her hands in her lap knowing the exact words that were going to come out of her mouth. "I'd rather die than make amends with you." Her response was tart, but he had a point. Calla knew pettiness wasn't helping, but when his face twisted with anger, it gave her satisfaction.

"You'd rather die, huh?" Finn got up and tossed his mug in the corner of the balcony. The broken ceramic pieces littered the now wet brick. "When you get into trouble, I pray to all the deities that your forest boy is there to save you because I won't be." Finn went inside, muttering things under his breath. Calla could only imagine what he was saying.

"Oh please, you'd be the first one to come to my rescue because I'm your responsibility. The only one you've had since you were handed Captain of the Royal Guard."

He turned towards her. "I don't think you want to go down that path, Calla." His eyes zeroed in on her, and he stepped closer.

"Why don't I?"

"You are getting in way over that pretty little head of yours, sticking your nose in things that are none of your business." Finn crouched in front of her, instead of his usual scowl, a smirk rested on his lips. Calla's breathing stalled, having his face that close to hers.

"The last I heard, Captains were supposed to earn their positions." She narrowed her eyes on Finn, his jaded eyes bore into hers. She could feel the chilling air swelter with tension.

"The last I heard, I'm Captain, and what I say goes." His voice was strong yet laced with something Calla couldn't pinpoint. It only added to the growing tension.

Calla's upper lip curled smugly, "Aye aye, Captain."

Finn backed up. His face had lost its edge. He clasped his hands behind his back. "Goodnight, Hybrid." His face fought a satisfied smirk as he showed himself out.

Tired of fighting, she let him have the last words, this time. Calla let her shoulders slump forward as she took calming breaths. Her skin felt the cold again as the fire that had surrounded her floated away.

Calla's mind fumed on the balcony. She could only think about Finn and everything wrong with him. A log fell and rolled in the fire inside, and the crack snapped her out of such deep thoughts. She curled herself under the blanket and drank the cider while she stared into the distant reflection of the fire.

"Psssst!"

Calla jumped out of her skin as she felt vines creep through the stone railing behind her. She turned to the balcony, and her favorite head of green hair came into view. Smiles spread across their faces, but Calla held a finger to her lips. She got up as Vihaan climbed over the railing, sending the vine back down. Something was behind his back.

She peered inside the room. Lucy was sitting with her back to the balcony. Her head lolled to one side and her gentle snore caressed the room. Calla closed the curtains to the balcony, then the doors themselves, careful not to make a noise. She turned, and Vihaan's arm wrapped around her in an instant. "What are you doing here?" She made sure to keep her voice low.

Vihaan nuzzled his nose into her hair and whispered, "I didn't know it was a crime to miss you?"

"You could knock on the door, like everyone else."

Vihaan brought the hand that was behind his back between them. Calla gasped at the flower in his hand. "If I was like everyone else, I don't think you'd like me very much."

Calla grabbed the flower, and she recognized it immediately. A deity rose. The ancient book and her dreams didn't do this flower justice. Under the moonlight, the white flower danced in iridescence. Each layer of petals cupped into the one underneath in a never-ending semi-sphere of the corolla, opening towards Calla. Her knuckle graced the silkiness of the petal. Unlike her dream, no thorns burst from the ground. "I thought these didn't grow outside the Falls?"

Vihaan's lips caressed her forehead, "You made them grow. These were the sprouts from a week ago. It's amazing! Like how Yocsho's animals came to our aid when The Corrupted attacked. They knew." Calla's face dropped at his words. Vihaan continued with excitement in each word, "The realm knows you're the Hybrid, Calla. It is sending you signs!" She untangled herself from his grasp as her heart spiraled into the ground. "What's wrong?"

Calla hugged herself against a chill from the autumn air. Her breaths came in short and erratic puffs. She wanted to scream, but that was the worst thing she could do. Instead, their eyes locked, and a tear fell down her face. It caught the moonlight, sparkling as it continued its descent. Sobs finally broke from her lips, "Vihaan, I'm so scared."

Vihaan held up a finger to her before he took the blanket and spread it out on the ground. He broke her self-made cage to guide her to the blanket. She sat down, still sobbing quietly. She'd hate for Lucy to come out now. He sat behind her and pulled her in close, then threw the blanket over them. Vihaan's strong arms wrapped around her. "Shhh, it's okay Calla. I'll protect you," he whispered to her between soft kisses to her ear.

Calla sniffed, finally able to catch her breath. "Promise?" Calla fell back against him. Her head came to rest over his heart. The gentle rhythm grounded her.

"I promise, Calla. With everything that I have."

Calla glanced up and his lips were right there. Calla pressed her lips to his with tears still clinging to her eyelashes.

Their kiss boiled with passion for a fleeting eternity, then Vihaan broke away. He gave her a few light kisses to bring them both back. She rested against his chest again.

"From the heavens above," Vihaan sang as gentle as a lullaby, "the deities came. Fast but swift with only love. When their feet touched the ground, they staked their claim..." The soft vocal silk of his baritone voice lulled Calla's eyes close. He followed suit, still singing, but trailing off into a hum and finally a soft sleeping pattern.

Calla's eyes opened to see wisps of sunlight melt the night. She smiled, even though sleeping like this wasn't comfortable, she would do it every night if she could. Calla never wanted to leave this spot.

"You're finally awake," he whispered into her hair.

"You've been awake?"

"How could I sleep with such a radiant beauty in my arms?"

Calla turned to rest on her knees, "You spoil me with your words." Their eyes met, and Calla couldn't get enough of how purple they were. Like she was diving into an endless pool of glittering amethysts.

Vihaan ran his fingers down her jaw to cup her chin, "Quite the opposite, I don't spoil you enough." Their lips touched for only a moment, as if it was a forbidden kiss. Vihaan rose and helped her up. He grew a vine from the ground.

"You can leave through the door, you know? I don't think Lucy would care."

Vihaan smirked at her, "Now, where is the fun in that? I enjoyed our secret night together." Vihaan kissed Calla's left hand, "I'll see you at the South Gate before the evening bells?"

"Please don't be late," Calla joked, but it wasn't a joke to her at all.

Vihaan hopped over the railing and grabbed the vine. He flashed her a smile. "I wouldn't dream of it."

Twelve

Each toll of the evening bells made the pit in her stomach open wider. Calla couldn't help but look around for Vihaan. He wasn't at the South Gate as promised. At Finn's request, she had been there long before the bells signaled the twilight. She spent the time meeting the group of men and women who would be protecting her, their names lost in the slurry of introductions. Mixed in the convoy were scouts, archers, and warriors. The variety of druids, trolls, and vampires dressed in warmer traveling clothes, with all the prestigious armor and banners stowed in favor of less flashy attire. Inconspicuous was what Finn wanted, and he got it. If she hadn't known the guards were to be protecting her, Calla never would have guessed who they were. During the introductions, Calla put aside her fear and resistance towards the situation to thank them. It was the least she could do.

In her downtime, as Finn supervised last-minute preparations, Violet obsessed over her. She had overpacked Calla's bags, so it seemed the entire contents of her suite sat divided on each side of her pinto mare's saddle. Calla had dressed in thick trousers, a long sleeve shirt that tied across her chest, a warm traveling cape and her gloves. While she was donning the gloves, happy to not look at her sigil for once, Finn warned her that she was not to take them off for any reason. He didn't need to ask twice, not after remembering what happened in Japhia.

Calla toyed with her fingers as she watched an empty path.

"Staring at nothing isn't going to help." Violet stepped up next to her.

"He said he would be here. The bells are almost done ringing." Bile bubbled in her stomach from nerves.

Violet sighed curtly. "I looked for him earlier. I couldn't find him. I stopped by the garden house and the other groundskeeper, Hawke, had no idea either."

Calla didn't know what to say. She felt stupid, sad, and betrayed all at the same time.

Violet patted her shoulder. "Vihaan will come. I have a feeling."

Nakosi and Shea came up to Calla as the final bell was tolling. "Lady Calla, we wish you luck with the Oracle and a safe journey." Nakosi gave her a look that reminded her of their conversation.

"Yes, may the deities bless you with a safe journey," Shea tacked on.

Calla bowed her head to Nakosi because Shea still got under her skin. "Thank you."

Finn came up to them and bowed his head, "Everything is ready to go, My King."

"Very well then. You have portals to come back?"

Finn's hand graced a distressed leather bag that had seen better days, "Yes, Philomena made sure. As long as we keep to the schedule, the portals will last."

"We will pray that you are back before the snow falls," Shea said. Her and Finn shared a quick look Calla couldn't decipher.

"Indeed," Finn agreed with Nakosi. "A moment, Lady Calla?" Nakosi and Shea left them as they descended back in the castle via a long windy path. "I want to make sure you understand the rules."

"I didn't know there were rules," she replied with a tartness in her voice.

Finn's eyebrows dropped low, fighting his rising temper. "There are always rules. Rule one, you listen to me and only me. This isn't a vacation. These guards will die to protect you. Do them the courtesy of listening to me or their lives will be on your hands." Calla nodded her head, frightened at the thought. "Rule two, those gloves stay on at all times when you're not in a safe house, designated by me."

Calla held her hands up to show her covered hands, "You already told me, so that should be rule one."

Finn scowled at her. He knew she was testing his patience, but he continued, "Rule three, scream as loud as you can if you're ever in trouble, or even uncomfortable. Follow those three rules, and our journey will be quick and easy."

"Quick and easy, my ass," Calla murmured with her eyes darting around.

Finn ignored her and turned to the guards milling around the gate, "Mount up! We leave on my command."

The guards hustled to their horses, but Calla couldn't move as she scanned the chaos. "Where are you..." she whispered. Her nerves were all over the place.

"Lady Calla, I said..."

Calla spun to him on a dime, her hair whipping behind her, "I heard you!" Her voice was as threatening as a viper's hiss.

Finn crossed his arms and stood next to his black stallion, "I knew he wouldn't show." He had a small cocky smile on his face that Calla wanted to smack off.

"He said he'd be here."

"His time's up. He knew when we were leaving. Now get on your horse, or I'll throw you on it myself."

Calla walked to her horse as slow as she could, petting her side for a moment trying to stall.

"Why so glum, Lady Calla?" It was from a little bit away down another path that led to the front of the castle.

The sound of that voice filled her lungs with joy, "What took you so long?" She slapped Vihaan's arm as he came up to her, leading his horse by the reins. The slap was meant to be playful, but it had a slight edge to it. She glanced at Finn, who couldn't hide his angst. He turned and mounted his horse. "Take that, Finn," she mouthed to him.

Vihaan slid down from his horse with a small hop in his landing. "I had to make sure my garden house would be in good hands during my absence. Took a bit longer than expected, but I made a promise to you with all intentions of keeping it." Calla opened her mouth to refute, but Vihaan held out his hand. "May I, Lady Calla?"

Calla furrowed her brows at how at ease he seemed, but she took his hand and he helped her up on the horse, then mounted his own. "I truly thought you weren't coming. I didn't know what to do. I knew Finn wouldn't wait. Where were you, really?"

"I told you, the garden house. You can trust me. I would never abandon you. Not for anything." He flashed that smile that turned her inside out.

Calla smiled and gripped her reins tighter. She'd never ridden a horse alone before. Violet ensured Calla that her horse was a sweet mare with only the highest patience.

The heavy gates creaked open just as the sun dipped below the Edulis Mountains. That's the way they were headed, west towards the setting sun. "Ready?"

"Yeah," Calla said, but she knew it was a lie. She wasn't ready. She wasn't ready for any of this.

"Move out," Finn led the expedition through the gate. Calla turned to the small group of servants who had helped them prepare, Violet was among them. They had said their goodbyes earlier when it was quiet. Still, they waved before the gates closed between them.

Once the gates closed, Calla sighed and turned to look forward. As the convoy started moving down the road, they spread out along each side of the road to box Calla and Vihaan in. Finn led the convoy from the front. If this didn't scream obvious that they were protecting her, Calla didn't know what obvious was. Nonetheless, Calla held her tongue. Finn was in charge out here. He made that clear, and she didn't want to rock that boat too much.

Vihaan sidestepped his horse closer to hers. Their legs touched with each sway of the horse. "How do you feel being outside the castle again?"

"Well," Calla began, hyper-aware of how close everyone was, "I hope I get to sleep under the stars."

Vihaan chuckled, "I don't believe that will be an issue, but why?"

Calla tried to find the early stars hidden in the dusky sky behind the entangled treetops of turning leaves. "When I was younger, my mom and I would go camping in our backyard." Vihaan smiled, and Calla mirrored it. "We would lay out mats with sleeping bags on top and fall asleep watching for shooting stars." Her face fell, "We never saw one." Despite the sad ending, Calla remembered her adoptive mom as if they camped out yesterday. Each day Nancy's presence in her mind became more the sweet remembrance of times together and less the pain of her absence. Just as everyone told her it would.

"Maybe we'll see one along this journey? We'll be traveling at night and resting during the day."

"Wouldn't that be nice," Calla agreed, trailing off, lost in her thoughts.

"She sounds like a good mom." Calla brought her eyes over to Vihaan again. He had lost his parents too, but at least he had gotten to spend a little time with Bastiaan before he passed.

"The best." A thought popped into her head, "The Oracle said the deities created me?"

Vihaan shrugged, "I wasn't there to hear it for myself, but yes."

"What if I have parents somewhere... Do you think the Oracle knows?" A feeling she's long past buried was surfacing, it felt like a new beginning. The feeling was strange, but she welcomed anything that wasn't anxiety or fear.

"Calla, don't get your hopes up," Vihaan said gently. "No one knows what the Oracle has for you besides your powers. Best to clear it out of your mind and focus on the journey, not the destination."

Calla pondered his words, "Those words... they sound like they came straight from Violet's mouth."

Vihaan laughed, "Oh, I got it from Violet." Calla joined in with Vihaan's laugh, their laughter bouncing off the trees.

"Quiet down back there. This isn't a carefree vacation," Finn warned from the front.

Vihaan gave Calla a look of annoyance. "My apologies, Captain," Vihaan punctuated the end. "I was only doing my job to keep Lady Calla in good spirits." She gave Vihaan a wide-eyed look but noticed a few guards smile to themselves. He asked, "Where are we heading to, anyway?"

A guard spoke to Calla's left, "Coriocris. A druid village in the middle of the forests between the castle and East Shimmer." The guard had short black hair and soft brown eyes. His hard patches had taken over his whole face except his right ear. Calla struggled to recall his name. It had something to do with rocks. It clicked in her mind, Stone.

Vihaan made a face, "Coriocris? Why there? Those druids don't take kindly to visitors."

Finn turned his horse to face the convoy. The front lines yanked quickly on the reins to avoid collisions. His face had gone red, and his jaw pulled tight. "Because I know people there who will let us stay. Especially because of..." Finn paused as all eyes converged on Calla, "our mission. And if you can't handle that, you can go back because I make the rules here." He scoffed, "Or get lost, for all I care."

Vihaan's teeth ground together. Calla gripped his arm. His muscles were tight under her fingers. "Hey," she whispered to him. Vihaan looked at her, and his face softened. "Relax. He has a plan."

"Can't wait to see Coriocris," Vihaan announced after taking a moment to relax.

"Continuing on then." Finn turned his horse to continue down the well beaten cobblestone path.

Everyone fell into a silent trot, but Calla was confused with Vihaan's behavior. "Are you okay," she whispered.

"I hate the way he treats people."

Calla grabbed his hand from the reins and kissed his calloused knuckles. "We all do. Focus on the journey, not the destination. Right?"

He smiled at Calla, grabbed her hand, and smoothly brought it to his lips. Calla wished the gloves were gone, but she thought of them as a necessary evil. "Throwing my words back at me, huh?"

Calla winked at him and smiled flirtatiously, "Violet would be so proud."

Numb. Calla had lost feeling in her butt hours ago and still they rode on into the night. At some point they had veered off the road to continue by weaving through the forests. No one else seemed as concerned as Calla, but they'd been doing this their whole life. She was grateful for the break they were on now, she got to stretch her legs. "Are we almost there?"

Finn frowned as his reply. Calla rolled her lips together. Finn turned back to the map he was holding, turned it upside down then held it at arm's length.

"We're lost? Aren't we?" She looked at the dense forest surrounding them. There wasn't much to see in the way of landmarks. After their issues in the beginning, no one had been in a talking mood.

"We're not lost, I just don't know where we are..."

"That is literally what 'lost' means," Calla quietly bellowed as she threw her hands up in exasperation. "What are you looking for?"

"A tree," Finn answered after folding the map again.

Calla and Vihaan exchanged similar looks then looked at Finn. "We're in a forest," they said in unison.

"Thank you for stating the obvious. I need to find a thick tree with a mark on it. It's a big square... Once I find that I'll know where I'm going." Calla looked around her, and while it wasn't a thick tree, there was one which was leaning to one side. Calla grabbed Vihaan's hand, not wanting to be alone and stood in front of the leaning tree. She ran her hand down the bark, no mark.

"Mount up, everyone," Finn said while he stuffed the map back into his bag. "It's this way." He pointed out the direction they had been traveling.

Calla went to turn but a huge tree in the distance caught her eye, she squinted to get a better look. "I found it," she sang.

"Where?" Finn's head snapped towards her, as did everyone else's.

She made a grand gesture to the tree. Finn hopped off his horse, making a beeline for the tree to run his fingers over the carving. Calla watched in anticipation with Vihaan right behind her tracing circles into her shoulder. Her breath caught in her throat when the wind shuffled the leaves and the moonlight shone over Finn. It reminded her of the first time she met him when he saved her life. Before he turned to a monster in front of her eyes. "Well?"

"You found it," Finn replied as he went to his horse. "We'll be there in two days."

"That far?" Calla heard a nearby guard laugh at her complaining under their breath.

"It's a good time to think, Lady Calla," a female vampire scout added. Her eyes were a dark blue covered by wispy, short brown curls. "Or enjoy the scenery." Calla remembered her name, Kalise.

"Too bad it's dark," Calla mused.

"It was only a marker to make sure we're going in the right direction." Finn whipped the reins, and his horse stepped forward. Vihaan helped her onto her horse. She didn't feel exactly graceful

"Lady Calla, up here," Finn called from the front.

Calla's head snapped to Vihaan and her eyes went wide. He gave her an encouraging nod. "Want me to come along?"

"You'll hear it if I need help," Calla muttered with a light whip of the reins. The horse broke into a faster trot to catch up to Finn. "So," Calla started as her horse fell into step with his black stallion, "You summoned me, Captain?" That was becoming her favorite way to get under his skin. His jaw ticked every time.

"When we get to Coriocris, you must not speak to anyone. These druids keep to themselves, and if they do let outsiders in, it is with extreme caution."

"How do you kn..."

"I lived with them for six years."

"Six years? Wow, how did you get into this village? Last time I checked, you're not a druid."

Finn gave her a side glare.

"From the kindness of two druids. Zinnia and Cypress, an older couple who found me at..." Finn stopped talking. He chewed at his lower lip while looking anywhere but at Calla. "When we get there, let me do all the talking."

"Where did they find you?" She felt she was digging into an old wound, but she'd noticed Vihaan come closer during their conversation. Having him near gave Calla a sense of comfort. Despite all that they had gone through, she still had to be careful. Vihaan talked of longevity with their budding relationship, but she had doubts.

"Forget I said anything." Finn whipped the reins to his horse. His horse went into a light gallop which Calla's horse matched easily. It was difficult to navigate in the dark, but trees had thinned to sporadic meadows with moonlight shining in the clearings.

"Tell me." Calla gave him a gentle smile. "We're making amends, right?"

Finn scowled. "You prefer death over making amends if I remember right."

Calla bobbed her head, hearing her words being spit back into her face. "I did say that, didn't I?"

"Get back in the formation."

Calla scoffed, but with a vindictive tone she replied, "Aye aye, Captain."

The night had come and gone, and the mid-morning sun shone over the horizon. Calla was enjoying the serene forests, happy to take in nature. Some of the leaves had changed, and it was a beautiful sight to see them mixed with the green. A long yawn escaped her mouth. The continuous travel was wearing on everyone. Finn had agreed to stop for an hour to rest and eat something proper just after sunrise, but that was hours ago.

"Captain Quinn," one of the guards, Calla had learned his name was Malak, called as he rode back to the convoy. "There's a clearing up ahead." Malak's face turned hopeful, "It would be a good place to rest for an hour or two?"

Finn turned around, and his eyes scanned over the convoy. He was met with tired faces, begging for a break. He sighed, "Fine." He hid his exhaustion well, but Calla knew he also needed to rest.

Calla slid down from her horse and sprang up on her tiptoes for a much-needed stretch. The clearing must have been a popular place to stay. There was an area in the middle that had the dirt tamped with remnants of a fire in the center. A stream babbled nearby. "Oh, it feels good to stand."

Malak threw his bow behind his broad back, while another guard, Lena, followed suit. "We'll be back with," Lena looked to the sky, "breakfast." Calla had seen the pair suck a woodland animal dry overnight. She knew they were vampires from that. It just occurred to her that she'd never seen Finn drink blood. The two hunters gave Calla warm smiles as they passed. Malak's eyes were a vivid hazel, and Lena's were a deep brown. They both had hair that made her miss dark chocolate.

Finn nodded, "Be swift, we need to keep moving."

"Yes, Captain," they both answered in unison.

Vihaan came over to Calla and took her hands. She immediately smiled, "I want to show you something."

"Show me what?" She gave him a sly look to tease him. Vihaan tucked a fallen piece of blonde hair from her braid behind her ear.

Vihaan looked around the camp, more specifically at Finn. He was busy looking at the map. "Come with me to find out."

"Lead the way, but not too far."

"I'd take you to the Cape myself if I could." He turned his head to wink at her.

"Finn would lose his shit." Calla followed Vihaan.

He didn't answer her, but instead led her to the edge of the clearing. He gestured behind a thick maple.

Calla gave him a skeptical look when they stopped. "You want to show me something behind a tree?" A small smile quirked on the edge of her lips. "Oh my mom warned me about men like you."

"Did she now?" He crooked a finger for her to follow. Sure, she still had doubts from yesterday, but that discussion was for another time. Calla went to the tree, having an idea of what Vihaan wanted. Vihaan snaked his arms around her, backing her up to the maple. His lips hovered over hers in an instant. "It's torture being so close to you, but not being able to have you."

Calla's eyes left his lips and flittered up to meet his. She could feel her heart thump in her chest. She loved and hated how he had this profound effect on her. He'd only been in her life for two weeks, but it felt much longer than that. "Tell me more," she whispered.

"I'd rather show you." Vihaan's lips crashed against Calla's with a passion that caught her off guard. She found her footing with him and began to kiss back, matching his passion. One of his hands was the buffer from Calla's head bumping the coarse bark. Hers gripped his emerald hair, lost deep in his tresses. He pulled her closer by the waist, breaking the kiss. Her head fell back, and his lips wandered down her jaw to her collarbone in a trail of smoldering kisses. Calla held back a moan, but a breathless gasp left her lips when Vihaan nibbled on her collarbone. When his lips left her collarbone, she went to protest, but Vihaan's lips captured hers again with a kiss laced with a passion that she never wanted to end.

"Name yourself," Finn shouted from a distance, drawing his sword with a sharp noise. Calla and Vihaan broke apart, but Vihaan kept his arms around her in a protective manner. They interlocked their hands to run back to the clearing quickly. "Lady Calla! Where are you?"

"I'm fine," Calla called as she ran back into the clearing with Vihaan close behind.

Finn narrowed his eyes on her when he noticed her flushed face and heavy breathing. Her eyes fell on the man who had Finn and several other guards on alert. He was a troll with aged, dark scaly patches leading down his neck, tufts of white hair on his head and a black cloth bandanna tied around his hairline. Through his drooping eyebrows, the trolls' golden-green eyes glinted with mischievousness. He held onto a long walking stick for support.

"I am but a traveler," the elder man spread his arms with both his hands showing.

"Leave us be, old man." Finn pointed his sword at him.

"Please, I only need to rest for a few moments. My bones are not as young and spry as they once were," the man chuckled to himself.

"Rest elsewhere," Finn growled. Calla marched forward, stopping next to Finn. "Stay back!"

"Have a heart, will you?" Calla reached out to beckon the man to come forward.

"Calla, I swear..." Finn whispered, "Remember the rules?"

Calla looked at Finn, "He's harmless, and it's only a few minutes."

Finn went up to the man and looked at him, eye to eye. Calla knew he was checking him for red eyes, "You have five minutes."

The man patted Finn on the arm and gave him a warm smile, "You're too kind. A few minutes is all I need, and I'll be on my way." The man sat on one of the logs in the center of the clearing and gestured to the other for Calla. She went with caution, feeling all eyes upon her.

"Calla," she stated, holding out her hand as she sat down.

The troll mumbled, "I thought you would be a man." He glanced down at her hand but didn't shake it.

"Excuse me?" Calla raised an eyebrow as she rescinded her hand.

"Forgive me. I'm Sigmund." He broke in a coughing fit. Calla grabbed a nearby waterskin.

"Are you okay, Sigmund ?" She offered the half-filled waterskin to him and glanced around the camp. Half of the guards were watching her, the other half were watching the forest. She felt guilty, but she knew in her heart he was harmless.

Sigmund waved her hand away. "I'm fine. Listen to me closely," Sigmund whispered through ragged breaths. "Imagine a weed in your garden..." He coughed, "what do you do?"

"There's someone here who might be able to help better than myself." Calla went to stand but his hand shot out and motioned for her stay. So, she did.

"What do you do about the weed?"

"Pull it?" Calla answered, confused.

Sigmund placed his walking stick across his lap, "Then what happens?"

"Uh... It comes back?"

"Hmpf," Sigmund muttered. The grip on his stick was tighter. "What must you do to..."

"All right, times up, old man," Finn stated as he gripped the back of the old troll's clothes.

"Leave him be, Finn," Calla snapped, coming to Sigmund's rescue.

Sigmund held up a hand, "No need. I am well enough to continue on my journey." He stood up and straightened out his clothes.

"That's right you are."

"Farewell travelers!" He gave a small wave behind him, "Perhaps we'll meet again soon."

Calla narrowed her eyes on Finn, "That wasn't even two minutes."

"He's lucky he got one." Finn followed the old man as he made his way out of the clearing.

Vihaan came to Calla's side kneeling before her, "What did he say to you?"

Calla watched Sigmund until he blended in with the trees. Finn felt the need to watch him too, but for different reasons. She turned her head to meet Vihaan's curious gaze. The answer finally clicked in her head. A memory of Nancy and her spending an afternoon in the garden floated in her head. She could almost hear Nancy's guiding words, but instead, her mouth recited those words, "Don't forget to dig up the roots."

Thirteen

Calla knew she was in deep shit after her stunt with Sigmund. Finn wouldn't even look at her, let alone talk to her. Part of her was rejoicing because it was exactly what she wanted, for Finn to leave her be. Vihaan had taken advantage of the situation to become more forward towards Calla. They stopped treading lightly about their affection, but Calla knew a storm was coming. It had to be. It was Finn after all.

The sun was halfway behind the Edulis mountains that loomed closer as the hours ticked by. Never-ending thick clouds filled with snow obscured the mountain tops. Vihaan warned her that the passing through the valley would be miserable, long, and cold. Part of her wanted to get it over with, but that meant she was that much closer to the Library of Midelle. She let her shoulders fall but perked up when the trees broke. Over the immense city walls, the crowns of buildings towered into the sky.

"Halt!"

The convoy stopped before a massive city gate. Sharpened iron bars jutted out from the huge doors of the gate. The iron pikes also appeared everywhere along the massive walls, angled steeply downward. Vines crept up the bars to add beauty to the defenses, but the message was clear; everyone keep out. Finn wasn't kidding about them not liking outsiders. A shiver ran down Calla's spine, and her heart sped up. Finn glanced back and gave her a reassuring nod, but Calla didn't believe it. Not after he ignored her for two days straight.

Calla turned to Vihaan, and he whispered, "Don't look so scared."

Calla's eyes glanced towards the two druids defending the entrance to the village. What caught her attention was the weapons pointed at them. "It's not like they don't have weapons," she forced her eyes off them, "sharp ones at that."

The druid to the left had black hair that hit his shoulders. His sharp spear angled out to stop feet before Finn's stallion. "Turn around now, and there will be no bloodshed."

"We're here to see Cypress and Zinnia," Finn said as Captain-like as he could muster. "I command you let us in," he pulled out a rolled letter from his messenger bag, "by order of the King."

The other druid sneered at Finn. His hair was a very light brown, almost blonde, and his eyes were brown. "You think a piece of paper is going to let you in?" He dropped his sword to his side and strode up to Finn to snatch the paper from his hand.

A loud snort left the nose of Calla's mare, and she stomped a hoof into the ground. Calla ran her fingers down the mare's neck to calm her, leaning forward to the mare's ear and shushing her. The black-haired guard peered over to look at her.

Finn smirked to the light-haired man, "I thought you'd remember me, Basil."

Basil's eyes narrowed in on Finn. "I knew you looked familiar, vampire." He looked at the black-haired guard. "Flint, remember when you broke his nose and slashed his face?"

"I'd prefer if you used my actual title, Captain of the Royal Guard." Finn gestured to the message, trying to hide his smirk, and ignoring the bait.

Basil scoffed. "You? A Captain?"

Flint grabbed the message from Basil and began to read. Calla bit back a smile at the situation.

"I'd no sooner kiss a mule's ass than..." Flint nudged him and pointed to the message. Basil's face scrunched as he ripped the message from Finn's hands. His eyes scanned over it. "Fine. They can come in, but you stay out here. You're not welcome here anymore, not like you ever were."

Calla's eyes darted up to Finn. His fists curled by his side and his lips went into a straight line. They were all beyond exhausted at this point, and they were only days into the journey. "I'm afraid it's non negotiable. If you read the..."

"I read it! You are not entering Coriocris!" Basil brought his sword up and everyone had their weapons drawn. Even Vihaan had a sword, all in a blink of an eye. Calla felt vulnerable as she had nothing, but her eyes dipped to her hand. She had the most powerful weapon here, whatever that was.

"Finn?" Everyone looked beyond the city defenses to an older female druid with white hair. A basket filled with baked goods hugged her hip.

"Zinnia!" Finn smiled with a tiny wave. Calla's mouth dropped. She'd never heard joy in Finn's voice before.

"For the love of Midelle, Basil, open those gates," Zinnia scolded as she came closer to them.

Basil grumbled, he unlocked the entrance, and handed the message to Zinnia. Finn motioned for the convoy to follow as he pranced his horse through the gates. He whispered to Basil, "Let me know when you're going to kiss that mule's ass. I won't want to miss that," Finn almost chuckled. "It's good to see you, Zinnia," Finn beamed as the elderly druid stood on her tiptoes to attempt to hug him. Finn could only get an arm around her from that angle.

"And why haven't we heard from you since you left?" She gave a quick look at the convoy coming in. The gates shut behind them with a loud clang. She cast her head down reading the message, then looked up at Calla. Was it that easy to tell she was the Hybrid? Did she look that out of place?

Finn ran his hand through his hair, in a loss for words. "A lot has happened... As you read."

"Is it..."

Finn nodded. "Yes. I was hoping we could spend the night here. I wanted to rest in a safe place." He glanced around the village. It was simpler than Japhia, with bungalows, open-faced shops, and rough cobblestone streets.

Calla felt relieved when Zinnia finally looked away from her. "I never thought I'd live to see the day. Come! Where are my manners? I insist you stay a couple of days." Zinnia started rushing off down the main path in the village.

Calla noticed other druids of all colors coming out, curious about what was going on. Most of them had scowls on their faces, unappreciative of the approved trespassers. Zinnia broke free of her tunnel vision to scold the gathering crowd. "Mind your business everyone! These are esteemed guests from the capital, and I approve of them to be here." That did the trick for some, but others still lingered, eager to see what was going on. Calla even saw sneaky onlookers, pretending not to care, but still very curious.

Calla turned to Vihaan, "I thought my identity was a secret?"

Vihaan gave her a reassuring smile, "We're safe here. They have guarded their village with pride ever since the First War. Don't tell Finn this, but I'm surprised he got us in."

"But The Corrupted could still get in. You saw how many there were in Japhia. That had guards and walls too."

"I'll protect you, remember?" Vihaan reached over, his lips poised for a kiss. Calla turned her head at the last second to have his lips grace her cheek. Vihaan gave her a puzzled look, but the worry ingrained on Calla's face made Vihaan understand. "Please relax, okay?"

Calla nodded, feeling anything but relaxed. Out of the corner of her eye, she saw that Finn had hopped down from his horse. He had helped Zinnia up as he walked alongside her and carried the basket she held when they arrived.

"Is Cyprus well?" Finn asked, giving the go-ahead for the convoy to follow.

"Very," Zinnia smiled, "he will be ecstatic to see you and," she looked back at Calla. A warm smile went her way, but she could feel eyes on her from every direction, "everyone else as well."

Calla peered inside a window of a two-story home. Her eyes connected with those of a little boy whose head barely made it over the sill. She wondered if he knew who she was. The boy waved and smiled at her. Calla waved back with a gentle smile. Perhaps he did.

Cypress and Zinnia's two-story cottage was nestled in the back of the village. Calla thought it was cute, back away from everything. The house was bigger than all the others they had passed in town. Explosions of colorful flowers lined the walkways and walls. Calla froze when the guards dismounted their horses. Zinnia was directing them where to set up camp. This house had so many things her mother's house had. A wave of sadness came over her and she tried not to cry.

"Cypress," Zinnia shouted as she stepped into the house.

Vihaan touched Calla's shoulder and her wave crashed, "Are you okay?"

"Yeah, this house," she smiled instead of letting a tear fall, "it reminds me of my mom's."

"She had good taste in flowers." Vihaan smiled at her, and it was still the same dazzling smile that made her weak in the knees. "As does her stunning daughter."

Calla was about to reply when Finn called her over. The first words he's spoken to her in two days. She let out a sigh, not knowing if it was out of relief or annoyance. Vihaan squeezed her hand, "We'll continue this later."

Calla slid off her horse without help. Vihaan took the reins to lead their horses over to a makeshift feeding trough. "Hello," Calla said, coming up to Finn.

"Inside." Finn pointed up the stone steps.

Calla passed him, but stopped and turned her head, "A please wouldn't hurt, you know." Finn didn't move. "Just saying," Calla stepped inside. The whole house was warm and cozy with a soft spicy aroma floating around. A soft glow from the fire bathed the open floor of the home. The main room housed the kitchen, an eating table, and a fireplace. Armchairs and a couch gathered around the fireplace. Two sets of stairs sat in the back, one leading up to a loft and then another leading downstairs. The warmth of the cottage made Calla never want to leave it.

"Why did the front guards not like you?" Calla whispered to Finn just past the threshold to the house.

"I had a dramatic exit. Don't pretend like we aren't going to discuss the other day. You deliberately disobeyed me."

An older male with a bald head and long white beard came up from the stairs, stopping their conversation. "Finn? Is it you?" His midsection was rotund and puffy cheeks dominated his face. Zinnia followed behind him, her smile couldn't have gotten any bigger.

Finn held his arms out in a simple gesture, "In the flesh." They embraced as a father and son would. "How's your back?"

Cypress rolled his shoulders. "I'm still walking, aren't I?

"For now. But when you hurt it again, who's going to go hunting with your sad sack of bones?" Finn smiled in jest.

"You haven't changed one bit," Cypress let out in a billowing laugh.

"He's Captain of the Royal Guard now, Cypress," Zinnia tacked on with pride like she was his mother boasting his accomplishments.

"You don't say!"

"And," Zinnia came over to Calla. Cypress watched her with a loving gaze. She grabbed Calla's hands, despite the frailty of Zinnia's hands, they were warm, "this is Lady Calla. She's..."

Cypress gasped and gripped Finn's shoulder, "Finn, she's beautiful." Calla furrowed her eyebrows when the old man continued. "When's the wedding?"

A laugh burst out of Calla, but she quickly covered her mouth with both hands. Finn narrowed his eyes on her. "Never!" She managed to get out before another laugh burst forth.

Finn cleared his throat, "Cypress, there's no wedding." Calla glanced at him. His cheeks were aflame with red.

Zinnia stifled a laugh. "My dear, no. She's the Hybrid. If you took two seconds to look outside, you would see the convoy escorting her to Cape Toria."

Redness grew in his jolly cheeks, "The Hybrid?" Calla nodded her head as Finn and Zinnia confirmed in unison. "You?" His light eyes wrinkled with joy. Calla nodded with hesitance. She rubbed her thumb against the glove, knowing where her sigil laid on her skin. "The deities have heard our prayers!" Cypress ran to Calla and hugged her. He smelled of pine.

Calla stiffly wrapped her arms around the man. She glanced out of the corner of her eye, and could have sworn that Finn smiled.

"What is it like? Are you prepared to fight The Corrupted? Is the prophecy coming true? Did you come from the human realm like the Oracle said you would?"

"Cypress," Finn cut into his barrage of questions, "let's catch up outside." Cypress let go of her. "I'm sure Lady Calla could use some uninterrupted rest." Finn gave Calla a quick look, pleading her to play along. He didn't need to ask. She was grateful for the time alone, but something deep inside knew that Finn wouldn't be far away.

"So," Cypress began as they made their way to the door, "Captain of the Royal Guard, eh?" Finn nodded proudly. "You've come a long way, but think you can help this sad sack of bones chop some wood?"

"Still have my ax?"

Cypress chuckled, "Needs a good sharpening, but it will be good as new."

The door clicked shut behind them. Calla pulled back the ivory curtain that had seen better days to watch the convoy set up their camp in the front yard. She smiled when she saw Vihaan nuzzling the neck of his sweet stallion. Deep down, she wanted to throw herself at him and never leave the touch of his tan skin and emerald tresses. She sighed and she dropped the curtain. She knew that as much as she wanted to indulge, she couldn't. It would only end in heartbreak. She also knew that her will would falter once he smiled at her. Vihaan's smile was nearing the top of her weaknesses.

"Come and sit Hybrid." Zinnia patted the armchair closest to the fire. "I have to start dinner if everyone is going to eat before midnight," she mused.

Calla turned to the elder druid, watching her cross the house. "Thank you, but it feels good to stand after riding for hours on end."

Zinnia pulled out a basket of vegetables from under the counter. "I can only imagine. You have quite the journey ahead of you. East Shimmer is about a week out. Crossing through the Shimmering Peaks takes a few days, depending on how long you rest for." She was rambling at this point. "Then the plains," she scoffed, "the most boring thing you could ever cross, endless fields of wheat and..."

"You can call me Calla," Calla cut in with a smile, "Hybrid sounds so..." Her eyes danced all around as if the ceiling had the answers.

"Formal?"

"In a way."

"Well then, Lady Calla, it's an honor to have you stay with us. When the realm trembled, everyone came alive with this hope that only you could bring." Zinnia chopped the carrots into thick medallions.

Calla went to stand next to Zinnia, "I keep hearing about that." She let silence fall over them for a minute. "Your home is lovely. Thank you for letting us rest here."

Zinnia's fingers were nimble with the knife and carrots, "No. Thank you, my dear. Finn, or should I say, Captain Quinn, helped us rebuild it after ours burned down."

Calla crossed her arms, feeling insecure. Suddenly she could feel every bruise Finn had given her, no matter how long healed. "What happened?"

"Seven years ago," she said in deep thought, "a terrible storm came through. Lightning hit our home and it went aflame in minutes. Cypress and I weren't home, praise the deities. But our son, Tedka, was. He never made it out, and..." Zinnia paused, placing the knife down, "we lost him that night."

Calla's face fell as she placed a hand over Zinnia's shoulder for comfort, "I'm so sorry."

Zinnia gave her a weak smile, "Thank you. We removed the remnants of the old house and buried Tedka. After that, we were in the woods marking trees to cut down for the new home when we found Finn."

"What was he doing in the middle of the forest?" Calla asked with a casual tone, trying not to sound nosy.

Zinnia's face furrowed as she began cutting potatoes, "You don't know?"

"We don't exactly talk much."

Zinnia pursed her lips, torn in her mind. She then sighed, "If I were you, I wouldn't tell Finn I told you this. We found him slumped against a tree. At first, I thought he was dead. But no, he was amid a blood rage."

"Why was he in one?"

Zinnia gave Calla a questioning look which made her a little uncomfortable. "He was newly turned and couldn't cope. You do know he's from the human realm? Right?"

Calla kept her face still, but her insides began churning with rage. "I actually didn't know that."

Zinnia dropped the carrots and potatoes in a large pot nestled over the fire. "Well, as I said, don't tell Finn. Luckily, we found him unconscious, with animals sucked dry at his sides. We broke village rules by bringing him back here, but we had just become elders and that gave us some liberties that the young folk in this village didn't have. We tied him down, so he wouldn't escape.

"After a couple of days of taking care of him, he finally woke up and had come down from the rage. We rationed how much blood he got, and when we untied the ropes one day, he stayed. Finn promised to help us build a new house, and he did. He also said he had no one to go to and asked to live with us. The village labeled him as an outcast, but Cypress and I were elders. We flashed our status a little and the folks of this village couldn't ignore us or our request. There was a consensus to let him stay as long as he didn't cause trouble."

Zinnia looked at Calla and continued, "He got into a fight one day, with Basil and Flint. You saw him at the gate. Finn almost beat Basil to death two years ago. He left before a decision was made about his punishment, thank the deities. The council was thinking of exile. One morning, he told us he had to go figure some stuff out, and he was gone. Then he came back today... Captain of the Royal Guard, escorting you... the Hybrid."

Before she could stop herself, Calla scoffed and pulled back the sleeves on her shirt. Bruises, in their final healing stage, riddled her arms. "I can sympathize with Basil."

Zinnia covered her mouth to shield a gasp, "Finn did that?"

"Yeah," Calla rolled down her sleeves, "to make my powers come to light. He beat me senseless for days on end. It didn't work. Sorry, but the Finn that you knew is not the Finn I know."

Zinnia pulled out a rather large jar of dark-colored liquid from a hole in the ground covered by a trap door. Meat swirled inside as she placed the jar next to her. Calla's stomach rumbled as she thought of warm soup. The days were getting cooler and crisper, the nights more so. "I won't say that I approve of his actions, but his anger has always been a source of conflict in him." Zinnia paused, her eyes darting to Calla's arms. "I have a salve for those bruises you can use after we all eat." She stood up to dust her hands off. "Help me with dinner and consider us even."

Calla didn't bother trying to plead her case, Zinnia knew about his anger. At least she knew what he was capable of. Instead, she grabbed a jar and helped her gracious host. "Thank you, Zinnia."

"You're welcome, Lady Calla. I'm proud to have you in my home. You, the Hybrid," Zinnia smiled, "in my home. I hope you'll stay for a bit, now that I can prepare a little bit, I can do a roast for tomorrow."

"Finn has us on a tight schedule of his own making. I'd love to stay. Trust me."

The druid patted Calla on the back, "I will have a word with him, I'm thinking at least a day for you to rest and recuperate." She had a coy smile on her face. "I think there's a big storm coming. The birds are silent today. It will be the perfect opportunity to rest."

"I'd appreciate that. All of this has been a lot to deal with. If there is a storm tomorrow, remind me to thank the birds."

Zinnia moved to an elongated pantry. Her fingers curled on the corner of a large sack of flour.

Calla stared at the soup, wishing for it to be ready.

"A watched pot never boils."

Calla smiled to herself, "My mom used to say that."

"Your mother? But the legend said you were born from the deities…"

Calla turned to the woman and shook her head. "My mom in the human realm took me in. The only mom I've ever known. She died a few months ago."

"I'm sorry to hear that. You know, in a way, I am Finn's mother here in Midelle." She chuckled to herself, "Funny how that works."

Calla stayed silent watching the fire kiss the underbelly of the cast iron pot.

"Finn may not be our blood, but he's like a son to us." Calla felt Zinnia's words penetrate deeply into her heart.

Fourteen

Zinnia was right, a nasty storm was coming in. The sky had been bright and blue at breakfast that morning, and while everyone was milling about at daybreak Finn had announced that they would stay until the next day. Calla was relieved that Zinnia had come through with her promise to prolong their stay at Coriocris. Meanwhile, Cypress and Zinnia had opened their home to the entire convoy. Everyone had taken shelter inside from the imminent storm.

Much to her dismay, Finn had insisted she sleep in his old bedroom instead of the great room's floor. Calla never would have guessed in a million years that this was Finn's room. A calm serene gray material covered the walls, a fireplace that promised comfort from the corner, and the softest furs lined the bed. She'd half expected a coffin, but Midelle vampires were different from the myths she grew up with. Still, the thought of sleeping in Finn's bed was weird, but her full belly, aching body, and tired mind had pulled her into a deep sleep the instant her eyes closed.

"And there you are, Lady Calla," Lena draped the damp braid of golden hair over Calla's shoulder. Calla traced the smooth lines, "Thank you, Lena. I wish I could braid as well as you do." Lena had popped in an hour ago to check in on her and Calla hadn't had the heart to send her away. At first, she feared it was Vihaan. Ever since they had arrived at Coriocris, she'd been wary of how passionate they'd become. Their limited time together and the situation with the previous afternoon left an uneasy churning in her stomach. She glanced outside. The sky was darker now. Lena laughed, "You're welcome. All my little sisters begged me to braid their hair growing up."

Calla turned to the vampire archer, "Little sisters? I don't mean to be rude, but how?" She gently asked.

"Vampires get to adopt orphaned druids when they experience the loss of a baby in the womb. Which is all the time." There was a thin smile on her face. "Druids are the only creature in Midelle that can withstand a change."

Calla grimaced. "Is it painful?

"I wouldn't know," Lena shrugged. "It happened when I was a baby before I could remember anything. But if you're that curious, you should talk to Captain Quinn or Queen Shea. The first thing they'll tell you is that vampire's blood tastes like death."

Calla knew about Finn from yesterday but hadn't thought about the Queen. "Queen Shea, a human? Is that how you turn? By drinking vampires' blood?"

A sharp knock ended their conversation too soon for Calla. "It's Captain Quinn."

"Come in, Captain. We're finished," Lena said.

Calla groaned to herself. Finn couldn't leave her alone. Now that she'd had breakfast and had cleaned herself up, she wanted nothing more than to be alone. Sorting out her thoughts would be a good use of her time.

Finn stepped inside and held the door open. "Leave us be, Lena."

"Yes, Captain." She gave Calla a fleeting look from her big brown eyes as she left the two of them alone in the room.

Calla turned away from Finn and rested her head against the window. She could hear the soft patter of raindrops dance on the roof.

Finn cleared his throat, "I thought we had an understanding about the rules."

Calla remained silent, making a promise to herself to not say a word. She knew anything she would say would only make matters worse. Then Finn would yell at her in front of everyone, and Calla would never want to leave the room. The scene played out in her head... Finn yelling at her, Vihaan bursting into the room, the two of them getting in a shouting match or even fighting.

"Was I unclear at any point?"

Calla broke her promise to herself she made moments ago, "I get it. Okay? I fucked up. I broke the rules. What are you going to do? Beat me again?" Calla turned to him and pulled the neckline of her loose tunic aside to show Finn her fading bruises. Zinnia was right, the salve did work. One night of application and the green and yellows faded even more than usual.

Finn averted his eyes, in what appeared to Calla, in shame, and said, "What do you want me to say? I can't go back in time." Calla turned back to the window. "Trust me, I would if I could." Finn sighed as she digested his words. It sounded like an apology without being an apology. Calla told herself not to move her eyes off a tree she was focusing on. Playful chipmunks picked up on the impending storm and dashed away inside a hole in the bark. A long roll of thunder drummed in the air. "That man could have been dangerous, Calla, and you disobeyed me. You put yourself in danger out of spite for me."

"His eyes weren't red, "Calla scoffed. "And why would I intentionally spite you? Aren't we on the same team here?" A scowl formed on her lips.

"It doesn't matter, Calla." Finn came to the opposite side of the window. "I know you don't want to hear it, but I'm honor-bound to protect you."

"Yeah, yeah, protect the Hybrid," the anger and frustration rose in her voice. "No one gives a shit about me, Calla Moro." She broke her focus from the tree to look at Finn. He was much closer than she expected him to be. There was a tiny scar on his cheek that resembled a lopsided 'x' that she had never noticed before. Calla jumped a little when lightning flashed.

"No, that couldn't be farther from the truth," Finn paused as thunder rumbled. "I..." Finn swallowed the word.

Calla sensed his hesitancy, "Do you think The Corrupted are after us?"

Finn stared at her, pondering her question. "Not here. You took out any Corrupted in Japhia with your powers. They must know of our basic plan and will be waiting to ambush us at points along the way. That's why I have us taking an odd route, following the Long Road, but not on it." Finn took Calla's hands. She missed wearing the gloves, but skin to skin contact felt good. His hands were warm, and it caught her off guard. Calla wanted to rip her hands away, but his grip loosened, giving her the choice. She kept her hands in his as a weird gesture of trust.

The storm was now overhead, the flashes of lightning illuminated Finn's sharp jawline. Calla assumed years of fighting gave him a jagged nose, but strangely, it fit his face. Her eyes landed on his jade eyes, which had already been looking into hers. It clicked, she finally understood why she was so on edge. "I'm terrified of what's to come." The admission lifted the dark veil that has been covering her since they left. Even if she had professed the same thing to Vihaan days prior, the fear never really went away.

Finn's Adam's apple bobbed. "I know. We all are. But I'd die before I let a Corrupt mongrel touch a hair on your head." In sync with his words, one of Finn's hands traced the rope of her hair. His fingers kept going over the end that wasn't braided, not wanting to let go.

The moment unnerved her. Calla pulled her hands away at a clap of thunder. "Why didn't you tell me that you and Shea were from the human realm?"

Finn's fingers dropped her braid. It landed softly against her chest. "What did you say?" Finn's voice lost the softness it had.

"You heard me." Calla's voice trembled.

In an instant, Finn had caged Calla with his arms. Her back pressed up against the cold damp panes. A shiver went down her spine, but she wasn't sure if it was from the window or the man in front of her. "Who told you about our past?"

"A little birdie." It was obvious about who it was, but Calla didn't want to give Zinnia or Lena up.

Finn rolled his eyes and muttered something about Zinnia. "Let's get one thing straight here. Do not talk about my or Shea's past. It's no one's business, especially yours." Calla noticed his fangs grew to rest on his lips. "Why do you even care?"

Calla squared her shoulders back to meet his menacing gaze. "Call me curious."

Finn moved closer. His fangs grazed her ear. Fear and anticipation paralyzed her. "Remember that curiosity killed the cat." Calla closed her eyes, feeling his presence next to her diminish. "Oh and, Calla?" She opened her eyes. Finn was by the door. "You should talk with your boyfriend." Calla opened her mouth, but Finn continued, "He wasn't stuck at the garden house the night we left as he said. He lied to you."

Calla stood there, dumbfounded, as Finn slipped out of the room. "No," she laughed to herself. Finn's doing this on purpose. How would he know? The storm raged stronger. She kept pacing around the room, stewing over his words. "I'm going to ignore Finn," Calla whispered with conviction. "Afterall he's given me like zero reasons to trust him, and I can't fall for whatever trap he's setting. And I've asked Vihaan more than enough times for the truth and he promised me he was being honest."

Calla fell on the bed and threw her forearm over her eyes. She forced herself to replay the conversation with Finn in the room. Did she really admit to him that she was scared? It was certainly easier to admit to Vihaan, but telling Finn made her feel better. She didn't understand it.

She sat up. No. Finn didn't get to ruin this day. Calla was going to spend just as she intended to, with Vihaan. She heard Cypress come in with a barrel or two of ale earlier and she wasn't about to wait until the barrels were empty to join in. It was past time she joined the convoy and relaxed with them. They all deserved it for having to deal with Finn.

She left the room. The guards were milling about the house, chatting. Most had mugs of ale in their hands. Calla noticed the conversation dimmed when she closed the door behind her. Finn was up on the loft, looking down with a hint of something in his eye that she couldn't place. Cypress and Zinnia were next to him. Calla met his gaze, but then dropped it to see Vihaan smiling at her on the couch near the fire. He scooted over, patting the space. She took his silent invitation and plopped next to him. Despite being so close to the fire, she could only feel the warmth of his body next to hers. The buzz of conversation picked up again, but she knew people were watching, one in particular. She melted against Vihaan. She'd missed his touch. His arm wrapped around her shoulder. "Hey," he whispered as he rubbed his thumb up and down her shoulder.

Calla gave him a warm smile, "Hey, yourself."

"Feeling better?"

Calla nodded. "I was just feeling overwhelmed by everything, and I'm sorry." A group of the guards began singing at a lively pace, a song about the mountains. The people sang in a slur of notes only to hit sharp crescendos and come back down. Calla wished she knew the words, it sounded like a fun song to sing.

Vihaan shushed her quickly, "Don't apologize. I should be apologizing to you." Vihaan nuzzled into her hair. "I can't help myself from giving you attention. I know it must be a lot. You're strong and brave, far more than me."

Calla felt the fear she's been feeling begin to melt away. "Me or the Hybrid?"

Vihaan pulled back, lightning flashed. The chorus of guards cheered as thunder crashed over the home. Light from the fire gave Vihaan's face a warm glow. "You. Damn all the Hybrid talk, you are courageous, kind, spirited and how could I forget, stunning. Midelle is lucky to have you as their hero. Hybrid or not."

Calla fought the urge to cry but failed as Vihaan wiped a tear away. "Thank you, Vihaan..." Calla sniffed back her tears, "I don't know where I'd be without you."

Vihaan whispered, "You know that offer still stands." Calla raised an eyebrow. "Where you stay here, with me." Their fingers interlocked.

"Vihaan, it's not that simple."

"Oh, but it is."

"I have a life back in the human realm, and I can only imagine what will happen when I come back. It will take months to put everything back together."

"Then don't go back."

"I can't leave my best friend."

"Felicia will understand."

"We've only known each other for," Calla exhaled hard, "Almost three weeks?"

"Love has no timeline."

Calla froze, her next excuse floated out of her brain in an instant. "You... love me?" She looked around the room. No one was paying attention to them. Everyone's attention was on songs and ale with the storm as an audience.

"Very much. Granted this wasn't the perfect moment to tell you, but I figured it would add a compelling point to the argument." He kissed her hand.

"I don't know if..."

"I don't expect you to. Take your time to make sure your feelings are true." Vihaan winked at her, "Which I can only hope they'll be."

Calla took a deep breath. Her cheeks were burning, and her palms were clammy. He loved her! Her heart was soaring into the sky, but she still managed to think of her next point. "The police will label me as missing, presumed dead, and that would break Felicia's heart."

Vihaan rubbed his stubble-laden chin, "Then we go bring to the human realm and bring Felicia here."

Calla furrowed her eyebrows, thinking of Felicia of all people in Midelle. "She's scared of bugs and I'm not sure she'd do well without technology and frappuccino's."

"I thought I'd at least get a maybe." Vihaan let his free hand drop and trace Calla's waistline with tenderness. "I have another suggestion then."

"And that is?" Calla raised an eyebrow.

"We finish what we started a few days ago."

Calla gasped and her cheeks flushed as she remembered Vihaan ravishing her against the tree. Her eyes darted to the window. The rain still fell in sheets. "But where do we go?"

Vihaan got up from the couch, pulling her with him, "I have a place in mind." His tone was low and husky, making Calla's stomach flutter. The mischievous glint of his eyes and the half smile on his lips made Calla want those lips on her.

Calla followed his lead only to look up to the loft before they went under it. Finn was watching, but it wasn't an angry look on his face like she anticipated. His fingers drummed on the railing and one of his eyebrows raised. He even mouthed, "Watch yourself," before he disappeared into the other end of the loft. The nagging voice of doubt called to her as Vihaan led Calla down the stairs into the basement. Her joy sank with every step.

The basement was colder than the main level. Goosebumps prickled her skin. Vihaan lit a lantern that gave only enough light to cast a soft glow on them. He turned to her, with only one look in his eyes. Lust. Calla wanted to match his look, but Finn's words kept echoing in her head. Still, her doubts did not affect Vihaan as his lips found hers. He pulled her flush against him as their mouths melted together. One of his hands found her behind and grabbed onto it. Calla moaned for him. Vihaan wasn't as gentile this time around, he was hungry for her. For her touch. For her womanhood. He wrapped both hands around her bottom. Calla wrapped her legs around his waist. His kisses became hungrier, biting on her bottom lip. Not enough to hurt her, but he was walking the line, and she loved it.

Locked in their passionate embrace, Calla's butt thumped clumsily on a table behind her. She was so lost in the kiss she hadn't noticed him walk her backwards. Vihaan pressed himself to her. He kissed and nibbled down her jawline onto her throat. Calla ran her fingers through his hair, teasing strands from his ponytail. He bit her collarbone, and a loud moan escaped her lips. "Shhh, my love." He placed a softer kiss over the scant bite mark.

Calla rolled her lips in and let her head drop back, completely flushed. Vihaan's hands roamed every inch of her body.

"Watch yourself."

Calla's eyes snapped open at the voice inside her head, but Vihaan didn't notice. She was hearing Finn in her head, now, of all times. Vihaan's fingers toying with the hem of her tunic made Calla push any thoughts of Finn out the window. She grabbed both sides of his face and kissed him with a demanding passion. She heard a deep moan surface from the depths of his throat, and he pulled her tunic off in one movement. They broke apart as Vihaan tossed his shirt off over his head. She reached for him, anxious for the touch of his skin on hers, but Vihaan had stepped back.

A great sadness washed over his face. Calla folded against her flat stomach, fearing it was her body. But she knew it was the bruises that made him stop. Her shoulders hunched forward to hide the bruises covering her collarbone. Her stomach and back were the worst. "Zinnia gave me a salve to make them heal faster. It works. I figure in a few more applications, they'll be gone."

Vihaan shook his head. He moved to her to cup her face with one hand while the other rested on her lower back. "I swear by the deities, I will kill him." His thumb rubbed down her spine, leaving a trail of goosebumps.

"He was only doing what he thought was right."

"Are you..." his face twitched, "defending him?"

"No!" Calla placed a hand on his chest to calm him. "It's in the past. What's the point of getting angry about it?"

Vihaan rolled his eyes. "What's the point? He beat you for sport. And it's not in the past! Look at you!" He backed up with a short sigh, watching her hop off the table to grab her tunic. "I hate him."

Calla pulled the tunic down over her head. "I know you do..."

"Don't you?"

Wrapping her arms around herself, she nodded. With hesitancy, she answered, "Yeah. I do."

"Then why are you defending him?" A sharp noise made Calla jump as Vihaan slammed his hand on the table.

Her eyes widened at the change in his demeanor. "I'm not. I choose to let it go because there is so much other shit I have to worry about," she said, raising her voice with each word. Calla crossed her arms with a huff. "Does Midelle expect you to save it from an unspeakable evil that terrifies everyone? Do people look at you with hope, but you only smile at them because you're even more scared than they are?"

"Calla, please calm down." Vihaan reached out a hand in her direction.

Calla swatted the air, "No! I thought you were on my side!"

Running his hand through his hair Vihaan sighed, "I am on your side. Always. Trust me. You have to... please." Thunder and lightning crashed together from above. "I'm doing everything I can to protect you from him, that asshole. Can you admit..."

"Finn's an asshole! Okay? Is that what you wanted to hear? And while we're on the topic of assholes, you stood there and watched him beat me. Not just one day, but every day!" Calla marched up to him and shoved her finger in his chest. "You want to talk about assholes, take a long look in the mirror."

Vihaan's face grew tight. "You think that I'm on the same level as he is?" He scoffed. "Maybe I should have missed the convoy. Philomena wouldn't stop talking."

Calla blinked, digesting his words. "You lied to me?" She took a step back remembering the moment back at the castle. Her heart hurt in an emotional way that felt physical.

"No!"

"You told me that you were making sure Hawke had everything under control."

"I was there before that, but you don't..."

"He was right."

Vihaan froze as his eyes narrowed. "He who?"

"Finn. He told me you were lying. And I didn't want to believe it, but he was right." Her arms wrapped around herself, fending off a chill.

"You listened to him?"

"I told you I didn't want to believe it!" She fought the tears that wanted to fall.

"But you did! And you don't trust me!"

"Can you blame me? We hardly even know each other. Plus, you were acting weird, and you promised me you'd be there!"

"I was there!" His voice filled the damp cellar.

"Barely!"

"You should have trusted me!"

"Trust you? You lied to me!"

"For all the right reasons! You never should have believed Finn." Vihaan turned and went up the stairs, not once looking back to her. Calla noticed that the singing had stopped upstairs, and everyone had heard everything. Calla winced when she heard the front door slam. She knew she couldn't stay down in the cellar forever, but the thought was tempting. Whatever party was going on upstairs she had ruined. Still fighting the tears, she squared her shoulders and climbed the stairs.

Calla felt everyone's eyes upon her, but she kept her eyes straight ahead as she walked to her room.

Zinnia cleared her throat from the loft, "Mind your own everyone."

An awkward chatter filled the bungalow as people forced themselves to look elsewhere. Calla glanced at the loft to nod her head to Zinnia as a token of thanks, but she was gone from sight. Her eyes caught Finn looking at the door that Vihaan had exited through. A full smirk spread across his lips, but then his head turned. Their gazes connected. Calla's eyes narrowed in on him, but the smirk on his face fell before he turned away from her as well.

Thunder shook the cottage as Calla shut herself away in Finn's room with only her tears.

Fifteen

The peaks of the Edulis Mountains loomed over Calla. A hazy light shone behind them in what should have been the moon, but it was gone. As was the sun, stars, and the deep velvet blue of the night sky. A small field lay between her and the base of the mountain. The grasses grew tall, interrupted by the occasional thistle. She could cross this in a few hours. Determined, she took a step into the field. The grass tickled her bare foot, but she didn't laugh. She watched as the grass that touched her skin wilted and crumbled into nothing. Calla cocked her head to the side and took another full step. The same thing happened, but it kept going, like dominoes falling. She took off deeper into the field, racing against the wave of dead grass to reach the living blades. Her running slowed as she couldn't get out of the field of lifeless weeds.

A sharp snapping sound behind her made her look where she had come from. Out from the death, vines covered in thorns shot up from the dead ground and stretched out towards her. Calla took off again, but this time to outrun the thorns. She ran towards the mountains, but the light faded as the thorns got closer. Her bloodied feet stumbled, and she fell face-first into the dead grass. Unable to stand or run on her feet, she sat up, but wouldn't give up as she crawled backward. Calla faced the wave of thorns that raced towards her at an alarming speed. The light illuminating the mountains was nearly gone. She could barely see the wave. Her arms gave out, and she sat there, unable to go on. The wave of thorns was yards away from her. She braced herself for the pain she knew was coming. The last traces of the light faded into black. Calla could see nothing, but she heard the vicious snap of the vines. She held her breath. The vines swarmed over her and tore into her skin.

A blood-curdling scream left her lips.

Vihaan dropped his handful of deep purple berries. "Calla!"

He ran to her and cradled her in his arms. Her eyes were clamped shut, and her body thrashed about in his arms. One agonizing scream after another left her lips. "Calla," he whispered into her hair as he held her even tighter. The guards and Finn formed a circle around them.

"Shut her up!" Malak tossed a rag at Vihaan. "She'll give away our position."

Vihaan narrowed his eyes at the troll, "Shh, Calla. It's okay. It was a bad dream. Come back to me."

Calla's eyes snapped open. Her tears fell and she fought to be free from Vihaan's arms. He let her go and watched her chest heave. Her hands trembled as she ran them over her arms and legs.

"Lady Calla, are you..." Finn stopped when he noticed her lip quivering and tears rolling from her icy eyes.

"The thorns..."

"What thorns?" Vihaan asked. His voice had a gentle edge to it.

"The thorns in my dream. They felt so real." Calla's breathing slowed, but she ripped off a boot and sock and ran her fingers over her foot. Unlike in her dream, her foot was fine. "My feet were bloody... I..." She swallowed, her throat was bone dry. "It felt so real."

Finn cleared his throat, "All right then. Pack up and move out on my command. We reach East Shimmer in a few hours. No need to arrive in the dead of night."

"There we cross the Edulis Mountains?" Calla's voice trembled. Finn nodded as he watched her with intense scrutiny put her sock and boot back on. "We can't cross there." Her lip trembled as images of the thorns flashed through her mind. "There has to be another way."

Finn knelt in front of her. Despite the chilling weather, her skin glistened with perspiration. "There is no other way. Unless you can magically fly now? Know any dragons?" He laughed, and a few others close to him chuckled as well.

Calla narrowed her eyes and lips. Over the past eleven days she had barely said a word to either Finn or Vihaan. Finn shrugged it off, but Vihaan tried to no end to get back into her good graces.

Finn rose and towered over Calla. "That's what I thought. Sorry, you had a nightmare, Lady Calla. We're heading out soon, so collect yourself. We've made excellent time and will arrive at East Shimmer before nightfall."

Calla dropped her head into her hands, and glanced towards their destination. The mountains stood tall past the trees, their peaks hidden behind a whiteout blizzard. She remembered others saying that it snowed that high all year round.

"Are you okay?" Vihaan asked, coming by her side. She turned to him wanting to collapse in his arms, but they were still quarreling. The rational part of her knew she was being stubborn, that she should have forgiven him days ago. But the sting of his lies lived embedded in her brain and reinforced her ire.

Calla stood on shaky legs. Vihaan went to help, but Calla swatted his hand away. "And you pretend to care now? Leave me alone."

"Calla, please!"

"No!" Her legs wobbled when she went to walk. Calla planted her feet on the ground, not wanting to move. "It was a bad dream, okay? I have to roll up my mat and," she sighed then pushed the hair back that stuck to her face.

Before she even asked, Vihaan rolled up her mat for her and hoisted it over his shoulder. "How many times do I have to say it..." His sweet purple eyes looked to her, "I'm sorry. If you'll give me a chance to..."

"To what," Calla scoffed, "tell the truth? You should have done that two weeks ago when we left."

Vihaan's eyes darted around them, but then went back to her. He shifted his head to face her and in a low voice, he said, "Calla, please. I couldn't tell you before."

"Thanks for getting my mat," Calla muttered then hobbled off in a different direction to find her horse.

There was something about the scenery that had changed. Gone were the forests clad in fall arrays of golds, oranges, and reds. The leaves had withered, browned, and fallen to crinkle under the horses' hooves. The night air had a chilling bite to it, but the day was tolerable when the sun was out.

"Lady Calla," a druid scout with tight brown curls said as she rode next to her. The curls were wild from weeks of neglect.

"Kalise." She had spoken with her a few times since they left Coriocris. She was the youngest scout, but still years older than Calla.

Her ever watching midnight blue eyes crinkled in the corners. "I wanted to make sure you were okay. You've seemed off since we left Coriocris."

"I'm fine." Calla knew what was going on, she had seen Kalise talking with Vihaan a few days ago. Even though Vihaan was using Kalise as a middleman, Calla still gave her a thin smile. It was hard not being mad at Kalise at this moment, but Calla knew it wasn't right. Finn and Vihaan demanded all her anger, split right down the middle.

"All due respect Lady Calla, but you've isolated yourself since we left. It's not," she paused as her brown horse gave a nervous whinny. "I'm concerned about you. We all are. Your nightmare today solidified that. You should forgive Vihaan." Calla rolled her eyes. "It's affecting you in a bad way. Even you have to admit it."

"Did he tell you to say that?"

Kalise raised an eyebrow to Calla, "No. I went to him because we all heard you two fight."

Calla wanted to crawl into a hole in the ground from the embarrassment. Most had done her that courtesy of not talking about the day she and Vihaan fought.

"You're stressed and holding onto that anger won't help you. You know how people turn Corrupted, right? They hold onto anger, for years and over time it builds up..."

"Are you saying I'll become Corrupted because I'm mad at Vihaan?"

"No, but it is not a good idea to hold onto anger." She pursed her lips. "If it helps any, I asked him to tell me the truth."

"And?" Calla asked laced with curiosity.

"He wouldn't tell me. Vihaan wanted you to hear it from him." A smile cracked Calla's lips. "You should forgive him."

"I'm not ready to forgive him yet."

"But you will?"

"I have more to think about before that happens."

"Oh, please, Lady Calla..."

Finn sounded a sharp whistle and held up a hand to halt the convoy. Kalise immediately perked up, and her eyes flitted around them. "Scouts, on your feet and go ahead," Finn commanded in a strong, but hushed voice. He hadn't moved one inch, but his eyes scanned the forest ahead.

Calla's eyes grew wide as Kalise and two other scouts dismounted, then disappeared into the tree line. She didn't know the other two scouts very well, they favored Finn over her. Finn came by her side, his hand on the hilt of his sword. "What's happening?" she whispered.

"I heard something up ahead, and we're close to the Long Road. We need to be cautious." He looked to her to bring his finger to his lips, "Now." He tapped his finger to his lips three times.

Calla nodded. Her face held stoic, but her heart pounded. A fat black crow burst from the trees, cawing a sharp-tuned call. It perched nearby and watched them. Calla raised an eyebrow and motioned to the bird with her head.

Finn dismounted, still on edge. "Stay here," he murmured as he pointed to a handful of guards. All the ones Calla rarely ever spoke with. They were all big, burly, and intimidating. Finn drew his sword and pointed to the right of where he was. He beckoned the other group to follow him to the left. Calla watched the two groups of men disappear into the trees with silent grace.

The remaining guards grouped up around Calla, Vihaan included. "It's okay Calla." He rested his hand on her arm which she had hanging down her side.

Calla wanted to rip her arm away, but her other hand knocked him off gently instead. "Just focus, please." Her voice was light. "I still need to think more." Knowing that was the answer he was waiting for.

Vihaan let out a soft sigh that finished with a soft smile. His hand fell down her arm and lifted her hand. Before Calla could react, he kissed her hand, unfortunately, covered by her glove, but that warm feeling in her stomach surfaced again. She knew that she was putty in his hands, but she wanted to keep her distance for a little while longer.

Calla fidgeted on her horse. Her muscles were tight from riding all night long and sleeping on the mat. She knew Finn was anxious to get to East Shimmer, but his paranoia at every noise made stops like this more frequent.

The previous Captain of the Guard, Jedrek, was at East Shimmer, and she knew they would be safe there. Finn said Jedrek would never allow any of The Corrupted in the village. A twig snapped from behind them. They turned so fast, she scared her horse into a nervous snort. Nothing was there. Calla placed a hand on her mare, "They're taking longer than usual."

Lena drew her bow, nocking an arrow. "Don't worry, Lady Calla. One of the groups will whistle if they're in danger or come back."

"We'll protect you," a wide-stance troll with graying black hair ensured. Calla had never talked with him, but she knew his name to be Zenji. He pulled his mace from its holster, "No need to worry."

Calla's facial features fell flat. "You all drawing your weapon says otherwise."

Vihaan drew his sword from its sheath last. "Only a precaution."

Another twig snapped ahead of them. It had to be one of the scouting groups. Vihaan stepped in front of her. This formation encased Calla in a circle of protection with Lena to her left and Zenji to her right. The forest became silent. Calla held her next breath in.

A sharp clang sounded from the forest, spooking Calla's horse. The mare galloped off as Calla gripped onto the reins, not knowing what to do. "Help!" The horse sped off into the woods, leaving Vihaan, Lena, and Zenji behind. She yanked the reins to regain control, but the horse reared onto its hind legs and threw her from the saddle. Calla hit the ground unable to brace herself. Her eyes found her horse in time to see the mare vanish into a denser part of the forest. "Vihaan?" She heard a commotion in the distance, but she was all alone.

Calla cautiously turned to take in her surroundings and came face to face with a Corrupted woman. She had short, dark brown hair, but her eyes were bright red. Calla gasped, the scream stuck in her throat. A burly arm snaked around her, and a hand covered her mouth from behind her. Calla struggled in vain, the man behind had her locked down. Calla thrust her elbow back into the man's gut, frantic to get away. The man only grunted and held her tighter. The woman walked closer to her and pushed back a tendril of golden hair out of Calla's face. "I can't believe we did it," the woman said with glee. "We captured the Hybrid! Our plan worked! We have to get her out of here while her guards are busy."

Calla bit hard onto the man's hand. He pulled his hand away with a terse shout. Blood dripped from the wound. A tangy metallic taste filled her mouth. The moment her mouth was free, she let out a high-pitched screech and fought his hold on her. The man shoved a piece of cloth in her mouth and tied it behind her head.

"You'll pay for that!" The man hissed, holding Calla's arms tight and looking at her in the eyes. From his long hair being slicked back, she could see his eyes. They were dark red, almost black, and they terrified Calla to her core.

"We're ordered not to hurt her, Ash." The woman tied Calla's arms back with rope. "Our Queen would kill us." Calla tried fighting against the rope, but the knot was too tight.

"Quiet, Hazel," Ash yelled. "Our Queen wouldn't second guess a few bruises." She wished that he wouldn't bruise her, for her old ones were finally gone. He grabbed a handful of her hair and twisted it in his hand. A tear ran down Calla's face, where were the guards? Vihaan? Finn? Anyone?

Hazel smirked, then got within inches of Calla's face. "As long as you keep it to bruises, this will be our little secret. Queen Belladonna would never find out. Right Hybrid?"

Calla turned her head from The Corrupted woman, trying to hide her tears.

"Give me one minute, then conjure the portal," Ash sniggered against Calla's cheek. She screamed into the gag and struggled harder as he spun her around to face him. Calla. "Now, now, Hybrid," Ash whispered. He roughly touched the spot on her cheek where he wanted to hit her, "The more you struggle, the more it will hurt, so stay still and..."

"Touch another hair on her head, and I'll rip your beating heart out and make you eat it," Finn's voice boomed. Blood stained his clothes and his sword dripped with fresh blood. Calla tried to struggle again, but Ash only pushed her to the ground. Without hands to catch herself, she fell face-first on the forest floor. Her jaw throbbed at the sudden impact. She rolled over to see the man catch a massive, long sword thrown by Hazel. She had a long and thin sword of her own and an evil look in her red eyes.

"It is you who will die and be feasted upon by the crows." Ash and Finn circled each other.

Calla attempted to get up, but a sword to the throat stopped her in her tracks. "You're not going anywhere," Hazel hissed. Calla fell back on the ground as Finn and Ash's sword clashed together with a deadly clang.

"Two against one?" Finn mused while he side-stepped to avoid a jab. "Since when is that fair?"

"Your other guards are being slaughtered right now," Hazel taunted. She gripped the back of Calla's hair and pulled back. She cried out against the gag with more tears falling down her face as she thought of the guards who were dying for her. Calla's heart stopped beating as she feared for Vihaan. "We thought this would be a challenge for the..." she smirked, "...Captain of the Royal Guard."

"Let's play then," Finn growled and thrust his sword forward. Ash dodged to the right, but Finn slashed his sword to the right.

His blade bit into Ash's side. He hunched over to check his wound. Before waiting for him to stand up, Finn thrust his sword through Ash's stomach until the blade came out his back. The Corrupted peon fell to the ground with a thick thud. His dark blood pooled on dead leaves.

"Ash! No!" Hazel cried, raising her blade and charging Finn. Their steel blades crashed together, and Finn absorbed the impact by taking a step back. His foot twisted in a hole disguised by leaves and Finn fell on his back. Hazel quickly kicked the sword out his hand. Calla's eyes went wide as Hazel raised her sword over her head to deliver the fatal blow to Finn.

Calla could feel his only hope, her sigil, burning. It was glowing again. She didn't have to see it glow, she could feel her power coursing through her veins. Closing her eyes to keep focusing on her power, she pressed her hand into the ground behind her. A vine shot from the ground and wrapped around Hazel's sword hand. In shock, her sword thudded on the ground. Her eyes narrowed in on Calla. Finn watched another vine spring up from the ground and wrapped around Hazel's other wrist.

Calla opened her eyes, concentrating on what she wanted to happen. The vines tightened and pulled back into the ground. Her energy faded, but she willed herself to continue until The Corrupted woman was dead.

Hazel fell to her knees with her hands bound by the vines.

Finn kneeled next to the trapped Corrupted soldier. "Your leader is next," Finn said as he pushed her shoulders, causing her to fall on her back. Calla made thick vines snake around her ankles and her neck, locking her down completely.

"You will lose, my Queen will win, and the Hybrid will destroy everything," Hazel choked out. "Belladonna will make the Hybrid kill you, I wish I could see that."

"Says the one about to feed the crows." Finn picked up his sword and cut a line from her navel to her chest in one effortless slice. Hazel screamed in agony and fought against the vines.

Calla let her hand roll away from the ground, her vision doubled. She felt arms cradle her, but when she expected to see Finn, she found Vihaan. Her heart skipped a beat.

"I'm sorry, Calla. I'm so sorry," Vihaan said as he untied the gag.

Calla's vision was fading, but she could see blood on his face. Rustling in the woods behind her made Calla turn her head. Her vision quadrupled at the quick movement. "Come out here and fight me, you Corrupted bastards!" The voice yelled through the trees. The voice seemed miles away to her.

"Finn?" A deep voice asked. Calla couldn't keep her eyes open anymore. They closed, but she was struggling to stay awake. "What's going on here?"

"You missed the action. Corrupted ambushed us." It sounded like Finn. She saved Finn. "I've lost some of my guards."

The last thing she heard was the deep voice say, "Is... Is that the Hybrid?"

Calla was sitting in a tree, her legs dangled off the branch, and she wore a soft white dress. The layers of the dress floated in a breeze as she kicked her legs back and forth. A braided crown of thorns sat on her head with a withered white deity rose nestled at the center.

She looked down at the corpses of Hazel and Ash, her eyes connected with theirs, even though they were dead, their eyes were open. Hazel's eyes were a vivid green color, and Ash's were blue as the nighttime sky. Crows now feasted on their bodies as Finn said they would.

The biggest crow cawed and turned its head towards Calla. The crow's eyes were gleaming red. Ignited with anger, Calla said to the crow, "I'll kill you." Her marked hand tightened into a fist, making her glove taut across her hand. A thorn pricked her head at the hairline, and blood started to mix in her golden waves.

"No, you won't," A dark voice hissed around them. The crow went back to picking at the dead bodies.

"Who are you?" Calla asked with a shaky voice as a drop of blood streamed down her cheek. "What do you want from me?"

"Your powers." Calla's sigil started to burn, she ripped off her glove, and it was blazing red. "It is only a matter of time until you succumb to The Corruption!"

Sixteen

This feeling was familiar. Her body ached, and her head pounded. Calla rolled over and met the soft embrace of a down-stuffed quilt. When she opened her eyes, her eyes adjusted to the small lit candle by the door. The room was small, cozy even, with the bed as the main piece of furniture. Light bled in from the outline of the door, as did the soft murmur of voices.

Calla pulled back the quilt and got up, in spite of her body's protest at every inch of movement. She opened the door, only to meet the sad eyes of nine of the people she had been traveling with. No one had to speak. Calla knew that they were all that had remained of the convoy. Vihaan was closest to the door. His face offered sympathy. It was hard to look past the dried blood that colored his clothes. Finn had his arms crossed in the corner of the room by the fireplace. He leaned against the mantle, as his eyes dropped to focus on the flames.

Calla was thankful that Lena and Zenji were in the room. She checked everyone in the room, and mourned for Kalise and the other guards not there. "What happened?"

Finn didn't take his eyes off the fire. "We were ambushed. They had double our numbers. My group found the scouts, dead, just as The Corrupted jumped us. We managed to kill our attackers, and then we split up to find you." Finn finally looked up to connect his gaze with hers, "I made it just in time. We would have lost you if it weren't for Jedrek and the East Shimmer patrol. They were close, heard the commotion and came to help."

From across the room, Calla could see the sorrow in Finn's eyes. He didn't even try to hide it.

"The Corrupted were hunting you," Vihaan added, keeping his head low. "Despite our best efforts, we never saw them coming. We owe our lives to him and his men."

Calla's lip quivered, "Is this--" She broke eye contact from Finn.

"We're all that's left," Lena filled in.

Finn cleared his throat, and the sorrow left his eyes. The emotionless exterior he so often wore fell over him like a veil. "Yes. We're all that's left, and that's why we keep moving. Their deaths will not be in vain. They all knew what was at stake, but there is a silver lining. We finally know their leader's name. Belladonna, or Queen Belladonna as she prefers." Calla could still see the admiration in Hazel's eyes as she spoke Belladonna's name. "Get a good night's rest. We start the crossing tomorrow morning. Jedrek is arranging that now."

"How long was I out?" Calla asked. She gazed out a large window by the cozy kitchen to see a dark sky.

"The sun had set not too long ago, so most of the afternoon," Lena responded with a weak smile. She shed her thick cloak, revealing a bandage that wrapped most of her left arm. Other guards had bandages over their bodies, and blood stained their skin and clothes.

An overwhelming sense of guilt washed over Calla. "I'm sorry," her voice trembled on the edge of a sob. "None of you would have gotten hurt if it weren't for me, and the fallen guards wouldn't be dead." She wanted to cry as a horrible feeling landed in the pit of her stomach.

Zenji stood. He had a long wound on his cheek, right through a patch of hardened skin. Blood had dried down his face and neck. "Lady Calla. If I was one of the ones to fall, and I could go back knowing that my life ended... I would choose to protect you once again."

Another guard stood. Calla remembered his name as Corbin. "As would I, Lady Calla."

Two other druid guards, whom Calla thought were brothers, each broad in the shoulder with strong arms, also stood. "We stand with you, Lady Calla." Their names clicked in her mind, Bear and Wolfe.

"And I," another man stood. Hard patches covered his entire body.

"I too, stand with you," Lena stood tall next to Calla.

The last man stood, tall and proud with his gray hair slicked back and his eyes a dark hazel. Calla had no idea what his name was. He was one of the ones who stuck close to Finn and intimidated her. "I pledge my life to you once again, Lady Calla."

Vihaan moved to her and wrapped his arm around her shoulder. "You know I'd die for you." Calla let her body relax under his muscular arm.

Finn straightened and cleared his throat again. "We're all with you. No one blames you, and no one is abandoning you."

Calla nodded, but the guilt still ate at her. "Thank you, everyone. I appreciate all of you willing to give their life for me, but it's too dangerous. We should turn back," Calla saw Finn's face darken, "get more guards and try again. There has to be a way to open a portal to the Library of Midelle and save time..."

"As I said," Finn started, "We will continue. I will not allow my brave men and women's blood and lives to have been shed in vain. We will get you to the Library of Midelle to see the Oracle, so you can awaken the other half of your powers. We leave at daybreak for the gates on the other end of town. Now if you'll excuse me." Finn stormed out of the house before anyone could say anything. Snow floated in when he passed through the door.

The door opened again moments later, bringing more snow breezed along with a woman and a man. Their faces featured broad smiles and hard patches all over. The muscular man had short brown hair and towered over the woman next to him. The woman's eyes were a bright brown like caramel, and strawberry blonde hair cascaded in gentle waves past her chest. The man took her fur cloak from her shoulders, and Calla's eyes were drawn to the baby wrapped to her chest, all bundled in furs.

The woman looked from the baby to Calla. "You must be The Hybrid." She had a gentle smile on her face. "We're so glad to see you've awakened. I'm Zula, and this is my husband, Jedrek."

Jedrek immediately bowed to Calla. "Welcome to East Shimmer, Hybrid. I wish our meeting had happened under more pleasant circumstances."

"And this is Saria." Zula smiled at her baby while unwrapping her.

Calla smiled, "Thank you, but please, call me Calla."

"Please, Calla," Jedrek motioned to a chair, "sit. You have come a long way from the Capital."

"I'm fine, thank you. It's been," she paused to look in the corner of the room where Finn had been, "a trying day."

Jedrek crossed his arms as he scanned the room, "I would believe it. Was Captain Quinn okay? He seemed off, when we passed him a minute ago."

People murmured things incoherently, but Calla said, "He needed some air."

"I can understand that." Jedrek nodded, "It's not easy to lose your guards."

Calla fidgeted until her icy eyes caught Zula's warm gaze. "You're safe here. Jedrek used to be Captain of the Royal Guard."

"Yes," Calla smiled, "Finn mentioned that Jedrek was his predecessor."

"There are no corrupted mongrels in this town. I can assure you. West Shimmer is also guarded. It's the least we could do to cut off this path from them."

Vihaan furrowed his eyebrows, "Did you hear about the attack on Japhia a few weeks ago?"

Jedrek sat by the fire, taking in its warmth. "Unfortunately, yes. Traveling merchants spoke of the event, but what I never understood was how many they spoke of."

"There had to be close to one-hundred," Calla cut in. She remembered how they flooded the streets and alleyways.

"Calla saved us all." Vihaan smiled at her. The fire caught the masculine sculpt of his jawline. "That was the day her powers came to light."

"How extraordinary," Zula chimed in amazed.

"A part of me wishes I could see that," Jedrek grinned, but Zula gave him a hard stare as she bounced the baby on her hip. "But my first duty is to these ladies." He smiled at Zula with admiration, who smiled back at him. The love they had for each other shone in their eyes.

Calla glanced at Vihaan, and another warm smile spread over his lips. Could love like theirs ever be hers? She chased the thought out of her brain, there was too much going on. How could she ever think about love when The Corrupted were hunting them down?

"A very good reason to step down," Vihaan agreed.

"Calla, I hate to ask this of you," Zula interjected as she walked closer to Calla. "We left so the Captain could regroup with his guards, but I have to cook. I am sure you're all famished. Would you mind holding Saria?"

Calla bit back a smile as she nodded her head. "No, not at all." Zula placed Saria in her arms. Calla moved to the rocking chair by the fire across from Jedrek while Vihaan knelt by her side. She admired the baby's chubby cheeks and bright brown eyes. She had the outlines of future hard patches on her face and arms. Saria cooed. She couldn't have been more than a few months old. "She's so sweet," Calla murmured as she rocked her in the chair.

"We're so lucky." Jedrek beamed at his only daughter. "I do miss the thrill of the guard, but fatherhood is a whole new different type of thrill."

Calla looked up from Saria. "As Captain of the Royal Guard before Finn, I have so many questions for you." Vihaan gave Calla a strange look. Coming over to the trio, Jedrek walked closer to Calla and held a finger out to Saria, and she wrapped her tiny fingers around his.

"Finally, someone who hasn't heard all his stories!" Zula joked from the kitchen. "He'll have you occupied until you leave in the morning." All the guards except Lena had dispersed from the room. She had moved into the kitchen to help Zula who appreciated her help.

"I'm not that bad, I promise," Jedrek assured.

"Why Finn?" Calla asked before she could stop herself. Vihaan nodded his head to agree with her question. "I don't mean it like that, I... I uh..."

"It's quite all right, Lady Calla. Hector was my second in command, and Finn was my third. By right, Hector deserved it. This made him lazy and complacent. I gave the honor to Finn because he unknowingly worked hard for it. Queen Shea also mentioned it to me, and the more I thought of it, the more I liked the idea. He also changed drastically for the better after time away from the castle." He paused, almost hesitant to continue. "Did Hector ever return to the Castle? He went missing after I gave the position to Finn. I was never able to say goodbye to him."

"Oh, we said goodbye to him..." Calla mouthed to herself as she dropped her head to watch Saria yawn. Calla looked to Jedrek and shook her head, "Not that I know of." She felt bad for lying, but at the same time, she didn't exactly lie. Hector didn't return to the Castle but went hunting her down back in the human realm. And that was where his body was, in the forests. She wondered if his body was ever found.

"I see." Jedrek sighed. "I was always hoping he'd come to his senses and become Finn's second in command. He was an excellent swordsman."

"It's Lucy," Calla said. "He picked Lucy Varden."

"Her aim is spectacular. She has the eye of an hawk and never misses. Good choice", Jedrek said to himself, almost like him giving his approval to Finn's decision. "Do his guards respect him?" He asked on the same train of thought. "That was my one concern because he was fairly new to the Royal Guard."

"Through fear," Vihaan answered without a moment's hesitation.

"His temper can get the best of him," Calla tacked on.

"You should have seen it when he first came to Midelle, new to being a vampire. He was fighting everyone and everything, as if he didn't care if he died. I never pried into his business, but one day he vanished. Queen Shea sent out scouting parties to look for him. After days of no signs from him, we all thought he died. Either from being in a blood rage or execution for crimes committed while in a blood rage. When he came back years later in perfect control, it was like seeing a new man for the first time." He shook his head in amazement.

"I understand that, but he's so," Calla paused. She thought of the word she wanted to use, but all she could think of was Finn hitting her over and over.

"He's awful," Vihaan cut in. "Do you know what he did to her when she first arrived?"

Calla gave Vihaan a sharp glare, "Vihaan."

Saria babbled and flashed a gummy smile.

Jedrek held up his hand, "Look I don't oversee what he does, but I can promise you he did what he thought was right."

"He beat her to make her powers come to light."

"Vihaan!"

"Oh, my," Zula gasped while listening in on the conversation.

Calla cleared her throat, to grab everyone's attention, "Listen. I choose to let it go and bury it in the past." She looked straight to Vihaan. "And we're done bringing it up. We don't need that looking down on us. Today has already been bad enough."

Vihaan huffed and kneeled next to Calla to be face level with Saria. His jaw was tight, but he said, "As you wish."

"Finn's tough. He'll overcome whatever he's facing. He's been through more than I could ever handle." Jedrek added, moving past Calla scolding Vihaan.

"Like what?" Calla prodded lightly.

"Queen Shea turned him to save him from his fate in the human realm."

Calla put Saria against her shoulder to rub her back in small circles. "What was his fate?"

"None of your damn business," Finn barged into the house. His intense look forced Calla to cast her eyes down. Finn turned into the room that the brothers disappeared to. She heard them acknowledge Finn as Captain and then the door closed loudly.

"I guess fresh air didn't help much." Calla broke the awkward silence after the door slammed. Saria stirred from her lull and Calla hushed her, not taking her eyes off the door.

The moon was shining in its glory after their late dinner. Everyone was asleep except Calla. She had slipped out back to think. Sneaking off wasn't the smartest move she had come up with given the situation, but she needed to be alone.

The blizzard spilled off the mountain tops and dusted the back yard with snow. When the moonlight caught the snowflakes, they glimmered like beautiful diamonds. The view of the Edulis Mountains from Jedrek and Zula's house was breathtaking. Calla could see the start of the valley where they were to cross the day after tomorrow.

She lay back on the cold ground with leaves under her back, looking up at the stars with each one shining brilliantly. Puffs of air left her mouth with each fall of her chest. She heard the door open and shut softly, then footsteps crunching closer to her. Her curiosity wanted to know who the uninvited guest was, but the dazzling sky won her attention.

"Aren't you cold?" It was Vihaan.

"A little," Calla said with a small frown on her face. "It numbs the pain of today." She sat up and a warm, fur-lined cloak settled over her shoulders.

"You'll get sick, and none of them would have wanted that." He sat behind her, and she fell against him on her own. Her stomach fluttered when he encased her fully in the cloak, shielding her from the elements.

A sigh left her lips. "Vihaan?"

"Calla?"

"I'm sorry for what happened at Coriocris. Everything is so stressful, and people died today! Died!" She turned to him, breaking out of her furry cocoon. His face was inches from hers as she rested back on her knees. "What if they got me? Do you know what they would do to me?"

"Hey now," he said with a calm tone. His eyes were soft in the moonlight. Calla wanted to dive into those pools of orchids that beckoned her so. "They won't get you. They'd have to kill me first."

Calla's lip quivered, "They almost did. I'm so scared. Now more than ever. I was talking with Kalise this morning! And now she's…" Her voice broke with a sob.

Vihaan rested his hands on the outside her thighs. He bit his lip in thought. "I have a plan to keep you safe. You have to trust me."

"A plan?"

"Look, I didn't want to tell you too early, but after today it's too late. The Corrupted found us and overwhelmed our strongest." Calla frowned. "You were right. I didn't tell you the truth about where I was before we left."

Calla's eyes got wide. "So, you did lie?"

"I couldn't tell you after we've been yelling at each other." His voice was quiet. "The whole damn house was listening then."

"You've had hundreds of opportunities," Calla whispered harshly as she crossed her arms. "Maybe instead of our little moment behind the tree, you could have told me the truth?"

Vihaan winced. "You're right, but all I want is to get lost in you." He pushed a stray wave back behind her ear. "Temptation is my greatest weakness with you. It always has been." Calla's shoulders dropped their edge. "But I will tell you the truth now and swear to you, no more lies. I was with Philomena."

Calla stayed quiet. Her stomach clenched with anger, but butterflies still fluttered around. It was an odd feeling. "She was giving me a portal potion, but it was in secret. I knew the closer we get to Cape Toria, the more dangerous it was going to be. I thought that if it was just us," he reached in his pocket to pull out a tiny drawstring bag, "traveling alone, posing as a married couple." He emptied the bag to have two gold bands clink in his palm. Calla's stomach flipped, and she could feel the heat rising to her cheeks despite them being cold. "We'd stand a better chance."

"What about everyone else?" She had too many questions, but that seemed to be the only logical one to ask.

"We leave behind a letter telling them, and if everything goes to plan, we all meet back at Japhia. We'd have to wait until we cross the mountains, but they would be safer and so would we." He held a ring out to her. "So, what do you say?" He flashed a cocky grin, "Will you marry me?"

Calla rolled her eyes, biting back her smile, "Do you think it would work?"

"I do."

Calla let the smile take over her lips and nodded her head. "Then yes. I trust you, and I will fake marry you for appearances only."

Vihaan slid the ring on her finger, "So am I forgiven?"

"You are." Vihaan went to kiss her, but his chest met the push of her hand. "But that still doesn't change the fact that I'm leaving Midelle when I'm done here."

"All right," Vihaan mumbled, dipping his face closer. The moonlight made his purple eyes gleam like amethysts.

"We have to keep this hidden and not to tip anyone off."

"Fine, fine. Can I kiss you now? I've missed your lips." He bit back a smile, "I've missed all of you, actually."

Calla's answer was to press her lips against his. He pulled her on top of him, and with a tiny squeal, they fell back onto the cloak. She laughed quietly as he peppered her skin with small kisses. The growing beard on his face tickled her. To escape the tickling, Calla rolled onto her back. Vihaan trapped her in an instant with his lips sucking at her neck. She bit back a moan, but her eyes fluttered open to look towards the stars. "Not here." Her voice dripped with disappointment.

Vihaan rolled on his back to match her. They shared a smile before he admired the sky with her. "The day I get you alone, I hope you're prepared."

Calla gave him a cheeky smile before hovering her lips over his ear, "I hope you're prepared." She nibbled on his ear lobe followed by the tiniest kiss before she fell on her back again.

Vihaan let out a long, controlled breath, the steam billowing in front of him. He looked towards the black sky filled with a universe of stars, "You are a fiery woman, Calla Moro, and I love it." He reached over to interlock their fingers, "Like I love you."

A brilliant streak of light flashed across the sky and Calla gasped. "A shooting star! Did you see it?"

Vihaan brought her hand to his lips to kiss her soft skin. "Of course, I did. It was a beautiful sight, but trust me, you are far more beautiful."

Calla held back tears, "I know that my mom sent that star to tell me everything will be alright. Do you think it will be?"

Vihaan pulled Calla onto his chest to where she listened to the steady beat of his heart. "Everything will be. I promise you."

Seventeen

alla stood before heavy, wrought iron gates as the winds whipped snow down the mountain. "Ready?" Finn asked, coming beside her. While he tried to be collected for the convoy, Calla could see through his pitiful attempt to put on a different face. She knew he would be back to himself in no time. Calla was still rattled herself, but last night had her flying on a high.

The convoy and the guide wore heavy furs and leathers, as dictated by the weather. The guide was a short, old man with graying brown hair. Jedrek had assured Finn that he was the best guide on this side of the mountain. He looked excited about this crossing, and by who he was guiding.

"Sure, I guess. How long is this crossing again?" Calla winced and threw up her fur-lined hood against a strong gust that flew off the mountain. Underneath her copious layers Vihaan's ring dangled from a chain. The constant warm feeling of it on her skin reassured her of his promise.

"A few days if we keep on schedule." Finn fiddled with his thick gloves. "There are caves along the way where we rest. Jedrek crossed years ago when they came from Ebonrun to take back Japhia against King Raoul. He said if you can get past the cold, it's a sight worth seeing."

"Right, right," Calla remembered the story. She hopped on her horse with little struggle. They couldn't find her mare after the attack, but Jedrek and Vihaan gave her a new horse that morning. This new mare wasn't as sweet as her previous one, but she would do.

"Nervous?" The guide limped into the space between them.

"A little." Calla gave him a tiny smile. "It's my first crossing."

"Have no fear! I'm the best guide there is," he shouted against the howling wind, "The name is Jack Ramte the fifth. I've led the crossings back and forth since I was a lad. Learned from my dad, he was the best." He rested his hand over his heart for a moment and looked to the sky. "May he rest peacefully with the deities." He dropped his hand, and there was a glimmer in his eye. "And might I say, it is an honor to assist the Hybrid in her journey. Remember my name, Jack Ramte the fifth. When the scribes record the events of your glorious victory against The Corrupted, I want my name in there." He winked at Calla.

"Of course, Jack." Finn rolled his eyes. "Are we set to leave?"

Jack mumbled something incoherent and fumbled with a key in his pocket. "Saddle up everyone, we're leaving!" He shouted as he limped over to the massive gate.

Calla waved to Jedrek and Zula. Bundled under furs, up against her mother's skin, was Saria. Calla missed the baby's soft skin and big eyes already.

Vihaan rode up to her, "Have I ever told you that I hate the snow?"

"No," she laughed. Finn turned away to mount his horse. Even though Finn made his exit quick, Calla didn't miss the scowl on his face.

"Well," he gave her a sarcastic look, "I hate the snow. I much prefer the sun and warmth."

"I could use a little warmth right now..." A screeching noise caught her attention as Jack pulled the gate open. Calla gave a sultry look to Vihaan, and he matched it. When Jack whipped the reins of his horse, it broke them from their intimate moment.

Calla watched Jedrek and Zula descend back towards town, which sat below the end of a slight hill. She took a deep breath. "Do this for Saria, Zula, and Jedrek," she whispered. After the group had passed through the iron gates, Jack dismounted and locked the entrance behind them. The seemingly impassable mountains towered over her. The more people she met, the more she realized that they all were depending on her. She had to do this.

Snow covered their path upwards before dipping into the valley below. Calla couldn't tell if it was snowing or just being blown off the mountains. She would have stopped to admire the mountains, but Finn kept them moving at a fast pace.

Jack wasn't thrilled about Finn setting such an arduous pace, but he tried pointing out features to her as they went along. The thick scarves over Calla's and Vihaan's mouths prevented them from conversing much. She couldn't shake the heavy feeling that settled in her stomach since they crossed the gates. Flashes of the dream where she was running from the thorns to the mountains were relentless. Calla wanted the crossing to be over as soon as possible.

After they had traveled for a good part of the day, their path had plateaued. Jack slowed the convoy. "There's a cave up ahead! Only a few more minutes," Jack announced. "We'll stay there until daybreak tomorrow. Then we descend into the valley."

Vihaan perked up as he pulled down his scarf, "Jack?"

The guide turned despite the wind that whipped his face. "Aye?"

"With all this time to think, why the guide, the gates, and the lock? Is the valley that dangerous?"

"It used to be," Jack answered. "The controlled crossings started during The First War of Midelle. When we won, people were free to cross as they wished and if they wanted, they could pay for a guide. With the return of The Corrupted, King Nakosi ordered the Shimmers to control all of the crossings."

"I see," Vihaan said. Jack stopped before a wide-mouthed cave and signaled for everyone else to stop. Finn looked ahead for trouble.

"We're here!" Jack shouted. He slid off his horse and led the group inside. Everyone followed suit, eager to get out of the wind.

Calla waded through the snow into the cave. Her feeling of dread intensified with each step. She looked around the interior of the cavern. The main part of the cave was empty except for a fire pit in the middle. Thick logs provided seating around it. To the far left long wooden stakes penetrated the stone and beyond that lay only the dark abyss of the cave.

"Tie your horses up, I have hay for them. They get fed first since they do the hard work." Jack's laugh echoed deep into the chasm.

Soon the horses were tied and grazing on the hay. Calla, desperate for warmth, grabbed the flint and steel and hunched over the fire pit.

"I don't think I'll ever warm up," Lena remarked as she threw kindling into the fire pit and sat down next to Calla.

Calla looked at the kindling. "Right. Fires need wood."

"Ever start a fire before?" Zenji joked.

Calla rubbed the flint and steel together, her eyebrows furrowed in frustration. She finally sighed, letting the tools roll out of her hands. "One that actually burned? Can't say that I have."

Finn rolled his eyes at Calla and scooped up the flint and steel. "It's easy."

Sparks flew onto the kindling when Finn scrapped the steel along the flint. Calla replied, "Maybe for you." Smoke rose from the kindling and a small fire caught. Finn smirked and Calla rolled her eyes in response.

"The storm is picking up," Bear, or his brother, Wolfe stated as they carried a few small game animals. "Jack, I reset the traps for your trip back. Those rabbits won't ever learn." Jack nodded his thanks and turned back to his horse. Calla was sure it was Bear who dropped the rabbits in front of her. Their dark glassy eyes stared at her, and Calla frowned back. "Never skinned a rabbit before?"

The travelers in the cave laughed at her in light jest. She looked to Vihaan for help, but even he was biting back a smile. Calla's mouth dropped to show the betrayal playfully and to hide the sting.

"Can't start a fire, can't skin rabbits," Finn mused. He grabbed the dead rabbits by their ears to hand them off to the other brother, Wolfe, who went to the entrance of the cave with a thick knife and a mission. Finn closed a makeshift door to block the howling winds from entering the cave.

Zenji popped in to sit around the fire. "And your snoring is quite distracting when we're trying to get a moment of sleep."

Calla gasped, mortified. "I don't snore!" She looked at Vihaan, who only shrugged his shoulders and smiled. She huffed and crossed her arms. "What gives? Everyone is picking on me today." The group was only smiling at her, but Jack broke first. His howls of laughter filled the cave, and everyone else followed suit, except Calla.

Vihaan passed her, winked, and placed a tiny kiss on the top of her head. She straightened her shoulders back in defiance of the laughter. "Well, since everyone thinks I'm useless... Is there anything I can do to help?"

Jack popped his head out from behind his dark horse, still chuckling to himself. He dropped a wooden bucket in front of the horse. "The horses need freshwater. There's a stream further back in the cave. All you need to do is dip the bucket in the water. It's really..."

She grabbed the bucket from the ground. "I think I can handle filling a bucket."

Calla stared into the dark abyss of the cave, and that feeling of dread washed over he again. She grabbed an unlit torch and touched it in the now roaring fire. She carried the flickering light into the dark depths of the cave. That dread got heavier with each step she took towards the darkness, but Calla kept on. She'd had tons of bad feelings before that never amounted to anything, and she hoped this was no different. Soon, her torch was the only source of light, and she heard the trickling of the small stream Jack mentioned.

"Hybrid?" A soft voice whispered in the air. Calla did a full turn looking for the voice, but saw no one. Whispers started to fill Calla's head, all inaudible. They got louder whenever she faced the back of the cave. In a trance, Calla followed the whispers, but she wasn't scared. She became curious as she followed the stream and the whispers. The deeper she went into the darkness, the more walls closed in until finally her path was blocked.

"Calla?" A voice echoed. She turned, and the whispers stopped. Lena came around the corner with a torch and bucket of her own. "You didn't have to go this far into the cave for freshwater, you know."

Calla dropped to her knees and dipped the bucket into the water. "Fresh from the source." She gave Lena a nervous smile. "Did Jack not trust me to get water?"

Lena dipped her bucket into the stream. "No, the horses need more than one bucket."

"Oh good. I'm deemed worthy to fetch water for horses," Calla remarked with a tartness.

Lena rested a hand on Calla's shoulder, "We're only having a little fun."

"At my expense!"

"Come on now. The horses are thirsty." Calla followed Lena to the main cavern. She gave the darkness a parting glance, wondering if she was imagining the whispers. Calla hadn't heard them since she was in Japhia when they led her to the run-down apothecary.

After the convoy had their fill of roast rabbit, everyone spread out and tried to get some rest. Soft rays of the twilight crept through cracks in the makeshift door. A welcoming warmth emanated from the fire. Not so long ago Calla would not have thought it possible that she'd have to shed some of her thicker layers to adjust for the heat.

Gentle snores softly echoed through the cave. Jack sat by the fire. He carved something out of wood while he softly whistled a lively tune. Finn seemed to have dozed off, facing the door with his back to everyone. Calla knew better than to think he was sleeping. As far as she could tell, he never slept. Lena and Zenji slept by the fire. Their backs rested together, and they looked more comfortable than Calla was. She was near the back end of the cave, far away from everyone else. She tried one position after another to get comfortable, all to no avail. The cave walls were bumpy, hard, and sharp in too many places to be good for sleeping against. An aggravated sigh pushed through her lips. She readjusted away from a sharp rock that had dug into her shoulder.

"Come here," Vihaan said without opening his eyes. He patted his chest and spread out his legs. The temptation of being close to him coursed through her. He too had shed some layers, and the chain holding his ring was visible through the opening in his shirt.

Calla sighed shortly, still annoyed from his teasing earlier, "I'm fine. It's just this one part by my shoulder…"

Jack's fast-paced whistling stopped, and he looked up from his wood chunk. "Stop being stubborn and accept his offer." He shook his head, "Women."

Calla opened her mouth to say something, but Jack went back to whistling and carving. With a huff, Calla scooted over and sat between Vihaan's legs. She leaned back onto his chest. His arms wrapped around her stomach to hug her tight. He let his head rest against the rocks while Calla got comfortable in his arms.

Once more Calla closed her eyes. In Vihaan's half-asleep stupor he whispered, "I love you." She blushed at his words, not used to hearing them yet, and her stomach flipped with this strange feeling. She'd never loved someone past her mom and Felicia, but that's a different kind of love. This had to be the type of love that people yearned for their whole lives. She allowed her body to fully relax as she listened to the airy song that the wind and whistle provided.

Jack's whistling hit a sharp crescendo then the notes fell in dissonant chords. Calla did her best to ignore the eerie tune. She forced herself to focus on sleep. A soft yet deep rumble shook the cave. Calla sprung up from Vihaan's arms, wide awake. Her eyes connected with Jack's for a moment before their curious eyes roamed the walls of the cave.

Calla grabbed his arm and urgently whispered, "Vihaan, wake up!"

Vihaan jolted upright just as another rumble rippled through the cave. The others woke up in startled confusion.

"What's going on?" Corbin got to his feet by the horses and drew his sword.

"Nothing good, I can tell you that." Jack sprang up to untie the horses. "Get out now!"

Vihaan helped Calla up, pulling her flush with him, "Stay close to me." Calla nodded her head while a stronger rumble ripped through the cave. Bits of stone fell from the top of the cave to pelt everyone's heads. Vihaan led Calla to their horses, grabbed her hips, and threw her up on her horse.

Next to her, Finn jumped on his horse, "Calla, go!" A deep and loud roar echoed throughout the cave. Finn's eyes snapped to her for just a moment, "Now!"

A whirlwind of movement spun around Calla, but she was frozen in place on top of a horse ready to flee with or without her.

Finn reached over and gave a firm slap to her horses hind quarter. With that encouragement, Calla's horse made a bee-line for the exit, and Calla snapped back to reality.

"Go!" Jack shouted from his horse as he bolted forward, knocking down the splintered door. Bear and Wolfe disappeared into a faded glow of twilight swirled with snow. Lena, Corbin, and Zenji followed the brothers. A chunk of rock fell from the ceiling where Calla and Vihaan had been sleeping. "Head to the woods!" Jack yelled at the entrance to the cave. He looked back at the convoy with wide-eyes, "Let's go! I haven't lost anyone yet!"

"Come on Calla!" Finn kept his horse in line with Calla's.

The four of them burst from the cave. As Jack predicted, the cave opening's overhang detached from the mountain. It crumbled into large shards of stone, blocking the entrance to the cave. Finn, Calla, Vihaan, and Jack raced towards the opening in the woods, where the others waited. Strong winds drove the snow against their faces and the cold pierced Calla's skin. She shielded her eyes to keep the wind driven snow from blocking her vision.

A large flying figure dipped down in front of them and screeched. Calla's horse bucked to a stop and threw Calla off into the deep snow. "Vihaan!" Calla scrambled to her feet. The wind whipped snow all around her. She turned all around her, but everyone was gone... Vihaan, Finn, Jack, and her horse. "Not again!" She wrapped her arms around herself to stay warm, since her heavy furs were crushed under tons of stone back in the cave. Snow seeped into her boots, shocking her feet. "Help!" Her cry immediately got lost in the howling wind.

A deep and terrorizing roar rumbled from the sky, and Calla froze. Her eyes darted around the sky, but all she could see in any direction was white. "F-Finn?" Calla trembled when a huge figure hovered over her. She took off running but agile claws wrapped around her body, and Calla's feet left the ground. She screamed and pounded on the claws that imprisoned her.

"Calla!" Finn rode in fast on his horse. He looked up at the large creature in shock. Large wings flapped and the beast roared again.

"Help!" Calla screamed trying to pry the claws away from her.

Finn fought his terrified horse to stay put. He managed to stand on the unsteady saddle, and in desperation, Finn jumped. One hand managed to latch onto the foot that trapped her.

"What is this thing!" Calla pounded on the claw again.

"I don't know," Finn shouted as they ascended higher and higher. The free foot of the creature wrapped around Finn. Calla grabbed onto his arms as if her life depended on it. It probably did.

The creature roared, then ripped back its leg that held Finn. His hand slid from Calla's and through the heavy snow and wind, she could no longer see or hear him.

In desperation, she used her powers, but she couldn't focus from the chaos of the moment. She saw a chunk of mountainside explode in a loud bang through the blizzard. She didn't know if that was her doing. Her powers were still a mystery to her.

With every second that she used her powers, her energy drained away faster. With the wind, the cold, and her drained energy she knew she was about to pass out. In her fading vision, she heard someone call her name at a distance.

"Vihaan?" She saw him on the ground getting smaller and smaller, calling after her. Calla fought to stay awake and keep her sight on Vihaan. As she predicted, she fell unconscious in the creature's grasp seconds later.

Calla's eyes flicked open, and her body sat up in a jolt. "Vihaan?" A soft blanket covered her on a large bed, but wherever she was, the heat was overwhelming, and she was sweating.

"You're awake," Finn said in a breathless tone, coming out into the room from what looked like a bathroom. He had already shed his heavy mountain clothes. He looked comfortable in light pants and a tan short-sleeved tunic. His powerful arms crossed in front of him. He seemed relaxed, almost happy for once.

Calla looked around the room, it was large with high ceilings and very spacious. The walls were bare but had a texture like the cavern. There were no immediate windows, but slats at the top of the room let in some moonlight and drifts of snow. The cold and snow had no chance making it down to them from the sheer heat in the room emanating from strategically placed torches. She brought her attention back to Finn. "Where are we? What happened on the mountain? Where's everyone else? Why are you so calm?" Calla asked the questions in rapid-fire.

"One at a time please," Finn said with an annoyed look.

Calla sucked in a breath, "Where are we?"

"Inside the Edulis Mountains." Finn came closer to the bed.

Calla threw back the blanket, but she was still hot in her thick clothes. "I wasn't expecting that answer." Calla took a few seconds to take in her new surroundings again. "What happened out there?" She looked up at Finn in a panic, "Where is Vihaan? Jack? Everyone?"

"That's four questions," Finn noted as he sat on the edge of the bed.

"Give me a break." Calla sighed while she slid off her thick snow pants. She was thankful that Zula made her wear a thin pair of pants underneath.

Finn rolled his eyes and gave Calla another annoyed look. "Yeah, about that," Finn stalled as he raked a hand through his fiery hair, "the dragons picked…"

"Dragons?" Calla froze with one of her thick damp wool socks half off, her eyes wide in shock. "I thought they were all gone."

"Yes, Calla. Dragons. Can you listen for once?" Finn took her heavy clothing away from between them to move closer. She didn't like him being so close, something stirred in her stomach. "They've been hiding all these years in the mountains, awaiting the Hybrid to return. When they saw you on the mountain, one came to retrieve you, so they could bring you back here. It would have been just you but… I'm supposed to protect you, no matter what. Wherever you go, I go…" He gave her a cheeky smile.

"We need to go back for…" She thought about the next word, "…everyone."

"Absolutely not. They're offering to fly us to Cape Toria. Do you know how long it would take them?"

Calla shook her head trying to think of ways to get back to the convoy.

"A day. One day of flying and we'd be there. We would get there and back to the Capital before the convoy even left East Shimmer."

"How do you know all this?" Calla got up and stretched. Her muscles were tight from her unexpected ride.

Finn smirked, it continued to stir deep within Calla, she wasn't sure if she liked it or not. "Unlike you, I didn't pass out when they brought us here and their Emissary explained everything to me. There's a friend here who's quite anxious to see you again."

"See me? Who? I was trying to use my powers, but all I did was knock myself out, can you blame me?" Calla huffed while crossing her arms. "Plus, I thought we were in danger. What about the convoy? And who's the friend?"

"Stop with the barrage of questions!" Finn got off the bed, and Calla's stomach stopped stirring. "After I asked, a dragon revisited them to explain the situation to them. He hasn't returned yet to follow up. I did send the dragon with the extra portal, so the convoy could go back to Japhia and be safe."

Calla closed her eyes and wished for Vihaan to be here. She touched her chest where the ring was, and it was gone. Her eyes flew open as she patted down her chest, pockets and everywhere else. "Where is it?"

Finn gave her a quizzical look. "Where is what?"

Calla knew telling him would make his temper erupt. She didn't trust Finn to understand. "Nothing." She broke eye contact with him because she knew he would prod for answers. Calla looked around for windows, but forgot they were inside a mountain range. "So, what's the plan now?" All she could think about was Vihaan and fighting The Corrupted. The room felt like it was closing in.

Finn crossed his arms, leaning back onto one of the bedposts. "They are planning a celebration for you tonight, and then offered to fly us to Cape Toria in the morning. We'd be there by nightfall, Calla."

The long-ignored thought of fighting Belladonna seeped into her head faster than she could block it. Her breathing became shallow at the thought.

"I prefer a quiet night for us. Tomorrow will be a long day. Don't you agree?"

Calla stood in the cavernous room, letting everything settle in. It was all so overwhelming. Her eyes fell on the bathroom that Finn came out of. "I'll be right back. I need a minute," Calla said with a wavering voice.

"Are you okay?" He came to her side in an instant.

Calla held out her arm to keep him from touching her, "I'm fine. I just... Please." Her legs carried her faster towards the bathroom. Once her feet hit the cold stone, she locked the door and slid down against it. Her head fell in her hands while she feared for what was to come.

If all this was true, she would be fighting The Corrupted within a week, or two once Finn came up with a battle plan. She wasn't ready to fight, even if Vihaan was by her side. Everything was happening too quickly and to find out that dragons were real was the last straw. Calla shook her head and whispered, "Dragons." She sighed and rested the back of her head against the door, letting a small smile spread over her lips. "Holy shit."

Eighteen

"In," Calla wiped her face and took another deep breath, "and out." She was the Hybrid, and her duty was to save Midelle. Whether she liked it or not.

She took one last deep breath and left the bathroom. Finn stood up from a chair by the bed and opened his mouth. "What is it?" Calla asked harshly with crossed arms. "I'm honestly not in the mood to be berated by you."

"I was going to ask if you're okay but fine. I don't care." Finn threw his hands up in the air.

Calla sighed to herself, "I'm sorry." It was a whisper, but she knew Finn heard it by the way his body relaxed. "All of this is terrifying."

A knock on the door cut off Finn's reply. Calla and Finn turned to the door. "Pardon my intrusion, Captain Quinn," a silvery and feminine voice pierced the door, "but is the Hybrid awake?" Finn looked to Calla, and she nodded. She was curious to see a dragon.

Finn put on his Captain-Of-The-Guards mien and opened the door.

A tall woman with bright purple eyes and an excited look on her face filled the frame. She seemed older than Calla. Her silky white-blonde hair reached her waist and iridescent white scales lined her hairline down to her neck. Her simple periwinkle dress molded to her shapely body. A circlet of gold and opals sat upon her platinum blonde head.

"Lady Amethyst," Finn stepped aside with a deep bow, then extended an arm to Calla, "May I introduce the Hybrid, Lady Calla Moro."

Lady Amethyst took a tentative step into the room. She towered over Finn and Calla. Her eyes held Calla's, and Calla knew that this woman was important. She had expected an actual dragon to walk through the door, so this was a pleasant surprise.

Lady Amethyst curtsied. "Hybrid, welcome to the Edulis Mountains, the secret sanctuary of the remaining dragons of Midelle. I am the Emissary, Lady Amethyst. I hope Captain Quinn has explained a few things to you."

Calla attempted her pathetic excuse of a curtsy. After all this time in Midelle, she was no better than the first night she came here. "Lady Amethyst, I thank you for your hospitality." Calla swallowed. Her throat was suddenly dry. She played with her fingernails, "Captain Quinn has informed me of the situation. Has your messenger returned from our convoy?"

"He did. And one of Captain Finn's men was insistent that he come back here." She chortled lightly with her hand covering her lips.

"He's here?" Calla's eyes widened. Finn scowled.

"No. I had planned on Alec bringing only you back here." Her eyes narrowed in on Finn. "The vampire was an unexpected," her lips tightened, "surprise." Calla exhaled and her heart deflated, but she managed to keep a gentle smile on her face. She hoped it didn't look forced.

Finn cleared his throat. "When will your warrior be ready to leave?" He glanced at Calla, "We're anxious to reach Cape Toria. We should forgo the celebration to leave as soon as possible."

Lady Amethyst smiled and crossed her hands in front of her. "Captain Quinn, I thought you wanted to leave at dawn's first light? We've already started preparations for the celebration. It shouldn't be more than a few hours."

Calla heard a low growl in Finn's throat. "We can't leave tonight?" The tone of his voice was calm, but Calla knew he was anything but.

"I don't think a tiny celebration would hurt anyone. And a proper night's rest would do us both good." Calla placed a hand on Finn's arm.

"See? The Hybrid agrees." Lady Amethyst gestured to Calla.

"We will stay the night, but no celebration. It's not necessary. Thank you, Lady Amethyst."

Calla's smile evaporated.

Finn pointed his sharp gaze back to Lady Amethyst. "Getting to the library of Midelle is..."

"Important," Lady Amethyst finished. Finn nodded in agreement. "But I must insist. You're already here. Saving the realm can wait a few hours. We've been waiting for the Hybrid to return for so many years. Inside a mountain no less."

"Thirty years," Calla whispered, piecing together timelines. "The Hybrid could use a break."

Finn's face burned. A cheeky smile was Calla's reply. "We should rest," Finn said again, more demanding this time.

"You can rest. I will attend the celebration," Calla decided as she looked at the dragon. "I can't wait, Lady Amethyst."

Lady Amethyst clapped her hands together with a wide smile, "Wonderful! Please take some time to enjoy the Edulis Mountains. The celebration will be at the evening meal in the main cavern. Do not fear here, for you are safe. I can promise you that. You can be free from the Captain's humorless eyes." Calla wanted to speak more with Lady Amethyst. Her intense presence and piercing gaze that was currently lasered in on Finn made her rethink her fleeting whim.

"We're elated for your return, and we want to help in any way we can. When you explore, please forgive our excitement. It's been thirty years since we retreated into these mountains. Some whelps have never been outside the caverns, and some are forgetting what it's like to fly freely." Lady Amethyst took a step backward. She nodded her head, and her eyes sparkled with tears. "Forgive me for my rambling, you know what is at stake. I will take my leave now, again, please adventure out into the cavern. We dragons have nothing to hide. Ask for me if you find yourself in need of anything."

"Of course." Finn failed to hide his annoyance.

"Thank you, Lady Amethyst." Calla butchered another curtsy. Lady Amethyst left and the door clicked shut behind her.

Calla looked at Finn once the door shut, "She's a dragon?"

Finn nodded, "They can shift."

"Are they all that gorgeous?" Calla asked while Finn rolled his eyes. "I mean, she was breathtaking!"

Finn crossed his arms, "And also incredibly arrogant. You didn't pick up on that?"

"Maybe to you, but I," she stretched out her arms and spun completely around before him, "am the Hybrid."

"All this fame is going to your head." Finn frowned and shook his head.

Calla laughed, "Oh please, I am the humblest Hybrid ever."

"You're the only Hybrid ever."

She shrugged, "By default that makes me the humblest."

"And the least humble," Finn chuckled sarcastically. "Come on, we should at least walk around if you're feeling up to it." His face softened and he held his hand out to her. Calla gave him a curious look then raised an eyebrow at Finn, this was very unlike him.

"Fine," He muttered, taking his hand back and opening the door to her, "suit yourself."

"I'm not leaving, I'm like half-dressed and I have no shoes on!" She looked around the room and only saw Finn's messenger bag. He brought it everywhere with him. "Where is our stuff?"

"Inside the cavern still. Under heaps of stone. When I spoke with Lady Amethyst earlier, she told me that there were things you could wear in that closet." Finn pointed to a narrow closet at the far end of the room. "I'll be outside the door. Try not to take forever."

Calla took a step towards the closet and joked, "I must look good, I am the Hybrid after all."

Finn stuck his head through the half open doorway, "Humble my ass." He shut the door.

Calla turned to refute him but found only the shut door.

She looked over the contents of the closet. After a short deliberation Calla pulled out a short-sleeved, dark red dress, and simple slip-on sandals. The sandals were a touch too big, but she'd manage. Calla changed quickly and ran her fingers through her hair. She brought her hands out in front of her to look over her hands. The gloves were still as pristine the day she got them. The glover who made them had incredible talent.

Lady Amethyst's words echoed in her head. Calla bit her lip and then peeled off the gloves. There was a slight tan line near her wrist from all those days traveling. The sigil was the same dark peach color it had always been, but part of her would always see it glowing. Another reminder of what was at stake.

She went to grab the necklace that held the ring from Vihaan but remembered it was gone. Checking all her clothing for the ring, she was positive it must have broken back on the mountain. She didn't need it, but now that Vihaan was back on the mountain and Calla inside of it, the ring would have been comforting to have. She missed him already and could only imagine how upset he was.

"You okay in there?" Finn asked through the door.

"Yeah! I'm coming."

Calla stepped outside and everything came into view. She moved past Finn in amazement. They were on a high ring balcony that encircled the vast cavern. Dragons of all colors and sizes flew in the vast openness of the cavern. Some had shifted into human form, carrying on mundane tasks below.

A marketplace bustling with merchants occupied in the center of the cavern floor. Tall torches stood over everything to spread a warm glow and be the main source of light. Smaller torches filled in where there were gaps of light. Up above, moonlight shone through tiny holes in the mountain peaks. Calla stared wide eyed with a wild smile on her face. "Finn, do you see this?"

"I do. I never could imagine anything like this. It's amazing," Finn said, coming next to Calla. He turned his head to her, "Beautiful, in fact."

A dark green dragon glided past them with its wings extended. Calla gripped the railing to watch the dragon shift in the blink of an eye and have his feet land on the cavern floor. A sturdy man with dark hair melded into the crowds. "Did you see that?" Calla gasped.

"How could you miss it?" He started to step away from Calla to a stone staircase, "Are you coming? There's someone who wants to see you."

Calla looked back to Finn, "The friend?" She followed Finn down the stairs, but she couldn't contain her excitement. Calla had not felt safe for so long she wanted to burst past him, but she was so used to him leading her everywhere it would be odd at this point.

Finn turned around, still descending the stairs but at a slower pace. He stopped when his eyes fell on her hand on the wall. "Where are your gloves?" His question was harsh.

"Lady Amethyst said I'm safe here. You heard her." Calla brought her hand close to her chest. "Everyone knows I'm the Hybrid. There's no hiding it here."

"Did I say you could take them off? Remember the rules?" Finn scowled as he grabbed her wrist, "We know nothing about this place or how safe it is." He lowered his voice, "I don't trust any of them and neither should you."

"I'm not one of your guards," Calla hissed as she fought for her hand back. "You can't order me around!"

Finn let go and Calla fell back on the stone stairs. "Protect yourself then." Calla sat upon the stair, holding her marked hand close to her. She watched Finn stalk away and disappear into the crowd. She got up, brushed off her dress and continued down the stairs, determined to forget Finn's outburst.

The main floor was even busier than it seemed from the upper ring with dragons coming and going on feet and wings. A pang of guilt ran through her when she didn't see Finn, but she was safe here. She could feel that she was. The feeling of dread was gone. She thought it was best to let him sulk. Hopefully, he'd come around before the celebration.

The marketplace was full of exotic wares she'd never seen before. Every part of the Mountains intrigued Calla, especially the dragons. She would never get tired of watching them shift from a magnificent flying beast to a gorgeous human. Everyone towered over her, except the children. Calla stood out like a sore thumb, but it was like the dragons didn't see her. They carried on, preparing for the celebration.

Walking along a row of potters, delicate porcelains and ceramics caught her eye. She stopped to admire their craftsmanship from afar. She looked down, and there was a young dragon in front of her with a bouquet of pink flowers.

"Why hello there." Calla smiled as she bent down to meet the child at eye-level.

Excitement sparkled in the girl's deep amber eyes. She brushed her brown hair from her face then hid her face behind the flowers.

"What's your name?" Calla asked. "Mine is Calla."

The girl brought the bouquet down a little to show tan scales around her hairline. "Luella," she giggled through the flowers. "These are for you!" Luella held out the flowers and smiled a toothy grin.

Calla took the flowers and inhaled the sweet scent. They resembled rosy, pink daisies overflowed with petals. "Thank you, Luella." Calla smiled back at the little dragon.

"You're the Hybrid, right?" Luella asked with an innocence that stole Calla's heart.

"Yes, I am the Hybrid." The statement flowed off Calla's tongue with ease.

"Hybrid?" A woman, who was nearby, asked as her attention tore away from the lump of clay on her potters' wheel. People stopped what they were doing and looked in Calla's direction. Soon all were whispering with excitement.

"Finally," an older male with teal scales set down a heavy barrel with a loud thud, "she's awake!"

A crowd started to form around Calla. She looked around at the excited faces of the crowd. "Hello. I'm Calla Moro, the Hybrid."

"We've been waiting for so long!" A female voice shouted from the crowd. Calla brought Luella in close, afraid she might get trampled.

"Is it true you're from the human realm?" Another voice shouted from the crowd.

"Why did you wait so long to return?"

"What's the human realm like?"

"Are you going to kill all The Corrupted?"

Calla didn't know what question to answer. Now she knew what Finn felt like when she barraged him with questions.

A sharp bang snapped everyone's head to look at the source of the noise. "Leave her be." The crowd parted for an elderly man who hobbled up on a dark wooden cane. He stopped a few feet before Calla, and everyone was quiet. The man had dark scales on his face and down into his tunic. When Calla's eyes met his hazel ones, she smiled. Finn was right, he was an old friend. "We meet again," he laughed with a gentle wheeze at the end.

"That we do, Sigmund," Calla replied, meeting him the rest of the way.

"Go about your business!" Sigmund announced with a wave of his free hand. With hesitance, the dragons dispersed. Most glanced back at Calla.

Luella tugged on Calla's dress, "Does that mean me too?"

"I think you could be very helpful in the main cavern." Sigmund raised an eyebrow at her.

Luella nodded her head. "I was so excited to meet Lady Calla, even though Lady Amethyst told us to leave her alone."

"Luella!" A woman called through the crowd, stopping shy of the trio. The woman, who Luella was a spitting image of, grabbed the little girl's hand and bowed to Calla. "Forgive me Hybrid, my sister was being a little whelp and ran off to see you. She must have forgotten Lady Amethyst's announcement to not overwhelm the Hybrid." The older sister gave Luella a stern look.

Calla smiled, "It's quite alright. Please, call me Calla. Luella is so sweet." She raised the bouquet as proof.

"When she's not chewing on the bones at dinner," the sister joked. "We'll let you be, Lady Calla." The older sister's cheeks grew red as Luella fought her grasp.

"We'll sit by the stream, it's peaceful there," Sigmund said as he walked towards the corner of the market. "I'm sure you have a few questions."

"Goodbye! It was nice to meet you!" Calla waved to the sisters before she caught up to the elder dragon, "A few?" Calla laughed. "Try hundreds of questions."

"Sit." Sigmund sat on a crude stone bench. Calla sat next to him and was silent as he took deep breaths. "I am not the young dragon

I used to be." He chuckled to himself. "Now," he looked to Calla, "Where to start?"

Calla looked at his bright hazel eyes, "What were you trying to say in the woods?"

Sigmund pointed his old, trembling finger at Calla. "Let me start by explaining why I was there. Weeks ago, the whole realm shook, that was when you sent the signal to tell the King that you were ready to return to Midelle." Calla wanted to interject to tell him what really had happened, but she knew it wouldn't matter. "The prophecy foretold that part, but King Nakosi hid you so well. Everyone doubted that the Hybrid had returned."

"Wait," Calla held up a hand, "How do you know all this?"

"I knew I was forgetting a part." He mumbled something to himself. "When Midelle felt your signal, I volunteered to come out of our sanctuary to wait for more signs. It was to ensure that you had returned."

"But why are the dragons even hiding? Everyone thinks that you no longer exist."

"You see, we dragons are very powerful. During the First War of Midelle hundreds of years ago, it wasn't about the grit of the people or the deities. It was who had the most dragons on their side, and that was the people of Midelle.

When King Raoul became corrupted thirty years ago, disappearances began again. We dragons knew we had to hide, to protect Midelle against ourselves. We fled inside the mountain to where we've worked to bring it to what it is today." Sigmund paused, his face tightened, and he gripped his cane harder. "Forgive me, I can't remember where I was going with that."

Calla rested a hand over his, "It's okay Sigmund. I'm following along just fine. I asked why the dragons were hiding because you mentioned you came out of hiding to go to the capital."

"Oh right, yes." He took a deep breath in and out. "I volunteered because I am two-hundred and fifteen years old." Calla's eyes went wide. "I look good for two-hundred and fifteen, don't you think?" He chortled. "If I were to fall to The Corrupted, what use would I be to them?"

"Your wisdom would be of use to them," Calla said with encouragement.

Sigmund waved his hand and made a bored face, "Don't flatter me, Lady Calla. I may be the elder of the dragons, but I'm no fool. Where were we?"

"You volunteered because you are the elder." More light peeked through the openings in the mountain top. Moonlight splashed over them. Dark flowers by the bank of the stream opened to accept the lunar rays.

"Yes of course. I needed to see the Hybrid with my own eyes. I was to approach you in the capital, but then The Corrupted attacked. By the time I found you again, you were being carried back to the castle. I needed to warn you about The Corrupted. To do that, I followed your group where I thought it would be a good idea to approach you. But that vampire filth Captain of yours was being paranoid."

Calla winced at his choice of words. "Warn me?"

"I wanted to tell you that you can kill off the bottom layer of The Corrupted, but it is pointless unless you kill their leader. Until their Queen is dead, they will never stop."

Calla nodded, "I believe that was the plan. We've figured out the leader's name. Belladonna?"

"Belladonna..." Sigmund whispered as he rubbed his chin in thought.

"Grandfather?" A tall and muscular man came out from the crowds. He was taller than both Calla and Sigmund. Green scales lined his face around the same eyes that Sigmund had. She recalled that he was the same man that she saw transform outside her room. Calla dropped her eyes from him, she didn't need a handsome dragon mucking up already murky waters.

"Alec," Sigmund shouted even though he was feet away. "Come meet the Hybrid."

The dragon came closer and smiled. It was slightly crooked but still a very handsome smile. His hair was black and long enough to tie back into a tiny ponytail. Calla was drawn to the thick muscles that rippled beneath the short sleeves of Alec's shirt. A faint blush fell over his cheeks when he stopped before Calla and stumbled over his words.

"Speak!" Sigmund commanded with a grandfather-like tone. A whack to the leg with his cane made Alec bow with grace.

"Forgive me, Hybrid," he spoke as he straightened up. "I am Alec Greenmoore, great-great-grandson of Fiero Greenmoore, Hero of the First War of Midelle."

"The Hybrid doesn't care for your titles," Sigmund scolded. "She's the Hybrid!

Calla held up a hand to Sigmund to shush him, "Calla Moro." She held out her hand to Alec. "It's nice to meet you, Alec Greenmoore." Alec shook her hand with just the right amount of pressure to flex his muscles. Calla kept her eyes firmly on his. "Great-great grandson of Fiero Greenmoore, Hero of the First War of Midelle," she tacked on while stifling a laugh.

"It is truly an honor to meet the Hybrid. I look forward to fighting alongside you in the battlefield against The Corrupted." Alec frowned when he noticed the color draining out of Calla's face.

"Aron would have loved this moment," Sigmund said, letting his shoulders drop forward.

Alec turned to his grandfather, "Enough about Aron, he's gone. I came here because the council has requested your presence. An urgent matter has come up." Calla felt bad for him, whoever Aron was, Calla could tell he was a sore subject.

"Can they do anything without me?" Sigmund grumbled while using his cane to lean on to get up. He looked at Calla, who was now standing by Alec.

"It's urgent. The council needs all members present to discuss the matter at hand." Alec backed away from the group. "Lady Calla Moro," he flashed a grin, "we will speak more at the celebration." He grabbed her hand and before she could process, placed a firm kiss in the middle of her sigil.

"I'm sure we will," Calla replied as she felt her cheeks redden. The men backed up to give each other space. Sigmund first transformed into a magnificent dragon with Alec following. Sigmund's scales were a darker green than Alec's, painted with time. White spikes lined his back and ghostly white whiskers his chin. Calla watched with wide eyes as Sigmund and Alec flapped their wings and soared away into another cavern.

"Making friends, I see?" Finn appeared from behind a storage shack piled with barrels of grain.

Calla's eyes narrowed. Finn leaned on the open shed, his arms crossed, and one leg set in front of the other.

"Like you care. Are you done being moody?" Calla scathed.

"No." He frowned. "You should be wearing your gloves. We can't be too careful."

Calla crossed her arms, cocked her hips, and raised an eyebrow. "You don't trust Lady Amethyst? She said we were safe here." Finn made a face, short of a scowl. Calla was amazed his face wasn't stuck in a permanent frown. "Wait." Calla held up a hand, cutting him off. "I know what you're going to say, you don't trust anyone."

"You can learn a thing or two."

Calla's mouth dropped with the insult, "Are you calling me stupid?"

"Did I say, 'Calla, you are stupid?'" Finn bit back.

Calla opened her mouth, poised to say something downright venomous, but then firmly shut it.

Finn waited another beat before turning away towards the crowd of the bazaar.

Calla snapped. "Go ahead, walk away! That's all you ever do!" Nearby dragons turned to her.

Finn stopped and spun on his heels. Their eyes locked in a storm of jade and ice. So much for keeping her mouth shut.

"Do you think I'd ever walk away from you?"

Calla took a sharp breath in, "You always have, from my first night in Midelle to now."

Finn rolled his eyes and smiled at her. That confusing, dangerous stirring came back even stronger. "You doubt me. King Nakosi appointed me to protect you, Calla, and I take it seriously." Finn came closer to her. "You may not see me, but I'm watching. Always, even when you think I'm not. Didn't think I saw you ogling that dragon? I wonder what your forest boyfriend will think. You are going to tell him?"

Calla gasped. Her cheeks flushed, but she remained silent.

"Didn't think so. Did Alec mention that he was the one who caused the cave to collapse?"

"He wouldn't," Calla replied.

"Alec could have killed us all."

"How do you know?"

Finn came a little closer. "Lady Amethyst apologized on his behalf while you were unconscious. She said Alec was impatient to bring you to safety. He wanted to flush us out. His superior thinking thought that collapsing the cave was the best way to accomplish that."

"You're lying." Finn threw his hands up in the air. She knew he wasn't, but a quick change of the subject wouldn't hurt. "What was it like to fly?"

"Hated it."

"What? Why?" Her voice was louder than she intended. Dragons nearby looked over with curiosity, most of them eager to meet the Hybrid.

"I hate heights. Okay?" Finn turned away from Calla.

Her heart swelled with... something she couldn't put her finger on.

Finn walked away with his long, fast strides.

"Wait," Calla called after him.

He stopped and turned around with a handsome smile that caught her off guard.

Part of Calla knew that if they were at each other's throats for the next few days, it was going to be miserable. She had to extend an olive branch as he had done all those weeks ago. "Care to escort me back to my room? I want to rest before the celebration. It's all a little overwhelming," Calla gestured around them with a small smile on her lips, "and I'm sure it will only get crazier."

Finn crooked out his arm as a gentleman would, "It would be my pleasure." Calla pushed away those thoughts of Vihaan doing the same thing as she entwined her arm around Finn's bicep. They walked back to her room in a comfortable silence as they absorbed the dragons' livelihoods in awe.

A voice inside her head was screaming. Never in her wildest daydreams did she imagine their relationship would boil down to this. But it needed to happen, it was the two of them, and they had to work together.

Finn left her at the door to her room. She tamped out the torches, blew out the candle on the table and settled on the bed. In the darkness she tucked herself underneath the blankets. Everything ran through her mind, Finn, her powers, dragons, the Oracle she was to meet, and Vihaan. There was a part of her, deep down in her, that could feel her stark betrayal towards Vihaan. He professed his love to her, put himself in danger, and how did she repay him? By ogling dragons and letting Finn's deranged charm get to her. How could Calla ever face him when she returned to Japhia? She hoped that Vihaan would understand.

Nineteen

Two men marched through the broken and damp corridor that led to their Queen Belladonna. It was dark, despite the moon rising fast overhead. Decrepit trees outside lined the cracked windows, scratching the glass when the wind blew. The man on the left held the torch, giving them enough light to walk through the crumbling castle. "Has Ash's party returned yet?"

The other man kept his dark red eyes looking forward but shook his head from side to side with a deep grunt.

"Ash was sure he'd capture the Hybrid and return swiftly." The torchbearer laughed with a cynical grin. "He wouldn't stop talking about it. On and on and on. He was too confident if you ask me. Do you know what our Queen says, eh, Bram? Confidence is the wine of the fool, but the water of the wise…"

The man on the right slammed the other man against the wall and caused him to drop the torch in a puddle. The fire hissed and smoke snaked into the air. "Malcolm, do you ever stop talking?"

Malcolm swallowed hard and stammered, "I...I...Well–"

"Speak! You idiotic–"

"There you two are," a dark feminine voice rang out from the other end of the corridor. Bram immediately let go of Malcolm, and they turned towards her voice. Their Queen, Belladonna, stood there with her most trusted guard, Abaddon.

The guards dropped to one knee in respect for her. Abaddon struck fear in everyone, corrupted or not. He was taller and stronger than any other soldier. His face was marred with ugly scars which only added to his intimidation factor. Bram had tried to get close to him once, but Abaddon hadn't thought twice about him. His loyalty was to the Queen and no one else. He was at her beck and call, rarely leaving the Queen's side.

"Stand." Belladonna wore a billowing grey gown with a crown of dead deity roses upon her cropped, angled black hair. She showed her age well, as only a few wrinkles were set on her face. But her eyes were alive with a red that mimicked the dark blood pooled in her brass chalice. Belladonna looked at the two groveling guards with disdain. A scowl rested on her face. "I went to visit my prisoner to find that he hadn't eaten today."

Malcolm's body shivered, and his lip quivered, "Well you see... My... My... Q... Queen..."

Belladonna held up her hand with gentle grace, "Bram, go feed my prisoner. He will need to be alive for our esteemed guest." A smile spread across her face, "We've been waiting quite some time for her arrival."

"Yes, My Queen," Bram immediately said as he got up, bowed, and made haste for the dungeons.

"Shove the food down his throat if necessary," Belladonna hissed. Bram nodded his head, then he disappeared around the corner that he and Malcolm came from.

Malcolm tried to stand up, but Belladonna gave Abaddon a pointed look. He stopped the guard with a strong hand to his chest. Malcolm looked up at Abaddon with a nervous look. "I need to feed him."

Belladonna laughed, "The two of you were not able to do your task. It seems one of you is useless. There will be no dead weight in my rule. Abaddon, take him to the dungeons. Bestow upon him the graciousness that he has given my prisoner."

Abaddon grabbed him by the back of his neck. Malcolm whimpered, "But my Queen..."

Belladonna studied the guard, her eyes narrowing. "Abaddon," She looked past Malcolm to meet eyes with her trusted guard, "I have changed my mind."

"Thank you." Malcolm sighed a breath of relief, but Belladonna only laughed. She gave Abaddon a dark look, and he returned it.

"Do with him as you will," Belladonna said after a smile spread across her lips. "Make him an example of what happens when orders are not followed."

"No!" Malcolm whispered with pure fear in his red eyes. Abaddon grunted, and his grip tightened as Malcolm began to struggle. "Queen Belladonna! Please! He refused to eat!"

"So, you disobey my orders to fulfill the desires of a prisoner?" Belladonna sneered at him with a wave of her hand. Abaddon dragged Malcolm away as she turned her back to them. The sound of his desperate screams fading down the corridor brought a smile to her face. She raised the chalice to her lips and peered out the window. A tiny crack of moonlight streamed through the trees. Savoring the sweet blood as the dark liquid slid down her throat, she let out a content sigh. "It's almost time, Hybrid."

Calla couldn't help but smile. The celebration was in full swing with food, music, and dancing in the main cavern. It must have been windy outside as drifts of snow would whip around the top of the cavern. The little wind and snow that came in didn't dampen the celebration one bit. Grand fire pits were lit to heat the cavern. Calla forgot all about the freezing temperature outside, in fact, she was a little warm.

She sat at the center of the long table. Lady Amethyst had insisted Calla take her spot. Lady Amethyst was to her left, Alec was on her right, and Sigmund was next to Alec. Much to Finn's dismay, he sat at the other end of the table on the other side of the opalescent Lady Amethyst.

Calla was scooping out the last of the honeyed yogurt with candied nuts when Lady Amethyst leaned towards her.

"I've been thinking, Lady Calla."

Calla raised an eyebrow, glancing quickly at Finn who was sulking over his yogurt. He ate none of it but instead kept pushing the yogurt around the bowl. Her eyes darted back to Lady Amethyst, "About?"

"What will you do once you defeat The Corrupted?" An older man with bright red scales and a bald head took the empty bowls from Calla and Lady Amethyst.

"Go home," Calla replied after the server backed away.

"To the human realm?" Her voice was slow, almost as if she was judging her answer. Calla knocked back the rest of her wine. It was nothing like she would buy in the store, but she missed the sweet tang of the alcohol. In combination with the heat, it made her cheeks flush.

"Yes." Calla knew some of it was the wine but talking about the human realm made her want to cry. She thought of Felicia coming home to no one.

"I don't mean to upset you, Lady Calla. That was never my intention, but I ask you to stay." Lady Amethyst's tone was neutral, almost diplomatic. Calla looked at her wide-eyed with her mouth parted in shock. Loud and fast music played on instruments she had never seen before. Dragons crowded the back of the cavern near the musicians and danced along in pairs with the music. "Alec is our strongest warrior, and he brought up a matter to the council that concerned you."

"Me...?" Calla stammered not wanting to turn and look at Alec. She could feel eyes burning into the back of her neck.

"Alec would like your hand in marriage."

Calla suddenly choked on nothing. Finn immediately looked at Calla with the little coloring on his face gone while her face grew red.

Lady Amethyst waited until Calla stopped coughing to speak again. "The council and I agree that this marriage would be advantageous for you and the dragons. Not to mention all Midelle would come together to celebrate the wedding. Dare I say, the event would be more popular than the King and Queen's wedding." A light chortle left her lips.

"No," Finn interjected immediately after he stood up. "The King forbids it." He flashed an angered look at Sigmund and Alec. Sigmund's face was tight, but Alec met his gaze with one that matched Finn's intensity.

Calla wanted to sink underneath the table and run far away from the building tension.

Lady Amethyst raised an eyebrow and turned towards Finn. "Is that so, vampire?" She cleared her throat. "Pardon me, Captain?"

"Yes," Calla replied before Finn did. Lady Amethyst turned back towards Calla with a surprised look on her face. Calla licked her lips before responding. "King Nakosi told me himself. My one and only duty is to the realm, and not my heart." She had no idea where that came from, or why she said anything.

Lady Amethyst's face turned sour. "Pity. Once we are free to roam the skies, I will have a word with King Nakosi myself. Alec is our finest warrior, your children would..."

"That's not necessary," Calla interjected. "I'm going back to the human realm after The Corrupted are gone, remember?"

"Won't you consider it?" Sigmund pleaded, which caught Calla off guard.

"Grandfather, Lady Amethyst," Alec cut in as he stood up. "Lady Calla hasn't declined my offer, only pushed her answer back." Calla went to say something, but Alec continued, "King Nakosi is wise on his part." He took a few steps to stop in front of Calla, "Please do me the honor of joining me for a dance? This song is a favorite among the dragons." His hand extended to her.

Calla looked up at a face that without a doubt belonged to a warrior. It had hard features, a jagged nose and covered in faded scars. "I can do you that honor." She dared not look over at Finn. Calla placed her hand in Alec's outstretched hand. He led her down the raised stone that they were on to weave around tables.

"Oh Sigmund, think of it," Lady Amethyst said with a dreamy sigh. The three of them watched the pair meld into the dancing crowd. "Alec will be the next Emissary of the dragons, and Calla is the Hybrid." She looked at Sigmund. "Can you imagine their marriage? Their children? Their powers? They would bring in a new era of creatures, superior to all others."

Finn slammed a hand on the table, unable to take any more. "Stop talking about her like you own her."

"Do you, vampire?" She hissed. Her dazzling purple eyes narrowed in on Finn, as did Sigmund's. "I'm surprised you are Captain of the Royal Guard. The honor has certainly lost its," a scowl formed over her lips, "...prestige."

"Once there's even a shred of light out in the morning, Calla and I are gone." Finn stewed in a mixture of anger and jealousy as he watched Calla spin into Alec's arms. Her smile was infectious, her cheeks still a bright red. "I don't care if we have to walk down the mountain ourselves."

Lady Amethyst chuckled, "No need to be rash, Captain. Alec will take you and Lady Calla to the forest outside Cape Toria at first light. It should be nightfall by the time you get there. He is swift."

"Thank you," Finn forced through his teeth. He rose, intending to leave the raised platform. He'd had his fill of dragons for the evening.

"While we clearly have different views of the Hybrid's future, we do have one thing in common." Sigmund's voice was calm.

Finn turned around with deep-set anger on his face. "What is that?"

"To rid Midelle of The Corruption."

Lady Amethyst added, "We haven't flown the skies in thirty years. Some of the whelps have never left the caverns. We all yearn to be back on our Isle. Leaving home broke my heart." Her eyes glistened with tears. "Protect her with your life once you get to the Cape. The Corrupted must be planning something. The whole realm knows the Hybrid has returned. It is still too dangerous for us to leave the mountains. If dragons become Corrupted, it would be the end of Midelle."

Finn nodded his head, "I always have and always will protect her with my life. It is my only duty." He left the platform without waiting for a reply.

Alec twirled Calla by her hand, then kept her in a loose embrace during the jovial dance. Calla watched from the corner of her eyes as Finn left the platform. He got lost through the crowds of towering dragons. "Everything fine?" Alec asked with his crooked smile while his thumb caressed her hand.

Calla's attention snapped back to the handsome dragon in front of her. "Yeah, I worry about Finn sometimes. He's... uh...." Calla shook her head and bit her lip, "Sorry. You probably don't want to hear about Finn."

Alec slowed their pace as they drifted to the outskirts of the dancing crowd. "You're right," he laughed. It was boisterous but got lost in the absurd amount of noise in the cavern. "I'm much more interested in you. Marrying the Hybrid would be the greatest honor. I am a proud and strong warrior. I would build us a strong home," he pulled her closer, "we would fill it with children. I see no other creature in the realm better fitted for you than me."

Calla smiled. Her cheeks were still flushed. "Marriage isn't in the picture for me right now." Some part of her wanted to melt under his intense gaze and say yes. She could imagine little Hybrid-dragon babies running around in a home built by Alec. Then she thought of the same scenario, but this time, little green-haired children ran around. She was about to speak when the scene changed once again. Her brain had set the same scene except the children had coppery red hair, and that caught her completely off guard.

"After we defeat The Corrupted in a glorious battle, King Nakosi will allow you to marry. Correct?"

"Yes, but Alec." Calla pulled him away from the commotion. The corner of the room had a steady stream of cold air flowing in, she was grateful for it.

"Then it's settled!" He went to bring her in close.

Calla shoved him away and stomped her foot, "No, it is not!"

"You don't want to marry me?" His eyebrows furrowed as he reached back out for her, but Calla crossed her arms in defiance.

"No! How many times do I have to say it?" Calla regretted that last glass of wine. "I'm not marrying anyone. I tried to say it nicely, but Finn was right. Dragons are thick-headed and full of themselves!"

Alec scoffed. "It's him. The vampire. He's ruining everything."

"Stop calling him that because he's not ruining anything. You're being an arrogant ass!"

"Me? He's inferior to all other creatures in Midelle! Besides you, no creature is better than a dragon."

"Get a grip on how things work, Alec. You met me a few hours ago, and you're trying to seduce me with ideas of children and homes and..."

"Is it working?"

Calla groaned and slammed her palm onto her forehead.

"As I said, he ruined everything. I should have dropped him from the sky."

"Maybe your plan wasn't going to work? Regardless of Finn being here or not."

"Lady Calla, I have nothing but the utmost respect for you. I also look forward to the day where we fight next to each other, but you're blind."

"Excuse me?" Calla scoffed.

"That vampire has affections for you, and you have affections for him."

Calla felt his words as a slap across her face. "No, it's not possible."

"He's in love with you. It's sure as the sun rising every day."

A slurry of emotions tumbled inside Calla. In quick flashes, she could see their conversations replayed in her head. Denying Alec's words, she shook her head. "No. He doesn't. You don't know our history, and you have no right to say how anyone feels towards anyone!"

Calla walked away. She passed Alec but stopped a few steps away from him. "I bless the woman that marries your arrogant ass one day. She'll need all the help she can get."

A strong grip grabbed her arm. She whipped around to see Alec, sadness written all over his face. "I still hope that it will be you." His bright hazel eyes searched hers for a glimmer of hope.

"I promise it won't be." She pulled her arm back, and he let go right away. "I'll see you in the morning?"

Alec took a deep breath. "Can I at least escort you to your room?" A new song started to play, it was more sincere and slower than the jovial songs that played before.

"No. Thank you, but I know my way," Calla replied calmly, even though she was far from sure. Fire coursed through her veins from what he had said.

"Then I will see you in the morning. I'll be taking you and Captain Quinn to Cape Toria." Alec's formalized his tone, but she could see so much more that he wanted to say on his face. He stood still as Calla took tiny steps back.

She nodded with a polite smile, turned on her heels, and walked quickly towards her room. She dared not look behind her. She knew Alec stood there with twenty more ways to ask for her hand in marriage.

Once Calla got to the marketplace cavern, she slowed her pace. The same slow song still played in the background. The marketplace looked so empty with everyone at the celebration, eating, dancing, and drinking. She stopped to rest against a smooth wall and closed her eyes. She felt herself losing her sanity. The dragons were relentless about the marriage, and her head pounded from it.

Calla took a deep breath, opened her eyes, and looked near the stairs on the other side of the cavern. A person sat with their head cast down by the stairs, she saw a flash of ginger hair. A small smile came across her lips. This was one-time Calla was glad to find Finn alone.

She stopped before him. His head didn't rise from his hands. She tapped his foot with hers, and he looked up. His appearance caught Calla off guard. Finn's eyes glistened with tears, and the tip of his nose was a blotched red. Calla's heart dropped at the sight of him. Finn hastily rubbed the tears from his face and gave Calla a nasty look, "What?"

"Nothing... I was going to my room."

Finn dipped his head back down in his hands without another word. Calla stared at him, confused because Finn never showed anything but anger. Sadness was a whole new game, and she couldn't make headway of it.

Calla got an idea from the music that echoed throughout the cavern. She held out her hand to Finn. "Come on." Finn brought his head up, and his eyes landed on her hand before he gave Calla a skeptical look. "Dance with me," she commanded.

"Don't pity me," Finn scoffed as he pushed her hand away. He got up then looked at Calla straight on, "It was a moment of weakness. Everyone has them."

Calla laughed in her head. Yeah, like they had affection for each other. Alec was wrong.

Calla sighed, and with the exhale, she offered her hand again. "Last time I'm going to offer. No questions asked."

Finn's eyes dropped to Calla's hand again. The sigil on her hand was a glaring reminder of what was on the line. In one swift move, Finn wrapped his right arm around Calla's waist and captured her marked hand with his. He brought their entwined hands between them and rested his forehead on hers.

They swayed to the music, not uttering one word. Her brain had shut down, not knowing what to do or how to act with him so close. She never expected him to accept her offer, it was only supposed to be another olive branch, not an actual dance.

Whatever was happening, it was working as Finn whispered, "Thank you." His grip on Calla tightened. It wasn't a possessive grip like Calla was anticipating, but one that comforted her and made her feel safe. She didn't know how to associate Finn and safety in one thought.

"You've gone at great lengths to protect me, and I haven't always made it easy," Calla said, trying not to let herself seize up. "It feels like the least I can do."

Finn rolled his eyes as he brought his head up from hers, "So, this is a pity dance?"

"No, it's not!"

Finn spun Calla around to have her back against his chest before she could process what he was doing. His arms wrapped around her tight, their bodies now flush with one another. Her stomach fluttered, and her mouth went dry. "Tell the truth," he murmured into her golden tendrils.

Every siren in Calla's head blared with flashing lights as his actions proved to be more than friendly.

"I am." Their bodies stopped moving to the music. "Dancing helps when you're sad. It's a fact, and I wanted to help."

"Who told you that?" His grip around her loosened, but Calla didn't move away from him.

"My mom."

"You must miss her," Finn whispered. He rested his head against hers. Every time he exhaled, her ear caught his hot breath.

"More and more every day," Calla replied with her lip quivering. She couldn't cry now.

Finn moved to kiss the top of her head with a gentle sweetness she'd never seen from him before. The spot where his lips touched smoldered with heat. He took her hand from the front and lifted it over her head with a gentle pull to get her to spin. She followed his lead and turned in his arms to face him.

During the spin, tears welled in Calla's eyes, reversing the scene she had walked up to. It looked like Finn hadn't been crying minutes ago. His eyes were the jaded green that secretly captivated her from the beginning. Her mouth felt even drier than before.

"I promise on my life that you will go home after all this mess is over. From the start, this has never been fair to you." His arms locked behind her, securing their proximity to each other.

A tear fell down Calla's cheek as she whispered, "Thank you." Gazing up, she admired him for everything he'd done for her and how unappreciative she'd been.

Without thinking, Calla popped up on her toes to press her lips on Finn's. The kiss caught Finn off guard, but the shock wore off as he deepened the kiss after a beat. Her hands wrapped around his neck while her stomach erupted with butterflies. Calla couldn't deny it any longer, she did have feelings for Finn, and he had feelings for her. Alec was right.

Finn turned their bodies without breaking the kiss and pressed Calla against the wall. One of his hands left Calla's back and wound into her hair, locking his fingers in the light strands. Finn pulled back on her hair with a gentle tenderness that made a soft moan escape from Calla's lips. His lips worked up and down her neck leaving a trail of kisses that burned with pent up passion. He found her lips again and kissed her with a fiery passion that melted Calla's wits away.

Beneath the butterflies, an ugly truth that she would have to face was surfacing. Vihaan. Guilt drowned her as Finn relentlessly kissed her. With every ounce of clear thinking she had left, Calla put a hand against Finn's chest to break the kiss. Finn placed his hands on either side of her and looked at her, his eyes pleading with what he wouldn't say.

Their faces flushed with their intimate moment, and Calla shook her head in shame, "I'm sorry, Finn. This is... I shouldn't have... I can't," she choked out while fighting an onslaught of tears. Calla ducked under Finn's arms and darted up the stairs. His head cast down and arms stayed locked, caging in the memory of her.

Finn's hands curled into fists and one reared back to punch the stone wall. His hand trembled, and his fingers throbbed. No part of him cared because he knew Calla would never be his.

Twenty

Calla, dressed in thick traveling clothes, stood in the middle of a crowd of dragons. They adorned her to no end with well wishes and hugs that made it hard to part from them. After her questionable decisions last night, she barely slept. Finn had only come into her room to wake her up this morning. He'd said two words to Calla and then left the room before she realized what was going on.

As she made her way to where Alec and the Council were waiting, she saw Finn come into the cavern from the stairs. He too, had heavy leathers and furs with his shoulder bag slung under his thick cape.

"Lady Calla! Lady Calla!" A group of young dragons chanted in unison. Calla looked at them to give them all a collective hug.

"May the deities protect your way," A bright green-eyed, orange scaled girl said with a wide grin. Her scales were striking against her rich brown skin.

Calla held back a scoff, the deities got her in this mess in the first place. "I'm sure they will," Calla assured with a false sense of confidence. She stood up to walk to the group waiting for her. While Calla had met a few on the council at the celebration last night, there were others that she had not met. The council was a mix of male and female dragons of all ages. They all bowed and curtseyed to Calla who stood there with her heart pounding in her chest.

She glanced up towards the dark opening at the top of the cavern, all her time in Midelle was coming to a boiling point. What would happen when she got the other half of her powers? She had so many questions for the Oracle, they just had to get there first, and that meant flying on Alec's back. "Thank you for waiting."

"Lady Calla?" Alec asked with an edge on his voice, "A minute alone?"

"Of course," Calla responded with hesitance. She turned her head to look back where Finn was. He was leaning on some rocks, looking straight at Calla. All she felt was guilt and a touch of fear as she felt another impending marriage proposal from Alec.

Alec and Calla walked paces away from the group who respected Alec's request of being alone. "I wanted to give you something," Alec started right away by digging in his pocket. Calla braced herself about what it could be. "We have to get going if I'm going to get you and... him to the Cape by nightfall, but I think it's important you had this." He pulled out what looked to be the claw of a dragon but hollowed out and much smaller to where it looked tiny in his palm.

Calla eyed the claw with care, "What is that?"

Alec grabbed Calla's hand and placed the claw in it, "It's an heirloom of my family. My great-great-grandfather Fiero and a witch crafted it during the First War of Midelle. It's a dragon signal."

Calla's hands wrapped around the signal, "What do I do with it?"

"It's for whenever you're in trouble, blow through the tip, and it will sound throughout the realm. Only dragons can hear the call. Best to use it a few times so we can locate you. This signal turned the tide of the first war, and it may help us win the second."

Calla nodded her head and looked into Alec's eyes, "Thank you. I hope I won't have to use it."

"Don't underestimate the power of dragons, call for us if you need to. Once you get the other half of your powers," Alec paused, he stood a little taller, "If you could rethink..."

"I'm going to stop you right there, Alec," Calla said firmly. "For the last time, I'm going home after I defeat The Corrupted."

Alec smiled, "I'm not giving up quite yet."

Calla pocketed the claw and started taking small steps back to the group, "We have to get going. You said it yourself."

Alec sighed shortly but still had a tiny smile on his face. "I did say that, but have you ever had a dragon court you?"

Calla shook her head, "No and this is not the time to start either. Now, come on. We have to go." Calla was dying to get off this subject. Alec wasn't even on the radar of things to worry about. Not after last night. Alec followed Calla back to the group. "I'm ready."

Lady Amethyst clapped her hands with enthusiasm as they reentered the circle. Calla was not prepared for her energy this early in the morning. "This is an exciting moment for all Midelle. You are so close to meeting the Oracle and receiving the other half of your powers. Bring in the saddle."

"Saddle?" Calla questioned.

Two council members transformed into their dragon form, one gray and the other blue. They disappeared into one of the upper levels of the massive cavern. Calla forced herself to look away from the dragons and back to Lady Amethyst.

The group before Calla chuckled behind their hands. Lady Amethyst only smiled. "Yes. How do you expect to ride on top of a dragon without a saddle, my dear?"

"They aren't exactly the most comfortable thing," Sigmund quipped. He prodded his grandson with his cane.

Alec frowned, "Don't remind me."

"Crafted during the first war, these saddles held archers on our backs. They would shoot to advance our front line through theirs," Sigmund said. "At least that's what I remember my grandfather telling me."

"But are they safe?" Finn came closer to the group. Calla did everything in her power to not look at Finn. She could only think of his lips on hers, and that was the last thing she wanted to think of. She forced her thoughts on Vihaan. All she could focus on was how she threw weeks of growing feelings out the window to kiss Finn. The very same person whom she once detested.

"Of course, they are!" Lady Amethyst gasped with her hand going over her chest. "Do you think we would put the Hybrid in danger? We're not mongrels." Some of the nearby dragons laughed derisively at Finn.

"I am in charge of keeping her safe," Finn evenly replied.

Lady Amethyst's eyes narrowed in on Finn. "Despite my people being sad about the Hybrid's departure, I must say," she stepped in front of Finn to where she was looking down at him, "I'll be glad when you're gone."

Calla put a hand on both their shoulders. She felt Finn's shoulder relax. "Okay that's enough," she forced a laugh, "We're all on the same side here."

"The Hybrid has spoken," Finn mused, not even looking at Calla. She removed her hands.

With a gentle roar, the two council members soared through the air with a large two-person saddle that was latched in their claws. After all this time, it was still intact. Each seat had a chain attached to it and footholds etched into the side of the saddle.

Alec gave Calla a reassuring nod, and before her eyes changed into a large, dark green dragon. While the other dragons in the group and Finn were fast on their feet, Calla was felled by a gentle swipe of Alec's tail. Sitting on the ground, she stared at Alec in fascination. The two dragons fastened the saddle onto Alec's back.

Calla got up, brushed the dirt off her hands and approached Alec's head. He dipped his head down so his eyes met Calla's. He let out a gentle snort. His eyes were still the golden hazel that she remembered, but now they narrowed to reptilian slits. Calla ran her hand down the side of his head. His scales were smooth, but she could see where his scars were. But instead of rough scars, the scales were an uneven light tan. To her amazement, up close, it was still Alec.

Lady Amethyst tightened the buckle next to Calla, "Magnificent, isn't he?"

"He sure is something." Calla backed away from Alec's head. "What is it like to fly?"

Lady Amethyst replied, "The best feeling in the realm."

"He's set on this side," a voice shouted from the other side of Alec.

Lady Amethyst held out her arms to hug Calla unexpectedly. "May the deities protect you," she whispered in Calla's ear after Calla hugged the tall dragon back. "I shall pray for it."

Calla looked up at Lady Amethyst and smiled. "Thank you, for everything."

Finn cleared his throat. He stood by the foothold with his hand out. "Ready?"

Calla looked around the cavern, etching it into her mind. There were hundreds of people around them and several hovering as dragons. Calla's eyes fell on a teary-eyed Luella, who was being consoled by her older sister. Calla took a deep breath and looked into Finn's eyes. There was undeniable tension between them, yet she put her hand in his.

"Ready."

Finn helped her up on the saddle while she suppressed the images of them kissing that played in her head. Once Calla was up on the saddle, Finn ignored her efforts to help him up and pulled himself up to sit behind her. They pulled the restraint belts over their laps and secured them in place. Calla patted Alec's back, "We're ready."

Alec's wings flapped, jolting Calla and Finn. They soared to the top of the cavern with ease. Calla waved to Sigmund and the rest of the crowd.

As they rose higher, the frosty air nipped Calla's nose. She hadn't missed the cold at all. Calla turned around as best she could to look at Finn. His eyes were closed and he had a tight grip on the holds of the saddle. "What's wrong?" The wind started to whip snow around their faces.

"Nothing."

A slow smile came to Calla's face, "Are you scared?"

Finn's eyes snapped open, "No!" He looked down to the side and shuddered. His face went white.

"You are!" Calla laughed innocently. "You really are scared of heights!"

Finn rolled his eyes then closed them again, "Am not."

"Are too!"

Alec perched on the cavern opening and let out a deafening roar. Calla took one last chance to wave to the dragons down below, then Alec shot out into the dusky sky.

The wind whipped Calla's face, and she pulled a treated leather cloth over her face. Lady Amethyst warned that flying on the back of a dragon isn't fun, especially on a trip at high speed through wind and snow.

Calla sat back against the divider for the two seats and pulled on the chain that strapped her in. She smiled because it reminded her of a roller coaster, but this was one different roller coaster. Alec flew steady, only a gentle bump when he flapped his wings. This was going to be a long, cold, and boring ride.

She looked behind her again. Finn had his face covered and had hunkered down to sleep. There wasn't much else to do or look at. Plus, they would get to the Cape by nightfall, and the sun had only peaked over the horizon moments ago. Calla followed Finn's lead. This was going to be a long trip.

Vihaan rushed through the portal, in a complete panic. They had wasted too much time getting back to East Shimmer. Jack had gotten injured during the cave collapse, so the convoy took double the time to go back to the gates.

His hand clutched the necklace that held his ring. Granted, Calla didn't know what he had Philomena do to them, but it was for her protection. She would understand when she found out. His mind couldn't stop running overtime with her gone, knowing that the vampire bastard was with her.

Dragons were back, had tried to kill them all and they had taken Calla. He didn't trust the messenger that had come to tell them what was going to transpire either. Especially when he demanded the dragon take him to Calla and the messenger ignored him. A few other guards thought it was suspicious as well.

Onlookers to the main hall looked on as everyone came through the portal. Violet stopped at the top of the stairs, watching them come through one by one. She held her breath. Vihaan caught his gaze with Violet. "We have a problem. Where is King Nakosi?"

Vihaan pounded on a heavy wooden door that led to the King's advisement room. Violet mentioned he's been in there every day for hours on end. An elderly figure opened the door. Bert Mountor, one of the King's advisors, met Vihaan with a hard look. "Vihaan?" He never liked the troll much, he was a stickler for rules and protocol. He avoided him like the Corruption when he was younger. "It's early, and you're not due back for another month!"

"Let me speak to King Nakosi. It's important. Lady Calla is in danger." Vihaan was frantic, but he kept his voice calm. He knew the other guards were coming to back his story up, but he couldn't wait for them. Precious time was sifting away. He knew something was wrong, very wrong.

"Vihaan?" Nakosi called from beyond the door. "Bert, let him in immediately!"

Vihaan barged in, almost knocking Bert down. "My King, it is good to see you."

"You as well. Tell me why you are back so soon?" Lines of worry etched into his skin. Even though the day was young, he looked as if he had been awake for days on end.

Vihaan explained what had happened in the mountains. Some wanted to hear more about the dragons, but Nakosi's dark eyes furrowed with concern.

"It's true," Lena said, barging into the chamber. Bert gave her an annoyed look. "They wouldn't take us to her. I know Captain

Quinn wouldn't leave Lady Calla to come to tell us either, but it was very strange."

"But you don't know for sure she's in danger?" Bert clarified. "The dragons would never hurt our efforts to defeat The Corrupted."

Vihaan held up his necklace, the gold ring shone in the light of the room. "Lady Calla has the other half. Philomena charmed them for me, so I know she would be safe if we ever got separated. When she's wearing her half, the rings have a slight warmth to them. It's been stone cold since the dragon took Calla."

A younger druid adviser laughed, "Maybe she took it off?"

Vihaan shook his head immediately, "She would never." Granted they didn't know she and Vihaan planned to go off on their own and what the ring meant, even if it was fake.

"Could it have broken?" Another adviser mocked with a chuckle.

Vihaan pulled on his necklace. The chain remained intact, as Philomena crafted it to be. It didn't break or bend one bit. "See? It's in one piece. She's in trouble. I know it. You have to believe me."

Nakosi rubbed his bald head, his heavy golden crown cast aside on a nearby table. "What do you propose? We have no idea where they are. If Captain Quinn is with her, he will do everything in his power to keep her safe. If what the dragon messenger said was true both Calla and Finn will be home in three days time, and the Hybrid will have received the other half of her powers."

Bert stood and Vihaan did everything in his power not to roll his eyes. "I suggest we wait three days then."

Zenji burst into the room, knocking into another adviser. "She's in danger. I know she is."

Bear and Wolf came in, calmer, but their faces bore the same deep concern that everyone else had. "We also believe that she is in danger. Captain Quinn would never abandon us."

"Do you feel comfortable having the two of them in Cape Toria? Forty Corrupted ambushed us on our side of the Shimmers." Vihaan never fathomed that convincing Nakosi would be this difficult. The King had always been one for thinking carefully, but now he was wasting time. Precious time.

Nakosi's gaze swept back and forth over everyone in the room. They quietly waited for his decision. "There is too much at stake for us not to be cautious." Bert let out a drawn-out sigh at the King's decision. "Now, the hard part," Nakosi said as he paced the room with his hands locked behind his back. "How do we find them?"

Vihaan racked his brain, never having gotten this far in his thoughts. It clicked. "We do have a witch."

Nakosi turned his attention to an older female vampire, "Summon Philomena at once!"

"This is amazing!" Calla shouted with her arms stretched out wide and slid back and forth in her saddle. They were over the plains now. The snow had cleared up but a cold wind still whipped their faces. Heavy gray clouds covered the sky. Alec used them to provide cover over the frostbitten plains. She was so bored, she asked Alec if he wanted to stretch his wings and have some fun. He didn't wait one moment before he started to twist and dip in the sky.

Alec nose-dived then veered off to the side.

"I'm going to be sick," Finn groaned with his hood pulled down to cover his face.

Calla rolled her eyes. Flying on the backside of a dragon was a once in a lifetime experience, and Finn was the wettest blanket of them all. "Then puke already! You've been saying that for like the last three hours!"

"I think I will," Finn shouted. There was the temper that grounded and reminded her that, affection or no affection, Finn wasn't a good choice.

Flying for hours on end had given her a lot of time to think. Last night she had gotten caught up in the moment, and that was all it was. She was foolish to think they had affection for each other. If he brought it up, she would set him straight.

"At least you're behind me," Calla laughed as she turned around. Finn pushed his hood back, his face paler than before. Calla stopped laughing and sighed, "You don't like flying, do you?"

Finn gave her a venomous glare and pulled his hood down once again.

Calla patted Alec's neck, "That's enough Alec, thank you!"

Alec let out a deep throaty noise, then resumed his gentle soaring. Calla's heart pounded harder with each flap of his massive wings. They had to be more than halfway there since the sun was nearing its descent.

Philomena followed behind one of the more tolerable advisers, Riah Honde. She had no idea why King Nakosi had summoned her to the advisement room.

That morning, Violet pinned her braided lavender hair into a crown. This was one of the rare times it wasn't in her face or her work. She wore one of her favorite dresses, a deep gray dress embroidered with ivory pearls. Ever since the convoy left, she only had Hawke and Violet to talk to. She had spent a lot of her days in the garden house with Hawke.

Philomena was happy to help with anything that would bring Calla back to the Castle. She hoped that's why the King was summoning her, to bring Calla back. While she missed Calla, her absence did grant her some peace because Finn was gone.

Riah rapped on the door sharply, "I found her. She was in the garden house this whole time." She glanced at Philomena. Unbeknownst to her, the whole castle had been looking for her all day, and she had no idea. When Riah had found her, she had told her it was urgent.

The door creaked open, and they stepped inside. The room had a large round table in the middle with figurines scattered over it. Maps hung along the walls of different regions of Midelle. King Nakosi sat above the rest of the advisory panel. Vihaan and some of the other guards were waiting by a tapestry of the royal crest, a dagger stabbed in the ground. "Philomena," King Nakosi acknowledged her presence as she curtseyed to the room.

"Your majesty, I apologize for the wait. I hear I can be of some help?" She glanced over to Vihaan and the others. They looked sick with anxiety. The sight of them made her stomach go sour.

"Are you able to find the Hybrid?" Nakosi asked with very little patience in his voice. His eyes looked tired with the magnitude of the situation. "Vihaan, Lena, Zenji, Bear and Wolfe have come to believe she could be in danger."

Philomena nodded her head and glanced at Vihaan. "Yes, I have base portals ready to go. I'll need a few days. Maybe, um... I already have her hair to practice with, but I guess I'm not practicing anymore." Everyone's confused eyes in the room landed on Philomena, she was taken aback at their reaction. "What? You never know when you'll need someone's hair."

"How many days?" Bert snapped out of turn. Nakosi gave him a stern glare, and Bert straightened up immediately to clear his throat.

"I think I can have it ready in two days." Bert always made her nervous with his hard manner. "I don't want to mess up, and I only have enough for one try." She was nervous at the prospect of failing. If Calla was really in trouble, she couldn't fail.

The room went quiet as Nakosi was thinking. He had always thought of all his options with care.

Vihaan kept glancing at Philomena, and she gave him a look back with a small shrug of her shoulders.

"Start working on it," Nakosi commanded. "I never should have agreed to the convoy. There were other ways to get her there. We're finding more and more citizens Corrupted every day. In three days we will know if that dragon spoke the truth. Your portal will serve as a backup in case he's deceived us."

"Yes, my King. I won't fall asleep. I promise!" Philomena smiled with another curtsy before she left the room.

Nakosi pinched the bridge of his nose and closed his eyes. "Someone please accompany her."

Vihaan sighed to himself knowing three days would be too late. He yearned for Calla to be safe in his arms once again.

The moon was high in the ebony sky when Alec dove through the cover of the clouds and flapped down into a dense forest. Finn jumped off Alec and sighed a breath of relief when his hands and knees touched the forest floor. Calla hopped down in a less dramatic fashion than her companion. From the corner of her eye she watched Alec transform back into a person. The saddle thumped on the ground.

"Are you going to come into Cape Toria with us?" Calla's voice was soft.

"I can't risk it," Alec shook his head. "Lady Amethyst is expecting me by midday tomorrow and I need to rest for an hour or two. Before all this, I could fly here and back without resting." He scoffed. "Guess I need to work on my stamina."

Calla began to untie her cape. The air had a frosty chill to it. "Here, you'll need it to keep warm."

Alec rejected her offer with his hand. "Lady Calla, do keep it. You need it more than I do. Dragons run hot. The cool air feels good after all that flying."

"Well," Calla started after hearing Finn sigh impatiently. "this is goodbye then. Thank you for flying us."

Alec brought her in for a hug, catching her off guard. "The pleasure is always mine, Lady Calla." He kissed her hand. Her regular glove and a thicker glove covered her skin.

"Cape Toria is this way?" She asked after she broke from the hug. She pointed behind her. Alec gave her a wolfish grin as he pointed to her right.

"Or that way," Calla laughed. She patted her pocket and looked up at Alec. "I have the signal, and may the deities protect you on your way home." Calla felt strange reciting the words that so many had spoken to her. Especially when she had a bone to pick with these deities.

"You as well, Lady Calla." She watched Alec take a seat in a grove of trees. His head rested against a trunk, and his arms crossed his chest.

"Are you coming?" Finn asked a few feet away from her.

A cold wind ripped through the trees to send a chill down her spine. Calla turned to Finn and nodded. "How much longer to Cape Toria?"

"The trail is this way. I saw it on the descent."

Calla followed him, "Oh, so you opened your eyes?" She placed a hand over her heart. "I am so proud of you." Last night was a blessing in disguise. The high and mighty wall between them seemed to have crumbled.

"Shut it," Finn said under his breath.

"Make me," Calla retorted immediately without thinking twice about her answer. Finn turned around with a devilish look in his eyes, but she already covered her mouth in shock.

"It's late," Finn said in a more reserved tone as he kept walking. "We'll go to the Library in the morning. I doubt the Oracle will even be awake at this hour. I'm also starving. Are you?"

Calla nodded her head still mentally reprimanding herself for her response to Finn. She wrapped her fur cloak around her, the air was thick with frost. Even the moon hid behind dark and gray clouds. She looked back for Alec, but the forest night had swallowed him.

When the tree line stopped, so did Calla. Cape Toria came into view, and she could have cried from fear and excitement. The road leading to the Cape had sloped down slightly, then rose uphill to the entrance of the city.

What caught her eye and her heart was sitting at the center of a widely spiraled peninsula. The Library of Midelle. The cathedral-like Library overlooked Cape Toria and the sea. She could see the big stained-glass windows even from this distance. Tall spires filled with ancient knowledge pierced the clouds. The Oracle was housed there somewhere, holding her powers and answers to questions Calla had her whole life.

Finn waited patiently as she stared at the Library.

"We made it."

Finn looked at her with a look of sadness, "We did." Finn cupped his hands to catch his breath, and then rubbed them together. "Let's get going. It's freezing out."

Calla took a deep breath of the cold air, it reminded her of home, right before a snowstorm. The air stung her lungs with each breath. "Are you sure we can't go now?" She dreaded this from the beginning, but now that they were there, she couldn't wait to go.

Finn smiled at her. "First thing tomorrow morning. I promise. But before all that, dinner."

A woman nestled deep within a crumbling castle gazed into a hazy orb. It showed the Hybrid and her protector walking into Cape Toria. The corner of her lips curved into a sneer as she gazed around her workroom. Herbs hung drying upside down, ancient books sat open on random pages, and a smell of death permeated the air. The woman waved her arm through the orb. It broke into miniscule droplets. Her attention turned to a simmering cauldron.

The thick black liquid bubbled with vicious drawn-out pops. She stirred three times, then brought the pewter ladle up to check its consistency. A sharp rap on the door broke her from her concentration.

"Come in," she spoke.

Abaddon strutted in and with a grunt. He stepped aside, and Belladonna moved in, graceful as usual in a dark dress. Her piercing red eyes snapped to the woman.

"My Queen." The woman curtseyed.

"Where are they?"

The woman's red eyes dashed over to Abaddon, standing there with his intense grimace. She found his face hard to look at. Massive and hideous scars covered most of his face. Her eyes set back on her Queen, Belladonna. "They are going to the Library tomorrow morning."

Belladonna drummed her fingers on a nearby table. The woman pegged it as a nervous habit for her. "And how is this batch fairing?" The Queen clasped her hands in front of her and nodded to the cauldron.

The woman smiled as she gave another stir to check for consistency. An acrid smell wafted over to her, burning her nostrils. This was her most potent batch yet. "It is ready."

Belladonna smiled at Abaddon. "Prepare your team to capture the Hybrid." Her smile then dropped, and her eyes narrowed on him, her most trusted guard. "And do not fail me."

Twenty-One

Finn needed blood. He'd gone far too long without drinking. Today had taken a lot out of him for three reasons. One, he had never been at such a high altitude in his entire life. Two, he felt sick to his stomach the entire time. And three, the Library of Midelle stared at him in mockery.

He knew that tomorrow everything would change. Calla would get her powers, they would create a portal back to Japhia, and then devise their attack plan. When The Corrupted were gone for good, she would be too. He wasn't ready for that.

He stood in a tiny grove of trees outside the Inn. A tiny squeak next to his head brought him back to reality. He shifted his eyes to the tree next to him. A squirrel cocked its head. Finn could hear the beating of its heart, but when he focused, Calla's heartbeat took over. The constant thump that calmed him when his thoughts spiraled out of control.

Calla was past the grove, leaning against the outside of the Inn's pub. They were too close to the Library for Calla to be out of his sight, even if it meant that she sits outside while he drinks.

In a fluid move, Finn grabbed the squirrel, his fangs grew, and he sunk them deep into the creature. The squirrel squirmed but quickly fell limp, drained of blood. He dropped the tiny creature to the ground as his fangs reverted to their normal incisor length. That would hold him over until he got back to Japhia.

He looked past the grove and smiled when his eyes landed on Calla sitting there. She was looking off into the distance. He doubted she noticed him. Her golden waves framed her face and white clouds puffed in front of her mouth. The effect made her eyes seem icier than usual.

Finn traced the direction of her eyes until his eyes fell on the Library. He would give anything to hear her thoughts right now. Maybe she was just as scared as he was. After last night, his thoughts were all over the place. He tried to sort them out but to no avail. His duty to protect her and his heart's love for her had divided him since the moment he met her.

Calla's frosty eyes landed on Finn. A small smile spread across her face. "Are you done yet?"

Finn emerged through the trees with an idea brewing in his mind. "Yes. Stay right here. It's your turn to drink."

"My turn? I'm not drinking blood!"

Finn had already stepped inside the pub by the time she'd replied. Warm air wrapped around him and his eyes scanned the pub. Creatures of all shapes and sizes crowded inside seeking refuge from the cold. Drinks were flowing, people were boisterous, and Finn blended in with them.

After he glanced back and saw Calla safe, he made his way to the bar and placed a gold piece on the counter. A troll with a large gut looked at Finn while he poured ale into a mug. "What's your vice tonight?"

"A bottle of wine. Something drinkable but strong. Lady friend has the jitters." Finn peered behind him again. He could see her outside.

The bartender's jaw ticked in thought. "Besides a good toss in the bed, I got just the thing." He pulled up a bottle filled with dark wine. "Two pieces. I do run a business here."

Finn smirked, tossed another coin on the bar top and grabbed the bottle by the neck. He made his way outside. The cold air was refreshing from the drunken atmosphere inside the pub.

"For you." He held out the bottle to Calla. She looked at him with hesitance but still took the bottle. "Stop acting all high and mighty. Drink the damn wine. You're stressed, and it's stressing me out." Finn pulled the cork from the bottle then pushed it to her lips.

Calla sighed and drank. After her drink, she passed the bottle to Finn. "Your turn."

"If you insist." Finn took a swig himself, not believing that she did what he asked. He anticipated the wine mixing with the blood, it was euphoric for him. Better than any plain liquor he could pour down his throat.

They sat down and leaned back against the wood and stone of the Inn to look up to the black sky. The clouds were gray and thick where a distant galaxy hid from view. The only light came from inside. Finn passed the bottle back to Calla. She took it but gazed at him pensively. After all this time, she still took his breath away. He had hoped that she wasn't the Hybrid from the moment he saw her. Turns out, he couldn't have been more wrong.

As usual.

Calla's face softened, and she smiled at him, "Tell me what happened?" She drank and passed the bottle back to him.

Finn took a drink and gave her a curious look. "Happened when?"

"Before you came here."

Finn immediately stiffened, and a brick of dread turned over in his stomach. There's a reason why he kept his past to himself. Calla took the bottle out of his hands, took a quick drink, and passed it back to him.

With a slight shake in his hand, Finn drank to pass the bottle to Calla. It was going faster than he anticipated. At this rate, they would need another bottle or a 'toss in the sheets', according to the bartender. "Tell me something I don't know about you." He could talk about anything but his past.

Calla sighed and rolled her eyes. She tipped back the bottle, took a big gulp, and handed the bottle over to Finn. "We never talk unless you're yelling at me," Calla teased. "My birthday is coming up, at least I think it is."

Finn sat up and relaxed a little. "When is it?"

"December twenty-first, at least that's when the doctors estimated when I was born."

Finn drank.

"Yours?

"May thirteenth. You know, I'd say we're close to December." He passed the bottle back to her so she would have the last few sips. She frowned and tipped the bottle upside down.

"Okay," Finn chuckled. "I get the hint." He got up and went to the bar and placed four gold pieces on the bar top and held up two fingers.

The bartender nodded and slid the coins off the bar. Two bottles of wine took the place of the money and the bartender winked at him. "Gotta loosen her up, eh?"

"Something like that."

Finn took his previous spot, and Calla started giggling, "So why doesn't Midelle follow the months like in the human realm?"

Finn tossed the cork into the woods and took a hearty swig. "They follow the seasons rather than the months. It was hard when I first got here. I didn't understand most of their ways. All I knew was that I wanted to be a human again and go back to my own shitty world."

Calla took a long drink. "So, no Christmas?"

Finn swiped the bottle from her fingers with a playful grin. "No Christmas, no Halloween, no Valentine's Day," He took a drink, "No Saint Patrick's Day."

Finn handed the bottle to Calla. She took a small sip. "Are you Irish? I never put two and two together, but the ginger hair is totally giving you away."

Finn barked a laugh, "That I am. Straight from Ireland. The accent has lost its charm here though. Shea dropped it too."

"I didn't know that. What else?" She shifted her body to look at Finn straight on and drank again.

"Hand it over!" Finn smirked. He playfully snatched the bottle.

Besides Shea, no one knew how he came to be. He vowed to himself to bury his past, deep down. Finn drummed his thumb on the bottle in thought. The smile fell from his face, and the light died in his eyes. "Shea left home when I was nine. My grandma hid away money from our parents to get her a one-way ticket out of Limerick once she was eighteen. My own damn sister didn't even say goodbye..." His chest tightened with pain from the memories.

Calla's smile faded.

"One morning I woke up, and she wasn't there to walk me to school as usual." Finn's face was hard. He drank two large swigs, then placed the bottle in front of Calla. "It was me, my grandma, and them."

"Them?" Calla had a long sip.

"My parents, the selfish bastards. Between the drinking, the drugs, and the gambling, they spent every single penny we had on themselves. I don't remember much before my grandma came. What I do remember is that Shea and I were always hungry. Our parents treated us like we were nothing but an inconvenience to them."

Finn took a quick swig, and he held the bottle out to Calla. She grabbed it clumsily, her fingers brushed Finn's, and their eyes locked in a moment of softness. He had no idea what he was doing, but it felt right to tell Calla. She took a quick drink.

Finn cleared his throat and continued, "My grandma came to live with us after my grandpa died. She did odd jobs around town for money, babysitting and such, but Shea and I were her focus." Finn cracked a smile as Calla tipped the neck of the bottle towards him. Finn took it a long drink. "And that's how we lived for years until Shea left. My grandma tried her hardest and gave everything she had, trying to give us a good life. She promised she would get me out too."

"She sounds like a wonderful woman," Calla whispered before she took the bottle back from Finn.

"She was." Finn nodded in agreement.

The next words he wanted to speak stuck in his throat. This was the most painful memory of all. Tears welled in his eyes. "I was fifteen when my grandma died."

A rowdy crowd left the Inn, their drunken voices filled the silence.

"It didn't take long before my parents sold everything she had to get their next fix. They even sold my quilt that she made me. It had all my favorite things as a boy." A fast tear slid down Finn's cheek to get lost in his red scruff. His heart hurt. He felt vulnerable, but the broken parts of his heart were lighter.

"I ran away a few months later. Anywhere had to be better than that hell hole. Cops brought me back days later after a storekeeper caught me stealing food. They knew my parents quite well." Finn ran his hands through his hair. The tips of his ears were cold, despite the wine. Calla sighed a small puff of air that clouded in front of her. She set the bottle next to Finn. It was almost empty again.

"When I thought that it couldn't get any worse, my parents made a deal with a local farmer." Finn glanced at Calla with his broken sea glass eyes, grabbed the bottle and drank. "A farmhand for three years in exchange for a place to live for my parents since the bank had foreclosed their house. Shane was decent, he gave me warm food and a roof over my head. Far better than my parents ever did for me. So, I never said anything to anyone about their deal. Not even my teachers."

Finn picked up the bottle and swirled the dark liquid inside, "Here. You finish it." This wine was for her after all.

Calla took the bottle from him, then tipped her head back and drank the last drops of the wine. She wiped her mouth with the back of her hand and looked at Finn. His eyes were cast down with anger set hard on his face.

"What happened next?" she asked quietly.

Finn relived the stinging memories in his head. "I worked for him without complaint. Even though he had a lot to say about my parents, nothing good of course. Right after I turned eighteen," he paused for a moment, "my parents died from an overdose, drugs mixed with drinking too much."

Finn raised his head to look at Calla. Their eyes met and a small smile spread on his lips. "One of the best days of my life. Shane hired me as a paid farmhand. Everyone in town expected me to turn into my parents, but I kept my nose down. I wouldn't allow myself to become them."

Calla reached out to grab his hand, her skin was cold to the touch. She brought his hand to her cheek and nestled her cheek into his palm. Her skin was soft despite the chill. "That takes courage, you know?" She said softly. "To break out of the mold everyone expects you to be in."

Finn closed his eyes, savoring the feel of Calla's skin. His thumb caressed her cheek. "It took everything I had. Until Shea came one day and promised me a life worth living. I had no idea what she was talking about. All those years I held a grudge against her. I wanted to see where she lived. What life was she living that was so good that she couldn't have come back for her younger brother and grandma sooner? Grandma could have still been alive. Shea apologized, then she attacked me. I can't remember anything else until I woke up in a room at the Castle. And low and behold, I'm a vampire."

Calla's lips grazed his fingers. He knew the pain showed on his face, but he couldn't bury it in anymore. Finn would never forget her warm lips on his fingers. "I don't remember much, only overwhelming anger. I ran away the first chance I got, tearing down anything and everything in my path. I had become a monster in my own eyes. A monster who needed to die. I didn't want to drink blood, I didn't want this cursed life. All I wanted was to work on Shane's farm. I was good at it. I was happy."

Finn's voice became harder and angrier with each word. "After weeks of being alone in the forest, I was starved into a blood rage.

I drank every drop out of every animal I could find. I remember lying down at the base of a tree. My body couldn't handle all the blood. I was at peace because I thought death was coming for me. Finally."

Finn sighed and pulled his hand from Calla's grasp. He knew her compassion was out of pity. He rested his head in his hands, "That's where Cyprus and Zinnia found me, and I know you know the rest."

Calla got up to her knees and closed the distance between them. She grabbed both sides of his face to make him look at her. Finn couldn't stop staring into her icy, teary eyes. "You are far stronger than you think you are, Finnegan Quinn. Do you understand me?"

A tear streamed down Finn's cheek. A strong gust whipped them and Calla shivered.

Finn knew they had stayed out here too long. It was too cold for her. He welcomed the cold, it numbed his outside to match his inside, but now? It seemed that the glacier that ran rampant within him was melting.

"You're cold," Finn wiped the tear off his face. "Let's get you inside."

Finn stood and held his hand out for Calla. She looked at him. "Promise me first."

"I promise, okay?" Finn tried to hide the annoyance in his voice. He wasn't strong, he still saw himself as a monster. "Come on, you'll catch your death out here."

She accepted his hand and he pulled her up. Calla's little hop at the end made his own heart thump. He forced his hand to let go of hers.

Finn grabbed the extra bottle and led the way inside. He turned around when he noticed Calla hadn't moved. Her hand was outstretched with her palm facing the sky. A smile spread over her lips. She turned to Finn. "It's snowing!" As if by cue, heavy, fat flakes started to fall.

"We've already seen snow."

"Yeah, but we were on top of a mountain. That doesn't count." Calla closed her eyes, flung out her arms to spin in the falling snow. Finn would never forget the way she looked. Snow nestled in her hair, her nose and ears kissed red by the chilled air, and her smile that would always take his breath away.

Finn blew warm air into his hands and rubbed them together. "How does that not count?"

"We were up so high, it wasn't snowing naturally."

"And this is what you consider naturally snowing?"

Calla snapped her eyes open and looked at Finn. "Exactly."

"How is your first natural snowfall?" Finn almost stifled a laugh.

Calla caught a snowflake on her tongue, then she pulled her fur cape closed and shivered. "Good, but I'm cold, and I need more wine."

"Good thing I have another bottle. Let's go inside before we both get sick." Finn shook the full bottle. She cast a parting glance at the Library and followed him inside.

Calla and Finn passed through the bar. The bartender winked at Finn, and he nodded. Toss in the sheets? That would be his dream come true.

They went up the stairs, to the end of the corridor. Room sixteen, that was their room. Finn passed the bottle to Calla and fished out a heavy key from his pocket. The door opened in a creaky arc. She waited just inside the door until he had checked the entire room. They couldn't take any chances, not this close. He cleared the main room, the tiny closet, and the bathroom. "It's safe."

Finn came out from the bathroom, which was a poor example of a makeshift toilet, water pump, and a dingy tub, and Calla had the wine to her lips, drinking in a frenzy. Finn held back his shock, he'd never seen her like this.

She broke from the bottle, "I'm cold."

"I'll rekindle the fire, give me a second." Finn knelt in front of the fireplace. Soon enough the roaring fire warmed the room. He rubbed his hands in front of the fire, then turned to Calla. She had shed her heavy clothes, leaving herself in light pants and a long-sleeved shirt.

Something tight pulled in Finn's stomach when he saw her undressed. His brow furrowed. He saw that the wine was more than half gone. "Thirsty?"

"Nerves," Calla laughed as she drank more wine.

"You're nervous about tomorrow?"

Calla nodded her head. Finn thought her eyes looked sad.

"It would seem so."

"I'm going to go wash up." Finn held up his hands. "I've got ash all over me." There was a bucket of water in the bathroom. He should have warmed some up over the fire, but he needed the cold water to shock him back into the real world.

"How will they know it's me tomorrow?" Calla's voice floated in from the main room.

Finn let the frigid water drip from his face for a few seconds. "Huh?"

"How will they know I'm the Hybrid? Do we ask for the Oracle? Is it that easy?"

"I have a letter from King Nakosi in my bag. Remember the one I showed back at Coriocris? You had this whole trip to ask this. Why are you so curious now?" There was a part of him that thought Calla didn't know if she would make it here.

Finn splashed more water on his face. He dried off with his cloak then took it off. The heat had floated into the bathroom, and Finn stripped to his cotton pants. He wanted to put his shirt back on, but the wine distracted his brain.

"Finn?" Calla's voice cracked from the bedroom.

Fear dropped in Finn's stomach as he left the bathroom. She stood with her back to him.

"Calla?"

Calla turned. Tears welled in her eyes. Her fingers were wrapped around something. "Why do you have this?" She let her fingers uncurl.

Finn swallowed hard when his eyes landed on the necklace he'd taken from her. With shame, he remembered every second of his choice. Here, he had a chance to come clean, but everything was shutting down. The inner wall so recently breached he rebuilt at a rapid pace. "I don't know what that is."

"You know what it is!"

He winced at how broken her voice sounded. He could see the growing sorrow in her eyes. Even if it meant she'd never speak to him again, she deserved the truth. It was time to own up to his mistake. Time to be strong. "We had just gotten to your room in the mountains." Finn's stomach turned over. "I took off your boots and cape when the chain caught my attention. The second I realized it was a ring, I..." He swallowed the lump in his throat. He didn't know how to say that his world became tinted green without revealing his hand, so he reverted to what he knew. What he was good at. "Do you think your garden boy is being cute? Whatever the two of you planned, did you think it was going to work? I wasn't born yesterday! He can't protect you like I can!"

Finn made his retreat into the bathroom. He needed to separate himself from Calla before something happened that he couldn't take back.

"Leave him out of this. Vihaan is more of a man than you could ever be!"

Finn stopped mid-step then turned towards Calla. His face was set hard, and a jaded storm of green blazed in his eyes. "What?"

Calla's chest rose and fell with her angered breathing. "You heard me."

Finn's jaw ticked, and his eyes narrowed in on Calla. "Say it again."

The fire cracked while an icy wind howled outside. "Vihaan is more of a man than you could ever be. Him befriending me that day was... was," trailing off, she glanced at the fire as if it had the words she was searching for. Her eyes darted back to Finn, "divine intervention."

All Finn saw was blind green rage.

"Divine intervention," he roared, making Calla jump. "I'll show you fucking divine intervention." Finn couldn't stop himself as he rushed to Calla to crash his lips against hers. He anticipated a sharp sting across his face, but instead, Calla wrapped her hands around his neck.

Finn took his chance to deepen the kiss. He entangled his hands in her hair, desperate for this not to end.

The cold metal of the necklace hit his back and brought him out of his euphoric bliss. Finn broke the kiss, grabbed the necklace, and flung it into the roaring fire before Calla could object. They watched it pop and hiss in the fire for a few seconds. A light green hue grew and danced in the flames.

Finn advanced on her again, pressing her against the wall. Their tongues danced together sloppily. Moans escaping their lips. He left wet kisses down her neck but stopped right before her shirt. Finn looked up, and Calla nodded before she flung it off herself. Finn groaned as he grabbed her hips, pulling her to him to kiss her as if he'd never see her again. He brought her legs up and she wrapped them around his hips. Her bare skin warmed his chest. He desperately wanted, needed more.

Finn brought her to the bed. His body ached for Calla and was drowning in pure lust. He caged her with his arms and his lips hovered over her chest.

She moaned and arched her back to have her chest meet Finn's lips.

He brought a hand to the waistline of Calla's pants and teased it. Before he could make up his mind, she slid out of them, and the air left Finn's lungs. Her body was everything he could ever want. Soft and supple skin, perfect curves.

Calla raked her nails against Finn's back, bringing him back to here, to now, to Calla. She trembled when he ran his hands over her body. She parted her legs for him and bit her lip. She tugged at his pants.

Finn didn't need to be told twice. His pants were off in an instant. Finn pulled Calla up the bed, so her head lay over the pillows, and their lips crashed together. Their bodies melded with nothing between them. Finn's skin felt like it was on fire where Calla touched him. His wildest dreams were coming true.

Finn kissed down her body slowly, deliberately, savoring every inch of her. She gasped when Finn reached her most sacred place. He glanced up. Her eyes were glazed over with bliss. Finn stopped to caress her face, "Are you sure?"

A gust of wind made the rafters creak. Calla wiggled out from underneath him and playfully pushed him down where she was. She straddled him.

"More than anything."

He was dying to be inside her. Finn licked his lips and ran his hands down her waist. He was letting her set the pace, no matter how it agonized him. Such sweet agony. He looked at Calla. She was perfect. Her smile melted and healed his heart. He could get lost forever in the icy blue waters of her eyes.

Finn pulled her down to kiss her sweet lips. "I'll take care of you then." He moved to suck on her neck. A soft gasp left her lips. "Don't you worry. Tell me what you need."

Another howl of wind rocked the Inn and silvery flakes of snow kissed the window. Everything stopped when Calla whispered, "I need you."

Finn readjusted himself to let her sink onto him. He now knew what heaven felt like.

Calla's head fell back and a deep primal moan gushed from her lips. The snow fell and the wind sang its hollow tune. They rocked together in perfect harmony, bathed by the soft glow of the fire.

Light slapped Calla's face. She groaned, her head pounded. Last night was one big, blurry mess. Piece by piece, she remembered Finn starting the fire, her digging through the bag, the ring, the kiss, and the sex. Her body went rigid as her eyes flew open. There she was laying naked with Finn, who was fast asleep, snoring, and naked as the day he was born.

"No, no, no…" Calla whispered internally with growing panic. "Shit." She slid from Finn's arms, and her feet padded on the freezing floor.

The chill in the room causing her skin to rise in bumps. The fire had gone out while they were sleeping. The melted ring in the fireplace caught her eye while she tip-toed around the room to collect her clothes. Calla couldn't believe they had sex, not once, but she lost count after the third time. She remembered after what could have been the fourth or fifth time, they had collapsed to fall asleep in each other's arms.

She moved as quietly as she could. She put her clothes on and looked towards Finn's bag to grab the letter from the side pocket. Calla couldn't look, let alone speak, to Finn right now. All she felt was shameful regret, and it was something she couldn't deal with. Not now. Probably not ever, but a few hours away from Finn is what she needed to clear her head.

Calla dressed and tucked the letter under her fur cloak. She paused at the door with her hand on the handle. Guilt ran rampant through her when she looked at Finn. The morning sun shone over his body with the sheet sitting right at his hips. She could no longer deny how handsome he was.

Calla wanted to throw everything to the wind and jump back into bed with him, but she knew that last night was a mistake. One she would have to own up to when she got back to Japhia. She hadn't even begun to think about how she was going to tell Vihaan. Calla opened the door and slipped into the hallway.

The Inn was silent, as was the bar when she walked through the pub. She took in the peaceful, snow-covered town for only a moment. Everything was quiet when she stepped into the snow. The crunch under her boots echoed throughout the town.

Calla shivered. The Library was straight up the road. It seemed to be looking down at her. Deep within those walls were the answers she had sought her entire life, at least she hoped. Calla squared her shoulders back and trudged through the untouched snow to find out.

Twenty-Two

All her life Calla wondered where she had come from. Now she stood before the Library of Midelle that held all the answers. Her hand shook around the letter she gripped.

The sound of waves crashing into the rocks below filled the silence of the morning. With the drop in temperature and snow, Calla couldn't imagine how frigid the water was.

Calla stopped before the gate. Two guards towered before her. "Turn back now. The Library is closed," the guard on the left said in a deep, gruff voice.

"I know but..."

"Leave now," the other guard commanded. They were both huge in stature. Their helmets sat above their strong faces and armor covered the rest of their body. The armor over their chests bore King Nakosi's royal tabard.

Calla told herself to remain calm and that they were on her side, but her foot was on her verge of backing up. She pushed back her shoulders and held out the letter. "I am to enter, by command of the King."

"Command of the King?" The right guard scoffed. He snatched the letter from Calla's hand.

"That's the royal sigil!" The guard on the left pointed to the letter over the right guard's hands.

Calla eyed them with gumption. "Straight from King Nakosi."

Both guards gave her a look as one guard unfolded the letter, they read it simultaneously. "I'm sorry but no," the left guard said.

"How dare you defy the King and deny the Hybrid entry?" Calla shouted, ripping the letter from his hands. "Are you not under his rule? Is that tabard you wear a lie?" She couldn't believe she came all this way for nothing. "You will let me in!"

"Don't you dare doubt our loyalty for the crown," the guard on the left shouted back.

"Then let me in."

"We can't. We're under strict orders," the left guard said forcefully, on the verge of yelling.

"Whose orders trump the Kings?"

"The Grand Bookkeeper. Too many Corrupted running about. If one of them got in, they could do more damage than your pretty little head can muster." The right guard gestured to the tall spires of the Library. "Even if you're The Hybrid. We will pass on that you have arrived here to the Grand Bookkeeper. If you wait here, I will go at once."

Calla crossed her arms and cocked her hip. Her mouth opened, poised to say something decidedly unladylike.

A dark line sliced through the air on the other side of the gate. Calla's eyes grew wide, and the guards turned around to fall to their knees. The line grew wider to create a portal. Calla's breath hitched in her throat, while her heart drummed out of her chest.

A hooded figure stepped out draped in a black cloak. A gust of wind pushed back the hood on the figure. Calla knew in an instant that it was her, the Oracle. Shriveled with age, wrinkles embedded deep within her soft facial features. A braid, of her ghostly white hair, fell down her spine. Her colorless eyes blinked away the whip of the wind.

"Let her in," the soft voice spoke from beyond the gate.

"Oracle?" The left guard sputtered looking up from dropping his head. "Is it you?"

Ignoring the guards, the Oracle looked straight to Calla. "Time is of the essence." She waved her hand and the bars of the gate parted in the middle, creating a path for Calla. "Come Hybrid. We have much to discuss and very little time to do so." Calla paused before the guards, unsure if she could pass them. "Come child," the Oracle commanded again.

Calla stepped past the speechless guards to squeeze through the bars. "Oracle, it's great to meet you! I have so many questions." She stuck out her hand to the woman, but the Oracle's eyes didn't see her gesture.

"Quiet," she cut her off. "Not here. Too many eyes." The Oracle gestured to the portal. It was dark on the other side, and that unnerved Calla to her core. "Come."

Calla hesitated. The Oracle finally looked at her with her eyes. They were pure white with no irises. She was positive that the Oracle was blind. Her fear evaporated away with a surge of confidence. This was her moment. She stepped into the portal with the Oracle close behind.

Darkness choked Calla. The Oracle swept away the portal with a wave of her arm. In that instant the room was robbed of all light. Wherever the portal led them, it was darker than her eyes could process. "Oracle?"

"I suppose light would help."

A flash of light sparked behind Calla, and she turned around. The Oracle held a flame within her palm. It reminded her of when Philomena did the same thing, it felt like forever ago to her. The Oracle tossed the flame forward. Calla ducked out of the way before it landed on a torch down a never-ending hallway of darkness. She watched as the flame bounced from torch to torch, lighting the passage. The torches cast a bright light onto the walls next to the sconce, but the glow barely reached the high ceilings.

"Thank you," she whispered as the Oracle walked past her. Calla stood tall and closed the gap between them. The Oracle walked with confidence, and did not look down once, but Calla had to look down to avoid the holes in the stone. "Is this a better time for my questions? I have a lot and I was hoping you would have answers."

The Oracle stopped and turned to face Calla. She stopped on her toes to avoid crashing into the elderly being. "We are safe now. It is only us under here, deep under the Library. I shall answer the best I can for I do not know all the answers. However, we must keep moving."

Calla didn't know where to start. She played this moment over and over in her head until she had come up with hundreds of ways this could pan out. "Am I the Hybrid?" Calla mentally scolded herself after asking the stupidest question ever.

The Oracle turned around for a moment, then turned back and continued down the passageway. "You know the answer to that."

Calla's cheeks were red from embarrassment, but she knew it wasn't seen. The Oracle was blind after all. All her steps were perfectly calculated, and she did not need the light. Her sight seemed to be in the future. Calla was curious, but there were more pressing questions to ask. "Are my parents still alive?"

"As far as my sight can see, yes."

Calla's heart soared with a happiness that she couldn't describe. She knew in her heart that she had biological parents somewhere. Being born to the deities, Calla laughed in her head that she ever believed it. More questions swirled in her head, "Where are they? Have they been looking for me? Do they miss me? Do they know what I am?"

"They never stopped looking for you from the moment you were taken from them."

"Taken?" Her wave of joy crashed.

"Yes, by me. The deities willed it so."

Anger flashed in Calla. This shriveled navy bean of a woman was the reason for everything. She could have been normal. She could have a happy life with her parents.

"I can sense your anger. I will give you this. They will find you, rest assured."

Calla wasn't sure if she should be angry or grateful. Her parents were alive, looking for her and were going to find her if they hadn't already. She racked her brain to think if anyone fit the bill. "What's my mother like?"

The pathway started to curve as it followed the spiraled peninsula. Calla was anxious to see where the Oracle was leading her.

"From what I recall, Ellanora's eyes rivaled the coldest ice."

Her anger melted away. Finally her mother had a name. Ellanora. She had her mother's eyes. Calla bit back a wide grin.

"She loves you more than anything."

"How do you know?" Calla felt like she was ten years old, unable to hold her questions in. She didn't know how much time they had left. "Have you spoken to her recently?" The Oracle didn't answer, the silence that fell over them was deafening. Calla finally gave way to the silence, "What about my father?"

"When we parted ways, he was hopeful time would pass quickly."

Calla furrowed her eyebrows in confusion. "What does that mean?"

"I gave you the best answer I can. My memories have faded, and my sight doesn't see the past."

Frustrated, Calla sighed shortly. "Will I defeat The Corrupted?"

"I cannot see that far," the Oracle responded immediately. "I can only see minutes ahead."

"So much for an all-seeing Oracle," Calla said sardonically. She didn't care if the Oracle heard. She was supposed to have all the answers.

The Oracle moved silently for some time. "My sight stops moments before my death. I knew what I was doing when I accepted the prophecy from the deities. To have such a gift, you must give up physical sight."

Calla was impatient. "Why was I brought to the human realm?"

"The deities wanted to protect you from the dangers of becoming Corrupted. From birth, I sealed half your powers away and hid you among the humans. Your parents disagreed, but it was the will of the deities."

Calla pursed her lips. "So, they're alive?"

"I already told you…"

"No. The deities."

"Their spirits are. They locked Morta away in the heavens after the First War and stayed there to make sure she never escaped."

A dim light broke through the darkness, entrancing Calla. The pair stopped before a shimmering veil of blue mist.

They stopped and Calla looked to the Oracle, wanting one more answer. "If Morta is in the heavens, how come there are still Corrupted running about?"

The dirt beneath Calla's feet began to rumble, and the walls shook. Small chunks of rock dropped on over their heads. Dust shrouded the corridor they came from. "What's happening?"

The Oracle turned her head to face Calla. "We must hurry, The Corrupted are coming." The Oracle placed her hand on the shimmer and whispered words Calla didn't recognize. The shimmer fell into nothing, replaced by a plain stone wall. "Only you have the power to break it."

Calla took off her gloves and watched them hit the floor. It felt freeing in some way. "What do I do? I pass out when I use my powers!"

Another rumble ripped through the cavern.

"The Corrupted are breaking through the seal from up above, we must hurry. Trust your instinct!"

Calla placed her hand on the rock, closed her eyes and concentrated. Her sigil glowed to light the tunnel while her body trembled. Shivers shot down her spine. She felt her energy drain from her. Calla let out a deep shout and the wall blew outward.

Beyond the wall was a room bathed in soft white light. A pedestal occupied the middle of the room. Calla's vision was spinning, but she placed one foot in front of the other until she stopped before the pedestal.

"What now?" She tried not to faint. Her hand gripped the white marble pedestal and Calla turned to the Oracle.

"The end is coming." Tears streamed down the Oracle's face.

"What are you..." Calla started, but whispers clouded her head. The same incoherent whispers that had led her astray many times since she arrived to Midelle.

Calla's mouth became dry when she turned her head back toward the pedestal. The air left her lungs as a shining orb materialized in front of her.

The orb filled the room with bright, gold light. The inside reminded Calla of bubbles dancing underwater. Timidly, she reached out to the orb. When her fingertip touched the golden surface of the orb, a shock jumped across her fingertips. She ripped her hand away to coddle her tingling skin.

Another rumble shook the cavern. Shouting echoed from a far distance.

"Hybrid?" The whispers asked from the orb.

"Yes?" At that moment, she felt as if she was screaming but her voice was barely audible. The shouting became louder, mixed with small sobs from the Oracle. Calla covered her ears and closed her eyes. So many voices filled her head, and they all were saying something different. "Stop!" She cried.

The voices in her head converged to one, and Calla dropped her hands to her side. Every noise faded away until Calla heard, "Accept your powers." The command came from the orb.

The world came back in mere seconds. Calla was back into the thick of it. The yelling and sobbing hit her ears again.

Calla sucked in a breath. She knew time was running short. She dropped her right hand with her sigil on the orb, and it glowed brightly. A searing pain swept through Calla. A scream escaped her lips. Her legs gave out and she dropped to her knees, but she kept her palm on the orb. The orb's golden light intensified and so did her pain. Tears streamed down Calla's face as every cell in her body seemed to explode over and over again.

She was grateful when the pain faded along with the light from the orb and her sigil. Calla stayed on her knees, trying to catch her breath. She let her hand slide from the orb to hug the pedestal. Her body felt broken, but stronger in a way she'd never imagined. She felt a new and stronger power surged through her.

Calla's limbs shook when she stood up. She looked at the Oracle. The tears had stopped, but a grim look was set on her face. "We need to get out of here," Calla said to the old woman. The shouting was becoming crisper and clearer from the passageway they had come from. "Now."

"We're trapped down here," the Oracle whispered. "My sight is gone. I'm but a frail, blind, old woman now."

Calla rushed to the Oracle and grabbed her shoulders. "Now is not the time..." A whooshing noise caught Calla's attention, but it was too late.

The Oracle gasped as an arrow pierced her heart and stopped inches before Calla's chest. The Oracle's face contorted with pain and her legs shook. Calla gripped her arms tighter to keep her standing, but the woman was dying.

"Do not give in to them," the Oracle whispered, then she disintegrated into dust. In shock, Calla watched the dust of the Oracle meld into the rubble on the ground.

Calla's head snapped up. She looked down the corridor. An archer perched on a fallen chunk of the wall with a triumphant smile plastered over his face. The flickering torches revealed an endless crowd of red-eyed attackers surging out of the darkness. "There she is!"

"Take her alive and unharmed," a commanding voice boomed over the commotion.

Dread and panic settled in Calla's whole body as the horde of Corrupted charged at her. She pushed the hair from her face and took a quick breath. The Corrupted were getting closer, their faces twisted in anger.

"Okay powers, let's see what you can do." She held out her hand and concentrated on putting up a barrier to buy her more time. Broken boulders on the ground shook and flew back to recreate the wall that she had broken minutes before. She quickly celebrated the fact that she was no longer dizzy after using her powers.

Within seconds she heard The Corrupted shouting for a battering ram.

"Shit." Calla looked around for a way out, but she was completely sealed in. Her eyes rushed over every part of the room, but there was no way out.

"One. Two. Three!" The ram slammed into the stone. Pebbles tumbled down the wall as it started to crumble.

Bile rose in Calla's throat when she realized that she was cornered. Once that wall came down, she couldn't keep them all away.

She desperately tried to remember how she had incinerated the horde back in Japhia. Nothing was coming to mind. Her sigil didn't glow that bright white, and that feeling to protect was absent.

"Three!" More chunks tumbled off the barrier.

Calla looked again for a way out when an idea struck her. She bit her lip, turned to face the outer wall, and put her hand out. She forced her mind to go blank except for the wall. She concentrated on it.

"Three!" The barrier trembled again and the top crumbled down. Calla's focus broke as she looked back and gasped with fear.

"Come on," she spoke to herself. "Work for God's sake!" Calla looked from her palm to the wall. With a frustrated shout, she channeled everything into her power. Her sigil glowed, and the outer wall blew out.

The icy winter wind slammed her in the face immediately. She carefully walked to the edge and looked down. Her stomach dropped at the height she was at. Dark blue water swirled with the dangerous currents of the sea, all while spewing sea spray in the air. There was no way she would ever survive a swim in those waters, powers or not.

"Three!" The barrier split down the middle, but it stood, still intact.

Calla held the sides of the hole, debating her next move. She only saw one, and she knew it was a bad one.

"One," the horde chimed together.

Calla knew this was it.

"Two!"

Calla's hand gripped the wall, her knuckles white.

"Three!" The ram slammed into the wall, the barrier crumbled. The Corrupted rushed in. In a leap of faith Calla's feet left the ground.

Calla was in the air with the platform behind her, but the feeling stopped when an iron grip latched onto her arm. Calla's body and head slammed against the rock outside. She looked up and saw red eyes.

Calla fought for freedom, but it was no use. They were pulling her up against her will. She tried to get away by clawing at the hand around her arm and pushing her feet against the rock.

"Move!" That deep voice commanded as a body leaned down to grab her other arm. The two men worked in tandem to hoist her body up and over the edge. They dropped her on the hard stone, with her shoulder catching the brunt of the fall.

In a whirlwind, Calla stood up, poised to attack, but there were too many. She wanted to do something, but fear froze her.

"You're outnumbered," a Corrupted woman chuckled lowly.

"Leave now and I'll... I'll spare you," Calla shouted meekly. She spun around to keep an eye on all of them.

The group chuckled as a section parted for a hulking corrupted beast. In his hands was a large single shackle made from black metal. His massive size, scarred face, and ruthless dark red eyes would haunt Calla for the rest of her life.

Calla turned to face him head-on with her arm shaking uncontrollably. "Stay back!" Why did she ever think leaving Finn was a good idea? If she ever saw him again, what would she even say to him. The 'if' made her want to be sick.

The beast chuckled before he charged her. Before Calla could react, someone moved in behind her and grabbed her arms. She tried to rip her arms out of her captor's grasp.

"Hold her still," the one in charge commanded as he fitted the shackle around her neck.

Calla squirmed at every opportunity, trying to get her powers to work. She had no idea what to do. Her fear held back her powers. She hoped and prayed for something... anything.

"Enough!" The beast yelled. He brought his giant hand across Calla's face, and she saw stars just before she hit the ground.

Calla stopped resisting for only a moment when she felt the cold clamp of the shackle around her neck. She felt her new-found powers dim. It made her feel like before she opened the signal, weak.

The man in charge grabbed her upper arm and pulled her up. The beast had a sick smirk on his face. Up close, his face was even more hideous than she could have ever imagined. He was inches from her face, but when she tried to turn her head, he grabbed a handful of her hair. Calla let out a scream and gave way to his strong grasp. He smiled at her and said, "Welcome to The Corrupted, Hybrid."

Finn groaned as he rolled over onto his stomach. He was done drinking for a while but drinking led him to the best night of his life. He got to be with Calla, on her terms.

He could still taste her on his lips, feel her warmth, and smell her delectable skin. It's something he'd never forget. He was riding an incredible high and never wanted to come down. For once, the world didn't feel like it was hammering down on his shoulders.

Finn's hand broke out from under him to feel around the bed, to the left... to the right... more frantic with each passing heartbeat. He shot up from the bed, "Calla!" He darted to the bathroom, but it's as he had left it last night. "Calla! Where are you?" Deafening silence churned his stomach. "Damn her!"

Barely keeping his mental sanity together, Finn dressed in a hurry. He then rummaged through his bag, hoping he was wrong about her whereabouts. Everything was there except for the letter and the ring.

The last thing he had to put on was his belt that had his sword inlaid with gold. As he tightened the belt, his eyes caught the hardened puddle of gold and ash in the fireplace. A cold sweat broke out over his skin. "I knew I shouldn't have," Finn muttered. He clipped his cape over his broad shoulders, "No." He stopped himself from spiraling down that dangerous train of thought. "I'm coming to save you, Calla, I promise."

He thundered down the stairs and through the few early risers in the pub.

"Could you make any more noise?" An elderly woman scolded with a harsh look. Her eyes were cast down over her food.

"A blonde-haired woman came through here earlier, have any of you seen her?" Finn asked the small breakfast crowd, ignoring the old woman. He knew it was a wasted effort, but there was a chance one of them saw something. Finn looked at each of them before letting out an aggravated growl. "You're all useless!"

Finn whipped open the door. It banged on the inside wall of the pub. Outside, the glistening snow blinded him. He pressed on anyway. He couldn't waste one more second, Calla needed him.

He ran towards the Library with his eyes focused on the front gate. Even from a distance he could see something was wrong.

Bodies were strewn along the pathway leading up to the Library, and blood stained the fresh snow. He saw the gate wide open. Finn's blood ran cold. Calla was there.

"Now that I'm thinking about it, I saw your blonde-haired friend."

Finn spun around. The old woman was wrapped tightly in a plethora of layers. He looked at her round, puffy face, but her eyes were gone from view. "Where did you see her?"

The woman rolled her lips together, "I'm not sure where, my memory is," she waved her hand in the air. "Maybe down this way." She began to shuffle away from the Library. The snow moved out from under her feet. Finn's hand wrapped around the hilt of his sword.

"I don't think she went that way." He turned on his heels and began at a fast pace back towards the Library.

"Oh, The Hybrid is this way, I assure you."

The hair on the back of Finn's neck rose as shivers ran down his spine. He turned around with a suspicious look plastered over his face. His eyes narrowed.

"You have my attention."

"Good." The woman pushed her hood back to reveal what he already knew. Before Finn could draw his sword, a man burst from the shadows of the alley and tackled him to the ground.

Finn struggled against his aggressor, but his face was only pushed further in the snow. "Fight me with honor, you bastards," Finn growled while the man tied his hands behind his back.

A strong jerk brought him to his feet to come face to face with the woman. Finn bared his fangs at the old woman who smiled at him as a response. "I swear to the deities, I will rip you apart limb by limb!" Finn tried to escape the captor who held his arms down, but it was no use.

"That was easier than we thought," the male that captured him said. "So much for Captain of the Royal Guard?"

"Untie me and fight me with what little honor you have left! You piece of shit!"

Finn felt another set of cold hands wrap around his arms. The new set of hands tied his arms to his chest. His first aggressor came to face Finn with a cryptic smirk on his face, his gray hair covered an eye. "I can't wait to watch you die. I wish I was the one doing it."

Finn watched the old Corrupted woman bring out a small vial. He knew what it was as his eyes laid on the shimmering purple liquid, Finn swallowed hard but he couldn't give up. "Whoever tries to kill me, will die by my hands!"

The woman closed her hand around the vial. She scoffed before she crushed the vial in her hand. Blood and the portal potion dripped from her palm. "You dare think you can defeat the Hybrid?"

Finn's blood ran cold as the three corrupted around him laughed. "Calla would never..."

"Once she's Corrupted that will change," the woman said as she conjured the portal. She went into the dark abyss on the other side.

The two men pushed Finn through, and he landed on a hard floor. Finn picked his head up from the dirty ground to see a long line of cells lining the room. "What are you waiting for?" The old woman hissed. "Lock him up."

Finn couldn't get his footing. The guards lifted him by the arms and tossed him into an open cell. They kicked him a few times. He took the hits and bit back the pain. Finn's back and stomach throbbed where they kicked him. "Is that all you got?" He spat with fading vision.

The guards walked out of the cell laughing. The cell door closed and locked with a loud click.

The woman knelt before the cell and looked down at Finn. He was nearly unconscious. "I will take pleasure in your death."

Twenty-Three

Calla hit the dusty and wooden floor, hard. "Maybe now you'll learn your place and cooperate," a female troll hissed. Calla propped herself on her hands to turn her head. She saw the guard who had all but dragged her up to a room in this crumbling tower.

"Go to hell." Calla spat in her direction. It landed inches from her feet.

The guard rushed behind her to grab her hair. The long braids of the troll graced Calla's back. She fought the trolls grasp, but she only held Calla's hair harder. "You're lucky that you're the Hybrid. Queen Belladonna would never tolerate this insolence."

"Go ahead and hurt me," Calla got out through the sharp pains to her scalp. "I'd like to see what happens to you."

"Maxa, what is the meaning of this?"

The troll pushed Calla's face into the floor, then got off her and stood tall by the door.

"Teaching her a lesson. She fought me all the way up here. Queen Belladonna would never stand for this," Maxa glanced at Calla, "disrespect."

Calla finally mustered up the courage to get up. She put distance between her assailant by putting her savior in the middle of them.

Her savior was a middle-aged woman, dressed in a black cloak, with a rounded face and merlot eyes. "You were tasked to bring her here." Her eyes flicked to Calla and back to Maxa, "And only to bring her here. By not following the Queen's orders, you are disrespecting her command."

Maxa rolled her eyes. "Mind your tongue, hag."

The woman narrowed her deep red eyes and stepped closer to Maxa. Calla's back was up against the wall, and the rough stone bit through her shirt. Her heart raced. The shackle around her neck felt even tighter.

"Is this a matter for Abaddon?" The woman asked sharply. Fear danced in Maxa's eyes, and she was stricken silent by her question. "Well?"

"No."

"Now leave us. I must prepare the Hybrid for the ceremony." The woman gestured to a dress folded in her hand.

Maxa left the room in such a hurry that she tripped.

The woman closed the door then turned quickly to Calla. Like snow on a sunny day, the red melted from her irises. The mystery woman closed her eyes, dropped the dress to steel herself on the mantle of an unlit fireplace.

"Thank you, for saving me." Calla's voice was soft, unsure of what was happening.

"We don't have long, I am slipping to the Corruption already." The woman opened her eyes to show white irises. "I'm Rose."

"Rose, how did you turn yourself just now? Are you here to help me?" Calla tugged at the magic shackle around her neck, showing the raw skin underneath.

"I'm afraid I can't help you with that, only Abaddon holds the key, and my magic won't work on that."

"Magic? You're a witch?"

Rose nodded her head. "Yes. When The Corrupted were rising once again, King Raoul kept asking me to do horrid things. I was able to persuade him otherwise on most things. Then the siege of the Free Army happened, King Nakosi began his reign, and another witch was born, all was well.

When signs of The Corrupted started occurring a few years later, a bad feeling surfaced. I had a dream where I saw Philomena Corrupted, and that solidified my fears. The Corrupted needed a witch, like with the First War of Midelle, and they would stop at nothing to find one. I knew that they would get either me or Philomena at some point." Calla's eyebrows furrowed.

"I thought I would stand a chance at fighting them. Not sweet little Philomena, she'd turn in an instant, and be a slave to The Corruption. Like my dream foretold."

"You gave yourself up?" Calla's tone was accusatory.

Rose let a sad look take over her face. "I went into hiding, but within a few weeks, they found me by accident while I was traveling the Long Road. It wasn't long before I became Corrupted."

"How are you resisting it now?" Calla asked. "Your eyes turned from red to white."

"This is my first lucid moment. When the realm shook with your return, something changed in the air. Hope flooded the land and the hearts of the people. That's when I felt the strength to hold back The Corruption within me for the first time. I waited for you to come here to act. Like my own capture, I knew it was only a matter of time."

She tucked a piece of dirty blonde hair behind her ear. "Before I lose myself, there are things you must know. Belladonna has found a way to turn innocents Corrupted. My first task when she captured me was to make a potion from the blood of those monsters to turn someone Corrupted. I refused at first, but the torture was too great."

Shame washed over her face. "I watched myself do everything she asked, and I couldn't stop myself because I was afraid of death. I was a different kind of monster, and I hadn't even turned Corrupted yet."

She paused for a moment, her breath shaky. "When I tested the first batches of the poison, there were horrifying failures that turned some mad upon consumption. Others? They are her most loyal soldiers. Once it was undoubtedly successful, she made me drink my poison, and I've been Corrupted until this moment."

Calla's lip quivered as she connected the dots. "Am I to drink..."

Rose nodded as she pulled a vial from her bust that had a black liquid swirling inside of it. "That's been the plan all along." Calla wanted to vomit. "I kept tabs on your journey thus far, so I was ready to help you when the time was right."

"Help me how?"

Rose shook her head. "I can't help much because I feel I am losing my grip on sanity. I need to hurry, forgive me." She twisted the tiny vial in her fingertips. "Under no circumstances do you drink this. It's my most powerful concoction. On our one test subject, he became Corrupted within seconds. You won't be able to fight it, I promise you."

"But I'm the Hybrid, the deities made me to stop The Corruption."

"That doesn't make you immune!"

"What if I am immune? Are you positive I'm not?"

"Why do you think she's been trying to capture you since you arrived?"

Calla sighed shortly, "If I become Corrupted..."

"Midelle will fall to The Corruption, and it will only know hatred and darkness." Rose hid the vial back in her chest. "You cannot drink it. No matter what she does to you or others."

Calla held up her hand to interject, "Can't she shove it down my throat?"

"She can, but one of the most crucial ingredients, the deity rose, protects the drinker. When it's forced by another hand, the poison doesn't work, I was never able to figure it out, but Belladonna knows this. You must drink it on your own accord for it to work, which is why you can't drink it. I promise you, if you drink it, you will become Corrupted. And all will be lost."

A shiver ran up Calla's spine. The possibilities shuffled through her head. Neither of them had anything to say, but the wind outside filled the silence with high pitched shrieks.

Calla turned away from Rose and drummed her fingers on the frosted glass. "There has to be a way out of here." The snow outside swirled in the air. "Can't you make a portal to anywhere but here?"

"I'm locked out of my storeroom," Rose admitted sadly. "I need the key from Abaddon. He still doesn't trust me after all this time. I suppose for good reason."

Rose made a choking noise before her legs started to buckle. "I'm losing control. I'm sorry Calla. I wish I could..."

Calla rushed to her and grabbed her arms to support the witch. She noticed Rose's eyes were turning dark as the red swirled over the white. "Stay with me!" Rose became an unyielding, fluid statue as Calla shook her. "Rose, please!" Her eyes grew darker, and she stared off, absent-minded, into the distance.

Calla's lip quivered as she begged, "Please don't leave me." Calla's head hung low before Rose, and she couldn't bring herself to let go of her arms. "I can't become Corrupted," whispered Calla. "Please."

"You will let go of me, Hybrid."

Calla jumped back. Fresh tears streamed down her face. Calla knew Rose was gone, her lips were set in a taut line, and her eyes were devoid of any emotion. She tried to form words, but her brain was going faster than her mouth, "I... I..."

A hard slap snapped against Calla's cheek. It was in the same spot that the hulking beast, which she suspected to be Abaddon, slapped her at. Her left side of the face pulsed with a dull pain. She pressed the stinging skin with her hand while fighting the urge to cry more.

"You will speak no more words unless told to respond. Do I make myself clear, Hybrid?" Afraid to speak, Calla nodded. "Good. Queen Belladonna expects you to wear the dress. If you don't change on your own will, I am told that Abaddon will assist." She gestured to the misshapen, folded dress by the fireplace. Rose looked confused. "I must prepare for your ceremony. Time is of the essence."

Calla watched, still as stone, as Rose left the room and locked her inside. She waited a minute before dashing to the door to pull on the handle. To no surprise to her, it was definitely locked. Calla pulled, pushed, and kicked with all her might until her breaths fell in heavy pants. She broke away from the door, fighting tears.

Calla looked for a distraction and picked up the dress to inspect it. It was onyx in color with long lace sleeves, a regal skirt, and a neckline with a slight plunge to it. Under any other circumstance, she would wear it, but with anger, she tossed it in a corner. Dust billowed up from the disturbance.

She wrapped her arms around herself. Her lip quivered from the cold and fear. She moved in front of the fireplace and fell to her knees, desperate for a warmth that wasn't there. Tears fell faster than she could process. The wind howled, knocking against the cracked windows outside the room.

"Deities?" She asked against the tears. "You probably can't hear me." A tear fell from her chin. "I'm in trouble, and if everyone in Midelle believes in you, then help me." A sob broke from her lips. "Help me bring them peace. I don't know what to do."

She paused, looking around the barren room for a sign. Only the wind howled in response. "I'm such an idiot!" Calla's hands fell to the side and her hand brushed against something hard in her pocket. She dug in her pocket and frowned. "The dragon call," Calla opened her hand to see the magical claw in her palm.

With an idea brewing, she went to the window and unlatched the lock. It cracked open a bit, but the ice-crusted on the edges kept it from fully opening. "Please work," she begged, and she brought the signal to her lips. She moved her face close to the opening, sucked in a big breath then blew into the hollowed-out claw. Nothing. She blew again and again and again. Alec said only dragons could hear it, but she doubted it even worked. There seemed to be no air going through the claw.

A sharp turn in the wind forced the window shut. The cracked pane of the window knocked the claw from her hands. She watched the ancient whistle shatter on the floor.

Heartbroken, Calla scooped the broken pieces in her hand to cradle them. "Damn you," she whispered at the broken signal. Calla's hand curled around the pieces only to throw them across the room in a sudden burst of anger. They clattered on the floor by the dress.

Calla wrapped her fingers around the shackle that constricted her powers. She closed her eyes to try and focus her powers, but

Calla felt nothing. She yanked at the shackle, ignoring the pain, but it didn't budge. "Damn it!" She kicked an empty crate, only to have a piece of the wood crack.

Calla took a deep breath to calm down, then sat down on the floor. She could feel the cold's grasp through her clothes. The snow swirled in a flurry outside that Calla couldn't take her eyes from. "Damn you too, stupid snow."

Silence fell over the room. With a sigh, she let her head fall back on the wall. "I never should have left the Inn. You'd find a way out of this, Finn. I know it."

Pain. It was everywhere, and every move Finn made caused him more. He couldn't find it in him to sit up. For who knows how long, he stared into the darkness above him. All he could think about was failure. He failed Calla.

She was alone in this castle somewhere, and he was here. His mind wasn't having trouble coming up with situations of what they were doing to her. He knew his body was cold, hungry, and he needed a healer. But mostly Finn was numb with failure.

Groans echoed from the hallways, it reminded him of his dungeon in Japhia. Never did he imagine that he would be on the other side of the bars.

"You alive over there?" A man's voice cut through the desperate echoes. The voice was strained and belonged to an older man.

Finn turned his head to face the raspy voice, but all he saw was darkness. "Me?" He coughed as a sharp pain ripped through his lungs.

"Who else? Everyone in here has either gone mad from Belladonna's experiments or from resisting The Corruption."

"Which are you?" Finn held back a groan.

"A pawn in Belladonna's games," the man paused, "Which are you?"

"I'm not sure yet, but what I do know is that I'm as good as dead."

"Aren't we all?" The man laughed. A small smirk played across Finn's lips, if this old man had some humor left in him then Finn couldn't give up, not yet. He owed Calla one more attempt.

A heavy clank told him a door had unlocked. Light flooded the long halls of the dungeon. Finn covered his face with his arm and let out that groan.

"Shut your mouth and eat up. Queen Belladonna ordered that you get one more meal," a new voice commanded as he wheeled a cart in. He grabbed the unlit torch near his cell then tipped it in the lit flame from outside the dungeons.

Finn caught a glimpse of the man in the cell across from him. The man had long tattered hair that looked to be brown, was skinny and wore tattered clothes.

The bald guard tossed a loaf of bread at Finn, which bounced off his shoulder and fell onto the floor. A full waterskin fell a foot short of him, he could hear the water slosh inside. Finn didn't move.

"Are we going to have another problem?" He was addressing the man across from Finn.

"No."

"That's what I like to hear, Queen Belladonna won't allow you to starve."

"How considerate of her," the man hissed. Finn heard him take a bite of the loaf, it crunched too much.

The bald man turned to Finn again, "Are you going to eat, or will I have to shove it down your throat too?"

Finn agonizingly sat up, holding back his cries of pain, and took a bite of the bread. His stomach churned, stale. "Happy?" He muttered through a full mouth.

He had to switch hands because his two fingers were swollen and colored with bruises in their earlier stages. He regretted punching the stone wall back inside the mountain. The bald man scoffed then continued wheeling the cart down the hallway.

Finn spit the bread out to empty his waterskin. The frigid water soothed his parched mouth.

His gaze landed on the man, staring into the distance, across from him. "Best if you use the water to soften up the bread." He laughed. "Learned that trick months ago."

"How long have you been here? What's your name?"

He turned to Finn, his face devoid of emotion. His bright eyes were wide and sunken into his gaunt face. "I wish I knew. You can call me V. Yours?"

"Finn." He mirrored V's mysteriousness. "Why is Belladonna keeping you alive?"

A pointed look overtook V's face. "You haven't been here for a day, and you know why." He moved closer to the light, he was older than Finn thought. V had to be in his late forties.

A puzzle was coming together in Finn's head, but he had to work on this a minute to figure out this piece. "To kill you?" The old man nodded his head. "But why wait so long?"

V laughed, "You know why."

Dread settled in Finn's stomach as golden tresses and baby blue's flashed through his mind. "Calla."

"Calla," he whispered so soft that Finn almost missed it.

"She's the Hybrid. She has everything to do with this, doesn't she?"

V nodded. "If she falls to The Corruption, nothing and no one in Midelle will be able to stop her. These lands will fall to the darkness and evil that bleeds out from The Corruption."

Finn pressed his body to the bars of his cell to get closer to his informant. "Who is going to kill us?" His mouth went dry, and his heart was heavy. He didn't have to ask the question, but it materialized out of panic. V was silent but didn't break his gaze. "Who is going to kill us?" Finn begged too loudly, clinging onto the bars of his cell.

"Where is he?" A voice roared from the corridor beyond the open door. Finn braced himself for whoever was coming through that door. The guard passing out the bread scrambled to the front, ignoring Finn's outburst. He dropped to one knee, in fear of what was coming.

Barging into the dungeons was a massive man with blazing red eyes, impossibly thick arms, and a twisted scowl of a face.

"Abaddon," the guard acknowledged with a cool edge to his voice.

Finn locked eyes with Abaddon. He had to be the one in charge. New energy coursed through Finn, and his pain faded away with adrenaline.

Abaddon snarled as he stopped before Finn's cell, not breaking eye contact. "Unlock the cell."

"Queen Belladonna's orders were strict..."

"Bram! Now!"

In a rush, the bread giver, Bram, grabbed a ring of keys jingling from his waist and with a shaking hand, unlocked the cell. Before Finn could prepare himself, his feet were off the ground, back against the wall and the red-eyed beast was inches from his face. "Where did you get it?" He growled.

Finn tried to push his assailant away, but he didn't move an inch. "Get what? I don't have anything!"

"Tell me!" Spittle flicked on Finn's face.

"Abaddon, what is the meaning of this?" A calm yet curt voice cut the tension of the situation. Finn's feet plopped on the ground, but he didn't dare move a muscle.

"My Queen, we need to start the ceremony. Now," Abaddon snarled.

Finn couldn't see the Queen because Abaddon was too close to him. The sounds of the dungeons dimmed as the sharp click of her heels echoed throughout the endless row of cells. "Step aside."

Abaddon obeyed without protest.

Finn watched Belladonna come into the light of the torch. She was the smallest person here but had the most power in that dungeon. Finn was no fool, he knew if he was to attack her, he would surely die. "You must be Belladonna."

Abaddon shoved Finn's shoulder back into the wall and it burst with pain. "You will address her as your Queen."

Finn sucked his teeth for a moment as his eyes darted over to her, "Excuse me, Queen Belladonna."

"So, you are the thorn in my side," her eyebrow raised, "Captain Finnigan Quinn, is it?"

"Of the Royal Guard," Finn felt like being the thorn she thought he was.

"How could I forget? I can't stay long, I must see to my most esteemed guest. The Hybrid."

Finn stiffened. "Don't you touch her!"

A smile came across Belladonna's dark lips, "Did I hit a nerve?"

Finn took a step forward, but Abaddon slammed him back against the wall again. More pain ripped through Finn's shoulder. He kept a straight face.

"I shall tell her that you send your regards."

"I will make sure you have the most agonizing death of them all if you even look at her!" Finn pushed against Abaddon's grip.

Belladonna turned toward the door, "Come Abaddon, I must visit the Hybrid to prepare her for the ceremony. I see your point, there is no use in waiting until tomorrow. She must be anxious."

Abaddon's knee slammed into Finn's stomach, and he doubled over in pain while Abaddon locked the cell. "Bram, stand alert outside the dungeon. Kill anyone not our Queen or me who tries to enter the dungeon." His voice was gruff and menacing.

"Yes, Abaddon." Bram bowed to Belladonna as she passed him.

The heavy, wrought iron door to the dungeon closed, but light still illuminated Finn and V's cells.

Finn sucked in a breath and wrapped his arm around his stomach. There wasn't a part of him that wasn't in pain or bruised. It reminded him that this feeling once belonged to Calla by his doing. Oh, how he wished he could go back in time and start over.

"You're lucky he didn't hurt you more. I've seen him beat men dead before."

Finn glanced at V, he still sat in the same place, "They still need me, right?"

"You're playing a dangerous game."

"I'm a dead man walking anyway. What do I have to lose?"

V shifted his body and with a grave look on his face he answered, "Everything."

Twenty-Four

Calla opened her eyes. The room was devoid of light. She turned around in small steps. A gilded mirror stood out from the dim aura around it. Despite the darkness, she saw herself in the mirror, dressed in a black gown. The very same gown she had discarded earlier.

Dark lace encased her arms and when she turned, the skirt's ethereal fabric billowed out around her. Calla ran her hands up the bodice in the mirror. Her fingertips brushed her neck, her red lips, and stopped when they reached her eyes. They were still a vivid color, but red instead of blue. Calla didn't feel fear, she only stared back at herself. A small smile spread across her lips in the mirror.

Calla jolted awake and gasped for air. Her heart raced as perspiration soaked her skin. She didn't remember falling asleep. She hadn't thought sleep was possible in this situation. She crawled to the window to peek out the ancient, colored panes. The sun had dropped halfway below the horizon.

She caught her reflection in the glass, and to her relief, her eyes were the same blue they always have been. Calla rested her forehead on the cold glass.

"I couldn't find it in myself to wake you."

Calla slowly brought her head up from the coolness of the glass, she could see a figure reflected in the panes from across the room. She froze as her heart leaped into her throat.

"Do not fear Hybrid, for all the confusion you have been burdened with is nearly over. It is time for the ceremony. We must make haste, there is no time to spare."

Calla took in a sharp breath to steel her nerves and turned to face her enemy. Calla knew from the withered deity rose crown, the dark lips, and deep red dress exactly who it was.

"Belladonna, I presume?" She clasped her hands together to stop them from shaking. The woman's face was bereft of any emotion. Her eyes tracked every tiny movement Calla made.

Then the woman smiled. Her fangs emerged for an instant, then were buried behind her lips. "Beautiful, smart and powerful. Exactly as I imagined my Hybrid to be." Her eyes traced up and down Calla. "Pity you didn't change into the dress. It would look lovely on you. I saved it just for you to wear on this occasion. And now you," she glanced to where it lay in the dust, "have tossed it aside. I won't have Abaddon put it on you but let me make something clear. This will be the first and only time you disobey me, Hybrid."

Ignoring Belladonna's obsession with the dress, Calla's lips formed a scowl. "I'm not your Hybrid. I fight for the people of Midelle! For freedom from your diseased Corruption."

Belladonna glanced to the left, the right, then back to center at Calla. "I don't see the people you fight for. Where are they? Seems they've all abandoned you."

"They are coming." Calla made fists at her sides. For the first time in her life Calla fought an urge to kill someone. The urge became stronger with every passing second.

Belladonna snorted a light smile.

"As is your protector?"

Calla's nails dug into her palms.

"What is his name again?"

Calla remained silent. She desperately tried to form a plan in her head.

"No? Something Quinn? Am I right? "

Calla's shoulders tensed.

"I must be getting closer. He and his guards did kill many of my soldiers. Seems fair I repay the acts of carnage. Oh my, what is his name?"

"Finnegan." Calla spat the name at Belladonna and immediately wished she hadn't. If she had just stayed by his side this morning.

"That's it!" Belladonna snapped her fingers. "Finnegan Quinn, Captain of the Royal Guard!" She moved closer to Calla. "Where is he?"

"Coming to kill you."

"Kill me?" Belladonna gasped mockingly and placed a hand over her heart, "Don't you want him in your army? To keep him close? I hear he is an excellent swordsman. I was told you two have grown quite fond of each other."

"You know nothing of me. If I don't kill you myself, he will!" Calla leaped and knocked Belladonna to the floor and wrapped her hands around Belladonna's throat.

Immediately a strong hand grabbed the back of her shirt and yanked her off The Corrupted Queen. She caught her fall before her face caught the floor. Calla sneered at him, the monster. The monster with the hideous face at the Library who had shackled her.

Belladonna got up and dispassionately dusted off her gown. She walked towards Calla but stopped short. The monster loomed right behind her.

"I'll forgive you this time. I did hope this meeting would go better."

"I thought I'd already used my 'last and only time' to disobey you?" Calla spat.

Belladonna froze for an second, then moved through the door slowly. "Come Abaddon. The time is upon us, we have a ceremony to attend to. Midelle will soon know what it is like to live with a clear mind. One free of emotion and aches." Belladonna turned just outside the doorway, "I also think it's time the Hybrid met her army."

Calla planted her heels in the ground in a pitiful attempt to stall. Her only shot had been poorly planned and executed.

"Come," Abaddon growled. He yanked Calla out in front of him. "Now walk, or I'll drag you down the stairs." Calla took a tentative step, but the brute behind her pushed her along. The three of them descended the staircase at a quick pace.

Calla turned to get a closer look at Abaddon's face. It was as mangled and scarred as she remembered it. Deep scars layered over his face and throat.

"Just let me go," she whispered. "Please. I'll leave Midelle and never come back." She couldn't believe what came out of her mouth. Even if he let her leave, she didn't know if she could. Abaddon ignored her.

They walked through an endless maze of high-ceilinged corridors. Calla passed several partially burned tapestries that hung by threads. Chunks of the walls were missing, as were with sections of the roof. Snow and dead leaves collected in some nooks and corners.

There was one unnervingly missing thing, people. The castle was silent, and that made Calla want to unravel more.

Somehow, she held herself together.

"Where is everyone? Your army that you keep talking about?"

"Awaiting your arrival. I was worried that the snow wouldn't stop, but I'm pleased that it did. They're all waiting outside for you. The perfect place for you to join us." A thin smile spread across her lips.

Dread settled in Calla's stomach.

"I won't become Corrupted," Calla seethed.

They walked on in silence. An echo of cheering seeped through the walls. It became louder with each step they took down the vast, dank corridor. Tinted light washed over them from the far end of the passageway. Calla's heart pounded in her chest. Every cell in her body screamed at her to flee, but with Abaddon so close she knew it would be a wasted effort.

The cheering had become a deafening roar. Late afternoon light streamed through a cracked window and blinded Calla.

Belladonna waved her arm and Abaddon pulled back on Calla's shackle. She halted with a sputtering cough. "You'll," she coughed, "kill me!"

Abaddon scowled at her, "Wait."

Calla swallowed. It burned.

Belladonna disappeared into the light and the roar grew even louder and then went silent. Calla froze. Her heartbeat drummed in her ears. "The time has come, my loyal subjects! We have captured the Hybrid!"

The Corrupted burst into a cheer that died down quickly.

"The Hybrid harbors the three deities' souls, but what of ours? What of the most powerful deity of them all? What of Morta? We shall change that. Tonight, under her watchful eye from above, the most powerful creature in all Midelle will become one of us. Tonight, her eyes will gleam red, and we will follow her into a glorious battle. Tonight is the night that The Corrupted will claim their reign over all of Midelle!"

The army roared so loudly Calla couldn't hear herself think anymore.

"No longer must we hide in the shadows! Behold, our champion, the Hybrid!"

Abaddon shoved Calla so violently she had to step forward to catch herself. Calla scowled at his towering form. He pointed towards the light. She hesitated, then stepped outside. The strong sunlight on the snow blinded her. The Corrupted army cheered continuously.

Calla's senses adjusted and she walked forward. She and Belladonna were on a rounded balcony. Stairs curved down on each side. What frightened her more was the horde on the ground in front of her. Druids, vampires, and trolls all stared at her with red eyes. Their lined formation went on as far as Calla could see. There were hundreds of them, each clad in armor with deadly weapons in hand. All of them, ready for war.

"Come take in your army, Hybrid!"

Calla turned from the endless lines of The Corrupted army and looked at her. She stood at the front of the balcony next to a pedestal with a small black cushion on top.

Calla turned back to Abaddon. He stood before the shut doors of the balcony, trapping her there. Her eyes caught a movement above the doors. She saw the body of a man locked in a suspended cage high above the balcony and her stomach turned. He had no clothes on and had huddled his body close to protect himself from the elements. There was no doubt in her mind that he was dead, for his skin was a pale blue.

A strong gust of snow-studded wind stabbed Calla. The cold made the shackle that sapped her powers feel like a block of ice.

Calla stepped forward. Each stride brought her closer to complete despair. She stopped and looked at the black poison that rested on that pedestal.

Rose's warnings echoed in her head. She looked past Belladonna to the front row of The Corrupted horde. Rose stood tall in the middle of the line, her eyes gleaming red, admiring her poison.

There was a cage of some sort near the left stairs, but Calla couldn't see inside because a thick tarp lay over it. Calla could only imagine what, or who was inside.

Belladonna held the poison out to Calla. She was too entranced with Rose to notice her pick it up and step closer to her.

"Do you know what this is?"

Calla shook her head, "No."

"I ask that you drink it. No harm will come to you," Belladonna whispered and pulled the cork from the bottle.

"No."

"Hybrid, you must drink the potion."

"No."

Belladonna grabbed Calla's wrist. Her skin was ice cold, and her pointed nails dug into Calla's skin. She felt a hard pressure on her arm, but her skin was numb. "This is the last time I will ask you."

Calla yanked her arm. Nail marks lingered on her skin. "Ask me a hundred more times, my answer will always be no."

Belladonna inhaled air sharply like she had anticipated Calla to say yes. "Just remember, I asked you, more than once."

Belladonna looked over Calla's shoulder to Abaddon. Calla watched him nod his head and descend the stairs to the cage.

A dark feeling settled in Calla's stomach.

Belladonna wore a triumphant smirk on her face.

"You can't fool me. I know what it is. I'd rather die than drink The Corruption poison."

Belladonna narrowed her eyes to Calla. "After your eyes shine red, you will tell me who the traitor is, and I will end their life, personally. They made this far more difficult than it had to be."

A whoosh caught Calla's ear. She looked to see that Abaddon had ripped the tarp from the cage. Both Calla and Belladonna looked to the rusted iron cage. Two hooded men were being escorted up the stairs with their hands bound behind them. Abaddon directed the two guards, one guard for each man. One prisoner struggled against the restraint, and a second guard rushed to his side.

They brutally subdued him.

The Corrupted Queen had a deep smirk on her lips.

Calla backed away from Belladonna. With every second that passed, the dread in her bones intensified. Both men were pushed to their knees in the center of the balcony. The passive man's clothes hung in tatters, as if he'd been a prisoner for a very long time. The feistier man Calla hoped was Finn. At the same time, she prayed it wasn't. If it was him, then no one was coming for her.

The energetic man started shouting something incoherent through a gag and the hood.

Calla hesitantly turned her back to the men.

"Now," Belladonna hissed, "drink it, or their lives are over."

Calla swiftly replied, "Who are these men?" She felt the eyes of The Corrupted army upon her.

Belladonna swirled the vicious poison in her hand. "What an excellent question. Abaddon, prepare to unmask them."

"What is she waiting for?" a shout came from The Corrupted army. It was impossible to distinguish who it was, but the army murmured in agreement.

"Silence!" Belladonna commanded. A forced hush swept over the ranks.

Belladonna grabbed Calla's hand with gentle grace and forced the vial into her fingers. Despite the chilling weather, the vial had a subtle warmth to it. "The fate of these men depends on your next action. Say no, and their lives will come to a slow, agonized end. Say yes, and their lives will be spared."

"You're going to hell," Calla whispered, staring straight into the Queen's eyes.

"I've been in hell for years, my dear." Belladonna didn't break the stare, "I'm the Queen of this realm, and you will fight for me. It is your destiny."

Calla scowled and turned away from Belladonna, her hand still curled around the black poison. Everything in her wanted to destroy the vial, but that would all but seal the fate of the masked prisoners.

The Corrupted army behind her howled with cheers and laughter in anticipation of death for the two men.

This time Belladonna didn't quiet them.

She stopped before the calmer man. Abaddon ripped off the hood. The man looked at her with wide eyes. He couldn't say anything from the gag in his mouth, but a single tear fell from his deep amber eyes. His matted, and befouled hair was in such disarray, Calla couldn't tell its natural color. This man was a stranger to her, yet his life was in her hands. Calla reached for the gag, keeping him silent, but Abaddon swatted her hand away.

He nodded his head to the second man. Calla held her breath and Abaddon yanked the hood off him. Calla gasped but kept her lips stiff to suppress a sob.

Finn looked at her with disappointment in his eyes.

Calla dropped to her knees in front of him with tears streaming down her cheeks. "Finn, I'm so sorry. I never should have left you. I'm so sorry!"

Calla couldn't make out his muffled words through the gag, but he nuzzled his head to hers.

"I can't drink it," she whispered, "but I can't lose you either."

Finn pushed Calla's head up with his, so her eyes met his. Her hands went to cup his cheeks. He felt so cold. His eyes said what his mouth couldn't. They both knew what needed to happen, but Calla didn't know if she was strong enough.

Finn nodded. His sad eyes knew what was to come. Calla glanced at the older man, whose head hung in the defeat he had accepted years ago. She still couldn't place him.

"Kill them! Kill them! Kill them!" The army below chanted, eager to see death.

"We don't have all day," Belladonna sighed. "What is your choice?"

Calla felt time slipping away from her.

She rubbed her thumbs along Finn's jaw. The stubble brought life to her numb fingers. She gave Finn a nod then turned to Belladonna. "Who is the other man?"

"I suppose you wouldn't recognize him. He did let himself go a bit during his time in the dungeons." The ranks of The Corrupted roared in laughter again.

"Abaddon, let him tell our Hybrid who he is. I believe he's been waiting for this moment for almost twenty-six years."

Abaddon loosened the gag, and it fell from the man's mouth. He looked at Calla but refused to speak. Another tear fell from his eye. Abaddon grabbed his tangled locks and whispered something in his ear.

The little color left in this man's face was replaced by terror.

"I..." He swallowed.

Calla's heart pounded.

"I am the Forgotten Prince Vallen Pragma. I am your father."

Calla froze.

Everything in her body shut down. Calla stared at her... father?

Before he could speak another word, Abaddon shoved the gag into his mouth and tightened it. The universe crashed around Calla.

All of this was wrong, so wrong.

Finn pleaded with her silently, his eyes said too much.

Yet with Vallen, there was hope.

"My patience is wearing thin, Hybrid. Make your choice."

Calla stood there frozen, the vial still warm in her hand. All she could think about was when she was little, she would sit on her tire swing crying to the stars while she begged for a chance to meet her parents. She had begged and pleaded until she could beg no more, and now, here he was. In front of her. His fate in her hands. She couldn't find any words to say. What would he say to her? What would she say to him?

"What is your choice?"

Calla faced Belladonna, unable to say anything. All the air was gone from her lungs. Her reality turned to sand and was rapidly slipping through her fingers.

"Kill them!" Belladonna shouted in anger, "Start with the Captain."

Belladonna stomped past Calla and faced the army. The Corrupted chanted for an execution. Abaddon's sword sang as he removed it from its sheath.

Like the bell tower in the morning, it woke Calla up.

Without thinking, Calla popped the cork on the bottle and downed the vile contents. Every place the poison touched in her mouth, throat, and stomach burned with what she knew death would taste like. "Stop!" Calla shouted loud enough to halt Abaddon's sword inches from Finn's neck. Both looked in time to see the vial empty.

The army cheered. Belladonna rushed to Calla grabbing her arms, "Hybrid, this is only the beginning. We will rule Midelle!"

Calla's vision doubled while darkness seeped into the very fiber of her being. She dropped the vial, and it smashed into little pieces on the stone floor. She fell to her knees. Pain stabbed her body. She forced her eyes shut to escape the agony.

Calla stood alone in a vast field. Darkness crept through her mind. Panic rose as she tried to move but could not.

Lines of black fire burst forth from the horizon, raging towards her from all angles. She braced herself for impact. When the black fire moved in close, it met a hazy semi-globe of a golden metallic sheen. The semi globe encased her, but the fire engulfed the perimeter of the semi-globe. The dark fire tried to penetrate the globe, but it only fizzled against the shield. Calla closed her eyes, knowing she needed to wake up.

It was time for her to fight.

Twenty-Five

"**I**s she alive, Abaddon?"

"Yes. I don't know how, but yes."

"Take the suppressor off of her."

"Yes, My Queen."

Calla's body still coursed with pain, but she could hear the shackle clang to the ground. The deity's power surged through her once again, fighting the poison. Her chest heaved, in and out, in and out.

Her eyes opened.

"My Queen, the Hybrid is awake."

Calla saw an aged woman inches from her face. The old face was familiar, but she couldn't place it.

"Her eyes haven't changed yet, but seeing that she hasn't gone mad, it's only a matter of time until they do." The old woman turned to Calla, "Now get up and acknowledge your Queen."

The woman helped Calla to her feet. She was still sore, but the burning pain in her body had subsided.

A dark fog filled her brain. She couldn't navigate through it. She caught glimpses of two figures on their knees. They had familiar faces, but she had no idea as to who they were. Her attention snapped back to Queen Belladonna.

Calla curtsied as gracefully as she remembered how to do so, which wasn't very graceful at all. "My Queen. It is an honor." A pit settled in her stomach.

Belladonna's eyes lit up at her obedience.

"Calla, no," the redhead cried through his gag.

Calla? Was her name Calla? The fog in her head was so dense she couldn't find her name.

Calla heard the man being kicked by... Ab... Abaddon behind her. Patches of clarity were starting to disperse the fog, but not quick enough.

Belladonna grabbed Abaddon's massive sword from his sheath and moved in front of the red-haired man. She bent down to become face level with him, "It will be my pleasure to see you die." She turned to Calla and held the sword for her to take. "Your first assignment as the Hybrid is to kill both of these traitors."

Calla nodded her head without hesitation. Her fingers wrapped around the sword's hilt. She swung it a few times in the empty air to get a feel for the blade. Something about swinging a sword held a vague familiarity to her. It was heavier than she had expected it to be.

She moved next to the man Belladonna ordered her to kill.

She raised the sword over his neck.

Her arms stopped mid-air.

Her fog-filled brain froze.

"Kill them!" Belladonna hissed.

The crowd beyond the balcony roared so loudly Calla couldn't focus.

She forced her attention to the man underneath her blade. This wasn't right.

"Kill him! Embrace the darkness," a voice in her head insisted.

"No..." Calla said to herself. She dropped the sword behind Finn. Finn! The man was Finn! And next to him was her father! All her memories came back as a whirlwind that banished her fog.

Her powers now surged freely. Calla stuck out her hand in Abaddon's direction. A block of stone flew from the wall and slammed into his chest. The blow sent him tumbling down the stairs.

Calla focused her power again and slammed her palm onto the balcony. The aged bricks crumbled under her hand.

Calla knelt between Finn and her father. Brick by brick the balcony crumbled away. Belladonna fell with a shower of bricks that piled onto her army. Calla lifted her hand and stopped the balcony underneath them from falling.

She turned to Finn and removed his gag. She pulled it down then grabbed Abaddon's sword to cut the rope that tied his arms.

Finn pulled her to him the second he was free. They were freezing, and the sun faded faster and faster, but all that she needed at that moment was his body next to her.

"I thought I was dead back there," Finn whispered against her skin.

Calla broke from the hug, remembering her father. She looked back to Finn before giving him a frightened look. "So did I."

Calla moved to Vallen and untied his gag, then freed his arms. He wrapped her in the most anticipated embrace of her life. It was everything she expected a hug from her father to be, warm, loving, and comforting.

"Dad, is it really you?"

Vallen nodded. "I never thought I'd see you alive, but here you are. You have to listen..."

"Hybrid, I command you to kill them," Belladonna shouted from the ground as she climbed from the rubble.

"Calla, we've got to get out of here!" Finn shouted as the army was surrounding the remnants of the balcony.

"Yup, well aware!"

The ground rumbled again, but not from Calla. It affected the whole field as everyone fell to their knees or grabbed onto anything stable. She looked over to Finn with her eyes wide. "What's happening?"

"The deities have heard our prayers," Vallen gasped through chattering teeth.

The tremors intensified. Behind them in the snow-covered field a swirling purple rift sliced open the air. The light emanating from the rift seized everyone's attention.

The rift widened under the fading daylight. Calla's heart raced faster than she ever thought it could. She could make out people on the other side. Hazy, but most certainly people.

"I don't think it's the deities," Finn smiled.

"Calla," Vallen whispered, grasping onto her arm. "Listen to me..."

Calla looked at her aged father. His face was pinched with pain. "Shhh, don't talk. We will speak later. Save your strength to get back to the castle." She rested her hand over his, looking away from him. "Finn, what do we do?" Finn's eyes were glued to the snowfield. "Finn! We're outnumbered!"

Finn turned to her. Their eyes connected intensely.

"I don't know about that."

A familiar voice yelled, "Charge!"

Calla's head snapped to the widening portal.

Lucy charged through the purple mist on a gray stallion with the entire Royal Army close behind. In the wave of allies, Calla saw Bear, Wolf, and Zenji near Lucy with their weapons raised.

Their war cries filled her ears.

With a renewed sense of hope, Calla watched The Corrupted soldiers leave the perimeter of the balcony to charge at the mounted army.

The Royal Army flanked The Corrupted soldiers with ease and met them in a clash of steel on steel. The Royal Army kept coming and coming through the portal until they outnumbered The Corrupted army.

Finn grabbed Abaddon's sword lying near them and jumped down from the balcony.

"Are you crazy?" Calla shouted.

" I fight with my soldiers!" Finn answered as he stabbed an unsuspecting Corrupted troll in the back. "Stay up there!"

Calla didn't charge in as Finn had. Her battle was not there, so she watched from the safety of the broken balcony next to Vallen. His breaths were short and shallow while his body shivered from the cold.

Calla's breath hitched when she saw a beautiful white stallion burst through the portal. She recognized the rider instantly, Vihaan. Her heart swelled as he spotted her across the field. He pulled the reins on his horse when they made eye contact over the chaos. Vihaan whipped the reins and disappeared around the other side of the castle.

A motion below caught Calla's eye. She saw the hem of a dark red dress billow through a wooden archway. Calla jumped to the ground with one thing on her mind, Belladonna must not escape.

"What did I just say?" Finn parried a thrust from a Corrupted vampire. The Corrupted hissed. Finn hissed back, then kicked him onto his back and stabbed him in the heart.

"I can't let her get away," Calla shouted. She ran after Belladonna. Inside the castle she had to hurry because the light was fading fast. It was hard to see in the crumbling yet massive labyrinth.

"Calla!" Finn's angry voice filled the vast but empty room she was in. She stopped and thought about going back.

Abaddon's voice echoed up above in the stairs. "Hurry my Queen, I will get you to safety!"

Calla immediately ran as fast as she could in the direction of Abaddon's voice. She couldn't lose Belladonna. This had to end and end tonight. She reached the bottom of a long, spiral staircase in time to see a glimpse of Abaddon and his Queen exit the stairs about halfway up.

Calla couldn't wait a moment longer. She took two steps at a time and made sure she avoided the gaping holes in the stairs.

The corridor they exited into was silent. Goosebumps raised on Calla's skin. She checked every room along the passageway as quietly as she could.

All the rooms were empty. The corridor ended in what looked to be an old atrium, some walls still stood tall, but the roof was gone. The large room reminded her of the rooms back in the Edulis Mountains. Big and cavernous. Stairs wrapped up the wall around to a large balcony above.

Calla was in the middle of the atrium when Abaddon jumped down from above. He had a crazed look on his face. The Corruption coursed through him.

"I told you we were being followed. Kill her!" Belladonna commanded from the balcony. She turned on her heels to disappear.

"Yes, My Queen," Abaddon growled.

Calla backed up against the wall. Her hand shook when she raised her palm to him and concentrated. Calla could feel her Hybrid powers pulse through her to concentrate through her sigil.

Abaddon charged.

Calla released her energy.

Large blocks of stone tore from atop the crumbling walls and slammed into the monster's chest. Abaddon was knocked back into what used to be a bookcase.

Calla scrambled for the stairs, eager to catch Belladonna. Something grabbed Calla's ankle.

Abaddon.

She fell forward but tried to yank her foot out. "Get off of me!"

Abaddon roared and pulled Calla from the stairs. He threw her on the ground like a rag doll.

Pain tore through Calla's arm, but still she attempted to get up.

Abaddon's hand went to her throat. The monster picked Calla up like she weighed nothing. His fingers curled in.

"No," Calla shouted through her closing airway. Her hands flew up to his. She tried to pry his grip from her throat.

Calla couldn't get air into her lungs. Bright flashes filled her fading vision.

Her resolve faltered.

She begged for something, anything to save her, but nothing happened.

This was it.

She felt her life slipping away.

Calla had failed everyone.

Vihaan, Finn, Nakosi, Sigmund, Philomena, Zinnia, Saria, everyone...

A thundering roar cut through the silence.

Calla saw nothing but the fading face of Abaddon. Suddenly Abaddon dropped her. Air filled her lungs again. She coughed, her face against the cold stone floor.

"Brother! What has become of you?"

Calla rolled to the face the sky. A familiar man was standing on the stairs.

"Alec? You heard the call?" Calla wheezed before breaking into a coughing fit. "Brother?"

Alec acknowledged Calla with a quick nod and she nodded back, in pure shock.

"You come here now?" Abaddon shouted from the bottom of the stairs. He locked eyes with his kin. "After all these years you still call me brother?"

Abaddon turned to Calla, "I should have known that you had the dragon call, and not Quinn."

"I see you tried to rid yourself of who you are," Alec growled, getting his brother's attention back on him. "Cut off your scales?"

Calla pulled herself up on a broken piece of furniture. She looked at the two men.

The closer she looked at Abaddon, the more she saw it. They were both tall, with the same stature and black hair.

Abaddon was a dragon.

A Corrupted dragon.

Lady Amethysts' worst fear came true.

"You don't get to judge me! It should be I who judges you!" Abaddon's face contorted and malevolence gleamed in his eyes.

"We settle this in the sky! Remember our traditions, Aron?"

Alec morphed into the brilliant forest green dragon that Calla remembered.

Aron?

He was dead or at least was supposed to be, according to Alec and Sigmund.

"Fuck your traditions!" Abaddon roared and fell to his knees. His skin ripped. Oily black scales erupted through his skin. He grew taller, longer, and bulges pushed out from his back. The bulges burst into massive black wings with red spikes that outlined the sharp curves.

The two massive dragons stared at each other, then took off into the skies together.

Talons raked against scales, ripping and slashing. Time and again Aron went for Alec's throat, biting at it with his colossal mouth full of jagged teeth.

Calla watched them fight in the twilight sky, dipping down in a tangle of anger only to soar back up into the clouds.

"Calla! Where are you?" Finn's voice echoed up to the atrium. Calla ran towards him, but something stopped her.

The thought of Belladonna, being all alone now, pulled her attention from Finn.

She dashed up the stairs, following the path The Corrupted Queen had taken.

Vihaan rounded a corner. His heart raced. Calla, his light, was there on the broken balcony. He found the balcony, but it was empty.

Calla was gone.

"Calla!"

He knew his voice had gotten lost within the chaos of the battle's cadence.

He couldn't lose her, not again.

A hand grasped his leg, "She went after them."

Vihaan looked down. An old man looked back at him in desperation. He dismounted his horse and grabbed the old man's shoulders with more force than he'd intended.

"Went after who?"

"Belladonna," Vallen said with hushed intensity. "We need to hurry."

Finn waited for Calla to answer, but all he heard were the sounds of the battle outside. "Dammit," he whispered, then continued up the stairs. He had already failed at his duty once and couldn't afford to fail again.

He wouldn't fail again.

A dark mass flew by a gaping hole in the wall. Finn stuck his head out and saw two dragons engaged in a life-or-death battle. His mouth dropped in shock. Deep wounds riddled their scales, and bite marks peppered their bodies. The dragons flew by a high tower, locked into their battle.

His eyes found Calla climbing a broken battlement. She gleamed like a shining star in the dark abyss.

"Calla!" he shouted through the window. He didn't expect for her to hear him, and she didn't react.

He gazed down on the snowy battlefield. Finn filled with pride for a moment as he watched Lucy lead the royal army with confidence. She was taking down The Corrupted just as he had trained her, perhaps better than he could. Maybe she could keep the Captain title and he could...

Finn pushed his self-indulgent thoughts to the side.

Finn took the stairs with a renewed vigor, two at a time.

It was time to end this.

Every time Calla caught a glimpse of Belladonna, she found some way to escape. But their game of cat and mouse was about to end. They were moving higher and higher into the decaying tower, leaving fewer places for her to escape to.

The sun would stay below the horizon until morning, and stars dotted the clear sky. Calla's breath puffed in front of her with a cold snap.

She expected Belladonna to reappear out of a tower that she had been inside before. Belladonna emerged out of the door, looking left and right in a panic. Her dress was torn by long rips and the deity rose crown was gone.

Fear shone in her eyes.

"Enough running!" Calla shouted. Her sigil glowed. She covered the door with vines from the side of the tower.

Belladonna pulled her shoulders back and hissed. Black smoke rose from her hands.

"It's a pity the poison didn't work on you. I could have turned you into something truly... special." Belladonna took a step closer, "A true hero."

"Give in," the dark voice hissed again in Calla's head. "It's not too late."

Calla fell to her knees. Her vision went dark. The pain from drinking the poison erupted once more throughout her body.

Calla closed her eyes. When she opened them, she was staring at a mirrored reflection of herself.

Bright blue eyes stared back at her. Her reflection walked to her, grabbed her shoulders and whispered, "Fight back!"

Calla opened her eyes.

A powerful energy had awakened within her. Her hands glowed with a golden light. She had to find her powers that the deities gave her. It was now or never. "I don't need to be your hero. I am the Hybrid!"

Streams of bright energy burst from her hands.

Belladonna put up her hands, letting her dark mist drink in the light.

Belladonna brought down her hands and a rush of black mist enshrouded Calla.

She waved her hand through the mist. It evaporated with a hiss as it touched her sigil.

"Hybrid?" Belladonna laughed, "Don't you see that you and I are one of the same?"

Belladonna's hands curled, and the remaining mist evaporated without Calla touching it.

Calla shook her head, the glow on her hands grew brighter. "You're a monster! Look at all you've done! The chaos and turmoil Midelle has had to bear, all because of you!"

Rage washed over Calla. A golden rope of light shot out of her hands and met the dark mist around Belladonna in a shroud of sparks.

Belladonna turned the dark mist into sharp points, all pointed at Calla. The dark needles flew at Calla at an alarming pace.

Calla threw up her hands to shield her face and a bright light encased her. She had no idea how her powers worked but winging it was, at least, keeping her alive. The needles pelted the shield with a noise that reminded Calla of hail on a roof.

Once all the needles were gone, she thrust her arms out to expel the shield. Pieces of the shield turned into sharp shards of light that hurled through the frosty air and towards Belladonna.

The evil Queen dodged the light shards and rose to her feet. A mass of dark mist formed over her head.

"If I am a monster, then so are you."

The ball of mist shot towards Calla and hit her square in the chest. She fell into a broken wall, the breath knocked from her lungs. She could feel the open air under the same arm still pulsed with a dull pain from being thrown by Abaddon.

Calla tried to move away from the edge, but Belladonna stood over her. Black mist dripped from her hands. "I don't need you to bring true peace to Midelle, Hybrid. I can do it on my own, the voice was mistaken."

The black mist twisted in the air and creeped up Calla's body. Where it touched her, it burned her skin. She refused to die here.

Calla grabbed Belladonna's arm and pulled her to the ground. The mist sunk into nothing as Calla tried to move The Corrupted Queen closer to the edge.

Belladonna fought to escape. She dug her nails into Calla's arms.

Calla rolled, and with all her remaining strength pushed Belladonna towards the edge. .

Belladonna fell over the edge and Calla scrambled away from it. There was silence.

Calla couldn't hear herself breathe, but she did hear a gentle call.

"Calla," Belladonna called from beyond the edge. "Please help me..."

Calla cautiously peeked over the edge.

Belladonna's fingers desperately held onto a hole in the battlement. She hung there, within arm's reach. The great maw of the dark sky waited to swallow her whole and spit her onto the ground.

"Kill her," the dark voice in Calla's head whispered.

Belladonna clung tightly to the wall, but the stones crumbled under her fingers. Her eyes were frantic with fear. The wind whipped Belladonna's drees about violently, and chilled her nose and cheeks a deep shade of red.

Dark thoughts clamored in Calla's head, but she knew they were evil.

"Please," Belladonna begged after one of her hands slipped from the crumbling wall.

The dark voice quieted when Calla focused on the women begging for help. Without another hesitation Calla stuck out her arm to help. Belladonna used her free hand to lock onto Calla's wrist.

"I'm no monster." Calla yanked the woman up.

The second Belladonna steadied her footing the black mist around her hands returned. "It's such a pity the wrong side got to you first. You could have been great."

The deity's power came alive in Calla once again. She felt it in her sigil, then it moved through her veins.

The golden glow returned to her hands.

"It's such a pity you've lost yourself," Calla mocked, "this ends now!"

The golden light burst brightly from the lines of her sigil.

Calla yelled and the light beamed from her hand into Belladonna. The powerful blast tossed the Queen backwards. A sharp crack filled the air as Belladonna hit the wall.

The world went silent for Calla.

She felt her powers dim inside her as her breathing calmed.

The evil Queen's eyes were closed. Her chest rose and fell lightly. Dark blood seeped from her head and pooled under her.

Belladonna's eyes opened slightly. The red started to fade from her irises. "We aren't that different, after all..."

Calla stood there, in terrifying awe of what she had done and why she wasn't helping the woman. Was this who she was becoming? Calla berated herself for not coming to this woman's aid, but, how could she? Belladonna was the source of everything evil. Was Belladonna, right? Was Calla no different than her?

Her world grew smaller.

She couldn't feel the cold.

She couldn't feel the wind.

Strong hands gripped her shoulders.

The cold slapped her face.

Calla blinked. She was staring into the sea glass green eyes of Finnegan Quinn. He brought her into his chest and whispered, "I'm here. You did it."

Calla sobbed. Her knees buckled, but Finn wrapped his arms around her more tightly to steady her.

"She's not dead yet," Calla cried against his chest. "I couldn't do it."

"Stay here, I'll kill her. You did good, Calla. I knew you could do it. The deities were right to pick you."

Finn backed away from Calla and drew his sword. He held it over Belladonna's heart.

Calla turned away. She couldn't watch Finn end this woman.

"Looks like you've lost, Queen." Finn raised the sword high.

Belladonna's eyes shut tight, and her lip quivered.

"Stop," Vallen yelled from a distance. "Don't hurt her!"

Finn let the sword drop to his side. "What? Are you kidding me, Vallen?" Finn threw the sword against a far wall, a spark fizzled. "After all she's done to you?"

A pained dragon roared in the distance, followed by a loud crashing sound. Everyone felt the rumble in the stone beneath their feet.

Calla hoped it wasn't Alec.

Vallen rushed across the battlement and pushed past Calla. Tears filled his eyes and he dropped next to Belladonna.

Calla didn't understand why her father would choose to ignore her, after all these years.

Vihaan was close behind the Forgotten Price, but he stopped next to Calla. Everything she missed about Vihaan rushed into her mind. He brought Calla in for a hug, and she melted into his arms. Fresh tears rolled down her face. His arms wrapped around her, and he kissed the top of her head. "I'm here, Calla. I'm so sorry. I'll never leave you again," Vihaan whispered into her hair.

Finn watched the reunion with a scowl on his lips. He walked to the edge, turning his back towards everything.

Vallen scooped up Belladonna's body in his arms to sob into her dark hair. "My love, my sweet, sweet Ella. I'm sorry I couldn't save you. Open your eyes, Ella, one more time." All eyes on the battlement turned towards the grieving man, in shock.

"Your love?" Finn yelled with his face contorted in anger. "How could you love that corrupted... thing?"

Vallen paid no mind to him as he kept whispering to the woman he loved.

Vihaan wrapped his arms around Calla tighter, "Perhaps you don't understand love, Captain?"

Finn growled and clenched his fists.

Calla placed a hand on Vihaan's chest, giving Finn a sad yet sympathetic look. "Both of you stop." Her voice froze them both instantly.

"Vallen, my love?" Ella coughed. Everyone fell silent, wanting to hear what she had to say. Vallen showered her skin with soft kisses mixed with tears.

"Where is she?"

Calla's head sprang up from Vihaan's chest.

"Where is our daughter?"

Vallen turned to Calla and gave her a sad look.

"Me?" Calla's lip quivered.

What had she done?

Vallen held out his hand to her.

Calla went to Belladonna... or Ellanora's side. Her eyes opened with a shaky sigh.

Calla felt completely empty. Icy blue eyes stared into Calla's.

"I have your eyes," Calla whispered. Tears spilled down her cheeks. "Is it really you?" Calla paused as she found the word that she buried a long time ago. "Mom?"

Ellanora nodded. Calla noticed how much blood she had lost, she was kneeling in a pool of it. "Calla, I love you," Ellanora whispered with a small smile on her lips. Her eyes closed and opened again with a tear streaming from the corner of her eye. Her chest barely moved with her shallow breathing. "You two were my dream come true..." Ellanora closed her eyes with a soft sigh. Her head lolled limp back into Vallen's hands.

"Ella?" Vallen asked the wind as he held his wife. Tears ran down the man's face. "Come back, my love. This isn't the end of your dream." A sob escaped his throat, "Our dream."

"Mom, please?" Calla sobbed against her cold hand. "Don't leave me! I'm sorry. I didn't know it was you..."

Vallen brought her head close, crying into her hair.

Vihaan came behind Calla to pull her into him where she fell into his arms sobbing. "What have I done?" Calla whispered into Vihaan's chest through sobs. All she could think about was how she had killed the woman who birthed her. She had yearned all her life for this answer, and a singular thought kept running through her head. Belladonna was right. "Maybe I am a monster after all?"

Twenty-Six

After what seemed like an eternity, morning came. For Calla there was no warmth of the rising sun. A painful emptiness hung heavy on her heart. Her mind could only focus on Ellanora, her mother dead, by Calla's hand.

Everything after the tower was a blur. Calla managed to get through the portal back to Japhia. She managed to sneak away from the clamor of returning to find solace. After aimlessly wandering around, she found herself at Philomena's bedside. At first, she thought the little witch was dead, but she was unconscious instead.

"Has she come around?"

Calla's eyes remained on Philomena, her chest rose softly. She knew that voice, one of the first she heard when she came to Midelle. The calm voice brought a sense of peace to the turmoil inside her.

"No. What happened to her? I wanted to be alone, and I found her like this."

Violet came next to her, sitting on the edge of the bed. Her hair was grayer than Calla remembered it. The severity of the situation bore onto her face.

"To make the portal wide enough for the army, she had to cast a separate spell on an existing portal. She knew it was too much for her juvenile powers, but she wanted to do it. She said saving you would be worth it. Once she completed the spell to widen the portal, she collapsed. Hawke brought her away from all the chaos, to here. She needed to rest. Philomena is strong. She'll wake up, I have a feeling."

A small smile played across Calla's lips, "You and your feelings."

"I also had a feeling that I would find you here. You ran so fast from the portal, some thought you didn't make it through. Did you know where you were?"

Calla shook her head, fighting the need to cry.

"The Isle of Dragons. It was the perfect place to raise an army without anyone noticing."

Calla brought her head up to look at Violet with tears pushed up to the brim of her eyes.

"Oh, my dear," Violet sighed as she pulled Calla close to her for a hug, "you did it. I knew you would save Midelle."

Tears fell down Calla's cheeks. She wrapped her arms around Violet and sobbed. "Belladonna, she is," her voice cracked, "she was my mother."

Violet brought Calla at arm's length, "We all know now who Ellanora is. I refuse to think of her as Belladonna. You should do the same. I came searching for you to see if you were all right."

Calla pulled away from the hug. She considered her next words carefully.

"I will be." Their eyes fell to Philomena in the same beat. Calla wiped her face with the sleeve of her shirt. Dirt, dried blood and who knows what else stained the fibers of her clothes, but she didn't care.

"I have her eyes, Violet," Calla said as she brought her gaze up to her friend.

Violet sighed shortly, "There is something you have to understand, you did not kill your mother. Corrupted Belladonna was not the woman who birthed you. That was Ellanora Bellcott. You killed the evil that held your mother captive for all these years. She wasn't strong enough to survive the battle."

Calla held back tears as she pictured life leaving her mother's eyes, over and over.

"I met her a few times," Violet said, breaking the chain of the replay in her head.

"Ellanora?"

Violet nodded. "I had no idea that Prince Vallen, or Vallen I suppose, and Ellanora were planning on running away together. She was kind, brave and smart, oh so smart," Violet smiled. "It's not a surprise that Vallen fell in love with her against his father's wishes. After Queen Alina died, King Raoul's soul went with her. It took every part of him to stay sane, but when Vallen left... he fell to The Corruption under the facade that he was looking for his son. Everything that happened fits. We were all pieces in a puzzle of our own design."

Silence fell over them with the crackle of the fire filling the void. "When I think about it, you're a miracle of the deities' hands. They created you to right our wrongs, to put the puzzle together, but most importantly end The Corrupted once and for all."

"Me? A miracle," Calla scoffed as she wiped her nose.

"With Ellanora being a vampire, her chances of her having a healthy baby were nonexistent. It's happened before, but it's accepted that vampires..."

"Have stillbirths," Violet nodded her head at Calla's words.

Silence fell over them again. Calla couldn't hear it over the hundreds of questions swirling in her head. "Where is Vallen... uh, my father now? We need to talk about some things."

"I last saw him in the courtyard."

"Thank you, Violet," Calla sprang from her chair. The overwhelming sadness that threatened to consume her faded before this new-found determination to find answers.

"Calla?" Violet called after her. Calla popped her head back through the doorway of the makeshift recovery room. "You bring a special light to the castle. I've missed you so much. We all have. You've been gone for too long."

"I agree." Calla smiled, it felt wrong. "I missed you too, Violet."

Calla burst into the stairwell. It was utter chaos, but it was all leading down the stairs. Soldiers leading remnants of The Corrupted army in chains down into the dungeons. Some part of

Calla wished that those men and women in chains were no longer Corrupted, but it was over. Their leader was dead, perhaps it took time for the Corruption to fade away for good.

She could hear Finn's voice echo up to her, but he was out of sight, and Calla wanted to keep it that way for now. After everything that happened, she didn't know how he would act.

She rounded a corner lost in thought and smacked straight into someone. Calla jumped from the sudden, hard impact. She quickly realized it was Alec, of all people.

Alec steadied her by holding onto her arms, "Lady Calla." He stepped back and bowed. "Or should I say, Hero of Midelle?" He flashed his debonair smile.

Her eyes did a once over on him. Uncountable wounds covered his body, but they didn't seem to faze him. Mud and blood covered his ripped clothes. His shirt barely hung on to his broad and muscular chest.

"How about Calla?" She corrected. "I'm surprised you're not tired after your battle with," she paused, unsure if she should continue that way. "You fought with bravery and discipline last night."

Alec gave her an appreciative look. "As did you. You were smart to use the dragon call. I never would have known you were in danger. I came at the right time. Lucky for you, I didn't wake up until morning. When I took flight, I saw the aftermath of The Corrupted storming the Library. I looked all over town for you. After I got a few townsfolk to talk, some recalled seeing you and," he paused to fight the grimace on his face, "the Captain.

"When I heard the call, I knew exactly where it came from, but I couldn't believe it. I took off for the Isle of Dragons immediately, hoping I wouldn't be too late."

"You had perfect timing." Calla popped on her toes to place a chaste kiss on his cheek. His fingers traced where her lips had just been. "Thank you for saving my life. I'd be dead if it wasn't for you. I hope you don't need the whistle back." She averted her eyes of his gaze, "I kind of dropped it, and it broke into pieces."

Alec patted her shoulder, "You put it to good use. Please don't worry about it. The war is over, and The Corruption will fade in the survivors. We won't need it again."

Calla did another once over of him while picturing The Corrupted dragon next to him. Despite the red eyes, the similarities were overwhelming. Alec noticed her taking him in, and he smirked at her.

Calla's cheeks grew red, and she averted her eyes immediately. She didn't need to give him any reason to ask for her hand again. "I have to ask, is Abaddon really your brother?

Alec's eyes danced around the corridor like they held the answer. Calla waited for him. "Yes. My twin. The one grandfather mentioned in the Edulis Mountains. His name was Aron. We thought he was dead."

"Is he dead now?"

"No. I managed to subdue him in our aerial battle. However, my twin is dead, I don't know who that monster Abaddon is." Calla opened her mouth, but Alec continued to speak, "Before you ask, I'm the older one." He gave her the tiniest smile.

Calla rolled her eyes. "That's not what I was going to ask." She saw him tense up, almost preparing for the question. "What happened to him? Did you know he had succumbed to The Corruption?"

"Dragons are proud creatures, Calla. We fight gallantly, live modestly and love vigorously. With Aron and I being twins in a line of great legends, everything was a competition. Who could do their duties faster? Who could eat dinner faster? Who could fly faster during training? We were inseparable, or so we thought." Alec ran his hands through his hair.

"When we were young, our Emissary came back from Japhia with disturbing news. She told the council that King Raoul had become Corrupted, and Prince Vallen had disappeared. An emergency council meeting followed. They decided that the dragons would go into hiding in the Edulis Mountains, our sacred home, where the first dragon was born. The council knew that we dragons could never risk becoming Corrupted. Hiding would protect us until the Hybrid came. It felt very reminiscent of the accounts of the first war."

He gave Calla a quick look. "When Aron and I learned this, Aron said he would never leave his home and that he was duty-bound to protect the island." Alec stopped talking with difficult memories surfacing.

"What happened?" Calla prodded.

"Aron wanted us to stay and protect the Isle. I wanted to leave. We were so young and foolish. He thought he could defend the

Isle if The Corrupted ever came to it. He wanted to be a hero. I foolishly let him hide on the wild side of the Isle.

When it came time to leave, Grandfather asked me where he was, and I lied to him. I told him he left with the first group. By the time we got to the Edulis Mountains, we searched far and wide for him. A scout even went back to the Isle to check for him, but he must have stayed out of sight. No one could find him. I kept his secret, even when everyone thought he was dead." A tear streamed down his face. If Calla wasn't looking at his face, she would have missed it.

"Lady Amethyst kept asking me where he was. I told her I didn't know every time. I was a coward, afraid to defy my brother's wishes. Everything would have been different if I had just..."

"Alec, stop. You can't blame yourself. Aron made his decision. And with more time, The Corruption will fade without Belladonna to bolster it."

Alec placed a delicate kiss on Calla's cheek. His lips left a warm tingle on her skin. "You're right. Only time will tell. I don't know if I can stand united with my brother again, but that's my problem. What will you do now?"

"I need to find Vallen. Do you know where he is?"

"In the courtyard, but before you go," Alec cupped her face with one hand while his thumb traced along her jawline. "I want you to know that my offer still stands. Imagine how the realm would rejoice at our union, especially now."

Calla thought on his words for a few seconds. "I need time to digest everything that's happened. I can't agree to something until

I know completely what I want," Calla responded as gently as she could.

Alec nodded his head. "I see your point, and I hope to see you again soon, Lady Calla. Please excuse me, Lady Amethyst is expecting me back at the mountains. I have much to inform her of. When the deities will that our paths cross once again, I hope you will know what you want."

Calla hugged Alec, taking him by surprise. In one swift move, he wrapped his massive arms around her. "See you around, Alec," she whispered. He continued on his way, but not before giving her one last smoldering grin. Calla watched, shaking her head, as he disappeared around the corner. He was something else.

Every step closer she got to the courtyard, her heart beat faster. She may have lost one parent, but she wanted to incorporate Vallen into her life. Calla was sure that he would want her in his life as well. She opened the courtyard door to slip out. The glare from the sun bounced off the snow. She shielded her eyes as they adjusted. A gentle winter breeze tossed her hair back and bit her nose.

A lone figure was on the other side of the courtyard, at the inside edge of an outcropping of trees. It was Vallen. He sat hunched over by a tall and mighty tree. Calla remembered sitting by that very same tree, escaping from the world in the warm sun. It's where she had met Vihaan.

Calla's heart beat fast. She crossed the courtyard. Her mouth was dry, and her hands were sweaty. She paused a few feet away from him, scared to speak.

Vallen wore new clothes and a thick cape. His skin had brightened up a bit, but he still bore signs of malnutrition.

"What do you want," Vallen asked deadpanned. He didn't even bother to turn around.

Calla wrung her hands together, "Well... I thought I'd see how you're holding up." Calla mentally chided herself for the dumb question, she could only imagine how he was.

When he didn't answer, Calla's nerves took over, "You know, I've been thinking about you my whole life. What you're like, what makes you happy, if I looked like you? I think I have your hair, it's a tad dirty, but it still looks blonde to me." Calla paused again, he still didn't say a word, and his back was still to her.

"I didn't know that you were my, um, father when we were on that balcony. I never meant to gamble with anyone's life. I left my guardian's side in Cape Toria, he's Finn. Uh... Captain Quinn, actually. It was kind of stupid, I thought I could handle The Oracle on my own, but we were ambushed..."

Vallen murmured something, but Calla missed it over her ramblings. She paused to see if he would say it again "I didn't catch what you said," she admitted after dead silence.

"Stop talking," Vallen said with a hint of anger in his voice. Calla pressed her lips together and held her breath. "You dare show your face to me? You ruined everything." Calla gasped as if all the air vanished from her lungs. "You killed my sweet Ella."

Vallen turned around, his eyes were bloodshot from crying, "You're nothing to me. Go back to the human realm, and never come back to Midelle!" Vallen placed his forehead on the tree, fighting the oncoming sobs. His fingers turned white as they curled into the deep bark lines of the tree.

Calla backed away slowly, her world falling endlessly through her stomach. Nothing seemed right. Her lungs wouldn't fill with air, and the outside seemed to close in on her. Her feet ran back into the castle, unaware of where she was going. Every cell in her body was screaming to leave Midelle, and she was listening to them.

There was a distant chatter coming her way, Calla placed her hand on the wall to feel something solid. Her lungs began to fill with air. Her vision stopped spinning. She looked up to find Nakosi and Finn walking around the corner.

Nakosi's face brightened when he saw her, but Finn looked upon her with concern. "There's the Hero of Midelle! We've been looking all over for you!"

Calla couldn't find words. All she could think about was how her father hated her.

"You need to meet with the scribes so they can gain a first-hand account of what happened for the archives. Shea thought of a great idea. A celebration held here in the Capital, for all Midelle. To celebrate what is being coined as Liberation Day. You, of course, will be the center of attention."

Calla finally caught her breath and gasped, "No."

Nakosi gave her a quizzical look, but Finn watched her with a cautious eye.

"No?" Nakosi repeated, confused.

"I want... no. I need to go home. Back to the human realm. To-day," Calla said with a wavering voice. "Now. Find another witch to make me a portal home. I can't stay here."

Nakosi sighed. A dreadful feeling settled into Calla's stomach. "There's good news and bad news I need to tell you. Which would you like first?

"Good." Calla kept her eyes on the King. She always picked good first, it softened the blow of the bad.

"Before Philomena fell ill, I tasked her to make a portal back to the human realm. I wanted to give it to you before you fought The Corrupted. A gift of being in the human realm for a few days after you got your full powers. She completed it without incident, so another witch isn't needed. There is a portal for you to use to return to the human realm."

Calla raised an eyebrow. "And the bad news?"

"I'm afraid I can't let you go back to the human realm."

A blanket of rage swept over Calla, "What? I did as you asked! Everything!"

"That was before you drank the poison. Captain Quinn gave me his detailed account of the events before the Royal Guard arriving."

Calla gave Finn a venomous look, but there was something different in his eyes when he glanced back at her. Calla couldn't place it.

"You are in no condition to leave Midelle. There is a slim chance you could become Corrupted, and we must keep a close watch on you."

"It's impossible, I'm immune! Captain Quinn saw for himself. Wasn't that in his detailed account? I killed the leader of The Corrupted. My own flesh and blood. The woman who brought me into this world. Dead. Because of me. I kept my end of the promise, now you keep yours. Let me go home."

Finn cleared his throat, "What if she had a keeper in the human realm?"

"Like a babysitter?" Calla scoffed as she rolled her eyes. "Yeah, great idea. Send me back with a ten-foot troll. No one would notice."

Nakosi rubbed his chin in thought, "Yes," he murmured to himself, "that could work."

Finn and Calla waited for Nakosi to speak. They only exchanged glances once in a flurry of emotions.

"I believe Captain Quinn's idea could work. A keeper is exactly what you need. Someone expendable, but still trustworthy. Someone who can blend in with your kind of people."

"Someone like me," Finn offered as his eyes bored into Callas.

"Yes, Captain Quinn. If you would be willing? I know you once lived in the human realm. First Commander Varden has been an excellent Captain in your stead."

"I would be honored."

"It is settled then. I shall gather those that I can in the throne room to give you somewhat of a proper goodbye." He dipped his chin in silent agreement.

"It is not settled," Calla shouted to stop the madness unfolding before her.

Finn touched her arm gently, pulling her aside from Nakosi. "I need to talk to you," he whispered. Nakosi tilted his head and watched them.

"What if I don't want him as my keeper? At least do me the courtesy of choosing my keeper," Calla said to Nakosi, ignoring Finn. They were back in Japhia now. Things were different, and he had to understand that their time together was a mistake.

"Very well. I expect you in the throne room by the midday bells. If you have not chosen your keeper by then, it will be Captain Quinn, or you don't leave Midelle."

"How could you do this to me," Calla scolded Finn as soon as Nakosi was out of earshot. "Why would you tell him that?"

Finn took her into his masculine arms but kept her at a distance, so his face was only inches away from hers. "Just listen, for once."

Calla's eyes flitted up to Finn's.

"You have got to be the most infuriating, hard-headed and down-right annoying person I have ever met. But none of those things could stop me from falling in love with you. I fought my feelings for you from day one."

His hand tucked a piece of hair behind her ear, but then cupped the side of her face. Calla felt the air in her lungs disappear again, for a billion different reasons. "I love everything about you. Because even you know that our hearts belong together. I had once regretted the course of my life, but once I met you, I'd live my past a hundred times over if it meant that it would lead me to you."

"Finn... I..."

"I'm sorry for every tear I made you shed. I couldn't confront my feelings, so I hid behind them in shame and anger. But being with you made me realize that love is nothing to be ashamed of. When I thought my life was ending, all I could think about was you. Calla Moro, I love you with all my heart, and I know you love me too. I will do everything in my power to make you as happy as I can." His thumb never stopped caressing her skin.

He pressed his lips to hers. Calla melted against him. His hands moved to weave into her hair as she opened her mouth to let him deepen the kiss.

Calla slowly pulled away, and she found herself lost in the haziness of his jade eyes. He placed a soft kiss on her forehead then met her gaze, but his eyes filled with sudden doubt. "Choose me now, or I'm gone forever."

Calla freed herself from his loving grasp but stayed close. "You can't expect me to make this decision now. I need to talk to Vihaan."

Finn placed another lingering kiss on her lips, savoring her. "You've made your decision then. I hope he makes you happy." He let her go, turning on his heel then stalked away at a quick pace.

"Finn!" Calla took a step towards the direction he went to chase him.

He stopped but didn't turn around.

She only took a few steps towards him. "You don't understand how complicated this is."

Finn turned around and she could see him trying to hide his pain. "As long as I have you, I can do complicated."

"Calla?" Vihaan's voice floated from behind her.

She turned from Finn with a smile forming on her lips to see Vihaan lightly jogging toward her. She glanced back to Finn in time to see him disappear around the corner.

Calla concentrated on the only thing that mattered, going home and convincing Vihaan to come with her. If it wasn't either of them, her last option was worse. Being stuck in Midelle for forever.

Calla stood there as Vihaan made his way to her. Her heart hurt. All this time Finn had loved her, and she had no idea. Maybe she did, deep down. Calla remembered how it felt to have her skin against his, be in his embrace until she so stupidly left.

A picture formed in her mind. One where she woke up that morning and instead of panicking, she smiled and rested her head on his chest to fall back asleep. A deep feeling of guilt settled in Calla, but then she remembered he walked away.

"There you are, I've been looking everywhere for you."

Calla's brain dropped every doubt about Finn as she met him in the middle, of what distance they had left, to kiss him like her life depended on it. Vihaan smiled through the kiss. Calla could feel his arms wrap around her. She felt safe again. Vihaan ended the kiss with a series of quick pecks on her lips.

"I missed you," Calla whispered against his soft lips. A flash of jade eyes crossed her mind, but as quick as it came, it left just as quick.

"As did I." Calla dropped her eyes down from Vihaan's eyes. His thumbs traced up and down her spine. "Is something wrong?"

Calla let her hands drop to her side. Her eyes lifted to meet his, "I've decided to go home." Vihaan's brows furrowed. "But," Calla smiled as Vihaan pulled her closer. Their hips became flush with each other. Calla blushed. "But to leave, I need a keeper."

Vihaan dipped his nose to her ear, nuzzling her with deep affection. "Go on," he said in a husky tone.

Calla's heart skipped a beat. "How would you like to go to the human realm and be my keeper?" When Vihaan didn't say anything, Calla kept going, "I know it's sudden, and I'm asking you to leave your legacy here..."

Vihaan pulled away from Calla as a serious look washed over his face. She could feel her heart beginning to shatter when she thought of his rejection. The thought of being stuck in Midelle forever made unease creep up her throat.

He grabbed her hands, then got on one knee. Her heart grew wings and began to soar up to the heavens, fixing all the broken pieces.

"I would go anywhere and do anything if that meant I'm by your side." Vihaan's breath hitched from nerves. His thumb caressed her hand. "My legacy is a garden house, but you are my future. My ancestors wouldn't want me anywhere except by your side and having our love flourish."

"But the human realm is different," Calla cut in as she looked into his vast purple eyes, "What if you don't like it?

"It wouldn't matter because as long as I have you, I'm complete." Vihaan raised her hands to his lips, kissing each one. "I'd love to see everything you told me about, the tall glass buildings, the cars, and meet Felicia. I love you with every part of me, and I want to be everything for you. If you'll have me."

A tear welled in Calla's eye. She didn't care as she tackled Vihaan to the ground to kiss him again. "I love you too."

The throne room was filled with faces familiar to Calla. The midday bells rang. Nakosi accepted Vihaan going in Finn's stead, which put Calla at ease. Vihaan waited at the center of the throne room for Calla to finish saying goodbye to all those who heralded her as a hero.

She stopped in front of Shea. The Queen's eyes narrowed in on Calla. She avoided her gaze and dipped into a curtsey, her balance still faltering, "Thought I'd nail it by now."

Shea moved in close, "What did you do to him?"

A heavy feeling settled into Calla's stomach. "Do what to whom?" Shea kept her face neutral because many eyes were on them. Calla mirrored her facial expression.

"You know who, Finn. He came up to me, said he's done being Captain and to not look for him. He ran from me before I could process what he said. I haven't been able to find him since."

"That's his problem, not mine."

Shea stepped back and gave a curt nod to Calla, not wanting to cause a scene. She moved onto King Nakosi, giving him another pathetic curtsy. She could feel Shea's gaze burn into her. Nakosi showered her with all the praise, but Calla could only muster a smile for she kept imaging Vallen saying to leave and never come back.

When she moved on to the last person, her heart hurt, making her regret her decision to leave.

"Oh, my dear." Violet cried. "I'll miss you so much." They hugged each other with tight grips, but Violet brought her out at arm's length. "You'll remember what I said?"

"I will. It's the only thing keeping me together."

"To us, you're a hero. Savior of the realm, and you always will be. Try not to forget us."

"I could never. Say goodbye to Philomena for me once she wakes up?" Calla asked, holding back tears.

"She'll be devastated you left, but I will," Violet handed her the small purple vial that was their way back if they ever needed it. Calla tucked it in her pocket before Violet crushed her in another hug. This time Calla savored it. Violet let her go with tear tracks staining her rough cheeks. "Go on now, you have a good man waiting for you."

Calla smiled then went to Vihaan. He was nervous, but he made a decent attempt at hiding it. Vihaan embraced her while he placed a kiss on the top of her head. "Ready to go?"

She looked up at Vihaan, his soft purple eyes gazed down at her. Her heart glowed with a welcomed and missed warmth. Calla hoped that this could be her new normal. Things would never be the same, now that she knew the truth. This was the future she wanted, and she'd fight for it until her last breath. Calla's fingers wrapped around the vial that would take them home while she rested her head on Vihaan's chest, "With you by my side, always."

Twenty-Seven

Time was a peculiar concept to Finn. He expected the days to fly by alone, but instead, each day lasted longer than the previous. Every day was the same. Wake up, eat, fix his cabin in the middle of the woods, eat again and find some way to wind down before sleep.

He couldn't get her out of his head no matter how much he tried to keep busy. It was the little things that were the hardest to forget. The way a breeze would toss her golden waves. When the corners of her lips would curve when she bit back a smile or laughter. The way she would look at him when she thought he wasn't paying attention.

Calla.

Everything in the castle reminded him of her, that's why he couldn't stay there. She broke his heart, and there was no fixing it. Living a simple life, in the middle of nowhere, was what he needed. Just him and this little house that he'd found in disrepair. Despite the cottage being in the Ashbury Woods, this was the perfect place for him. No tale of haunted woods would force him from his self-made paradise.

The wood splintered apart as Finn brought the ax down one last time for the day. Daylight was fading fast, and another snow storm was coming, he could feel it. A feeling of frost was thick in the air, and all the woods had gone quiet. He threw the last of the split logs into a crude cart he had rigged together and wheeled them into his little home.

He was thankful the storm held off for today. All-day he patched holes in the roof and the little gaps in the walls of his home. He was looking forward to a night where he wouldn't wake up to snow drifting onto him. Peace and relaxation were calling his name.

When he crossed into the threshold of his home, the aroma of rabbit stew hit him square in the face. His stomach growled in anticipation.

He parked the cart of wood by the fire and glanced at his makeshift timekeeper. He had carved a single line for each day, but soon he stopped that too.

It only made him think how long it's been since he saw Calla last. Since he last held her in his arms and had his lips on hers. She haunted his dreams every night. He woke up every night filled with regret and hatred. He had no idea how to stop it.

Finn tried not to pay attention to it, instead, he forced all his attention on rabbit stew. It had become his specialty.

Later that night, Finn was in his usual spot, a chair he'd made. The stars sparkled against the inky sky, reflecting the cold abyss that was his heart. He hoped the storm would hold off until he went to bed. If only he was that lucky.

"So lonely," a voice whispered in the darkness.

Finn was immediately on his feet and alert. "Who's there?" He looked around him, but it was only the trees.

"I can feel how angry you are." He couldn't tell if the voice was male or female.

"Show yourself!" He dashed inside to grab his ax. When he came back out, he didn't hear the voice again. He ventured out in front of the house with his grip tight on his weapon. He missed his sword.

As he listened for the intruder, all he heard was an owl calling out to him. Finn let the ax drop next to him as he pondered his sanity.

"Embrace it all, stop fighting it."

Finn whirled around to the voice and brought his ax up in the same movement. He stopped when his eyes landed on a dark figure against the hibernating trees. "This is your only warning, get off my land!"

In the blink of an eye, the figure was closer. Fingers snapped and a dark mist swirled from the ground. Finn was locked in place. His ax fell from his paralyzed fingers. It landed with a crunch in the snow.

"I can feel your anger and pain." A finger slid down Finn's face. The black mist held him motionless when he struggled. "It drew me to you, like a moth to a flame."

"Let me go," Finn managed to spit out through a clenched jaw.

"I'm afraid our time together has just started." The fingers snapped again and the mist enshrouded Finn's vision. Everything went black.

Time.

More time.

Eons.

Starved. Beaten. Chained. Tortured.

His thoughts had become dark and filled with hatred. Calla was the only source of light he had left, but even her glow had faded.

Finn lay there in the cold and dark cell with eyes closed wanting all the time he had left to go by. He had lost count of the days while locked in a light-less place.

The door opened, and not even light came in from there, but the dark figure did. He never got a good look at the figure. Maybe today. The figure grabbed the back of Finn's head to pull him up. His face became eye level with a tiny flame. He refused to give the figure the satisfaction of being in pain, so he bit back his cry.

"Open your eyes," the mysterious figure demanded.

Finn forced his eyes open, he knew the ramifications if he didn't. Instead of meeting the figure's cloaked face as he normally did, his eyes met a piece of reflective glass. Staring back at Finn was a pair of red eyes.

His red eyes.

www.ingramcontent.com/pod-product-compliance
Lightning Source LLC
Chambersburg PA
CBHW030055310726
48970CB00004B/1025